The Clay Sustains

Stacey
Enjoy
Sharon K Miller

The Clay Sustains

BOOK 3 IN THE CLAY SERIES

SHARON K. MILLER

Buckskin Books
Tucson, Arizona

ISBN: (Print Edition) 978-0-9961544-5-1

ISBN: (Digital Editions) 978-0-9961544-6-8

Raven image by Seabarium, Flickr.com (CC BY 2.0)

This novel is a work of fiction. The characters, places, and events are drawn in part from the archaeological history of Hohokam habitation in the Tucson Basin. Although the foundation for this story comes from the archaeological record, at times the author has taken liberties with that record for the sake of the story.

Many of the spiritual and cultural beliefs of the characters are borrowed from the Pascua Yaqui Tribe's ancestral people, the Yoeme, as well as from the Tohono O'odham. However, this story does not purport to represent either culture or tribe factually. Details of the daily life, beliefs, customs, naming practices, and behaviors of the characters should not be interpreted as a factual representation of either culture or tribe.

The story is set at the archaeological site known as Romero Ruin in Catalina State Park near Tucson, Arizona.

Any resemblance to real persons, living or dead, is purely coincidental.

Contents

The Clay Series

Praise for *The Clay Remembers*

"*The Clay Remembers* honors . . . the positive, the intimate, the beautiful and sustaining. The voices of the past, caught with deftness and sensitivity, guide Anna in her quest to restore balance to the present—to find her place in a tradition she can see and hear, and happiness with a man whose past is as haunted as her own. Alive with the light, scent and grit of the desert, this first volume compels from the outset. Its successors promise to uncover more of time, craft and enduring love."

~David Neilson, Author of the Sophie Rathenau Vienna Mysteries: *The Prussian Dispatch* and *Lay Brothers*

"Anna unearths the strength to stand up for herself in much the same way she uncovers the past buried in the desert dirt—carefully, bit by bit, until eventually something beautiful is revealed."

~Ilana Maletz, Author of *Cha'risa's Gift*

"I appreciated the author foregoing the cliché of women battling each other for the affections of men or career advancement. The women in the story support each other, and are trustworthy allies. A magical realism element binds together the generations of women who possess a clay pot."

~R. Nanna (NoMoreJDRobb), Amazon Review

Praise for *The Clay Endures*

"Esperanza's struggle to survive in an all-but-barren place becomes ever grimmer. There are threats on all sides, some to be faced without the husband whose obsession has brought them here. Yet she is never quite alone: Sharon Miller is convinced of the solidarity of women throughout time, and the pot connecting all three women in this trilogy-to-be is the symbol of the love, work, and suffering which binds them in shared experience."
~David Neilson, Author of the Sophie Rathenau Vienna Mysteries: *The Prussian Dispatch* and *Lay Brothers*

"I felt such a connection with Esperanza that I had my own ideas about how her story should end; but Sharon Miller has many plot surprises for the reader, and I was glued to each page with anticipation (and sometimes dread)."
~Wendy Barnes, Author of *And Life Continues: Sex Trafficking and My Journey to Freedom*

"A magnetic tale of love, survival, and courage."
~Patricia Day, Readers Favorite.

"I was easily swept into the story. I had trouble putting the book down! I felt like I was at the homestead along with Armando and Esperanza. I cried along with the tragedy. I didn't want the story to end!"
~Kindle Customer, Amazon Review

To those hardy women and men who dig through layers of time, unearthing the stories of the extraordinary people who came before us on this earth. Their devotion to those stories opened the door to the rich and colorful history of the people who occupied the Tucson Basin in the twelfth century. Because of their work, I have made a remarkable journey through time in the sandals of the Hohokam.

Acknowledgments

To my husband, Jim: I am humbled by your generosity and your goodness. You've been beside me for more than a half-century, allowing me the time and space to pursue my dreams. I'm looking forward to the rest of our century together.

To my advance readers: Linda "Lucy" Fernandez, Jeannie Waters, Donna Mathews, Renee Nanna, David Neilson, author of *The Prussian Dispatch* and *Lay Brothers,* and my sister, Betty Anne O'Ferrall Hood, I thank you from the bottom of my heart for your honest (and sometimes brutal) feedback. What is good about this book, I owe to you. And to Lucy's friend, Jill Holbrook, thanks for setting me straight on certain details about spinning cotton and backstrap looms.

Sincere gratitude goes to my advance readers, some of whom came back for a second helping: Jada Ahern, Linda Donahue, Donnie Endicott, Linda "Lucy" Fernandez, Donna Mathews, Markie Madden, of Metamorph Publishing, David Nielson, Keira, of Pirate Lady Pages, Carol Scott, Mary Semus, and Jeannie Waters.

To my "A-Team," Andy Ward, Allen Denoyer, and Allen Dart: I owe you all a BIG debt of gratitude for what you have taught me.

Andy Ward, you gave me the pleasure of clay, of holding it in my hands and connecting to the essence of this earth. The pot I dreamed of so many years ago came into existence through your exceptional instruction. Thank you for taking me to the West Branch of the Santa Cruz River to collect the same clay my character, Ha-wani, would have used to make her pot and guiding me from my first feeble efforts to the final product. It ain't perfect, honey, but I'm proud.

Allen Denoyer, you introduced me to the spirits that reside in stone and mud and fire. The points I knapped and the knife I made might not be museum quality, but, nonetheless, they connect me to a fascinating past. Your pit house at Steam Pump Ranch welcomed me to sit within mud-covered brush walls like those in my fictional village and imagine my characters sitting there with me. Your half-scale pit house from the Early Agricultural period in the Tucson Basin, served as a model for my departure from the archaeological record wherein I gave my village a granary a few centuries before granaries were in use. The subsequent burning of your model helped to create an important scene in my story. Thank you for patiently answering my questions and giving me superb instruction and valuable insights into the lives of my fictional characters.

Allen Dart, the value of my association with you and Old Pueblo Archaeology (OPA) for the past several years is something I cannot begin to measure. Your Prehistory of the Southwest class provided facts about and insights into the Hohokam. The field trips and other activities offered at OPA have been important in my archaeological education, such as it is. Thank you for patiently answering my persistent questions about specific issues I have included in the story.

Although I have thanked them in the previous books in this series, I cannot omit the archaeology staff at Pima Community College who gave me valuable, hands-on experience: Dave Stephen, Helen O'Brian, Leah Mason-Kohlmeyer, and Buff Billings. Thanks again. Your instruction has served me well.

Again, my thanks to Herminia Valenzuela, teacher and Yaqui storyteller, who introduced me to the Yoeme culture and the concept of seataaka in 1999, and to Felipe Molina, Yaqui/Yoeme scholar, who provided me with in-depth education on Yoeme history and culture and corrected my use of the Yoem Noki (Yoeme language). Although I have taken liberties with some of the Yoeme beliefs, I did so with the utmost respect.

To Stella Tucker, a lovely Tohono O'odham woman: thank you for allowing Arizona Sonoran Desert Museum members to come to your desert camp for the saguaro harvest several years ago. We used saguaro rib harvest poles to knock the fruits off the cactus and catch them in a bucket. My partner and I took turns, and, believe me, it's not as easy as some might think. After collecting the fruits, we cut them open (with the sharp base of the dried blossom) and scooped out the fruit to go into the huge pot over the fire. We experienced everything about the harvest but the "sit and drink."

And to my powerful editing team: Wynne Brown (www.wynnebrown.com) and Charlie McKee (www.editorsproof.com), thanks for your enthusiastic support, your impeccable skills, your recommendations, and your ability to find my persistent gremlins.

Map 1: The General Area

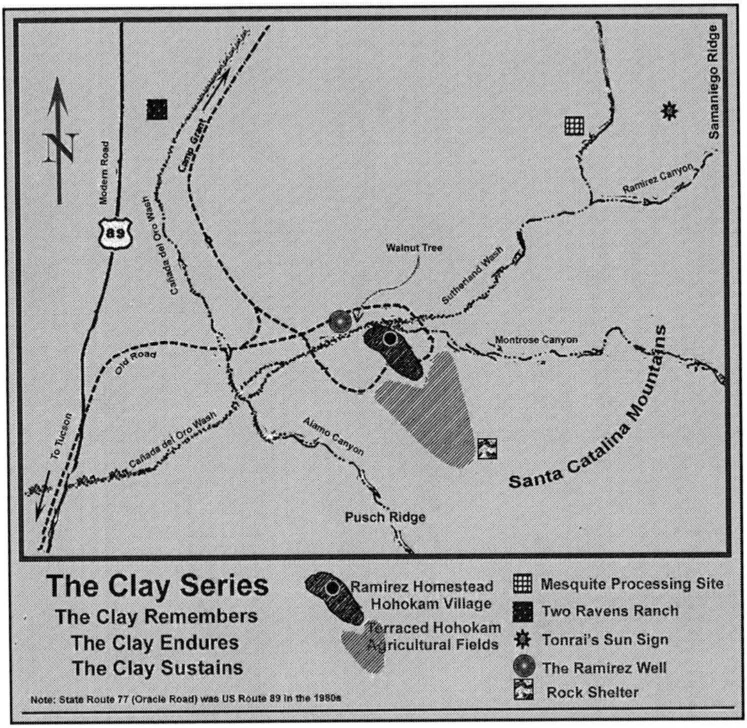
N
Modern Road
89
Cañada del Oro Wash
Camp Grant
Walnut Tree
Sutherland Wash
Ramirez Canyon
Samaniego Ridge
Montrose Canyon
Old Road
To Tucson
Cañada del Oro Wash
Alamo Canyon
Santa Catalina Mountains
Pusch Ridge
The Clay Series
The Clay Remembers
The Clay Endures
The Clay Sustains
Ramirez Homestead
Hohokam Village
Terraced Hohokam
Agricultural Fields
Mesquite Processing Site
Two Ravens Ranch
Tonrai's Sun Sign
The Ramirez Well
Rock Shelter
Note: State Route 77 (Oracle Road) was US Route 89 in the 1980s

In a small village beneath the massive towers of Great-Grandfather Mountain, Ha-wani, following traditions handed down since before there was remembering, crafts an ordinary clay pot, singing her spirit into the clay as she works it. It is a simple act, but one that will touch the lives of two women centuries after she has gone from this place.

One pot. Three women. Eight-Hundred Years

Map 2: Stone Towers Village

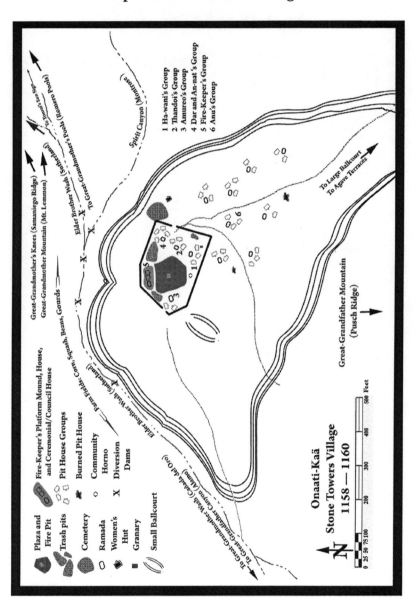

1 Ha-wani's Group
2 Thandoi's Group
3 Amureo's Group
4 Dar and An-nat's Group
5 Fire-Keeper's Group
6 Anu's Group

Spirit Canyon (Montrose)

To Tonsé's Son Side
To Great-Grandmother's Pools (Romero Pools)

Elder Brother Wash (Sutherland) To Great-Grandmother's Pools

Great-Grandmother's Knees (Samaniego Ridge)
Great-Grandmother Mountain (Mt. Lemmon)

Community Farm Fields: Corn, Squash, Beans, Gourds

Elder Brother Wash (Sutherland)

To Large Ballcourt
To Agave Terraces

Great-Grandfather Mountain (Pusch Ridge)

To Great-Grandmother-West (Cañada del Oro)
To Great-Grandfather Canyon (Alamo)

Fire-Keeper's Platform Mound, House,
and Ceremonial/Council House
Pit House Groups
Burned Pit House
Community
Horno
Diversion
Dams

Plaza and
Fire Pit
Trash pits
Cemetery
Ramada
Women's
Hut
Granary
Small Ballcourt

Onaati-Kaä
Stone Towers Village
1158 — 1160

N

0 25 50 75 100   200   300   400   500 Feet

xiv

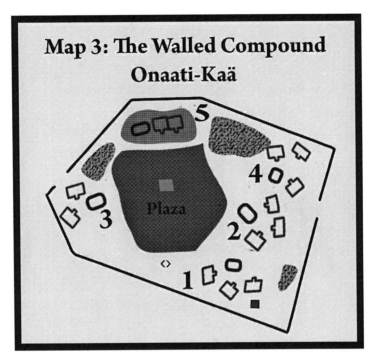

Map 3: The Walled Compound Onaati-Kaä

What's What and Who's Who?

Time Period: 1158 – 1160

Historical Events

- 1130 – 1140: severe drought
- 1140 – 1150: minimal rains
- 1150: approximate date when the walled compound was built at what is now Romero Ruin in Catalina State Park
- 1160: reliable rains return

Characters

Vachai's House Group (1)

- Vachai – Farmer
- Li-naä – Vachai's wife

- » Tonrai – Vachai's first son/Artist
- » Ha-wani – Tonrai's wife; Ra-naä's sister
- » Chanu – Vachai's second son/Flint-Knapper
- » Ra-naä – Chanu's wife; Ha-wani's sister
- » Wokkai – Vachai's daughter
- » Benai – Vachai's third son
- Nothai – Harvester
- Kokii – Nothai's wife
  - » Cheshonii – Nothai's first son
  - » Tarukii – Nothai's second son
  - » Chuwii – Nothai's third son

Thandoi's House Group (2)
- Thandoi – Chief Elder
- Thandoi's wife
  - » Tatanikii – Chief Elder's first son/Runner
  - » Tatanikii's wife
    - » Tatanikii's children
  - » Thandoi's second son and family
  - » Thandoi's younger children

Amureo's House Group (3)
- Amureo – Hunter
- Amureo's wife
  - » Akamai – Amureo's son
- Panereo – Amureo's brother/Builder
- Panereo's wife
  - » Panereo's children
- Kutareo – Amureo's brother/Wood-Cutter

An-nat and Dar's House Group (4)
- An-nat – Knowledge-Keeper
- No-wani – An-nat's wife/Healer-Woman
- Dar – Bead-Maker
- Usareo – Dar's brother/Flute-Player
- Vaeleo – An-nat's brother/Drummer

Fire-Keeper's House Group (5)
- Fire-Keeper's House
- Ceremonial/Council House

Anu's House Group (6 – outside the wall)
- Anu – Farmer and friend to Vachai
- Mochik – Anu's wife
  » Sochik – Anu's oldest daughter
  » Sochik's husband
    » Sochik's children
  » Ma-taä – Anu's second daughter
  » Anu's other children
- Anu's mother

Other characters
- Robanti and Lantha – Ha-wani and Ra-naä's parents, living in Honey Bee Village
- Ladenki – Man from Twisted Snake Village
- Shamans from neighboring villages
- Messenger from Honey Bee Village

Village Place Names

- Onaati-Kaä (Stone Towers Village) – now Romero Ruin Site in Catalina State Park
- Sleeping Snake, Honey Bee, Seepwillow, and Rattlesnake – neighboring villages

Geography

- Santa Catalina Mountains
  » Great-Grandmother Mountain (Mt. Lemmon)
  » Great-Grandmother's Knees (Samaniego Ridge)
  » Great-Grandfather Mountain (Pusch Ridge)
  » Great-Grandmother's Pools (Romero Pools)
  » Spirit Canyon (Montrose Canyon)
  » Great-Grandfather Canyon (Alamo Canyon)
- Little Dove Mountains (Tortolita Mountains)

- Desert of Burned Rock (Sierra Pinacate in Mexico)

Waterways

- Great Water (Sea of Cortez/Gulf of California)
- Elder Brother Wash (Sutherland Wash)
- Big River (Santa Cruz River)
- Great-Grandmother Wash (Cañada del Oro)

Calendar

Derived from Tohono O'odham. Please note that calendar moons do not correspond precisely with our Gregorian calendar. Each month is marked by the "death" of the old moon and the "birth" of the new moon. All moons are associated with weather, plants, or animals. Modern months are indicated only as a reference and should not be seen as equivalent.)

- Cactus Harvest Moon (June)
- Big Rains Moon (July)
- Short Planting Moon (August)
- Dry Grass Moon (September)
- Small Rains Moon (October)
- Pleasant Cold Moon (November)
- Big Cold Moon (December)
- Animals Get Lean Moon (January)
- Deer Mating Moon (February)
- Green Moon (March)
- Yellow Moon (April)
- Bean Tree Moon (May)

The Enchanted Worlds (Yoeme/Pascua Yaqui)

- The Flower World (Sea Ania)
- The Wilderness World (Huya Ania)

A Message From the Author: Tips for Reading

Looking into someone's eyes is to trespass on their spirit. The eyes are literally windows to the spirit (soul).

Spirit names are known and used only by family and close friends. For example, Ha-wani *means* raven. Unwelcome use of someone's spirit name is often an effort to exercise power over them.

The spirit names of the main character's family are used throughout the book, but you will note people outside the family and close friends address them according to the role they fulfill in the village. For example, Tonrai *means* kingbird, but to the village he is known as Artist. Likewise, the names of villagers are associated with the role that character fulfills in the village, For example, the name Kutareo *means* wood cutter; Amureo *means* hunter.

Except for Healer-Woman (who has an important role to fulfill), women are identified in the community as someone's wife, daughter, sister, mother, and so on.

Author Notes are provided for:

- indigenous spiritual beliefs and practices,
- locations in Southern Arizona and Northern Mexico,
- geological and geographical features in the Sonoran desert,
- details from the archaeological record related to the Hohokam who lived in the Tucson Basin from approximately 200 BCE to 1450 CE, and
- words, terms, and names borrowed from the Yoeme (Pascua Yaqui) language.

An asterisk (*) indicates that readers can turn to Author Notes (page 352) for definitions, descriptions, context, and other information.

While I have tried to remain true to the facts, I have, at times, taken liberties with those facts.

Everything has its own spirit—even a broken pot. They say the clay remembers the hands that made it. . . . Women then must have spoken to the earth as they took its clay. They must have sung special songs for shaping the bowl, for polishing it, for baking it so it would be strong enough to last long after that tribe was gone. . . . They say that even now the wind finds one of those songs still in the clay and lifts it out and carries it down the canyon and across the hills.

It is a small sound and always far away but they say sometimes they hear it.

~ *When Clay Sings*, Byrd Baylor

Chapter 1

Yellow Moon 1158 (April)

Before the first sliver of the sun peeked over the ridge, the girl stretched out her arms, lifted her chin, and closed her eyes. The gentle breeze swept over her, fluttering her skirt against her knees. The sun would follow.

She came to this spot each morning to await the first kiss of the sun and to cleanse her body and spirit in the dawn wind.* Today, though, she was impatient. Lantha had injured her knee in a fall, and Ha-wani needed to grind the corn.

The sun should have brightened her eyelids, yet darkness remained. Frowning, she opened her eyes and stumbled back. A man stood before her, blocking the sun, denying her its blessing. Pale eyes, a color she had never seen, invaded hers. She could neither move nor break eye contact.*

A frigid wave flowed through her body, chilling her bones and raising coldbumps on her skin. It was nothing like the dawn wind. She shivered. The distant mountains and the surrounding desert slipped into a murky gloom that dissolved into total darkness.

Disoriented, she reached out, took a hesitant step forward, and then another. Finding nothing, she held both arms to the side, turning around and around until her hand finally touched a wall. Frantic, she circled, her hands searching the mud-plaster. No ladder, no hand holds, no footholds. Again and again, she circled.

Above, the rising morning light came through a small opening revealing the walls enclosing her. What is this place? How did I get here? Now, heat flowed into her, her head throbbed, and she struggled to breathe. Somebody, please! Somebody help me! *Exhausted and trembling, her heart pounding, she wrapped her arms around her middle and pressed her back against the wall, her face lifted to the small circle of light.* Please . . .

A low thrumming grew louder and louder until her entire body vibrated. She clapped her hands over her ears. When she could stand no more, the floor erupted in thick, white, writhing grubs. When the tangled mass surrounded her and started crawling up her legs, she refused to yield to terror, to scream. She willed herself to resist. She stomped her feet, crushing the hateful creatures; she snatched them from her body, squeezed the life out of them, and flung them against the walls which soon dripped with shadowed slime.

For a moment, she thought they were all gone, but one remained. It lifted its head, its brown head cap turning in her direction and fixed her with its gaze. In spite of her resolve, she panicked, press-

*ing her back against the wall. Unable to break
eye contact, she watched in horror as the creature
transformed into a huge black beetle, almost half
her size. She shuddered when it moved toward her,
its long, jointed antennae waving, reaching for her.*

*The moment an antenna brushed her cheek, a
harsh croak gurgled in her throat and echoed from
the walls. She had not made that noise before, but
she drew strength from it, and spreading her arms,
she pushed down and then up. Taking flight, Raven's wings lifted* her out of the darkness and into
the rising morning light.*

Standing once again on the ground with the village at her back and the desert surrounding her, she
let her breath out and concentrated on the mouth of
the man who stood before her. He smiled, his black-
ened teeth worn down to the gums, his fetid breath
and sour odor enveloping her. Lowering her eyes, she
focused on the beaded necklace and turquoise-studded shell pendant resting among a scattering of
sparse gray hairs on his chest. His breechclout hung
loosely from his sunken belly.

She found her voice. "What do you want?" She
sensed another smile, but she did not shift her focus.
If she looked into his eyes, she would be lost again.

She knew this man. She had seen him before. He
sometimes visited the village shaman. A fire-keeper*
from a neighboring village, she thought. He always
made her nervous, watching her every move if she
crossed the plaza or passed by. He often blocked
her path, something that required her to greet him
politely and request permission to go on her way.

"I want you, Ha-wani."

Gasping, she took another step back, folding her
arms across her naked breasts. "How do you know my
name?"

He chuckled. "I learned it when you showed me the raven. I need a woman with such a powerful spirit. I need you."

"I am not a woman," she said, hoping he would not sense the lie. In fact, she only recently went to the women's hut for the first time, but she did not yet have the blue chin lines that marked her status. "My father will choose a husband when I am ready."

He leaned toward her, his rasping voice slightly more than a whisper, bathing her with his putrid breath. "Ha-wani, you will be my wife."

Chapter 2

Yellow Moon 1158 (April)

In the dim interior of their pit house,* the girls knelt on woven mats, sitting on their heels, their hands folded in their laps while the visitors from Onaati-Kaä* met with their parents. Their father, Robanti, had refused to consider any of the young men in Honey Bee Village,* going instead to Onaati-Kaä where he proposed a union between his daughters and the sons of an old friend.

Since learning of her father's plan, Ha-wani had seen nothing of the strange shaman who had frightened her. Apparently, he had not spoken to her father. Glad to put that terrible experience out of her mind, she tapped her sister on the knee. "What are they saying, Ra-naä? Can you hear anything?"

She shook her head. "I can't tell. I heard a strange man's voice."

"Are you scared?" Ha-wani fidgeted with her long hair, now hanging over her shoulder. She would have to get used to wearing it loose. Their mother had unwound the knots they had worn above their ears for as long as they could remember.

"Of course not. Are you?"

"Maybe a little." Ha-wani envied her younger sister's adventurous behavior. "What if they don't like us?"

"Why wouldn't they like us?" Ra-naä pushed her long hair back over her shoulder. "I'm the prettiest girl in Honey Bee, and you—well, you—you make good pottery."

Blue, vertical lines, drawn from their mouths to their chins,* symbolized their passage into womanhood. For the first time, Ha-wani found a similarity between them. Ra-naä was slim, with a narrow waist and slender legs, and her face was more delicate than most. Her brows, narrow and arched, offered a brightness that Ha-wani feared was lacking in her own face. No one greeted her with a ready smile the way they did her sister.

Ha-wani didn't know what she looked like, but she suspected her mouth lines failed to lift when she smiled, and she did not offer the same brightness in her round face. Ra-naä's brown coloring reflected the golden light of the sun, while Ha-wani's deeper brown reflected little light. In spite of their differences, she did not envy her sister's looks. She saw herself as a sturdy and capable young woman, one who worked hard and did what her parents expected of her. She would bring that same commitment to her marriage.

Several villagers had sought Ra-naä for their sons—or perhaps the boys pressed their parents to ask for her. Boys followed her around the village, and she thrived on the attention. When her mother asked her to grind the corn, she might start, but if one of them came by, she abandoned the stone and walked out into the desert with him. When Lantha scolded her willful daughter, she only laughed. Ha-wani always took care of her sister's chores.

Now, their mother ducked into the entry and smiled. "Come, girls, and meet your husbands." When Ra-naä stepped ahead of Ha-wani, her mother put a hand on her shoulder. "As the elder daughter, your sister will go first."

Stepping aside, Ra-naä frowned at her mother.

Outside, in the sunlight, Ha-wani blinked. Naked from the waist up, with her skirt skimming her knees, she squared her shoulders and lifted her breasts. Her father took her hand and led her to the ramada where two young men waited. A man she assumed to be their father stood to the side. She glanced at each man, her eyes averted from theirs, wondering which of the two young men she was to marry. One was tall and muscular. An iridescent shell pendant at his neck flashed in the dappled sunlight under the ramada's brush covering. A beautifully carved horned lizard. The other man was shorter but equally muscular.

When her father placed her hand in the hand of the taller brother, her heart beat a little faster. She focused on the horned lizard resting against his dark skin.

Her father presented Ra-naä to the shorter brother, and the two couples, with their hands clasped between them, waited for their fathers to bring the matrimonial ribbons. Hand-woven by their mother once she knew her daughters would live to marriageable age, she had decorated each ribbon with tiny, colorful beads.

Robanti handed his elder daughter's ribbon to the tall man.

"Tonrai, I give my daughter to you for your wife. You may bind Ha-wani's spirit to yours."

Her heart pounded in her ears. Never had her father given her name to someone outside the family. *He knows my name. What if he doesn't like me?*

Tonrai turned Ha-wani's right hand over and laid the ribbon across her palm. Holding it between their hands, he used his free hand to wrap it over and around their hands several times. "Ha-wani, I bind your spirit to my own. You are my wife."

She sensed he inclined his head toward her, and she heard the soft rattle of shell tinklers.* Involuntarily, she glanced into his eyes, and his spirit opened to her. She broke eye contact and concentrated on his pendant.

Robanti handed the second ribbon to the shorter man, saying, "Chanu, I give my daughter to you for your wife. You may bind Ra-naä's spirit to yours."

Chanu took the ribbon, and, like Tonrai, bound them as husband and wife.

After the girls collected their extra skirts, sandals, and winter wraps into baskets, they said goodbye to their parents. As Lantha bade each girl to give her husband healthy children, Ha-wani could not stop her tears. "Will I see you again, Mother?"

"If the gods will it."

They left the village, Vachai in the lead, followed by Tonrai and Chanu, with Ha-wani, torn between loss and anticipation, and Ra-naä, chattering and laughing, walking into an unknown future with men they had just met.

The clear, blue dome of sky hung over a golden desert basin as the path brought them closer to the mountains east of Ha-wani and Ra-naä's home village. A slight breeze blew drying blossoms from the bean and green stick trees* along the trail, showering them with yellow petals. Birds chattered and fluttered in the scrub, and a jackrabbit hunched beside the trail. Ordinarily, she would have smiled at his attempt to look like nothing more than a rock as they passed, but instead she focused on her new husband as he walked out ahead of her. His long, black hair was tied back with a leather thong from which tiny shell tinklers hung. *Ah, that's the source of the music I heard when he inclined his head.* His waist was not quite as narrow as his brother's, but he moved with a powerful grace, his breechclout swinging easily with each step.

A light sheen of sweat glistened on his broad shoulders, and yellow blossoms clung to his hair and his back. He seemed to have come directly from the Sea Ania, the Flower World beneath the dawn. She plucked a few blossoms from her arms and her breasts and held them in her hands like treasure.

As they neared Onaati-Kaä, Tonrai and Chanu dropped back to walk with their new wives.

"Our village lies in the embrace of Great-Grandfather Mountain," he said, sweeping his arm toward the massive ridge to the south, "and Great-Grandmother Mountain." He nodded toward the east.

"We call that one 'Sunrise Mountain.'"

He looked surprised. "Do you not know Mother Earth and Father Sky put them here to watch over us as great-grandparents?"

"The mountains behind us watch over Honey Bee Village." She glanced over her shoulder and realized how small those mountains were and wished she had said nothing. Her new husband would think she was stupid.

Tonrai, silent for a moment, said, "Of course, Mother Earth and Father Sky no doubt put your mountains there to serve your village as they put these here for us." He smiled. "And the sun does rise from behind Great-Grandmother."

As they neared the village, they passed dwellings with families who greeted them, along with vacant houses and the remains of some burned-out homes.

"Our village has gotten smaller in recent years. Some of us live inside those walls you see up ahead, and others live out here."

It seemed odd they lived separately, but she had no time to ask because they entered the walled compound, where several family clusters of mud-plastered dwellings were scattered around a broad open plaza. Like those in her own village, the houses were rectangular with flat roofs and low entrances. She was surprised to see among them two houses raised higher than the others on an earthen platform mound. Tonrai's family greeted them noisily.

Ha-wani relaxed when her new mother-in-law took her hand. "Welcome, Daughter. I am Li-naä." Tonrai's mother was a handsome woman, somewhat taller than Ha-wani, with bright eyes and a ready smile.

"Thank you, Mother. I am Ha-wani." Her new mother-in-law gathered her two youngest children around her with a low, clucking sound, reminding Ha-wani of her father's sister-in-law, also named Li-naä. Their spirit guide was the quail, a desert bird very protective of her young.

Tonrai's younger sister smiled and took Ha-wani's hand, saying, "Welcome to our family, Sister. I am Wokkai."

Dove. It suits her.

Tonrai's sister lifted her chin, lengthening an already slender neck and met Ha-wani's eyes without hesitation. Her hair was parted in the middle and twisted into knots over each ear, indicating that she was not yet a woman. Ha-wani guessed she was not far from it.

Tonrai's brother, a skinny boy who had lived perhaps eight turnings of the seasons, did not step forward until Li-naä encouraged him with a quiet *tut tut*. The boy smiled shyly. "I am Benai. Welcome." His large, inquisitive eyes searched hers for only a moment before he averted them.

Horned owl. Impressive. But a lot to live up to. She smiled, hoping to put him at ease.

Never in her life had she learned so many names in such a short time. Her small family at Honey Bee only included her parents, Ra-naä, her father's brother, his wife and their three young children. It was, at first, a little overwhelming. She learned Vachai's spirit name was Maasii, for the deer. Within the family they, like everyone else, used their spirit names, but his powerful connection with growing the crops gave him a public name meaning "corn." His work was so completely tied into his identity that even the family had fallen into the habit of calling him Vachai.

Vachai's brother, Maisokai, his wife, Kokii, and their three sons shared a house group with Tonrai's family. Maisokai was known in the community as Nothai because he worked closely with his brother managing the harvesting for the village. Like his brother, even the family called him Nothai most of the time.

Li-naä invited them to put their belongings into one of the pit houses. The cool interior felt good after their long walk from Honey Bee Village. It was a house much like the one they were raised in, with a mud-plastered floor a short distance below the ground and brush interior walls and ceiling. Baskets and hides hung from nubs on the roof support posts, and pots of various sizes and shapes, along with covered baskets rested on the ledge that circled the interior at the base of the wall. Opposite, it held two throwing sticks, two bows, along with several arrows, a coil of yucca fiber rope, an ax, and several knives. The low fire in the shallow hearth, its smoke curling toward the entrance, filled the room with the fragrance of bean tree wood. "This is your home. You will live here with my sons." She ducked outside, leaving the two girls with mouths agape.

Ra-naä dropped her basket and danced around the hearth. "Our own house! We will not have to be quiet when we join with our husbands."

Ha-wani flushed. "You're eager for your first joining?"

"Of course. My first with him and many to follow." She paused and looked thoughtfully at her sister. "Don't you want to join with Tonrai?"

She hesitated. "I think so, but I'm scared." The sight of the rolled sleeping mats on the ledge in the back of the room made her stomach flutter.

"Don't be silly." Ra-naä tossed her hair over her shoulder, stepped closer, and whispered. "Relax and breathe in when he puts his man-part into you. You will know what to do, and you will like it."

Ha-wani's eyes opened wide. "Ra-naä! Where did you learn this?"

Her sister grinned and shrugged. "Tonight will not be my first time."

Ha-wani stammered, "Who!? When—?"

"Never mind who." She waved the question aside. "Boys can join with girls even if they haven't completed their manhood initiation. When their voices get deep and hair grows under their arms and around their man-part, they are ready."

At the same moment, Tonrai poked his head through the entrance. "Is everything all right in here? Can I do anything?"

Ra-naä laughed. "No—not yet anyway."

Ha-wani flushed again.

"Our village is here to welcome you." When he held out his hand, Ha-wani stepped forward and took it, but she hesitated. He smiled and said, "Don't be afraid, Wife."

Wife. He called me "wife." Her heart sang as she stepped, blinking, into the bright afternoon sunlight. Tonrai introduced an older man who stood under the ramada. "This is An-nat, our knowledge-keeper."

The man bowed his head and took her hand. "Welcome to Onaati-Kaä."

She tipped her head and focused on his chest, surprisingly muscular for an older man. The knowledge-keeper at Honey Bee was soft and wrinkled. "Thank you."

When another man stepped forward, displacing the knowledge-keeper, she recognized his sour odor. Gray hair, twisted into two knots, one on top the other, gave the impression of height, but he was no taller than she. A long pin, with shell tinklers and tiny beads hanging from the end, stuck from the knots. A turquoise-studded shell pendant rested on his chest.

Tonrai's introduction was brief. "Our fire-keeper."

She held her breath when he clasped her hand with both of his and rubbed a bony finger across her palm. "Welcome to my village."

Concentrating on the pendant, she said, "Thank you." When she tried to extract her hand, he held it, making her wait. When he walked away, her knees buckled, but Tonrai caught her before she fell.

She leaned against him, her heart pounding. With her head against her husband's chest, his heart beating in her ear, she willed her own to beat in time with his.

Later, she could not remember anyone else she met.

Chapter 3

Yellow Moon 1158 (April)

The gentle waves rushing in and out around his toes uncovered a small brown dome. When he cleared the sand around it, he discovered the top half of a large clam shell. Speckled brown and white grooves and ridges circled the outer shell, converging at the umbo,* where, when the clam was alive, the upper and lower halves of the shell hinged. The iridescent rainbow colors dancing in the concave interior took his breath away.

Tonrai held the bracelet in his hand and remembered, not so terribly long ago, when he found the shell. He rubbed his finger around the smooth circle, smelling again the salt air, remembering its taste on his lips, and almost feeling again the cool sea swirling around his bare feet.

It was his first trip to Great Water,* the summer of his manhood initiation, and he had been more successful than the other boys in trading for the finest shells. But the Bead-Maker, Dar, was beyond ordinary pride when it came to the shell* his apprentice found one evening on the beach.

Dar, laying a strong hand on his shoulder, said, "The gods have given you a matchless shell. You must keep it until they are ready to guide your hands. As good as you are, your skill must be equal to the shell's perfection. Do not ask for its spirit before you are ready." Tonrai had apprenticed with Dar from childhood, learning quickly and soon surpassing his mentor, crafting pendants, rings, and bracelets from the shells others had brought back from the sea.

Tonrai's dark eyes glistened. Would he ever be ready to do it honor? Dar handed him a bundle of sea grass and instructed him to wrap it for the trip back to the village. The presence of the shell in his burden basket made the other shells, trade goods, and salt lighter as he followed the trail back from the sea.

At home, he dug a niche in the plastered floor of the house his parents had built for him, his brother, and the wives they would someday take. He wrapped the shell again with a length of hide and covered it with dirt and a new layer of mud plaster. He thanked the gods, praying that his desire to craft the perfect gift for his future wife would do the shell honor and that they would guide his hands when the time came.

The following spring, after Robanti's visit to arrange the marriage, Tonrai retrieved the shell, carried it into the desert toward the agave terraces, and sat on a rock. With an unobstructed view of the massive towers and pinnacles of Great-Grandfather and the softer lines of Great-Grandmother, he sought their guidance. He cradled the shell and considered the relationship between these two mountains that held his village in their embrace. They had been here since before remembering, and he was certain they would remain here long after he was gone. He hoped his wife would be equally steadfast and that their life together would be long-lasting as well.

Closing his eyes, he ran his thumb along the knobs and ridges of the shell, tracing each circle to the bulging umbo as he asked the shell to reveal its spirit. Shortly, a frog leaped into his thoughts and made him smile. He cupped his hands around the shell in much the same way he might hold a frog and prayed his skill would honor the spirit who resided there. He stood and thanked both mountains for their guidance.

He had only taken a step or two toward the compound when a horned lizard darted across the path, its spiny horns lifting slightly as it paused to regard him with beady eyes. Tonrai smiled when the little fellow waddled out of sight into the brush. Perhaps there was room in the shell for both frog and lizard.

In the morning, he left the rising heat of the desert and climbed high into the canyon, past the rock pools where Great-Grandmother collected rain and snow melt, to her summit where the air was cool and her big trees stayed green through all seasons. Selecting a tall evergreen, he asked permission to collect its essence. With his ax, he removed a wide strip of bark close to the ground, and, using his knife, he scored the bare wood with V-shaped lines. Sticky droplets of sap pearled and then joined to flow toward the small bowl he had tucked beneath the lowermost V.

While he waited for the sap to run, he went to a nearby clearing and stood with his hunting stick* behind his shoulder. Unmoving, he listened to squirrels chattering in the overhead branches. One spiraled headfirst down the trunk of a pine across from him and scampered into the open. It stopped, head lifted, tufted ears alert, tail switching back and forth, its eyes on the strange figure. Because the figure remained still, the squirrel assumed no danger and turned to forage among the grasses. Tonrai whipped his arm, and the stick spun through the air with such speed the animal had no time to move. He thanked it for the stew Li-naä would make tonight.

Returning for the sap, he thanked the tree and the forest for its gifts. Covering the small bowl with a larger one, he wrapped them both in soft leather and placed them in his burden basket. He hung the squirrel on the sash at his waist, swung the basket behind him, and secured the strap against his forehead.

Back in the village, he put the bowl of sap close to the fire under the ramada where, in warming, it would thicken into pitch. While his mother skinned the squirrel, he sang a prayer for guidance to honor the spirit of the frog within the shell. He ground a hole in the center of the shell and enlarged the hole with a small hammerstone,* setting aside a piece to make a horned lizard pendant. Only the outer ring of the shell remained with the umbo intact. He ground it smooth all the way around, hoping it would slide easily over the hand of his future wife and settle on her wrist.

Using a small brush of yucca fibers, he applied the pitch to the bulge, creating the design he imagined. He worked painstakingly, straightening or rounding the margins as necessary. When the design was finished, he placed the shell in a small, clay pot into which he poured aged, fermented liquor from the giant cactus.* He sang a prayer for the spirits of the shell, the pitch, and the liquor to come together as one.

After the cactus liquor etched the unprotected parts of the shell and the pitch was cleaned away, he looked into the face of a frog. He examined its lines, its curves, and its expression, incising them and further defining the creature who lived in the bracelet. He polished it to a high gloss, wrapped it in a clean square of cotton, and put it in a new basket his mother had specially woven for this occasion.

In the days following their marriage, Ha-wani and Tonrai took long walks, talking but mostly seeking to understand the person they had pledged their lives to. One evening, they followed the path toward Great-Grandfather Mountain, surrounded by a still-golden desert. Yellow flowers covered the trees, and bees buzzed and hovered in and out of the blossoms. Sparrows flitted through the scrub, and a cactus wren scolded them when they passed too close to her nest.

Beyond the orange mallow along either side of the trail, the thorny branches of slimwood* were thick with green leaves and pointed their red blossoms at Father Sky. Soon enough, blossoms would fade, leaves would drop, and bare branches would stand guard over the desert waiting for rain.

They continued walking in comfortable silence. At first, Ha-wani thought if she didn't keep up a constant chatter, he would think her distant or unfriendly or—or—or something. She didn't know what he would think if she didn't talk. Gradually, his even temperament and patience won her over, and she learned the silence meant they were growing closer.

He pointed to a hollowed-out oval in the ground beside the trail. "Many years ago, before remembering, villages around here gathered for grand celebrations. Some say they played a kind of ball game* here."

"My village has one, too. I heard the same stories from my grandparents, but they said they learned about it from our knowledge-keeper."

"Now, it's all grown over with acacia and weeds. It's useless."

Ha-wani tried to focus on the lizard running on the path ahead of them, but she could not ignore the presence of the man beside her.

"When we were children, we pretended we knew what those people long ago did." He pointed to a rock beside the path. "We put a rock about that size at both ends and divided into teams. Each team had to try to break through the other team to steal it and make it back to our side without being caught. Sometimes it got rough."

He picked up a stone and tossed it up and down with one hand. He wound up and hurled the stone the length of the ball court, watching to see how far it went.

Standing there with him, she was drawn to the muscular contours of his chest and abdomen, but she remained fearful about the true joining with her new husband. It was expected, and it was natural. Growing up, she was aware of her parents' nighttime joinings, but Ra-naä's description on their wedding day had unsettled her. As was customary, that night, she averted her eyes in the dim light of the hearth fire, but her sister was both brazen and noisy, nothing like the quiet grunting of her parents. She had trembled so violently, Tonrai had not pressed her. She could not put it off for much longer.

Now, without realizing it, she focused on one of his nipples, dark against smooth brown skin. She had the urge to touch it, to touch him. Just as she lifted her hand, he grinned and flexed his chest muscles making his nipples dance up and down.

Ha-wani turned away, surprised and embarrassed. "I'm sorry—"

Tonrai put both arms around her from behind. "No. I'm sorry. I shouldn't have teased you." He kissed her on the shoulder. She shivered, and he stepped away.

When she turned back to him, he stood with his shoulders back, looking up. Above them, a pair of ravens flew with effortless grace, their wings whooshing. One glided into the top of a nearby tree. Tonrai focused on the other as he circled above his mate.

Examining him while his attention was elsewhere, she took in the tattooed lines streaking his cheeks beneath his eyes, one slightly thinner than the rest, and the sharp contour of his jawline. A thin scar bisected his upper lip. A head taller than she, his broad shoulders and muscled chest glistened, and the horned lizard at his throat reflected the sunlight.

When he turned to her, his dark eyes held hers. She sensed his spirit, circling her own, reaching out, stepping back, reaching again, inviting her to allow him in—not to steal her spirit, but to truly bind them. Taking a breath, she surrendered, and a powerful feeling washed over her—one of peace and strength.

He wrapped her in his arms, threading fingers through her long black hair and pulling her head back as he slid kisses from her lips to her neck and her breasts. A longing she had never experienced settled low in her body. Briefly, she wondered what it meant. Was she ready for a true joining? The only thing she knew for sure was that she wanted to be closer to him, to have him hold her and not let her go.

Tonrai stepped back and placed his hands on her shoulders, looking into her eyes. "We are one," he whispered.

Now, she understood the closeness she desired. *That's why it's called a true joining.* She opened her eyes to his gaze and said, "We are one."

Over his shoulder, Ha-wani watched the male raven join his mate in the tree, and she smiled, grateful for her spirit bird's blessing at this moment. Her apprehensions about her marriage and this strange new village dissolved, and she felt lighter. Her spirit, now bound to her husband's, was strong.

When they returned to the compound, Tonrai asked her to wait behind their house. He went inside and brought out a small, cloth-covered basket. He held it before her and lifted the cloth.

Ha-wani gasped, almost afraid to touch a bracelet more beautiful than she'd ever seen.

"It's yours, Wife." Tonrai's voice was barely above a whisper.

She took it, turning it around, examining the exquisite carving. "It's . . . it's beautiful."

Incised on the valve was the face of a frog, and the circle was polished to a high gloss. She held it up to the fading sunlight. Its iridescence matched the horned lizard hanging from his neck.

He slid the bracelet on her wrist, lifted her hand and brushed a kiss across her knuckles. "I pledge you my love and protection."

She gazed into his eyes. "I pledge you my love and loyalty."

They sat under the ramada, watching the moon rise over Great-Grandmother. Ra-naä and Chanu had gone inside earlier.

Tonrai held her hand, rubbing his thumb along the ring of the bracelet. "Do you miss your parents?"

"Yes. I miss them, but it helps to have Ra-naä here."

He nodded. "I think my brother is pleased to have your sister for his wife. And she seems happy as well."

Outside the walls, an owl hooted. Another answered from a distant tree. Tonrai stood and took her hand. "You are ready?"

"Yes, my husband."

They ducked into the dwelling where Chanu and Ra-naä slept, one snoring loudly and the other breathing quietly.

Moonlight filtered through openings in the side and back walls where the exterior mud plaster had deteriorated and embers glowed in the hearth. Tonrai led her to his mat. Standing behind her in the dim light, he placed his hands on her shoulders, and she knelt. He knelt, too, brushing kisses along her shoulders and the back of her neck. He wrapped his arms around her waist and pulled her against his body. She felt him, hard against her back, and, although she was afraid, she knew what was expected. Bending forward, on her hands and knees, she raised herself to him. As he broke into her, she sucked in her breath and lifted her head, breathing deeply, pressing her buttocks against his thrusting, and gasping with each thrust. When Tonrai pushed deeper, groaned, and stilled, she, too, stilled. He wrapped his arms around her and fell forward, stretching her out beneath his body and rolling to the side.

Lying in a shaft of moonlight, he pulled her against him, their knees bent together, her head resting on his arm, and she drifted to sleep remembering the music of their joining, of the tinklers in his hair.

Chapter 4

Bean Tree Moon 1158 (May)

Not long ago, dwellings covered the whole length of the ridge." Tonrai swung his arm around to encompass everything to the west. "Hundreds of them. Now only a few remain."

The sky was clear, the air cool as the sun rose higher over the agave terraces.* Trees beside the path, in the foothills of Great-Grandfather Mountain, and in the village promised a good harvest of beans. On either side of the path, red blossoms topped slimwood branches, and purple and red prickly pear and barrel cactus flowers foreshadowed an abundance of fruit.

"What happened? Where did they go?"

"I don't know. In search of a place with more reliable rivers, probably."

"They left all at once?"

"No. It took a long time—starting before I was born, so I don't remember when the village was so big. My father said people started leaving after our fire-keeper suddenly died and his son—our current fire-keeper—rose to the position."

Ha-wani shivered, unready to tell her husband about her previous encounter with Fire-Keeper. She had tried to stay out of his way since moving to Onaa-ti-Kaä, but, at unguarded moments, an involuntary shudder swept over her. She didn't know why. But one day she realized he was standing on his platform mound staring at her.

Tonrai took her hand and rubbed his thumb on the bracelet. "I was about seven years old when we began building the walls. Chanu and I helped collect the rocks. That's why you don't see a lot of those kinds of rocks out here." Around them, the desert sported large boulders or stones, very few like those in the walls.

"Why did your fire-keeper think your village needed such a compound?"

"In case of attacks by our enemies, he said."

"Who? What enemies?"

"I don't know. But he convinced the Council of Elders. Only my father and Knowledge-Keeper opposed him."

"We must act now." He stood before the others in the dim light of the Council House. "They are coming,* and if we do not prepare, we will be destroyed."

"Who is coming, Fire-Keeper?" Thandoi, Chief Elder for several years, was well-regarded by the people. He was an imposing man, taller than anyone in the village and broad across the shoulders. His badge of leadership, passed to the village leader since before remembering, was a shell pendant, carved in a circle much like a bracelet, that hung from a necklace of small turquoise and bone beads. Two short strands of beads with iridescent bird effigies hung in the center.

"Who? You ask who?" Fire-Keeper's shrill voice cracked, spittle dripped to his chin, and the shells dangling from the bone pin in his hair swung in circles. Of the council members around the hearth, he was the only one standing. "They pass by, fleeing their villages in the north. They travel long distances, looking for somewhere to settle." He pounded his staff against the plastered floor, the bells ringing,* the beads rattling, feathers* flying. "They are not like us, and they have different ways. They do not belong here."

"We've had no problems from those people, Fire-Keeper. We welcomed them and traded with them." An-nat's quiet voice resonated in the small pit house. The tattooed lines on his forehead crumpled with his frown. As Knowledge-Keeper, he held stories from before remembering on his calendar stick, recounting the people's history each winter when venomous snakes slept. Besides the Chief Elder, he was among the most respected leaders in the village. On the council, only Dar was older.

The shaman glared at him. "We welcome them at our peril. You think because they trade with us, we are safe from their intentions? Should we wait until it is too late to protect our village, our people, our livelihood?" He sneered. "You are a fool. Who will you tell the story to when we are no more?"

An-nat's eyes flashed with anger. "You dare call me a fool?"

Thandoi's broad hand urged silence. "What do you propose, Fire-Keeper?"

"We must build a wall around the village."

"A wall?" Chief Elder frowned. "Our village stretches the entire length of this ridge. How could we possibly build a wall around it?"

"Not the village as it exists now. We can wall in a smaller area where our most valuable citizens will live and provide the leadership our people need." He pointed his staff in the direction of Elder Brother Wash. "Above the wash, there is enough room for a small compound." He paused and looked at Amureo, the hunter.

"Fire-Keeper's right," Amureo said. "Think about your children. I want my only surviving son to grow to manhood. He will be a great leader—like me, a hunter of uncommon skill." He looked at the farmer. "And you, Vachai, do you want to risk your sons' lives through inaction?"

"Of course not, Amureo, but do we need to hide behind a wall?"

Fire-Keeper scowled. "You, like Knowledge-Keeper, are a fool." He spat on the floor at the farmer's feet.

When Vachai leaped up and started toward the shaman, Thandoi rose and stepped between them. "Enough! I will not permit such behavior in the Council House." He laid his hand on Vachai's shoulder, and spoke quietly. "Sit down, please."

Vachai returned to his seat. "I apologize, Chief Elder."

To the shaman, Thandoi said, "Insults of that nature are unacceptable here. We will show respect for one another."

The shaman twisted his mouth into a poor imitation of a smile. "Of course, Chief Elder. May I continue?"

"Please." Thandoi sat again.

"It is not just these outsiders we have to fear." He paced back and forth and then whispered, "I have had a vision." Among those around the hearth, only Vachai looked skeptical. The others sat straighter and focused on the shaman.

"Father Sky appeared in a blinding flash of light. He berated me, accused me of dishonoring him. Of failing to lead the people as he had instructed. He threatened to deny the rains we need. He threatened to close the eye of day and leave us in darkness. He said Mother Earth would swallow our seeds, but she would bring forth no crops."

At this, even Vachai sat straighter.

"With each pronouncement, the light around Father Sky dimmed. At last, I was enveloped by total darkness—a darkness like I had never known before. A terrifying, empty world with nothing to sustain us." He waited several moments. "It is a darkness we will know unless we regain Father Sky's trust and honor Mother Earth as we have been instructed since before remembering."

In vigorous talks throughout the night, only Vachai and An-nat spoke against Fire-Keeper's proposal.

The shaman stood firm, insisting that the outsiders were responsible for Father Sky's unhappiness with the people. "Mother Earth and Father Sky will no longer protect us or provide for us." He bored into Dar's spirit. "Do you not fear the day when Father Sky refuses to send the rains?"

With the shaman's eyes locked on his, Dar spoke, his voice dull and his tone flat, "Fire-Keeper is right. We must act now."

Dar's capitulation persuaded Chief Elder, and plans for the wall went forward.

Ha-wani shuddered, wanting to believe that the sha-man had lied, but she had grown up believing that fire-keepers spoke only truth to those they served. "How did they decide who would live inside the walls and who would stay out here?"

"The villagers had always worked together, my father said. They planted and tended the fields, built the dams, and hunted as one people. Even families with their own little plots, mostly for growing cot-ton, didn't mind sharing with others in times of need. Everyone shared the good harvests or, in lean years, what little the village produced. Hunters went out in teams, bringing animals—large and small—back to the village. The women gathered greens from the desert, collected the bounty of the bean trees, and climbed Great-Grandmother Mountain to gather acorns. Everyone shared the cooking, and no one went hungry. The people lived together in friendship."

She considered his description. It was not unlike her parents' village. Ha-wani's gaze traced the pro-file of Great-Grandfather Mountain's rugged ridge to where it sloped down to the desert basin. She searched across the distance for the notch and small peak in the Little Dove Mountains marking the place where her parents lived. "That's as it was in Honey Bee, although, recently, some of the men decided they will only be hunters, and they won't go into the fields to help with the planting and harvesting."

A pair of red-shouldered hawks sailed in broad circles above them. Tonrai followed their flight for a moment. "People tend toward their greatest talent, like hunting, or making jewelry—like this." He took her hand and pushed the bracelet around so the spirit of the frog could see them. "Fire-Keeper insisted that those who use special talents on behalf of the village would live inside the wall and the farmers and work-ers would live outside."

Ha-wani's blue chin lines lifted when she smiled at the frog. But then she frowned. "Vachai and his brother Nothai are farmers, and your family is inside. You have your own house group, and your father's on the council."

"My father and his father before him had always directed the planting and Nothai the harvesting. The village has depended on their knowledge and guidance for many years. As much as Fire-Keeper doesn't want to admit it, my father and his brother are important to the welfare of the village."

"I have only known your father a short time, but I have learned what a fine man he is." She laid a hand on his cheek. "You are very like him."

Tonrai lifted her hand and kissed the palm. "I can only hope that's true." He took her in his arms and kissed her—a long, lingering kiss with the promise of joining. He stepped back, took her hands, blew out a long breath, and said, "I know what I'd like to do this very moment, but . . . Let's sit and finish our conversation."

Ha-wani laughed and joined him on the boulder next to the trail. "You too easily distract me, Husband. What were we saying?"

"I was telling you why our family was allowed to move inside the compound. Where was I?" He thought for a moment. "Oh yes. Actually, Chanu and I, even though we were still young boys, were part of the reason our family came inside. Chanu was apprenticing with Chief Elder, making spear points and stone tools, sometimes even better than his teacher. He had already made his first kill, as had I, so everyone expected him to become a hunter and weapon maker. I was apprenticing with Dar at the time. These things suggested we would grow in importance. So, reluctantly, Fire-Keeper allowed us inside. He could hardly deny Chief Elder's apprentice."

Across the trail from them, a desiccated prickly pear with only a few orange blossoms, harbored a pack rat who had lined the path to his nest with wicked joints of the cholla cactus. The intent was to ward off a snake intrusion, but a determined snake would not be deterred.

She glanced again across the desert basin at the familiar notch and peak. "I don't think anyone in Honey Bee ever talked about building a wall."

"Interesting. You would think other villages might also distrust the strangers passing by." He hesitated. "The people of Sleeping Snake,* Rattlesnake, and your village have always been our friends, allies, and trading partners, but Fire-Keeper said even our neighbors could turn against us. But, in spite of what he says, he continues to meet with the shamans from those villages."

Of course. Fire-Keeper had been to Honey Bee numerous times, where she had somehow caught his attention. "My people are good people. Our fathers have been friends for years."

"I know. We might not be together now if they weren't friends." He took her hand and turned the bracelet so the frog sat atop her wrist and rubbed his finger across the image. "It would be nice if our friend here would bring the kind of rain we need. Maybe things would change."

"I will sing for the rains."

"Fire-Keeper was furious when my father allowed Robanti to enter the compound to discuss our marriage."

Ha-wani did not comment, wondering if the shaman knew she was Robanti's daughter. She shifted closer to Tonrai, needing to feel protected by his touch.

He put his arm around her shoulders and pulled her close. "He would like to take full control of the village, pushing Chief Elder and the Council aside."

She tucked her head into the crook of his neck and whispered, "You do not care for him?"

A runner-bird, his crest lifted and his long tail stretched out behind, dashed through the scrub and snatched a whiptail lizard that had just skittered past them on the trail. He paused to look at them with the lizard hanging from his beak before flying a short distance into thicker scrub.

"I don't. Not at all. I don't trust him with the future of our village."

Ha-wani breathed out a long sigh.

Tonrai opened a space between them so he could look into her eyes. "You're relieved. Why?"

"He makes me nervous."

"How?"

Leaning into him, she wrapped her arms around herself, squeezing her shoulders in tight. "He stares at me when you're not around. I feel him searching my eyes, coaxing me to look at him. I try to resist, but sometimes I'm afraid my spirit isn't strong enough."

Chapter 5

Bean Tree Moon 1158 (May)

Shortly after Ha-wani arrived in Onaati-Kaä, she observed the wood cutter making his rounds from ramada to ramada with firewood. Kutareo was a boy of some eighteen years who never spoke. Cutting and gathering firewood for the village and girdling sturdy bean trees in anticipation of collecting dead wood for roof supports were his contributions to the village. He had no wife or children, and his days followed an unvarying routine. Each morning, he slipped in and out of the compound with armload upon armload of firewood. He passed from ramada to ramada so quietly the villagers rarely noticed him, even when he knelt and stacked their wood in a precise pyramid. He delivered the shaman's first, then Knowledge-Keeper's, Thandoi's, Vachai's, and finally Amureo's group.

No one ever looked at him. No one ever spoke to him. She feared the boy had become invisible to the people; they might only miss him if, one day, he failed to bring them wood. One morning, hoping to engage him in conversation, when he brought the wood to her ramada, she greeted him. "Good morning, Kutareo. How are you?"

The boy kept his head down and finished stacking the wood. He stood quickly and hurried to deliver wood to his brother's house group.

Thinking she had made him uncomfortable, in the days that followed, she simply said, "Thank you," when he brought the wood. At first, he offered no response. Later, he simply grunted. And, finally, one day, he glanced up at her, meeting her eyes briefly, and she glimpsed a spirit that was stronger than even he might know.

Kutareo lived in Amureo's house group, which was separated from the shaman's platform mound by a low trash mound. The plaza lay between his group and all the others. There were but two houses in the group: one the hunter shared with his wife and son, and another for Amureo's brother, Panereo— the builder—his wife, and their four small children. Kutareo lived with Panereo.

One evening, Ha-wani noticed Kutareo sitting on the ground outside his dwelling, his knees drawn up to his chin, his arms wrapped around his legs, a blank expression on his face, rocking back and forth. Amureo's wife approached him, but he kept rocking and did not acknowledge her. She planted her hands on her hips, and, although her voice carried across the village, Ha-wani couldn't make out the words. The woman turned and walked away.

Panereo's children, who were playing under the ramada, squealing and laughing in their game, scrambled into the house when Amureo, a length of giant cactus rib in his hand, came back with his wife. Hunter jerked the young man to his feet and back-handed him. Kutareo stumbled back and fell, curling into a ball and protecting his head as his brother struck him repeatedly across the back with the rib.

Ha-wani took two steps forward, but Tonrai grabbed her arm. "No."

"But—"

"We must not interfere. We must not watch."

She glanced around at her family and those in the other households. No one paid attention except Tonrai's sister. Wokkai hid behind their house, holding her hands over her ears.

Tonrai gently turned his wife to face him, but she could not block out the sounds. She flinched with each slap of the cactus rib and each cry from Kutareo. Tonrai led her out of the compound, not stopping until they reached the boulder overlooking the agave terraces. He invited her to sit with him, but he did not speak. Ha-wani's breathing eased as she focused on the high ridge of Great-Grandfather Mountain, following it westward to its end and looking for the familiar notch and peak.

When she turned her gaze to him, he said, "You must get used to seeing that, or you must learn not to see it."

"He does this often?" She searched her husband's eyes for a denial.

"Yes, and not just Kutareo. He beats his wife as well. Do the men in Honey Bee not beat their wives and children?"

"Kutareo is not his child. He is his brother."

"The boy is like a child."

"In my village, some men beat their wives and children, but I never saw it so close. Here, we see what others might prefer to keep private." She hesitated. "Will you beat me if I displease you?"

"You are my wife, and you must do as I bid. But no, I will not beat you. I have never seen my father strike my mother, and Nothai has never struck Kokii or his children." He smiled. "Besides, I don't think you will ever displease me."

She squeezed his hand. "You said Kutareo is like a child. Is that why he is not married?"

Tonrai turned the bracelet on her wrist so the shell frog could join them. "He is not a man because he has never killed an animal—I don't think anyone ever took him hunting. He has not made the trip to Great Water. I doubt he will do either. He is fortunate to have a valuable role, but he is destined to be alone."

Ha-wani pondered his words. "I suppose I never gave much thought to what makes a boy into a man. I became a woman when my first blood flowed, and I went to the women's hut. I didn't do anything but stay away from the men until I was clean. Girls become women naturally. Our blood makes us women. Even though there are natural changes in boys as well, those things do not make them men? A boy is only a man when he meets certain challenges?"

Tonrai smiled. "The natural changes you speak of—when hair grows around our man-parts and our voices deepen—tell our fathers to plan our first hunt. But we don't have blood, so there is no need to hide from the women."

She remembered Ra-naä's words on their wedding day. "But a boy can join with a woman. He just can't get married."

"The desire comes to us naturally. Boys like Amureo's son and Nothai's son, Cheshonii, have both made their kills, as have a few boys outside the compound, but they have not made the trip to Great Water. So their desires go unmet because they cannot marry."

Thinking about her sister, she asked, "Do they seek out girls to satisfy their desires?"

"Some do, but if caught, the girl would be punished. She would be barred from ever marrying."

She hesitated, not saying aloud what was in her heart. "Is the boy punished also?"

"It depends. He might be cast out of the village, but that doesn't happen very often."

Realizing Ra-naä might not be with her at Onaati-Kaä if she had been caught, she said, "It doesn't seem fair."

"It is our way."

She tipped her head toward a jackrabbit crouching under a nearby bush. He turned his long ears in their direction. "If you had your hunting stick, you could show me what a skilled hunter you are." She wrapped her fingers around his upper arm and squeezed his muscle. "You could show me how you became a man." She grinned. "And we'd have rabbit stew for dinner."

"Yes, we'd have rabbit stew, but jackrabbits don't count. We must kill a bighorn or a deer, something of similar size. As boys, we learned first to use snares and a rabbit stick.* We practiced killing the rodents, gophers, and birds that raid the fields. We hunted rabbits and ground squirrels. Everything prepared us for the big hunt."

"Well, I'm glad you became a man. Otherwise, we would not be sitting here talking about such things."

Tonrai pulled her close. "Me, too."

She rested her head on his chest and listened to his heartbeat.

Behind them, the sun, hanging low in the west, painted the mountains pink, and evening coolness was upon them. Tonrai took her hand and said, "We should go back, now."

They set out on the path, but Ha-wani stopped and turned to her husband. "What about Flute Player and Drummer? They live in the same house, but they do not have wives. Have they never hunted or made the trip to Great Water?"

Walking again, Tonrai answered, "Usareo completed both, but Vaeleo has done neither. He never expressed interest. They were close friends as boys, and when we moved inside the walls, Knowledge-Keeper and Bead-Maker combined their families. Drummer is Bead Maker's brother, and Flute-Player is brother to Knowledge-Keeper."

"Why is there a vacant house in their group?"

"Originally, they intended for each of their brothers to have a house when they took wives and had children. But they are content to share a house."

After the sun set, the compound was quiet. Parents had called their small children in from play, and ramada fires were banked. The moon rose above the mountain, bathing the desert in the half-light of night.* As she started into their dwelling, Ha-wani noticed someone behind her mother-in-law's house. Tonrai's little sister sat hugging her knees to her chest, with her face lifted to the sky.

"I'll be in shortly, Husband." Ha-wani didn't believe the girl was simply watching for the stars to emerge. "May I join you?"

Wokkai turned, her face wet with tears. Ha-wani knelt before the girl and took her hands. "What is it, Child? Can you tell me?"

"You'll think I'm a baby." Like most children, she wore her dark hair parted in the middle with knots twisted and pinned above her ears.

Ha-wani pushed a loose strand of hair into place. "I won't. I promise."

"Kutareo. What Amureo did to him today—it was awful."

"Your brother took me out of the compound and away from it. I should have asked him to bring you, too."

Her tears flowed, and when she lifted her eyes to Ha-wani's, their spirits touched. Wokkai did not need to explain.

"You like Kutareo?"

"He's a good person." She choked back a sob. "He would never be mean to anyone."

"He's your friend?"

"Yes. And I'm his friend. He told me."

Ha-wani's eyes widened in surprise. "He talked to you?"

The girl drew the back of her hand across her eyes, wiping her tears. "I followed him one day. At first, he didn't pay any attention even though I walked along with him. He didn't look at me until I picked up some wood and handed it to him. When his arms were full, I came back to the compound with him, but I waited outside. I hid behind the acacias. When he came out, he couldn't find me, and I could tell he was sad. When I stepped from behind the bush, he grinned."

Ha-wani smiled and brushed another wayward strand of hair behind her sister-in-law's ear.

"Now, when I go with him, I talk, sometimes saying silly things. I point at the birds or rabbits and imitate bird sounds and hop around like a rabbit. When he laughs, his eyes light up, and he is handsome." She covered an embarrassed smile with her hand. "Before long, he started to make me laugh. Yesterday, when he had his last armload of wood before he came into the compound, I stood in front of him and . . . " She paused a moment before plunging ahead. "I said, 'I'm glad you're my friend,' and I looked into his eyes. Please, Sister, don't tell my mother."

"I won't." Ha-wani squeezed her hand. "What happened next?"

He looked into my eyes, and, when our spirits met, he said. 'You're my friend.'"

Before Ha-wani could think of what to say, Wokkai whispered, "Am I a bad girl?"

"Of course not, Sister."

"But when I let him look into my eyes, he saw my spirit. That means he knows my name now, but he's not family."

"You're right. That's a problem. He could misuse it and bring harm to your spirit."

"He would never misuse it."

"I hope you're right." Her sister-in-law's innocence could bring her trouble, but Ha-wani chose not to say it. "You gave him a gift, something no one else ever did, I think. You must allow his spirit to bloom in the richness of your friendship." Ha-wani left unsaid a word of caution about getting too close. Since she had not yet been to the women's hut, Wokkai might not understand.

"He has no other friends. Even Hunter's son is mean to him, and Builder's children throw stones at him. It's not fair."

"No, it's not. But we cannot control how his family treats him, but having you for a friend is a good thing."

Somewhere in the distance, coyotes yipped and howled, their voices carrying across the pale desert. "Our brothers are singing to us, reminding us it is getting late." She stood and held a hand out to the girl. "Can you go to bed now? You will be all right?"

After rising, Wokkai kept hold of Ha-wani's hand. She rubbed her finger along the bracelet. "I'm glad Tonrai made you my sister."

"Me, too."

When Wokkai reached the entry of her parents' dwelling, she turned and whispered, "Sleep well."

She slipped silently inside, and Ha-wani sighed. "And may the gods watch over you tonight and in the days that come."

When she reached her own entry, a cold hand gripped her shoulder. She cried out and spun around. There was no one behind her, but Fire-Keeper stood between her and the family ramada, the moon lighting his eyes and casting a long shadow behind him.

Tonrai rushed out, sweeping her behind him and scanning the area. "What's wrong? I heard you call out—"

"Fire-Keeper, he—"

But he was gone. No one moved in the plaza. The village was quiet. "It was nothing."

Chapter 6

Cactus Harvest Moon 1158 (June)

They're ripe," he shouted. "They're ready!" Benai and other boys had spent several days scouting the desert watching for ripened fruit to signal the time for harvest.

Benai skidded to a halt in front of his mother and Ha-wani, who were grinding bean pods under the ramada, dust rising in the still air and settling on the boy's feet.

Li-naä coughed and fanned the dust aside. "Are you sure? More than one offers the gift of fruit?"

"Yes."

"And the other boys say the same?"

"Yes. But I got here first." As he spoke, other boys dashed through the opening in the wall carrying the news to their families. It was the one time of year when the entire village, inside and outside the walls, came together in cooperation and celebration.

Throughout the desert, the giant cactus the people called the saguaro,* had bloomed weeks ago. The nectar from the waxy flowers atop their tall columns and arms drew cactus wrens, white-winged doves, and other birds during the day. At night, long-nosed bats poked into the blossoms. For the people, it was not the nectar they needed, but the sweet fruit that ripened when the flowers withered. The fruit nourished their bodies and their spirits and promised to bring them blessed rain.

"We have work to do. Run and tell Fire-Keeper."

Benai stepped backward. "F-F-Fire-Keeper?"

Ha-wani laid her hand on his shoulder. "I'll go. You stay here and help your mother." She smiled when relief washed over the boy's face. As she turned to go, she heard Li-naä tell her son not to be afraid of the shaman.

Ha-wani pondered his fear. He was scared to speak to the man, and she suspected he had a good reason. She had never seen Benai at Fire-Keeper's dwelling, but other youngsters—male and female—came out of the house from time to time, looking confused and somehow lost.

As for her, she should be fearful, but she would rather face him than let Tonrai's brother speak to him. She crossed the plaza and stood at the base of Fire-Keeper's platform mound, eyes downcast, and waited, her heart pounding in her ears. In her peripheral vision, his sandaled feet shuffled in her direction. When he stopped, standing above her, she focused on his bony toes. "Greetings, Fire-Keeper. Forgive me if I interrupt your work. The boys report the saguaro fruit is ripe."

"Ah, yes. There is much to be done to prepare for the harvest and calling down the rains."*

His feet brought him closer, pausing in front of her and disappearing as he circled her. From behind, he leaned so close his hot breath brushed her shoulder. Suppressing a shudder, Ha-wani wrapped a hand around her bracelet, casting her spirit to Tonrai, asking his spirit to stand with her.

He passed so closely, her skirt swept against her legs, and his body odor enveloped her. She forced herself to remain still, tightening her shoulders and wrapping her arms around herself. Holding her breath, she called on the raven to protect her from his intrusion and felt the reassuring brush of dark wings.

"Well done, Ha-wani," he whispered. "Your spirit is strong. It guards you well. You don't know how much you can do, but you are learning. Each time you call on your spirit, you are stronger, and you show me the power within your grasp. I can help you learn to use it." He laid a bony hand on her shoulder. "Let me in."

At the touch of his cold hand, she suppressed a shudder, opening her spirit only to her heart, holding it more deeply inside, sensing the dark wings protecting her. Through her sandals, the pull of the Earth gave her comfort, reminding her it was the source of her spirit, of her strength.

When the shaman stepped in front of her, he lifted her chin and traced a blue line with his thumbnail. "Ha-wani. You will let me in."

She stood rooted to the ground with her eyes barely open, holding her gaze on his feet. Behind her, she sensed the growing excitement among the people as the news spread from household to household. She asked, "May I carry the news to the villagers to prepare for the cactus harvest and calling down the rains?"

Fire-Keeper grunted and dropped his hand. "Go." He spat the word at her. "Tell the others we will leave the village upon the second sunrise."

"Thank you, Fire-Keeper." She turned toward Amureo's house group, released the breath she had been holding and relaxed her shoulders.

"Ha-wani."

Once again, her shoulders tensed.

"You will be mine. Do not doubt it."

While the men gathered in the plaza, the women packed burden baskets with household items, including pots for cooking the fruit, baskets of corn meal, dried cholla buds, and other foodstuffs to take to the camp north of Elder Brother Wash where hundreds of the spectacular cactus crowded together on a south-facing slope. They had come to this place every year since before remembering to call down the rains.

The men knew their jobs, but they waited with Chief Elder for the shaman to declare the saguaro harvest open. From his platform mound, Fire-Keeper raised his staff high and sang the blessing of the harvest. Around the village, the women interrupted their work to stand and listen.

We call upon our brother*
We call upon the sacred saguaro
To call down the clouds
To call down your gift of rain
We celebrate our brother
We celebrate the sacred saguaro

After the song, Thandoi, pointing at Panereo, said, "Take your men to prepare the ramadas and inspect the dwellings. Rebuild them if you need to." They would have suffered from a year of disuse. He looked at Kutareo. "Go with your brother and provide replacement timbers he will need, and collect firewood for everyone."

While Vachai and Nothai, along with some of the other farmers, went to Elder Brother Wash to dig wells and fill large jars with water to carry to the camp, Ha-wani and Wokkai helped Li-naä and Nothai's wife, Kokii, pack burden baskets with cooking pots, spoons, and baskets of various sizes. Telling her younger sons, Chuwii and Tarukii, to go and help Kutareo, Kokii cautioned them with a wave of the hand, "He has much work to do on our behalf. He will not speak to you or tell you what to do. When you approach him, simply say your mother sent you to help. Go with him and do what needs to be done."

As the boys scampered across the plaza, Wokkai smiled. "That was kind of you, Kokii."

Kokii shrugged and, waving both hands dismissively, said, "His brothers would never think of it, and he has a big job ahead of him." She was a short, round-faced woman with a habit of using her hands when she talked, reminding Ha-wani of the fluttering wings of her spirit hummingbird. She was unlikely to be as sharp-eyed as the little bird, though, since only one eye looked at the person she was talking to while her other looked somewhere over their shoulder.

Wokkai grinned. "Not as big as you might think. He's been to the camp several times. He inspected the ramadas himself, and all the support posts they need are stacked nearby. He's made a good start on the firewood. But he will be glad for the boys' help."

Kokii squinted with her good eye, saying, "And you know this how?"

"I helped him. He knew he would have a lot of work for the ceremonies. His brother will beat him if he doesn't have something the moment he demands it."

Kokii scowled and opened her mouth to say something, but Ha-wani called out, "Come, Sister, I need your help."

Chief Elder sent Amureo and several men, including Tonrai and Chanu, hunting for deer to provide a feast of celebration.

On the morning of the second sunrise, the village gathered in the plaza to sing and await the sun. Afterward, the grand procession set out on the dusty path under a pale blue sky, anticipating the rain the giant cactus promised. They would call down the rains, and all would be well. The day heated up quickly, and, from the scrub along the trail, cicadas signaled a hotter one to come.* Women, their burden baskets full, chattered and laughed while younger children ran in circles and chased one another. Benai and some of the older boys went ahead of the women to watch for rattlesnakes.

Others passed them as Ra-naä lowered her burden basket to the ground. "Do I have to carry this? It's heavy, and I'm sick."

"Let's put some of it into mine." Ha-wani pulled her head strap loose and set her basket down. She transferred several pots from Ra-naä's to her own. "You didn't eat anything this morning before we left. You're probably hungry."

"I couldn't even look at Kokii's corncakes. I had to go behind the dwelling and vomit." She moved a basket of corn meal into her sister's burden basket and tested the weight of her own.

"Let me help you." Ha-wani stood behind Ra-naä and adjusted the strap across her forehead. Balancing the contents of the basket, she asked, "Better?"

"Some, but it's still too heavy."

Ha-wani sighed. "I have no more room in mine. We're almost there anyway." She lifted her basket and slid the strap into place. "Let's go."

They had only walked a short distance in silence when Ha-wani stopped. She turned to Ra-naä, who had nearly bumped into her. She grinned.

"What?"

"You didn't join me in the women's hut this moon."

"I know. I'll need to leave during the rain ceremony and miss all the fun."

Still grinning, Ha-wani said, "I don't think so. I'm guessing you won't join me for several moons to come."

"What do you mean? Why wouldn't I—?" Ra-naä's eyes widened.

In her eyes, the bud of a tiny flower glimmered at the edge of Ra-naä's spirit.

Ha-wani took her sister's hand. "You will give Chanu a child."

"A child?" She laid her hand on her flat belly. "I'm going to swell up and get fat like Builder's wife?"

"Yes." Ha-wani grabbed her sister's hand. "Isn't it wonderful?"

Ra-naä frowned and set out along the trail.

Ha-wani shook her head and caressed her belly, hoping she, too, would soon carry a child for her husband.

Because the sisters had fallen behind the large group, by the time they reached the camp, most of the women had collected their harvesting poles,* left hanging last year in the bean trees there.

Li-naä said to her daughter, "Come, Wokkai. This year you are my partner."

Ha-wani had worried her sister-in-law was still upset about Amureo's treatment of his brother, but the girl's expression said otherwise, and she leaped to her feet. "Can I knock the fruit off?"

Li-naä smiled. "No. You'll be my catcher." The giant cactus was tall—in fact, many times taller than the tallest man—and there was only one way to reach the fruits before they burst open and birds, scavengers, and ants feed on them. "I will knock the fruit off, and you must catch it in your basket."

"When can I be the harvester?"

"Next year you can make your own harvest pole. For now, you will help me." Li-naä showed her daughter how the three long cactus ribs were spliced together and bound with yucca fibers making a pole many times taller than either of them. She handed the girl a length of yucca and showed her how to bind the ribs. "Each year, we must replace the yucca because the fibers dry out and break when we are collecting the fruit. And we'll take extra along with us in case one of them comes loose."

When Wokkai finished replacing the binding at one connection, her mother examined it. "Well done. Now, let's make sure the cross-piece is attached properly." Li-naä replaced the yucca binding on the short length of greasewood near the top. Lashed crossways, it provided a hook to pull or push the fruit from the cactus.

Li-naä lifted the pole, and Wokkai asked, "Can I hold it?"

Her mother glanced at Ha-wani and smiled before showing her daughter how to place her hands with one higher than the other on the bottom rib. "Pretend you are standing under a giant cactus. Push it straight up. Don't let it fall."

Wokkai took the pole, and, when she tried to push it upward, it swung wildly around. Ha-wani laughed and Li-naä rescued the pole before it hit the ground.

When the women and girls were ready to go, they gathered in a circle, sang a song of blessing and thanks, and fanned out along the slope.

Wokkai was so excited to take part in this grown-up responsibility, she raced ahead of Li-naä, staking out a many-armed cactus with multiple fruits on the end of each arm.

"Hurry, Mother!"

Li-naä caught up to her daughter and leaned on her harvesting pole, breathing heavily. Although she was fit for a woman her age, she said, "I don't run as fast as I used to, Child. And sometimes it's hard to get my breath." She pointed her pole at the fruit. "And they aren't going anywhere until we get started." She indicated the lowest arm on the cactus, still high above their heads. "We'll start there, but first we must greet our brother.

Saguaro, our brother
We come to you in peace

"Sing it with me." Together Li-naä and her daughter honored the giant cactus, their brother, with the song.

"Now, you stand beneath it and have your basket ready to catch the first fruit when I knock it off."

The girl shifted her position a couple of times, trying to find the best angle when the sun wouldn't be in her eyes.

"Don't miss." Li-naä raised her pole to the top of the curved arm and hooked the cross-piece behind the fruit. "I'm going to pull. Ready?"

"Yes."

When Li-naä snapped the fruit off, Wokkai moved her basket under it just in time. She burst out laughing. "I did it. Let's do another."

Li-naä leaned her pole against the main trunk of the cactus. "Before we collect more, we must thank our brother for his gifts. He is a member of our family, and we do nothing that would bring him harm." She lifted the fruit from Wokkai's basket and held it up.

Wokkai examined it. "The reddish-orange color is how we know it's ready? We don't harvest green ones?"

"That's right. Now, we must cut it open and take it into our bodies as a blessing. Then we will share it with Mother Earth."

"You brought a knife?"

"No. Our brother gives us the knife with his fruit."

Surprised, Wokkai inspected the fruit more carefully. "You're teasing me. I don't see a knife."

"Look at this." She snapped the hard, dry blossom off and held it up, showing her the flat, round disc where the blossom had been attached to the fruit. "Feel it."

Wokkai rubbed her finger along the ragged edge of the disc. She jerked her finger away. "It's sharp."

"Yes. We don't need a knife." She used the sharp edge of the disc to slice the fruit open.* Inside, tiny black seeds speckled the thick red pulp. Li-naä scooped some with her finger and invited her daughter to do the same. "Leave some behind. We must give it to Mother Earth." After eating their share, she scooped the remaining pulp onto the ground.

We thank you
Mother Earth
For your gifts
For our brother the saguaro
Who appeals to Father Sky
To bring us the clouds
To bring us the rains

Throughout the camp, Kokii and others prepared cooking stations, piling rocks to make a three-sided firebox to hold the pots above the flames. Anu's wife, Mochik, and her daughter, Sochik, joined them. Although they lived outside the compound and were considered by many to be a lower class of people deserving of little respect, Anu was Vachai's most trusted farmer and good friend. His family welcomed them to share their ramada during the harvest.

The baby strapped to Sochik's breast kindled Ha-wani's desire for a child of her own, but she cautioned her spirit to set aside envious thoughts and to be patient. To the women, whom she had gotten to know since coming to Onaati-Kaä, she said, "Welcome, Friends. We are honored to share your company."

The infant detached herself from her mother's breast and turned to the sound of Ha-wani's voice. She averted her eyes from the child's, focusing on her tiny mouth with mother's milk drying on her lips. Like feathers brushing lightly across her face, the young spirit explored Ha-wani, and the child smiled. Ha-wani answered with one of her own. She glanced at Ra-naä and was surprised to see a frown cross her sister's face.

Across the camp, the people cheered when the hunters returned, Chanu and Amureo each carrying a deer. While they skinned and butchered the animals, the others pounded stakes into the ground to stretch the skins to dry, and Tonrai dug the roasting pit. Benai and other boys collected rocks to line the pit below the fire and to place above it when the wood had burned to coals.

When the pit was ready, Kutareo brought firewood, and Fire-Keeper came to light the fire with the sacred coals. Activity in the camp stopped, and everyone turned to watch him prepare the first fire and chant with him.

Mother Earth
We thank you
For the blessing of the deer
We thank you
For the blessing of this fire

Kutareo, with the help of Kokii's boys, carried firewood to each of the ramadas, coming to Ha-wani's last. The youngsters knelt and stacked their supply as Wood Cutter always did. When they were finished, Kokii's middle son, Tarukii, announced, "He taught us how to stack the wood."

Her youngest, Chuwii, added, "Kutareo didn't need to tell us what to do. Wokkai told us before she came back here."

Ha-wani looked up in alarm. Chuwii had spoken the girl's name in front of Kutareo. Of course, he knew it, but others might be shocked. She glanced at Kokii, but she was busy preparing the fire. She didn't seem to notice. *I must remind Wokkai to talk to her mother about the wood cutter. If Kokii heard, she might tell Li-naä before the girl has a chance.*

Soon, Wokkai and the other girls delivered the first full baskets to the cooking stations and returned to the desert to collect more. Ha-wani, Ra-naä, and Mochik knelt beneath the ramada, snapping off the dried blossoms and slicing the fruit open. They scooped sweet red pulp into bowls, and Kokii dumped it into the water to soak. As she stirred more into the water, the color became a deeper red. Using a long sotol spoon,* she mashed the pulp to release its sweetness. Sochik tried to help, but the child kept her busy.

Twice, Ra-naä stumbled out of the ramada to vomit behind one of the pit houses. After her second bout of nausea, she unrolled her sleeping mat and curled up on it. Kokii cast a curious, one-eyed glance to Ha-wani, who only smiled. The older woman nodded and mouthed, "I see."

Before Fire-Keeper came to ignite their fire, Kokii let the pulp settle to the bottom long enough to ladle out a jar of sweet, red juice for them to drink. Although Ha-wani stood apart when he arrived to kindle their fire, the rest of the women made a circle around him and sang.

> *Mother Earth*
> *Thank you*
> *For the blessing of this fire*

She kept her eyes downcast as he passed her on his way to the next ramada. Although he did not speak aloud, she heard his voice clearly. *"Soon, Ha-wani, soon."* His sour odor lingered even after he was gone. She called upon her spirit.

> *Stand with me*
> *Guard me*
> *When he threatens*
> *Give me strength*
> *Give me courage.*

She turned to join the women in the ramada. There was work to do, and she would not allow the shaman to intimidate her again.

By midday, all the ramadas had sufficient water and wood for cooking the fruit, and the men and boys joined their families. The sweet fragrance of the cactus fruit lingered in the still air around them. Throughout the camp, laughter rang out among the adults while the children chased one another around the ramadas and the two pit houses. The women gossiped, and, like the other men, Nothai, Vachai, their sons, and Anu sat near the ramada smoking and arguing about when the rains would come.

When Chanu saw Ra-naä sleeping instead of helping, a flicker of anger crossed his face. Before he could raise a question, Ha-wani said, "Her stomach is upset."

"She's sick? What's wrong?"

"It will pass. Don't be concerned."

When Kokii was ready to strain the juice and contribute the family's share to the ceremony, Mochik stood, eyes downcast, and waited to be acknowledged. Kokii glanced up from the jar she was stirring and waved her spoon. "You do not have to wait to speak to me, my friend. Our family and yours are equal—in spite of what others might have you think."

Mochik pulled a folded cloth from her sash. "I wove this for you to strain the juice. It will separate more of the pulp and seeds than a basket."

Unfolding the cloth, Kokii held it up to the sunlight. "Such a fine, tight weave, my friend. I envy your skill at the loom. Of course, we will share the seeds and pulp with you for your winter stores."

Chanu and Tonrai helped Kokii strain the cooked fruit into smaller jars. In one of the two pit houses, the Rain House,* the juice would be left to ferment before the ceremonies to bring the promise of rain to the desert. The men from all the ramadas carried their contributions inside and poured them into the large fermenting jars.

While the men delivered the juice, Kokii, Ha-wani, Li-naä, Mochik, and Wokkai spread the seeds and pulp out to dry. Later, they would separate out the seeds and dry them further, roast them, or grind them into flour for cooking. The dried pulp would be saved and stored for sweet treats in the winter.

Finally, the work was finished, and the families gathered under the ramadas to rest. Ra-naä woke and joined them.

Ha-wani tapped her sister-in-law on the knee and said, "What did you learn today, Wokkai?" She suspected the girl understood what she had done this day was a first step toward womanhood because the giant cactus harvest was women's work. And, while her budding breasts indicated she might soon make her first visit to the women's hut, something else was budding between her and Kutareo.

Wokkai pushed loose strands of hair behind her ears and grinned. "I learned to catch the fruit when Mother knocked it off."

Li-naä laughed. "She did well."

"I wish I had caught them all because sometimes they split when they hit the ground, and they are lost." Wokkai pouted. "Chief Elder's daughter didn't lose as many as I did."

"You kept score?" Tonrai frowned at his little sister, but a grin tickled the corners of his mouth. "I didn't know women competed like men."

Wokkai's brown eyes sparkled, and her smile was wider than ever. "Yes," she said, pushing her shoulders back and lifting her tiny breasts. "We women can compete, too."

Tonrai's love for his little sister was plain to see, and Ha-wani was glad she had a husband who cared as much about family as she did. He put his arm around her, and she leaned against him, remembering her first harvest and how excited she had been. She and Ra-naä had both joined her mother with baskets to catch the fruit, and she had suggested they keep score so they would know who had caught the most. Ra-naä had refused.

"Who cares which one of us catches the most?" Her delicate eyebrows pressed together in a scowl.

Ha-wani had always marveled at how pretty her sister was, even when she frowned. She sighed and concentrated on catching the fruit, looking forward to the next harvest when she would make her own harvesting pole and learn to knock the fruit down.

But before the next harvest, both she and her sister made their first visits to the women's hut in quick succession, and Robanti had arranged their marriages. In some ways, Ha-wani was disappointed her mother had not had time to teach her to make the pole and harvest the fruit. She did not doubt Li-naä would be happy to teach her.

Her heart swelled with love for her new family and gratitude that her sister was part of it. She placed a hand on her belly and silently sang a song for the flower she hoped would grow inside her. She didn't want to be jealous of her sister, but she couldn't understand why Ra-naä wasn't bursting with happiness.

All their lives they had looked forward to growing up, getting married, and having children. At least she thought Ra-naä had shared her anticipation. *Of course she did. Why wouldn't she?* What had happened for her to behave like this when everything they had hoped for was coming true?

Ra-naä sat apart from her husband, only half-listening to the conversation around her. Ha-wani was probably right. She would give Chanu a child. When she ran out of the ramada to vomit, Kokii had frowned at her with those ugly mismatched eyes. What was she supposed to do when nausea rose in her throat? But that wasn't the worst of it. Would Chanu even want to look at her when she was swollen and fat, like Builder's wife?

She stared at Sochik and her baby. The young woman's belly was slack and hung loosely over her sash, and her free breast sagged heavy with milk. *I will look like that.* She closed her eyes and tried to block the image.

Everyone was acting like Chanu's sister's first saguaro harvest was so remarkable. Women were supposed to do it. Either that or, like Kokii, take charge of cooking the fruit. She didn't doubt that Ha-wani would be the one to go out and harvest next year, and she'd be stuck with the cooking.

Ha-wani. She's not even pretty, but everyone thinks she's special. She looked into my eyes and knew I was pregnant. How does she do that? When Chanu and I look into each other's eyes, we share our spirit. His blackbird and my brownbird are well matched. That's all I know. How does she look into someone's eyes and know everything about them?

When Tonrai put his arm around Ha-wani's shoulder and pulled her close, Ra-naä glanced at Chanu, who had laughed when his brother teased their sister. *Why doesn't he invite me to sit closer to him? Am I already getting ugly with this child inside of me?*

As the sun traveled beyond the midpoint of its journey, the heat of the day intensified, and lengthening shadows signaled the time to rest before the nighttime ceremony. Everyone unrolled their sleeping mats and spread out to take a nap.

When Chanu put his mat next to hers, she smiled. *Maybe I'm not so ugly yet.*

Chapter 7

Cactus Harvest Moon 1158 (June)

The haunting voice of a flute carried through the camp, waking the villagers. As the people began to stir, a soft drumbeat joined the flute. A plaza had been cleared in front of the Rain House and the old pit house Fire-Keeper occupied. Flickering shadows, cast by the large fire, danced across the faces of the people—men, women, and children—as they gathered, shaking gourd rattles to drive unfriendly spirits away.

Usareo sat on one side of the fire playing his flute; Vaeleo, pounding his gourd water drum,* sat opposite; An-nat—Knowledge-Keeper—sat south of the fire, his calendar stick in his hand. The flute, the drum, the rattles, and the scratching of their sandals on the desert floor rose into the night sky as they circled the fire, shuffling their feet and humming. After making one full turn around the fire, they stopped, facing the Rain House.

When Fire-Keeper stepped out, the people gasped.

Mud, the same color as the dry sand in Elder Brother Wash, covered his naked body, matching his pale eyes so perfectly he seemed an apparition bereft of sight. Only his hair offered a contrast. Instead of his usual double knot, long strands had been twisted into smaller knots, each one red with pulp, looking like ripe fruit burst open atop the giant cactus. Beaded necklaces, along with his shell and turquoise pendant, twined around his neck. Bracelets adorned his upper arms, and a woven sash without breechclout wrapped his waist. As the people stepped aside for him to pass, he held his staff high, its colorful feathers dancing, its bells singing with the rattling tinklers. His rasping voice carried into the night sky as he sang.

Our fires have burned
The eye of day has closed
The eye of night looks on
We come together
To sing for the liquor
To call the clouds
To call the rains

Families stood in groups as Fire-Keeper stopped before the fire. He pounded his staff against the ground twice, and the people joined the song.

We come together
To sing for the liquor
To call the clouds
To call the rains
We come together to sing

Again, they shuffled around the fire, scratching the desert floor with their sandals, loosening the surface so it might easily drink the rains they called. Again and again, they circled, calling the clouds, calling the rains. The dust they stirred hung in place around them. No breeze offered to clear or cool the air.

Fire-Keeper pounded his staff once. The people stopped and turned to face him.

He lifted his staff at the darkening sky. "Hear me, Father Sky. We await your rains."

His reedy voice grated on Ha-wani's ears. She struggled to put aside her dislike of him. The ceremony was too important. The life of the village depended on a generous rainy season. She squeezed Tonrai's hand and focused on her love of family and her desire for good rains and a successful harvest.

The shaman called upon Knowledge-Keeper to report on past rains.

An-nat stood and drew his fingers along the calendar stick. "The last time rain fell on our fields and the village was during Big Cold Moon. We have had none since."

The shaman called out. "After we last sang for clouds and rain, when did they come?"

"Big Rains Moon came and went with no rains on our fields. Only the mountains received the gift of rain, which we put to our use."

Fire-Keeper stood silent, doing and saying nothing for several moments.

Tonrai nudged Chanu. "What is he waiting for?"

Before Chanu could answer, the shaman shouted, "Silence!" His familiar thin voice was replaced by an unfamiliar one—a voice they had never heard from him. It carried the distant roll of thunder, a sound that startled them. He walked deliberately around the fire, searching the faces of the gathered people, his voice penetrating the depth of their spirits. "I feel the presence of spirits who would bring harm to the People."

He hesitated in front of Ha-wani's family. Although she kept her eyes downcast, she felt the heat of his gaze sweep across her breasts and neck and to her face. She tucked in her chin and closed her eyes, forcing herself to remain still and calling upon her spirit to protect her, to deny him entry. When the brush of wings enfolded her, she lifted her eyes to his, returning his gaze.

I tell you, Ha-wani, you will be mine.

Never. You will not have me. You will not have my spirit.

Do not deny me. If you continue to deny me, you will suffer.

I am not afraid.

A low croak issued from her throat, and, at that moment, a dark wall rose between her and the shaman. She focused on it, puzzled. She expelled the breath she had been holding, and Tonrai's back came into focus. He had stepped between them. While she appreciated his protection, she had not fully explored the power of her spirit to resist the shaman. She had made a start, but did Fire-Keeper accept her refusal?

The shaman continued around the fire, pausing before others in the crowd, but Ha-wani sensed many eyes on her. Did they know she had held his gaze? If so, had he planted a seed of doubt about her? Did the people think she would bring harm to them? Tonrai wrapped his arm around her and returned each one's stare. All wilted before his challenge.

Fire-Keeper returned to his place in front of the Rain House. All the men stepped forward, forming a tight circle around the fire, Tonrai and Chanu among them. The men began the first of sixteen circles and singing, while the women sent their young children back to the ramadas to be looked after by those who chose not to dance. Sochik had agreed to care for Kokii's boys and Benai.

Children nearing adulthood stayed, and, if their parents approved, they could dance and sing. With the men absent from the family group, Wokkai stood between Ha-wani and Ra-naä, swaying back in forth in step with the men, clearly excited about being included in the rain ceremony.

Before the men finished their circles, the moment came when the women joined the circle, each taking the hand of her man.

The singing continued.

> The little red spiders*
> And the gray horned toad
> Together they make the rain to fall
> Upon the children's land

Although some might choose a man other than her own to dance with, Ha-wani and Ra-naä took their husbands' hands, as did Li-naä and Kokii, leaving Wokkai alone outside the circle. Ha-wani was relieved to see Ra-naä looking radiant and happy as they shuffled around the fire singing.

> The waters run and overflow
> Upon the stream-bed and mountain
> The waters run and overflow
> Corn is forming
> Corn is forming
> Beside it, squash is forming
> In the yellow flowers
> The bees and flies hum

On one circuit around the fire, Ha-wani glimpsed two figures dancing by themselves in the shadow of the trees beyond the plaza. They were not making a circle, but simply side-stepping back and forth. Wok-kai and Kutareo. On the next circuit, they were gone.

At the edge of the world
The trees stand shining
The waters run and overflow
Upon the stream-bed and mountain

When the dancing finished, Ra-naä grabbed Cha-nu's hand, and they ran back to the ramada. Tonrai drew Ha-wani into his arms and kissed her with pas-sion, signaling his desire to join with her. Such join-ings would be common all over the camp tonight; it was one of the pleasures of the rain ceremony. When he took her hand and started back to the ramada, she hesitated.

"Is something wrong?"

"No. Do you mind if I look for your sister before I go back?"

"Why?"

"I'll tell you later. Don't worry." Their eyes met, and his trust reflected back to her.

Striding into the shadows, Ha-wani did not intend to eavesdrop, but she hesitated when she heard Wok-kai say, "Why is your breechclout sticking out?"

Ha-wani did not wait to hear what, if anything, the young man said.

"Wokkai?" She stepped around the tree. "Time to go back to the ramada."

In the dim light cast by the dying fire in the plaza, fear animated Kutareo's face before he turned and dashed silently through the trees.

"Kutareo, wait!" When he didn't come back, Wok-kai frowned. "You made him run away."

"I'm sorry, Wokkai. I didn't mean to scare him, but I'm worried about your friendship with him. He's many years older than you, and you don't yet know about men."

"Kutareo's not a man. And he won't ever be one." Her voice carried her disappointment.

"And you've not yet become a woman, although I think it will happen soon."

"Do you think so?"

Ha-wani smiled, remembering her own youthful anticipation. "When you are a woman and you take a husband, you will experience your first true joining with him. You understand true joinings, don't you?" She didn't know how to explain such things to a child.

"I think so. I've heard my parents joining at night. But what does this have to do with being Kutareo's friend? He's not a man, and I'm not a woman, so why must we talk about joining?

"Although he has not met the challenges which make him a man in the eyes of the village, he can join with a woman. It's not a true joining as husband and wife, and others frown on it."

Wokkai's dark eyes widened. "He can? How can that—?" She put her hand over her mouth. "Do you think he would like to join with me?"

"Possibly." Ha-wani did not mention what Wokkai had said before she interrupted them, and she didn't know if Kutareo even understood. She took the girl's hand and started walking back to the ramada.

When they came out of the trees, the moon was high, lighting the desert almost as twilight. Only a few pale stars shone in the night sky.

Wokkai turned and whispered, "What if I wanted to be his wife?"

Ha-wani turned to her. "I'm sorry, Child, he cannot marry. Your parents would not permit it. Fire-Keeper would not permit it, and the village would turn against him. Young men who have not made the trip to Great Water are not allowed to marry. It would disrupt the order of things. He might be cast out."

The girl's tears began. "And it would be my fault. Can I still be his friend?"

"I think so, but you must no longer keep your friendship a secret. You need to tell your mother."

"Will she be angry with me?"

"I don't know."

For the people, morning brought the day they had waited for. They would feast this morning, and in the evening the "sit-and-drink" would finally call down the clouds and rain.

Under the ramadas, the women cooked corncakes, cholla buds, and soaked cactus pulp in water for themselves and the youngsters while the men opened the roasting pit and divided the meat among the families.

"May I ask a friend to eat with us, Mother?" Ha-wani had not expected Wokkai to act so soon on her advice.

"Who, Child?"

The girl bit her lip. "Kutareo."

Li-naä frowned. "Kutareo? He's your friend?"

She answered quickly. "He's a nice boy, and Amureo is mean to him." She paused. "They didn't give him anything to eat yesterday."

"We will share our meal with him. He works hard for all of us."

Before Li-naä could say anything else, Wokkai dashed from the ramada.

Li-naä turned to her daughter-in-law. "You don't look surprised. Do you know something I don't?"

"I do. I told her last night that she needed to tell you she and Kutareo are friends. I was afraid she would put it off."

"This has been going on for some time? What should I know about this?"

"Wokkai will soon become a woman, and Vachai will begin his search for a husband. I fear the girl wants Kutareo for a husband."

Li-naä dropped her spoon and stared at Ha-wani. "Kutareo? Wood-Cutter? But he's—"

"Not a man?"

"That's not what I was going to say, but it's true. He is unlikely to go through the manhood initiation, so he cannot take a wife." She picked up the spoon and wiped it with her skirt. "I was going to say 'simple-minded.'"

Ha-wani said nothing.

"What makes her think he got nothing to eat yesterday?"

"He told her."

"But he can't talk."

"He can. He talks to her."

"He never talks to anyone. Why does he talk to Wokkai?"

"She treats him with kindness. She reached out to him, something no one else has ever done, I think. Wokkai is a girl of uncommon goodness."

"She is, but she cannot marry him. It's impossible."

"What will you do?"

"I don't know. I must discuss it with her father. He will not like it."

Between the morning's feast and the final ceremony, Kokii and Li-naä crushed red, yellow, and black clay with dried mesquite sap. They mixed each color with a small amount of water and, using a yucca brush, painted the women of their ramada. It would be a colorful celebration tonight.

Sochik, who needed to care for her infant, and Wokkai, who was too young, sat together watching.

Wokkai asked, "Will you paint me next year, Mother?"

"I do not doubt you will make your first trip to the women's hut before next year's celebration," Li-naä answered kindly. "So, yes, I will paint you."

The girl smiled and touched the hand of Sochik's babe, who wrapped a tiny fist around her finger without detaching from her mother's nipple. Wokkai's expression, Ha-wani thought, was not unlike her own when she thought of having a child.

Sochik looked fondly at Wokkai. "I'm looking forward to being painted and participating again, but this year we will stay here and care for my child."

"Will you show me how to hold her?"

"If you like."

Ha-wani sighed. *Don't be in such a hurry to become a woman, Sister. I fear you will not get all you hope for.*

Li-naä painted squash blossoms on Ha-wani's breasts with leafy tendrils flowing in a vine down each arm. If she caught the exchange between her daughter and the young mother, she didn't comment. She painted Ra-naä's breasts and arms with butterflies and sunflowers, including a large one on her belly with a long stem reaching from the middle of her back. Ha-wani smiled when her sister laid a gentle hand on the sunflower; she hoped it meant she was pleased about giving her husband a child.

Before Li-naä began painting her, Mochik said, "Once again, you have welcomed my family into your ramada, treating us with a kindness and respect we do not enjoy from others who live inside the compound." She looked at Sochik, who nodded. Together, they said, "Thank you."

Li-naä took her friend's hand. "You do not have to thank us. We only do what everyone should do, and it gives me pain to see how some of our neighbors treat others. Your husband and mine are friends. They are as devoted to one another as brothers. To us, you are part of our family." She paused while Mochik wiped away a tear. "Now let's get you painted for tonight."

On Mochik's abdomen, Li-naä painted the outline of a quail, whose babies trailed around her back, over her shoulder and down one arm. When her friend realized how many babies Li-naä had painted, she laughed and said, "I will not have that many children. My mother-in-law is watching my young ones right now, and I don't plan to have more babies." She raised one eyebrow and whispered, "I talked to Healer-Woman. She gave me something to keep me from having babies."

Ra-naä looked up sharply but said nothing.

Ha-wani painted the wicked-looking seed pod called ram's horn* on one of Li-naä's breasts and bear grass on the other. Beneath them, she drew a basket similar to the last one Li-naä had woven. Mochik painted stalks heavy with corn growing up Kokii's legs and reaching all the way to her breasts and wrapping around her back.

The men joined the women to collect the leftover paint. They dragged their fingers through it and traced lines on their faces, chests, and arms.

At last, the flute and drum called them to the plaza. The remnants of last night's fire had been removed, and a small fire—one which would not frighten away the clouds and rain—burned in its place. Fire-Keeper waited, his covering of mud now dry and cracked. He looked to the sky, chanting quietly. A jar of cactus liquor sat on the ground before him.

The tension was high as they assembled around the fire—the men sitting in the inner circle, the women standing on the outside. Never had they needed rain as much as they needed it now.

The shaman lifted the jar and held it high. "The rains will begin after the third rising of the sun." A murmur of approval rose from the people.

> *I came to your sacred house and saw*
> *The winds that there lay*
> *The clouds that there lay*
> *The seeds that there lay.*
> *One was seated there*
> *Who swayed like the wind*
> *Who blew breath like the clouds.*
> *He left me moistened and healed*
> *And brought forth the growing things*
> *Saying come forward and drink*
> *Drink my sacred liquor*
> *Bring forth the clouds*
> *Bring forth the rains*

Fire-Keeper put the jar to his mouth and drank deeply and long. Afterward, he poured liquor into his hand and tossed it into the air. "Bring forth the clouds."

Again, he poured liquor into his hand, but this time, he sprinkled it on the ground. "Bring forth the rains."

At this, three men stepped out of the Rain House carrying tightly-woven baskets containing the liquor. One man went to Knowledge-Keeper, who laid aside the calendar stick, another to Usareo, who set aside his flute, and the third to Vaeleo, who silenced his drum. After they drank, two of the men served liquor to those seated in the circle, while one passed among the women, who were invited only to taste; the men bore the responsibility of bringing down the rains.

The men continued to drink until a pleasant dizziness swept them. When the first man stumbled from the circle, bent over, and returned the liquor to the earth, the others cheered, and someone announced, "He is the first to throw up the clouds!" He accepted the honor and returned to the circle to drink again.

The ritual of renewal had begun. They would take the fruit of the Earth into their bodies and restore it to the Earth, making it ready to receive the rains— rains that would nourish the fields and provide a good harvest.

Darkness fell as more men threw up the clouds. The women wandered back to the ramadas and their children, confident the new year would bring the rains they needed.

Chapter 8

Big Rains Moon 1158 (July)

Dark clouds, heavy with moisture, gathered over Great-Grandfather's towers and rugged peaks to the south and roiled along Great-Grandmother's smooth ridges to the east. After the saguaro harvest, the villagers had closed the camp and returned to Onaati-Kaä, planting and singing for the corn with optimism. Fire-Keeper had promised the rain would come after only three risings of the sun, but a full moon had passed and none had blessed the fields. Today, though, the promise of rain was real.

The shaman stood on his platform, his bony arms raised, his voice lost in the rumbling air, singing for the rain to bless the village and their fields. Sky fire drew jagged lines across the face of the mountains, and the first wispy finger of smoke rose from the summit of Great-Grandmother. By late afternoon, the clouds evaporated, taking with them any promise of rain.

Overnight, those who slept under the ramadas choked on the acrid stench drifting down the slope under cover of darkness. In the morning, the mountain and the ridge before it known as Great-Grandmother's Knees were enveloped in a smoky, spreading shroud.

Normally, the children would play games and chase each other around the plaza by this time of the morning, but today, they stayed close to their parents. Outside their dwelling, Ha-wani's family watched the fire grow, all but Ra-naä. She announced she couldn't stand the smell and went inside to take a nap.

Wokkai bit her lower lip. "Mother, will the fire take Great-Grandmother from us?"

"No, Child." Li-naä lifted her daughter's chin and looked into her eyes. "I have seen fires blacken Great-Grandmother's highest peak. The trees always come back. Sometimes they take more than one turning of the seasons, but they will be back, and Great-Grandmother will always be with us."

Benai stood silent, staring at the mountain with wide eyes. Ha-wani put her arm around his shoulders. "Listen to your mother. You shouldn't worry."

She could reassure the boy, but she couldn't dismiss her concern about Fire-Keeper's behavior and his failure to bring the rains. He told them he brought the sky fire, but he didn't explain why he brought it without rain and why he would let it burn Great-Grandmother. To intimidate them, she suspected. And, indeed, with some, he had been successful.

Growing up at Honey Bee, she knew sky fire and thunder were often followed by the heavy rains normally coming during this moon, and she had seen fires on these mountains and others far away. She doubted a fire-keeper at one small village possessed so much power over the skies.

That night, Ha-wani dreamed she was on the mountain surrounded by the fire.

Like hands — more hands than she could count — the flames reached out, touching her, withdrawing, reaching again, touching her once more. At the moment she expected to be consumed, a grinning Fire-Keeper appeared. He opened his mouth and spewed fire in her direction. She called on her spirit, but the raven did not come. No dark wings enfolded her. The shaman's flaming arms swirled around her, wrapping her so tightly she could not move. She could not turn her face away as he took it in his hands, bored into her eyes with his, and pressed his lips against hers.

The next morning, still trembling from the dream, Ha-wani stood outside the compound wall, her eyes watering and her throat burning. She lifted her face to the thick smoke riding down the mountain on the dawn wind and waited. When the sky turned from dark gray to purple followed by gold, she knew the sun had risen without offering the blessing of its first kiss. She closed her eyes and listened to people coughing, to children crying and gasping for breath, to mothers sobbing because they could not help their children.

Inside, she found Li-naä, kneeling under the ramada, her arms wrapped around her body, bent over, gasping for air, and struggling to breathe. She hurried to Knowledge-Keeper's house group and waited at the boundary, a respectful distance, knowing it was impolite to intrude on someone's living space without an invitation.

No-wani, Healer-Woman, glanced up from stirring the fire under a large pot. "Come, please." When she smiled, the wrinkles in the old woman's cheeks deepened and her blue mouth lines lifted. "Who needs relief?"

"Mother-in-Law cannot get her breath, and her cough is painful."

No-wani, a large woman, nearly as tall as Chief Elder and standing more than a head taller than most of the village women, pulled her considerable self upright and shook her head. "So many suffer the same." She gazed at Great-Grandmother. "By the gods, it is thick. I fear for the youngest and the oldest among us. But your mother-in-law is not so old I would have feared for her." Using a gourd dipper, she filled a small pot with hot water. "Has she coughed like this before, when there was no smoke?"

"Yes, mostly on windy days."

"Mmm-hmm. Our desert is not always kind. The wind stirs the loose sand and blows it into the village. We cannot help but breathe it in. Some are more sensitive than others." She dropped a pinch of dried leaves into the small pot and handed it to Ha-wani. "Give this to her, and tell her to breathe the vapors while it steams. After that, she must drink it—not all at once, mind you, just small sips until there is no more. Bring me a little basket, and I will give you the leaves so you can make the tea for her. And tell her to wrap a cloth around her head, covering her nose and mouth so she doesn't breathe the smoke into her body."

"Thank you, Friend, and may the gods bless you."

"And you."

The tea that Knowledge-Keeper's wife sent for Li-naä helped, and Ha-wani was relieved. It was the first time she had sought medicine here, and she was pleased with how quickly the woman offered a remedy. In Honey Bee, the healer-woman always demanded some payment—a nice pot or basket or food—in exchange for her help or advice.

For five days, the fire continued to burn on the mountain, blackening the ridge, suffocating the village, and transforming their world. Each day, an orange sun—one they could look at without squinting—traveled across a sky glowing red as it sank each evening in the west. At night, the stars hid behind the haze while a slivered moon shone deep red. The People worried and whispered. *What did it mean? Did Father Sky dim the sun? Would it disappear from the sky?* Some scowled at Ha-wani, muttering and pointing. Fire-Keeper had singled her out at the rain ceremony. She feared they suspected she had somehow caused the gods to abandon them.

On the afternoon of the fifth day, massive clouds formed over both mountains, rising dark and high into the hazy sky above the smoke. After a prolonged round of violent sky fire and thunder, life-giving rain pounded Great-Grandfather Mountain before racing along the ridges and extinguishing Great-Grandmother's flames. The people gathered to again sing for the rain to bless the fields and terraces. Instead, the storm hung over the mountains, and winds finally drove the blessed curtain of rain to the north, bypassing the village and their fields.

During the storm, when everyone, including Fire-Keeper, was concentrating on the rain, Vachai laid a hand on Benai's shoulder. "Take a message to Anu. Tell him to take two men to the terraces. They must make sure the dams and channeling borders can slow the runoff from Great-Grandfather and direct it to the agaves. And tell him to send his farmers to me. Be quick about it."

Vachai was not heavily muscled, but his slender form moved with grace and a certain elegance that reminded Ha-wani his spirit was the deer. When the first two farmers came inside, he told them to look for breaks in the diversion dams where Elder Brother

Wash and Spirit Canyon join and to repair any that were weak. He did not order them to do the work but spoke in a quiet voice conveying his respect for them. "We must channel the water Great-Grandmother sends to the fields." The men nodded and set out to follow his direction.

He sent Tonrai to speak to Thandoi about organizing a party to climb to Great-Grandmother's pools* to bring water to the village. The hand-dug wells along the wash had not replenished for several days, and, if the pools below Great-Grandfather had collected any water, it would be scant.

Ha-wani admired her father-in-law's efficiency. Everything was quietly put into motion to channel the run-off to the agave terraces and to divert Great-Grandmother's water from the wash to the fields. She understood why he was so respected by the men and women who worked the fields and why so many depended on his leadership.

Vachai was distributing seed jars to those who came into the compound carrying their hoes when Fire-Keeper approached. "What do you think you are doing?"

"One moment, Fire-Keeper, please." He ignored the old man's contorted face and turned to the farmers. "Plant the corn along the wash near the first two diversion dams, and sing for it. I will be down shortly to help."

Ha-wani suppressed a grin; not many villagers would ignore the shaman.

As the farmers left the compound with the seeds and their tools, Vachai turned to the old man and smiled. "It's a blessing, Fire-Keeper. Great-Grandmother and Great-Grandfather have collected precious water for our fields. Last night was a new moon, the perfect time to plant corn and prepare for planting beans and squash. We will sing for a good harvest."

"I have told you before, and I say it again. *I* read the moon. *I* decide when to sow the seeds. I will not tolerate your disrespect."

"Forgive me, Fire-Keeper, but I was certain you would order them to do so immediately. I did not mean to be impertinent. I know well that your knowledge of the moon and the planting cycles exceeds my own."

Ha-wani wondered if her father-in-law's attempt to disarm Fire-Keeper would be effective. He kept a respectful tone. "I anticipated your orders, knowing, as you do, the rain on the mountains did not last long enough for a sheet flood, and when Great-Grandmother pours what she has collected into the wash, we must be prepared to channel it to the fields. As you have said many times, we must never offend Great-Grandmother by wasting her precious gift."

Fire-Keeper glared at him. "You will regret this." He turned and walked away.

As Vachai gathered his tools and left the compound, Ha-wani thought she detected a spring in his step.

Chapter 9

Big Rains Moon 1158 (July)

Why is my husband going? Why didn't they pick Tonrai?"

"I don't know. The council made the decision." This morning, a group of men had been selected to climb to Great-Grandmother's pools and collect water for the village. The sun still hid behind the mountain when the people gathered in the plaza to sing blessings for a safe trip.

They only did this when the need was great. The pools likely held water all year round, but stories were told of days past when Great-Grandmother offered little. The recent mountain rain guaranteed they would be full.

The day before, Chief Elder had called the people to the plaza to announce that Vachai and his brother, Nothai, would lead a party into the canyon between the two mountains to the pools. The rest of the group included Chanu, Tatanikii—Thandoi's eldest son—Dar's brother Usareo, and Amureo.

When Thandoi finished naming the members of the party, the shrill *cr-r-r-r-uk, cr-r-r-r-r-r-uk* of a raven sitting atop Fire-Keeper's dwelling drew Ha-wani's attention. Others paid little notice and resumed their excited chatter, but Ha-wani's spirit reacted. The raven had sounded an alarm.

She scanned the plaza for Fire-Keeper. He and Amureo stood between the plaza and the shaman's platform. Amureo's back was to her, and she followed Fire-Keeper's gaze as he looked over the other man's shoulder. His narrowed eyes focused first on Vachai, then Nothai, and finally Chanu. When Amureo nodded and joined the rest of the party, the raven took flight from Fire-Keeper's roof, still calling the alarm: *cr-r-r-r-uk, cr-r-r-r-r-r-uk, cr-r-r-r-uk.*

Now, in the dim light of morning, the men set out on the trail from the village to the mouth of the canyon with many villagers joining the procession.

After they crossed the wash at the bottom of the ridge, Ra-naä touched Ha-wani's arm and signaled for her to slow down and let the others go ahead.

"It's not fair. Tonrai should take Chanu's place. What if something happens, and he gets hurt?"

"It could happen to anyone, but we must not speak of it. We will sing our blessings and hope Great-Grandmother hears them and sends your husband and the others back safely." Even as she offered assurances to her sister, the raven's alarm echoed in her head, giving Ra-naä's complaints a greater meaning.

"If something happens to my husband, I'll—I'll—"

"Sister, what can you do?"

"I don't know, but my husband better come back to me."

Ha-wani sighed and shook her head. Her sister had always been willful and a little selfish, and it disturbed her when Ra-naä behaved poorly here in their new village. If Li-naä criticized her for failing to help grind the corn or beans or making cakes, she pouted and stalked out of the compound. *Why does she behave like that? It can't be her pregnancy. Our mother would be disappointed. I should talk to her.*

The day before, after the announcement in the plaza, Ha-wani had raised the same question with Tonrai. "Why did the council name three people from the same family?"

He told her the trail to the pools* was dangerous in places and would be more so when they came down carrying the heavy water jars in their burden baskets. "My father and his brother have made the trip many times over the years. They know the trail, and they are skilled at climbing into the pools and handing up the heavy jars of water. My father suggested Chanu join them because he is so strong."

"All the same, I fear for their safety. The shaman threatened your father when he sent the farmers to the fields after the rain, and Fire-Keeper appeared to be plotting with Amureo after the announcement."

"Fire-Keeper dislikes my father and my uncle, and I think his magic is all show. He has threatened you—and I take that seriously—but with others, it's just empty noise."

"You're wrong. He is a dangerous man, and Amureo will do whatever he tells him to do. You don't remember what we talked about after the rain ceremony?"

The morning after the "sit and drink," the people had been slow to rise. The men had drunk long into the night, consuming all the cactus liquor and returning it to Mother Earth as it had been done since before remembering. They believed they had done well and Father Sky would smile upon them, sending the rains they needed.

The sun was above the mountain when the women rose and stoked the fires. They nudged their husbands and brothers awake and made corncakes for breakfast. Afterwards, they would pack up and return to the village.

Before breakfast, Tonrai took her hand and they walked among the giant cactus. They stopped next to a tall saguaro—one with several arms reaching toward the sky and another arm wrapped around its middle pointing to the ground. White-winged doves pecked at the remaining fruits that resembled red flowers now that they had split open in the sun. Ants crawled busily over the discarded fruits on the ground.

Tonrai took her hand and rubbed his thumb along the bracelet. "Can you explain what happened between you and Fire-Keeper at the ceremony?"

"He may as well have pointed to me and announced that I am a danger to the people. Already some of them stare at me with distrust."

"I know. He wants to intimidate you and trespass on your spirit. I realized what he was doing when you made a noise. That's why I stepped between you." He turned the frog around to face them.

"And I thank you, my husband, for protecting me, but—"

"But what?" His dark brows furrowed together, and he tipped his head toward her, the tinklers in his hair singing softly.

"I am just a woman. As my husband, you are pledged to protect me, and, as your wife, I am bound to obey you. I must do what you tell me to do. But . . ." She hesitated. "But I fear that my struggle against Fire-Keeper will depend more on me than on you."

"What do you mean?"

"If another man, someone other than the shaman were to threaten me, what would you do?"

"I would confront him. I would tell him to stay away from my wife. That if he brought harm to you, he would suffer at my hands."

"Exactly. Can you say those words to a shaman?"

"I would like to. But, no. I don't like him or trust him, but others in the village depend on him."

"I am the one who will ultimately need to confront him. I don't know why, but he is determined to capture my spirit for his own purposes. You cannot be by my side every time I encounter him and he threatens me. I must learn to resist his intrusions."

He wrapped his arms around her. "I fear for your safety."

She leaned into him, her ear pressed against his chest, listening to the strength of his spirit, his kingbird ready to defend his nest and his territory at all times.

As she did each time she laid her head on his chest, she willed her own heart to beat in concert with his. "I am not without fear, but if, as he suggests, I have a powerful spirit, I must learn to use that power to protect myself. What will he do when I continue to resist, continue to refuse him? He may become more forceful, even vengeful. I must call on the raven to keep me safe. I am learning to bring her forth, to use her strength and her intelligence. She comes to me more quickly now, and I must learn to use her power in my own defense."

"I don't like it, and I cannot promise I won't interfere in the future. I will try to step aside and let your spirit protect you. Fire-Keeper is powerful, and I don't want you to have to fight him alone. But I understand you might need to."

After they started back to the ramada, she touched his arm, and he stopped. "I'm afraid our whole family is in danger. For some reason, Fire-Keeper hates your father, but he doesn't want to capture his spirit. He wants to destroy it. He will do it by whatever means possible."

Now, as his father, uncle, and brother prepared to undertake this dangerous journey, Tonrai could find no reason to disagree with his wife.

Because the trip down the mountain would be slow and difficult with the large jars full of water, burden partners accompanied each man, carrying the empty jars; later, they would relieve them of the heavier burden of precious water when they returned at nightfall. When they reached the entrance to the canyon, the party halted in the shadow of Great-Grandmother's Knees, while they transferred the baskets to those who would climb to the pools.

Chanu transferred the cone-shaped basket from his brother's to his own shoulders. Woven from yucca and beargrass, it stretched on an x-shaped frame of giant cactus ribs. The long ribs helped distribute the weight of the burden, and because they extended above the shoulders, Chanu would be able to shift the weight from time to time as he came down the steep

and rocky trail. He adjusted the strap across his forehead and bent his knees down and up to test the balance.

Nothai's eldest son, Cheshonii, carried his father's
burden basket and assisted him in settling it on
his back. Tatanikii transferred the basket from his
father's back to his own, and Chief Elder wished him
a safe journey to the pools. Neither Amureo nor his
son spoke when the boy passed the burden basket to
his father. Anu, partnering with Vachai, offered him
a blessing along with the basket and empty jar. After
Valeo got the basket settled on Usareo's back, he urged
him to be careful.

Tonrai placed his right hand on Chanu's shoulder,
and Chanu did likewise. "May the gods guard you,
my brother." Then he bade his father and uncle farewell in the same manner, whispering to each, "Guard
yourself and each other. Know where Amureo is at all
times."

Each man acknowledged the warning with a nod.

Ra-naä clung to her husband and cried. "Please
don't go. Stay here with me."

Chanu took her forearms and released himself
from her grip, stepping back. "I will come back to you,
Wife. I promise." He kissed her and turned toward the
trail with the others.

She spun around, looking at Ha-wani and shouting. "It's not fair." Without waiting, she ran back along
the wash to the village.

As the men began their climb to the pools, the villagers who had come with them sang a blessing for
their safety. They started back to the village, and
Ha-wani and Tonrai fell in step with them, each quietly appealing to the gods to keep the men safe.

Chapter 10

Big Rains Moon 1158 (July)

The sun was still high when Chief Elder's son ran into the compound shouting. By the time Ha-wani and the others gathered, Thandoi had learned what happened. With Tatanikii at his side, he turned to the people and waited for silence.

"My son brings an unhappy message. On the way down from the pools, two members of the party fell."

Ra-naä grabbed Ha-wani's arm. "Chanu—"

"Hush, Sister. Don't speak it."

Chief Elder waited for silence, "Vachai and Nothai are injured. Vachai's son stayed with them. The rest of the party continues."

Tonrai and Ha-wani exchanged a glance as An-nat began to sing. Fire-Keeper stood quietly and listened, making no move to join the conversation or to sing for the safety of the men. Li-naä and Kokii wailed.

Ha-wani led them back to their ramada and knelt with them to sing for blessings.

Thandoi continued, "Who will go with me?"

When Tonrai and Anu stepped forward, Nothai's eldest, Cheshonii, joined them.

Tonrai laid a gentle hand on his cousin's shoulder. "You cannot go. You are not yet a man."

The boy lifted his chin and said, "Only because I have not yet traveled to the sea. I have successfully hunted, killing two deer and one sheep. I may not be able to take a wife, but you cannot deny I am a man. I will bring my father home."

It was true, Cheshonii had grown tall, standing shoulder to shoulder with his cousin. His square face and chiseled jawline projected confidence. He never shied from hard work, and his strength and endurance equaled that of many men in the village. It wouldn't be surprising if people forgot he had not made his initiation trip to Great Water.

Tonrai smiled grimly. "You are your father's son. He will be proud."

Nodding his approval, Thandoi instructed Vaeleo to lead the party of burden partners to meet the others at the bottom of the trail later.

Before leaving, Tonrai and Cheshonii came to the ramada to kneel before their mothers. Cheshonii took Kokii's hand. "I will bring my father home."

She drew in her breath, one eye looking over his shoulder and the other meeting his gaze. "You are going with them?" When he nodded, she said, "Guard your spirit, my son."

After making the same promise to Li-naä, Tonrai took Ha-wani's hand and turned the bracelet so the frog sat on top of her wrist. "An-nat will take you and others to one of the brush houses near the entrance to the canyon where you will wait for our return."

Unlike the camp they used for the saguaro harvest, this one was a small cluster of brush shelters and a ramada where, in better times, farmers had stayed when planting or harvesting crops on the floodplain below the canyon. With only scant rain, it had seen little use in the past few years.

The family took what they needed for an extended stay. Healer-Woman went with them to tend the injured men. The heat of the day was upon them, and Li-naä stopped to catch her breath several times along the trail. The men filled two large jars with water at one of the dug wells in the wash. Once they were settled in the brush house, An-nat asked Tatanikii what happened.

"We came through the slot, a narrow place passing between high rock walls. Once through, a tight curve in the trail passes a rock wall rising on one side with the other dropping off sharply. They were behind Amureo at the back of the group. None of us in the front knew what happened because they were still in the curve. Somehow, Vachai must have collided with Amureo and stumbled over the edge."

Ha-wani's stomach clenched. *Amureo.*

He glanced at Kokii and Li-naä, hesitating before continuing. "When Vachai cried out, we set our burdens down and ran back to see what happened. By then, his brother had already set his basket aside and started down the slope. We only had the ropes we used to lift the jars from the pools, but they were not long enough for the climb down the cliff side. We could do nothing but watch. Nothai was almost there when loose rocks gave way, and he fell, landing below the shelf where Vachai lay." His voice shook. "Rocks kept falling on him."

An-nat spoke. "Did either man talk to you?"

"We heard Vachai moaning, but Nothai made no sound."

Everyone was silent. Kokii spoke to Chuwii and Tarukii, her frightened sons. "Be strong. We must accept Great-Grandmother's will."

As Thandoi's group began their grim climb into the canyon, the others sang blessings for them.

The sun had slipped behind the mountains to the west by the time Dar led the burden partners to the mouth of the canyon to wait for the men bringing precious water down from the pools. When the tired and dusty men finally arrived, their partners relieved them of their heavy burden.

With his jar of water now safely on the ground, Usareo said, "We passed Chief Elder and the others on their way up. They will have to wait for morning to come out. The new moon will not provide enough light."

Amureo stood apart, silently watching the others. Ha-wani didn't doubt that he was behind what happened. He and Fire-Keeper.

Tonrai and Thandoi each carried a long yucca rope coiled around his shoulder. Anu and Cheshonii dragged two litters. At the outset, where it was reasonably level, they ran, and when it got steep and rough, they left the litters behind. These would be useless on the steep and rocky trail.

When Cheshonii scrambled ahead, up and over the rocks, Thandoi frowned. "We could have a third injury to worry about if he isn't careful."

Tonrai laughed. "Don't worry. I was with him on a high ridge beneath Great-Grandfather Mountain. He's as surefooted as the sheep he carried down on his shoulders. I feel sorry for young men like him who cannot yet take a wife."

"We may discuss sending a party to Great Water soon."

Surprised, Tonrai asked, "Does Fire-Keeper agree?" His father never mentioned any such discussions.

"He suggested it. He thinks we have displeased the gods by failing to go."

Tonrai was incredulous. "Didn't *he* tell us we shouldn't go? That's why we've missed two trips."

Thandoi only grunted. Tonrai decided now was not the time to share his suspicions about how his father and uncle's "accident" had occurred.

They glimpsed Cheshonii ahead of them from time to time as he worked his way around curves in the trail. At one point, he stopped and shouted, "They are right ahead. Hurry!"

Tonrai glanced over his shoulder at Anu, who had remained silent while they climbed. Tonrai tried to hide his smile, but Anu almost laughed aloud. Cheshonii had given Chief Elder an order.

Daylight had faded by the time they reached the place where Chanu waited. The sliver of the new moon was still behind Great-Grandmother.

On another occasion, Tonrai might have taken in the expansive view across the land to distant mountains, but he embraced his brother while the others dipped their gourds into Nothai's jar, which still sat on the trail, along with Tatanikii's. He had left it when he ran back to the village for help. Each man took a small sip, saving a little of the water to pour on the trail as thanks to Mother Earth.

Cheshonii knelt, looking down the rocky slope to where his father lay, partly covered by a pile of rocks. Tonrai squatted beside him.

The boy said, "He's not moving."

Chanu hesitated. "No. And he has made no sound." To Tonrai, he said, "Our father's spirit struggles. Sometimes I hear him moan, but the silence that follows is long. When he's awake, I think he knows I'm here."

Thandoi uncoiled his rope. "Who's going down?"

"I am." Chanu answered before Tonrai could speak. "I'm rested." He wrapped the rope around his thigh, securing it with a knot before wrapping it around the other thigh. He pulled it around his back and drew it through the opening between the loops on his legs and wrapped it twice more around his body. Tonrai took the other end of the rope and tied it to a tall pillar of rock at the edge of the trail. Thandoi also secured his rope to an outcrop, where a dusty lizard scuttled to the top as if to watch the rescue.

Tonrai tested his brother's harness and sang a quiet song thanking the yucca for the fibers braided into this rope. He called upon it to hold Chanu's weight. Thandoi and Tonrai held the rope as Chanu started down toward Vachai. He worked his way down the slope backward, leaning back and looking over his shoulder for footholds. The others played the rope out as he descended the rocky slope.

Cheshonii asked, "What do you need me to do?"

Thandoi glanced at the boy and Anu. "The two of you will use the other rope to help pull Vachai up when he is secured."

Chanu worked his way down the steep slope, avoiding the scattered cactus, moving from rock to rock, testing each before putting his full weight on it.

Cheshonii was on his knees again watching Chanu's progress. "Can't he go faster?"

"No. He could start another landslide." Tonrai did not doubt Nothai's spirit had already left his body. It would linger near him, and when he was home, they would sing his spirit to the Flower World, the Sea Ania.* It would be hard on the boy.

Chanu reached his father and knelt beside him. He shouted back up to the others, "Our father lives."

He lifted Vachai's shoulders and pulled pieces of broken pottery and the burden basket from beneath him. Anu dropped the second rope, and Chanu secured it around his father's thighs and shoulders and to his own harness. "Ready."

When he lifted him, the older man screamed. One leg hung at an odd angle. As Anu and Cheshonii pulled a moaning Vachai upward, Chanu held him steady while Thandoi and Tonrai kept Chanu's rope taut as he made his way up the slope with his father.

"Easy! Easy!" Chanu cautioned whenever his father cried out. Twice he stopped so he could adjust his grip on the older man. Inch by agonizing inch, they brought him up.

Finally, Chanu reached the others. Tonrai lifted his father from his brother's arms and laid him on the trail while Thandoi extended his hand to bring Chanu to level ground.

Cheshonii dipped a gourd into his father's water jar and handed it to Chanu, who knelt with Tonrai beside his father. "His leg is broken. We will have to make a splint before we can carry him down." Cheshonii filled the gourd again and dropped in a pinch of crushed creosote leaves Healer-Woman had sent along. He handed it to Chanu for his father. Even though the water was too cool to dissolve the leaves, he hoped it would lessen his pain.

Vachai regained consciousness and reached for his son's hand. "His— spirit. It—"

"I know. We will bring him home." Chanu held the gourd to his father's mouth, and the older man drank.

Tonrai stood. "I'll go down for our uncle."

Once Tonrai was harnessed, Anu and Thandoi managed his descent. When he reached the narrow shelf where his uncle lay, his body nearly covered with rocks, Tonrai knelt beside him. Nothai's head was twisted to the side, and flies hovered around dried blood on his face. His eyes were open as if looking to the far horizon, across the vast expanse of land where their village lay, so small in Mother Earth's hands. Tonrai fanned away the flies and explored his uncle's eyes. Indeed, his spirit had left him. He laid a hand on Nothai's forehead and gently closed his eyes with his thumb.

Come with me now
Come to the place where
Spirits say goodbye
Come with me now
Come to where
The flower world awaits

His song floated down the canyon and across the land below. On the trail above, Cheshonii began to sing when his mother's voice drifted up the canyon and joined Tonrai's.

The flower world awaits
Come with me now to
Where spirits say goodbye

Tossing the rocks, one by one, down the slope, Tonrai lifted the weight of death from his uncle. With each rock, the sound reverberated across the land. In the silences between, Kokii's spirit wailed.

In the brush hut, Ha-wani and the others waited. An-nat sang while Li-naä made corncakes. The men would be hungry when they came down. The adults were quiet, but the children ran around playing and laughing, neither quite understanding the situation. For Chuwii and Tarukii, it was an adventure to be away from the village in this strange little brush hut.

Suddenly, Kokii stood and folded her hands before her. She left the dwelling and stood looking up the trail into the canyon.

> *Come with me now to*
> *Where spirits say goodbye*
> *The flower world awaits*
> *Come with me now*

The children came to stand on either side of her, their games forgotten. They, too, began to sing. Ha-wani exchanged glances with her mother-in-law. *Nothai. It meant Vachai lived, but how badly was he hurt?*

In the morning, after she greeted the dawn wind without the first kiss of the sun, Ha-wani woke her sister.

"Ra-naä, come with me to meet them." Because the brush house was so close to Great-Grandmother's Knees, the sun still hid behind her summit, and the trail was cloaked in shadow.

Ra-naä shrugged her shoulders. "Might as well. It's boring here.

The trail was shaded and cool until they reached the place where it became steep and rocky.

Ra-naä pointed to the litters. "Why did they leave these here? I thought they needed them to bring them down."

"It may be too rough in some places to use them."

"You mean they have to carry them? Poor Chanu."

Ha-wani bit her tongue. She wanted to point out it was not Chanu who deserved the most pity. Instead, she said, "Let's keep going."

"Keep going? Up there?" She shook her head. "You can go, but I'm staying here. I'm tired and this baby . . . well, I'm tired." She took a seat on a rock beside the trail and folded her arms across her chest.

Ha-wani turned and set out alone in the dim light of morning. She trotted where she could and scrambled over the rocky areas. Ground squirrels and lizards darted out of her way as she concentrated on the climb. Shortly, Chanu, with the water jar on his back, came around a turn in the trail with the rest of the men behind him.

Vachai was strapped to Tonrai's back, his right leg wrapped around his son's waist, the other, with thin branches tied along the sides, stuck straight out. Cheshonii followed Tonrai and Anu, a grim look on his face, carrying his father's body across his shoulders.

Ha-wani stood aside, and, as Tonrai passed, she willed the strength of her spirit to him. The men worked together to move through the rough parts of the trail. Where the trail was steep and rocky,

Chanu, with Nothai's burden basket and water jar on his back, turned to help Tonrai keep his balance under the weight of their father. Behind Tonrai, Anu, bringing Tatanikii's water, supported some of Vachai's weight as Tonrai stepped down. When he knew Tonrai was on sure footing, he turned to help Cheshonii navigate the trail under Nothai's weight. Thandoi came behind to provide support. Ha-wani fell in line wordlessly. *Amureo might have done this, but Fire-Keeper was behind it.*

By the time they reached Ra-naä, the sun shone on the trail, and the heat was rising. Anu and Thandoi readied the litters and helped Tonrai and Cheshonii lay their fathers on them. Chanu lowered his water jar, and each man dipped a gourd and drank, again saving a small amount to return to Mother Earth.

Once Vachai and Nothai were secured to the litters, Thandoi shouldered Cheshonii out of the way. "I'll take him now."

"No." Cheshonii stepped between his father's litter and Chief Elder. "I promised my mother I would bring him home."

"Do you defy me, boy?" Thandoi glared at the younger man, looking directly into his eyes.

"I made a promise." Cheshonii met his gaze, his spirit offering no threat and no disrespect, simply his determination.

Ha-wani smiled at the pride shining in her husband's eyes for his young cousin.

Thandoi laid a hand on Cheshonii's shoulder. The boy had achieved a height almost equaling Chief Elder. "I will not argue with you. You have proven your strength, but think on this: no man is more important than another. Your pride will put others at risk." Thandoi turned and took Tatanikii's burden basket from Anu and started down the trail. Cheshonii took up his father's litter and followed Anu, who was pulling Vachai.

Ra-naä walked with Chanu, clinging to his arm and chattering in spite of her husband's silence, and Ha-wani walked with Tonrai.

"Did Cheshonii carry his father all the way?"

"He did. He refused to allow anyone else to do it. He angered Chief Elder, but the boy wouldn't give an inch." He shook his head. "He never stumbled once. He is strong, but his spirit is stronger."

"Kokii will need his strength."

"Yes, but he would do well to heed Chief Elder's advice."

Chapter 11

Big Rains Moon 1158 (July)

Nothai's battered and bruised body lay naked under the family ramada. Kokii knelt beside him, singing.

The flower world awaits
Vanseeka weene*
Go now Maisokai*
Sea ania vovicha*
Vanseeka weene

Her younger sons sat on each side of her. Chuwii held the palette with puddles of red, yellow, and black paint, and Tarukii made the brushes, chewing on a length of yucca to break it down into separate fibers. Kokii dragged a brush through the red. Drawing a line from Nothai's hairline, down his nose, across his mouth, chin, and down his body. When the line reached his genitals, she dipped the brush again and branched the red line down one leg and then the other, all the way to his long toe. By acknowledging his spirit self and his mortal self, his spirit, Maisokai, would not leave the man who was Nothai behind when it passed into the Flower World.

Go now Maisokai
The flower world awaits the tarantula
Sea ania vovicha
Vanseeka weene Maisokai

Fire-Keeper prepared to send Nothai's spirit on its journey by directing several men to open a pit beyond the wall where a dwelling had been dismantled when they moved into the compound. Nothai would lie flat in the center of the pit with room around him for the gifts he would take to the Sea Ania.

His body, with the long line Kokii drew dividing it in two, now wore the messages she and the children had offered. Tarukii had drawn a figure that, to him, represented a bird with a long tail, and Chuwii added a rabbit figure with long ears. Cheshonii joined them, kneeling on the other side of his father and adding a figure representing a bighorn sheep with spiraling horns. He took the paint palette from Tarukii, dragged his hand across it, and gripped his father's shoulder, leaving a colorful imprint and a promise to care for the family.

Kokii and her sons stood, each one scattering corn meal on Nothai's body and singing.

Go now to
Where spirits roam free
Sea ania vovicha
The flower world awaits
Vanseeka weene

Fire-Keeper, in ceremonial garb, stood beside Nothai's grave. Black lines painted his cheeks, and his turquoise-studded shell pendant hung at his neck, along with four beaded necklaces. His beaded bone pin stuck through his ever-present double-knotted hair. In one hand he held his staff, its feathers floating lightly around the top, its bells and tinklers quiet. In his other hand, he held a gourd rattle.

"My people! Mother Earth again called one of our own. She will do with his spirit what she chooses, what she determines is his reward or his punishment."

A confused murmuring rose from the gathered people.

Wide-eyed, Ha-wani nudged Tonrai. "Fire-Keeper will not send his spirit on smoke and flames? We will not see his spirit rise from the fire and blend into the sky while we sing him into the Sea Ania?"

"We did that before the wall, but, for those of us who live inside, it is different. For a time, babies, small children, and those who lived outside were still borne away on flames and smoke, but now that has changed too. Sometimes, for the adults, instead of the pyre and the collection of bones and ashes for burial, Fire-Keeper uses the old, abandoned dwellings. He places the body on the floor and burns what is left of the dwelling. No remains are collected for burial in the cemetery."*

Ha-wani frowned. "But he said Mother Earth will choose what to do with his spirit. There's no way to know, then, if the spirit has made its journey."

"That's something new he's added. I haven't heard him say that before."

Among the people, others may have been having the same conversation because Fire-Keeper pounded his staff on the ground, jingling the shells and swirling the feathers, their colors bright against the sky, and the crowd quieted.

"Mother Earth instructed me. Our spirits are hers to guide into the Flower World if we have earned a place there."

Again, the people glanced from one to the other in confusion.

Fire-Keeper shook his rattle and pounded his staff against the ground again. "You will bring your gifts."

One by one, those who came to honor Nothai knelt by his grave and placed their gift. Chanu gave him a spear point he had crafted; Tonrai wove a shell necklace through the stiff fingers of his uncle, and Li-naä brought a seed jar she had made with a small handful of seed corn in it as a gift from her husband.

Vachai was still in the brush shelter by the wash where No-wani was caring for him. He would not have the opportunity to say farewell to his brother's spirit.

When the presentation of gifts was finished, Fire-Keeper began to sing. Everyone joined in, expecting the traditional song for Nothai's spirit to pass safely into the Sea Ania.

In confusion, many stopped singing when they realized Fire-Keeper's song was different. His song did not direct Nothai's spirit to the Flower World, but to Mother Earth as if she would decide if his spirit was worthy. When he went on singing, repeating the verse several times, other voices joined in. By the fifth time, nearly everyone had joined the singing. Nothai's family stood silent as did Vachai's family and An-nat.

> *Vanseeka weene go now*
> *Go now to mother earth*
> *Iansu weene itom ae aniawi**
> *She will cradle you*
> *She will guide your spirit*
> *Go now to mother earth*
> *Iansu weene itom ae aniawi*

While most of the villagers returned to their homes, Kokii stood watching as Fire-Keeper directed two farmers to cover her husband with soil and the remains of the dismantled pit house for burning. Waiting with Tonrai, Ha-wani asked, "What does Fire-Keeper do for the children now?"

"For a time, they were still done in the old way, but now he refuses to sing for them or even preside over a ceremony. He claims a child is of no value to the village. There is no spirit to sing for."

"He is a hateful man, and he is wrong." She laid a hand on her belly. "If we lose our child, I will be pleased if Fire-Keeper is not there to sing his spirit into the Sea Ania. I will do it for him."

Tonrai suddenly stopped and turned toward her, his shell tinklers singing.

"Our child?"

She smiled. "I only missed one visit to the women's hut. If I miss another, I'll be certain." Her smile faded when she looked over his shoulder at Fire-Keeper standing by Nothai's grave. "The shaman was behind your uncle's death and your father's injury. And, now, he denies your uncle passage into the Flower World on smoke and flames."

When Fire-Keeper turned to look at her, dark wings rose within her and settled protectively around her. "I will never yield to him. He is not my shaman, nor will he ever be."

Chapter 12

Short Planting Moon 1158 (August)

With one hand, Ha-wani steadied the round jar resting on her head ring. The water she was bringing up from the well was too precious to lose, and the trail to the ridgetop was steep. Her skirt was tied under her breasts, which had grown heavier as her belly expanded. Her body was preparing for the child, making the life-sustaining milk to nourish him. She hoped to give Tonrai a boy-child. Wokkai followed, carrying a basket filled with sand.

Inside the compound, she lifted the jar from her head and, bending her knees, lowered it to the ground in the shade of her dwelling. Leaning down was more difficult as the baby continued to grow in her belly.

When Ha-wani set aside her head ring, which looked like a shallow basket with a large hole in the bottom, Wokkai picked it up and settled it with the small opening resting on her own head. Ha-wani watched as the girl squatted, keeping the ring balanced, picked up an empty jar smaller than the one Ha-wani had carried. After nestling the jar in the ring, she took a few steps around the ramada, her chin lifted and her hand up in case the jar should fall. "I will soon be able to carry bigger jars with water. My mother said she will show me how to walk up the rocky trail from the wash without dropping it."

"You're almost ready to put sand in it so you can practice with a heavier load." Ha-wani laughed when the girl spun around slowly without dropping the jar. "You're getting very good. But let's get this clay ready so you can learn to make pots."

Wokkai put the empty jar and head ring aside and handed Ha-wani chunks of the raw clay Tonrai had brought from Big River.* As she dropped them into the jar of water, she and Wokkai thanked Mother Earth for her gift.

Wokkai turned a chunk of raw clay in her hands. "This is hard. Is there really a pot in it?"

"Yes. After soaking it for several days, we'll separate the soil and stones from the clay so we can find out what it will be."

"Fire-Keeper said if we make pots, we'll be one with Mother Earth? Will we?"

"Look at this pot." Ha-wani knelt beside the one with the clay soaking in it. The jar was almost perfectly round with no painted lines or decorations on the reddish-brown sides. Dark, fire clouds smudged the surface. The opening was wide and slightly flared. Wokkai squatted beside her and watched as Ha-wani drew her hand from the lip to its base. "Wrap your hands around it. Feel it."

Wokkai caressed the roundness of the jar and traced the opening with her finger.

"What do you feel?"

"It's smooth. And cool."

"Clay is not simply a gift from Mother Earth; it is a piece of her. The clay carries her spirit, and she shares her spirit with us through the clay. When we work the clay, we are even closer to her than when we stand here, our feet resting on her back. Fire-Keeper spoke truth. When we take the clay into our hands and make something with a purpose, we blend our spirit with hers. In our own small way, we are doing what Mother Earth and Father Sky did when they created this world for us to live in."

Once more, the village had been denied rain, but a storm lingered over the mountains beyond her parents' village before sweeping off to the south. On the morning after the rain, Fire-Keeper gathered the people in the plaza and declared the storm a message from Mother Earth.

He stood above them on his platform, his staff in his hand, its colorful feathers dancing, its tinklers singing in harmony with the bells. He did not wear his ceremonial garb, but he wore his turquoise-studded pendant with no other jewelry except shell rings. When he raised his staff, the feathers twirled, the shells rattled, and the bells sang. "Father Sky has sent rain to refresh Mother Earth and fill Big River with flowing water. She waits for us to claim her gift and renew our kinship with her."

His shrill voice triggered a shiver down Ha-wani's spine. She chose a place in the middle of the gathered people, standing behind her husband, positioning herself so she could look at Fire-Keeper without attracting his attention.

Tonrai would think she was using him as a protective shield, but she gazed through the space between Tonrai's earlobe and his shoulder focusing on Fire-Keeper's bony frame. She could study him, the odd patch of hair on his chest, his skinny bowed-out legs, and his face—she could examine it without fear. His brow was heavily furrowed, and his hooded eyes were set wide beneath a prominent brow. Creased, hollow cheeks framed a broad, flat, nose, and his mouth—during moments of silence—was a narrow, almost lipless, straight line. She shuddered at the memory of the dream in which those lips had touched hers.

He went on, his shrill voice grating. "How can you expect Mother Earth to sustain us when you have paid her no tribute through the work of your hands?"

With new resolve, Ha-wani probed his eyes, discovering why they had disappeared from his mud-covered face at the rain ceremony. They were nothing like the warm, dark brown eyes of her family and everyone she knew. They were an almost transparent pale brown, the same color as the small scorpions hiding beneath pots and mats. While she considered his odd eye color, she realized that an image had begun to emerge. When the image cleared, a pale white grub writhed in his eyes, its brown head cap turning toward her, locking on her eyes, and transforming into a creature whose long, jointed antennae waved in slow circles and pointed at her.

She shuddered, remembering her first encounter with him and the terrifying experience in the pit. Feeling light-headed and unable to break eye contact, she vowed he would not take her there again. She called on her spirit to challenge him, to take control. Lifted by the push of dark wings, her light-headedness diminished. She felt the strength of those wings. But suddenly her spirit settled, and the creature faded.

She breathed easily again. When her eyes came into focus, she was staring at Tonrai's back, his dark skin glistening in the sunlight. He had shifted his stance and blocked Fire-Keeper's gaze. Without turning, he reached behind for her hand. She stepped close to him, rested her forehead on his back, and listened to Fire-Keeper's words, hoping the shaman had seen her resistance and her resolve.

"Women," Fire-Keeper shouted. "Too many of our pots lie broken and scattered. Mother Earth waits for you to take her into your hands and become one with her again."

The sound of his voice was discordant, but the meaning touched her. He was right. Too much time had passed since she had felt the cool clay in her hands and had sung her spirit into new pots and vessels.

A few days after she and Wokkai prepared the clay, Ha-wani explained to the girl that the clay had settled to the bottom of the jar, and now they needed to strain the top water through a length of cotton cloth and save it for when they began making pots. When that was done, she poured the thick clay into a basket and laid a woven mat over the top. "The clay still has too much water mixed into it. It will drain through the basket, but the clay will remain. When that is done, we can begin to make our vessels."

Around the village, other women did the same. When the clay was ready, several women in addition to Ra-naä and Wokkai gathered in Ha-wani's family ramada to make new pots. Among them were Anu's wife, Mochik and his daughter, Sochik. Chief Elder's

wife joined them with her daughter-in-law, Tatanikii's wife, who like Ha-wani and Ra-naä, was pregnant, but this time with her fourth child. Ha-wani
enjoyed sharing this work with the other women.
Throughout the village, inside and outside the walls,
women gathered under other ramadas to carry out
the shaman's instructions.

Ha-wani welcomed the women and invited them
to join her in the traditional song.

We give you thanks
Mother earth
For the gift of yourself
Guide our hands
As we honor you

As the women set to work, Mochik's second daughter, Ma-taä, came into the compound with Sochik's
infant and her younger brothers and sisters. Ma-taä
and one of Chief Elder's daughters were close in age,
and, together, they would watch over the younger
children while their mothers worked.

In the past, Wokkai would have joined them,
as she was barely older than they, but today she
was learning the craft of pottery. She had collected
sand in the wash and sifted it to remove stones and
debris. Now, Ha-wani scooped a handful from the
girl's basket and let it fall through her fingers. She
smiled and took what she needed to strengthen her
clay against the heat of the fire.

After sharing the sand with the others, Wokkai
took her place next to Ha-wani to watch and imitate
everything her sister-in-law did.

Ha-wani divided her clay, giving some to her sister and some to Wokkai, and she thanked Mother
Earth again for her gift. Like the other women, she
placed her clay on the flat rock before her and worked

the sand into it until the grit blended fully with the clay. There was little talk among them as they each prepared it for creating the vessel Mother Earth intended it to be. Kneeling, Ha-wani rocked back on her heels, and, with her arms straight, leaned into the clay, folding it over itself, and leaning into it again. With each fold, she sang silently.

The earth is our mother
Who sustains us.

Over and over, she kneaded, folded, and kneaded again. She tore chunks from the worked clay and threw them against the rock, again and again, compacting the spirits of sand, water, and clay into a single spirit into which she would fuse her own. Through the work of her hands and with the addition of fire, she would honor Mother Earth.

She flattened a disk of clay in her puki,* a small, shallow saucer that would hold the pot while she built up the sides with coil after coil. She was so intent on her hands and the clay, she paid scant attention to the conversation among the women when they, too, began to make their pots.

Ra-naä absently rolled the clay between her hands, making little round balls that would likely have no function. She had never liked making pottery, but her mother had insisted she learn something that would contribute to the family and to the village. She had also tried weaving, making a useless skirt that hung crooked with an uneven weave. She hated strapping the loom around her waist and sitting on the ground, endlessly shuttling thread in and out of the warp.

It required too much concentration. Basket-weaving had been another failure. Her aunt finally gave up and took her basket away, saving the grasses for a better one. Pottery had been her last hope, but her vessels always broke in the fire. Ha-wani told her it was because she didn't knead the right amount of sand into the clay.

At least she could make corncakes.

Around her, the conversation was all about having babies. She looked at Tatanikii's wife, large enough to be close to giving birth. *Her fourth!* Ra-naä could not imagine having that many children. She rubbed her round belly. "I can't do this anymore. I can't get comfortable."

Anu's wife said, "Try to sit up straight. You might find it more comfortable. When you slouch like that, you're crowding the baby, and your back will ache when you stand."

You should know—with seven children. She lifted her shoulders, straightened her back, and lifted the corners of her mouth into what might pass as a smile. "Thank you. I'll try to remember."

She lined up the clay balls on her stone. "Why does Fire-Keeper think the pots we make today are so important?"

Tatanikii's wife replied. "We need to reconnect with Mother Earth and restore harmony. We haven't used her clay for some time, so if we make pots today, the rain we need will come."

"We never stopped making vessels in our village. Why did you stop?" Ra-naä's clay sat idle on her puki while she scraped clay from beneath her blunt fingernails.

"Fire-Keeper said we would waste water." Her sister pointed to the small jars of top water—the water the women brought to keep the clay moist while they worked. "If we strain this water through fine cotton cloth, we can use it for cooking. Or we can water the corn. We don't have to waste it."

Ra-naä narrowed her eyes and furrowed her otherwise clear forehead. "So you're saying Fire-Keeper is wrong?" The other women stopped working and waited for Ha-wani's answer. Ra-naä enjoyed her sister's momentary discomfort before she answered.

"No. Of course he's not wrong. Some of the water strained off was lost to the ground."

Ha-wani glanced at Ra-naä's little clay balls in a row on her stone. "It looks like you're making beads instead of a pot."

After a moment's hesitation, Ra-naä replied, "Of course. What else would they be?"

"That's a wonderful idea. Will you let Tonrai make them into a necklace for you?"

She shrugged. "If he wants to."

Ha-wani's face brightened. "You could make the hole so he can string them, and you could decorate them with lines—different patterns, so each one is distinctive."

Ra-naä stared at her sister. "That's what I was going to do."

Everyone returned to her task—even Ra-naä, who seemed to have a renewed interest in the clay. They each worked in silence, privately singing her own song to Mother Earth who honored them with her gift.

Happy to think only about her creation, Ha-wani's dark hair hung long in front of her shoulders. Occasionally, she shrugged it over her shoulder and wiped perspiration from her face with her forearm.

Ha-wani's clay invited a relatively small pot with a short neck and a wide opening, smaller than those the other women were making and different from those she had made before.

Even on this warm day, the clay was cool in her hands as she sang her spirit and her song into the pot she made. It would hold them and bring blessings to the people.

The earth is our mother
Who sustains us
She honors us with gifts
From the earth
The earth is our mother
Who sustains us

Under the ramada, Ha-wani sensed the brush of dark wings as she focused on her hands, bringing the pot into being and stopping only to pluck out a bit of leaf or a twig stuck in the clay or to dip her paddle into the precious top water she had saved from processing the clay. With renewed energy, she pounded the pot's sides and bottom until they were thinned and the clay was evenly distributed. Her long, brown fingers wore the stains of the clay and danced of their own free will.

She did not have to think about her work; her hands did what they needed to do. She dipped her fingers into the water and began to build the short neck and rim, and, using a smooth rock, she polished both the inside and outside. After the pot cured, she would paint red, interlocking scrolls—square instead of round.

Like most of the women, she made several pots that day—pots to be shared among the villagers for cooking and storage purposes. This pot, though, stood apart from the others, having little utilitarian use. The opening was too small for a gourd dipper, so she would not use it for drinking water. It was too small to make a rabbit stew for the family's dinner and too large for Vachai to use for seeds. Mother Earth might someday let her know what its purpose would be. In the meantime, she would keep it beside the entry of their house.

Chapter 13

Short Planting Moon 1158 (August)

While Li-naä stayed with Vachai in the brush hut beneath Great-Grandmother's Knees, Ha-wani took care of Wokkai and Benai, who from time to time went down to visit with their parents. Cheshonii had taken up his father's duties in the fields, working with Anu and the other farmers. After a full turning of the moon, Tonrai brought his father back to the compound. Vachai's broken leg had nearly healed, but he could not straighten it, and his back was twisted. Although Chanu made him a sturdy walking stick from a sotol spike,* coming up the rocky trail to the compound had been difficult, but both Li-naä and Vachai were glad to come home.

Tonrai built his father a bench under the ramada because both lowering himself to the ground and rising from it caused him pain. Soon, he learned to lower himself to the bench and to stand with the help of the stick, although his sons insisted on helping when they could.

Because his father needed to be busy and productive, Tonrai sought out Chief Elder to discuss his father's role in the community.

"My father is no longer able to work in the fields with the farmers."

"I'm not surprised." Chief Elder paused to watch a hawk circling above the compound, red tail flashing in the sunlight. "He's not a man who will be happy sitting around."

"You know him well."

"I do. We grew up together. We hunted rabbits and hares, competing to see who could throw the rabbit stick more accurately and who made the most kills. We made our first trip to Great Water together."

"He speaks highly of you."

"We competed in foot races." He smiled at the memory. "Most of the time he won." His smile faded. "And now . . . "

Tonrai waited, anticipating he would say more.

"I have been thinking about this since his injury. Regardless of what Fire-Keeper says, no one knows the fields or understands planting as well as Vachai, and, without Nothai, we may well depend on his wisdom for the harvest also."

Again, he concentrated on the hawk, and Tonrai wondered if he was looking to the hawk for guidance.

As if a decision had been made, he said, "I will go and speak with him now."

Tonrai fell in step behind him.

Under the ramada, Vachai took his stick and started to push himself up when Chief Elder approached. Thandoi held his hand up, palm out. "Don't stand, friend."

Tonrai caught a glimpse of fear in his father's eyes. Not standing for a conversation with Chief Elder was beyond rude. It was unacceptable. Tonrai suspected his father thought he was being dismissed as unworthy.

But Thandoi knelt, so he was level with Vachai and laid his right hand on the other's shoulder. Vachai returned the gesture. With their arms aligned in this sign of mutual respect and friendship, Tonrai saw his father's fear dissolve.

"It is good to see you, my friend. I am pleased your spirit remained with us."

"I, too, am glad to be here, glad I can still walk the Earth, but . . . " He laid a hand on his twisted leg. "I don't do that very well any more. I fear I am not of much use to the village."

After they unclasped arms, Thandoi remained on one knee to continue the conversation, maintaining a respectful demeanor. "That's of no importance. Others will do the work in the fields. We still need your knowledge and your wisdom. When you distributed seed corn in time to catch the water Great-Grandmother sent into the washes, you knew how much water to expect, giving out no more seed than could be expected to grow and thrive with the available water. Our farmers diverted those waters to the field and dug wells to capture them. That small field is doing well, and the harvest should be better than in the past."

Vachai nodded. "I passed the corn field when I came back to the village. The beans need to go in soon. I cannot visit the terraces," gesturing at his bad leg. "My nephew tells me the agaves out on the terraces are fine."

"Agaves take their time, but our channeling borders directed the little run-off from Great-Grandfather to our purposes."

"This news gives me peace. But if I cannot join the farmers in the fields, what can I offer?"

"You have much to offer, my friend. With the lack of sufficient rain to keep our fields productive, our seed supplies are dwindling. We are too haphazard with planting and harvesting. I'm thinking we need to do things differently and become more purposeful. Unless we get the needed rain, we may lose more than we harvest. We have to do a better job of maintaining the common stores for the village. Too often, we have failed to separate the grain and crops into categories to best serve our needs."

"What are you thinking?"

"The people are often hungry, and it is far too tempting—especially now with scant rains—to consume everything we grow. But without a seed supply, we will deprive ourselves of a future."

"Of course. We must have seeds for the next planting. Fire-Keeper will tell us what he needs for the sacred supply."

"Exactly."

"What is it you want me to do?"

"I'm thinking we need a place to store the harvest, a granary* of sorts. And, because you have knowledge most of us lack, you should manage the distribution and storage of the harvest, setting aside the seeds for each planting. At council meetings, you will tell us about the food and seed supplies and recommend any changes that will best serve the entire village, especially in lean times."

"I don't know what to say." Vachai's voice caught in his throat.

"Of course, I have to bring this to the Council of Elders for their approval,"

Vachai glanced at Tonrai. "Fire-Keeper will oppose it."

"Maybe, but we will overrule him. I believe Knowledge-Keeper and Bead-Maker will agree."

"Thank you, my friend." Vachai hesitated. "But . . ."

"What is it?"

"If the council approves, my obligation to them must be restricted to matters related to the granary, to farming, and to irrigation. As one who is serving the council, I shouldn't vote on anything related to my work." He nodded towards Tonrai. "May I suggest that my son join the council as a voting member, replacing me?"

Tonrai had never realized just how close his father and Chief Elder were until he listened to this conversation. It was now clear to him that they had a bond.

He glanced over Chief Elder's shoulder to Fire-Keeper, who was in the center of the plaza brushing away yesterday's sun shadow marks.* Daily, he tracked the sun's journey across the sky by marking the length and position of the shadows of a stick in the center of the plaza. He told the people he would know when Father Sky might abandon them, something he assured them was possible. If the sun no longer made its daily journey, it would be because the people had failed to follow the laws and listen to what he tried to teach them.

Now, he scowled angrily at Thandoi. Tonrai suspected he was outraged that Chief Elder knelt before a farmer.

Day after day, the weather remained hot with no promise of rain. Each afternoon, clouds formed over the mountains only to disperse into the pale blue sky.

Chanu and Tonrai sat under the ramada with Vachai, who was making sandals. Benai had collected a supply of narrow yucca leaves for his father to weave everyone in the family a new pair. No matter what came of Chief Elder's proposal, he would not sit around doing nothing. He would be useful and productive.

Cheshonii and his youngest brother, Chuwii, had gone to the terraces with Anu, who had picked up Nothai's duties along with Vachai's. This day, Anu was helping the field workers shore up the check dams and extend the channeling borders to capture additional runoff for the fields—if, indeed, rain should finally fall. The women and girls had gone into the desert to collect prickly pear fruit.

Tonrai was using shell fragments to make beads. Tarukii sat next to him, a flat rock between his knees. He was making holes in broken pieces of pottery with a stone drill. They would be spindle whorls for the village weavers. Chanu was fashioning a new spear point, and Benai squatted beside him, a hammerstone in one hand and a piece of chert in the other. Each time Chanu struck a flake from his rock, Benai did the same.

"Do you think the council will go along with Chief Elder's plan?" Chanu glanced at his father, who pulled cordage through the sole of the sandal, making the toe loop and the ties.

"I think they will—that is, if Fire-Keeper isn't particularly persuasive. I worry about Bead-Maker. He is sometimes too easily swayed." He continued to focus on the work of his hands.

Tonrai did not doubt the shaman would oppose it. "Why does he dislike you?"

Vachai laid the sandal on his knee and directed his gaze to Great-Grandfather's towers and pinnacles. "I'm a farmer and have no business living inside these walls with the people he deems most important.

He reminds me often that I wouldn't be here if my sons were farmers. But that's not the only reason."

Chanu frowned. "But Nothai was a farmer, and his sons had not yet revealed their talents."

"He was part of my family group outside, so, naturally, he came inside with us."

Ordinarily, children paid little attention to adult conversations, and they knew better than to interrupt. Tarukii, however, rarely hesitated to join in. He set his spindle whorls aside, put his head down, and said, "I miss my father."

Tonrai laid his hand on the boy's shoulder. "We miss him, too. His spirit may have traveled to the Flower World, but he is still with you and your brothers."

The boy's eyes filled. "I know. He talks to me."

Vachai leaned toward the boy. "What does he say?"

"He tells me to behave, to help my mother, and to run faster than all the other boys."

Vachai chuckled. "Do you know why you are named Tarukii?"

"Because I run." He wiped his tears with the back of his hand.

"As a small child, you never walked anywhere. You ran before you walked. Our people are excellent runners, but you, my boy, will be the best ever. Yours is the spirit of *taruk*,* that funny looking bird with the long tail that runs through the desert catching quail babies, snakes, and lizards. You catch lizards just as easily."

When the boy smiled, Tonrai was reminded of the depth of his father's wisdom. It was not limited to farming.

Bringing the conversation back to its beginning, the boy frowned and asked, "Does Fire-Keeper dislike me and my brothers, too?"

The men exchanged glances, and Tonrai wondered if they should have spared the boy their comments about Fire-Keeper.

Vachai's mouth tightened into a straight line, his brows coming together above his nose. "We should not have spoken in front of you about Fire-Keeper."

Because Benai remained silent during the conversation with Tarukii, continuing to strike flakes off the edge of the chert, Tonrai would have sworn he paid no attention to the conversation. But when Benai laid his chert aside, it was too heavily flaked on one side and was unlikely to be a useful point.

Chanu, who had also remained silent, picked it up and examined it. "If you were angry with the spirit of the stone, you should have laid it aside sooner."

Ignoring his older brother's comment, Benai glared at his father, and demanded, "You said being a farmer is not the only reason he dislikes you. What else is there?"

Vachai sighed. "If I tell you," he said, looking at both youngsters, "you must swear by your spirit you will never speak of it to anyone—ever."

Wide-eyed, both boys nodded.

Perhaps regretting his outburst, Benai scooted toward his father, tucked himself under Vachai's bad leg, and lifted it to his shoulder. "Thank you, my son. That relieves the ache."

Tonrai reached for Tarukii's hand. "Come." He lifted the boy to his knee and put an arm around him. The child leaned against him, tucking his head beneath Tonrai's chin.

A pleasant breeze stirred the air as Vachai began his story. "We called him Star-Watcher. He sat outside most nights, watching the sky. Sometimes we thought he was counting the stars, which was impossible—except maybe to him. I wasn't much older than

Benai, and he was about Chanu's age. His father was our fire-keeper.

"At night, he crossed the terraces toward Great-Grandfather, often not returning until after sunrise. For a long time, it was a mystery where he went and what he did.

"It occurred to us that he had secrets unrelated to star-watching. But his mysterious trips toward the mountain roused our curiosity. Each morning when he returned, he was more arrogant than ever.

"He would strut around the plaza, and if he encountered either one of us, he would shove us out of his way. He trespassed on our spirits, trying to make us look into his eyes. My brother and I and my friend, Rabbit-Stalker, stuck together as much as possible. We were afraid to let him catch us alone."

Tonrai assumed Rabbit-Stalker was Chief Elder, but he didn't say anything. It might be best for the boys not to know.

"One night, Nothai and I followed him. We were determined to find out what he was hiding. We discovered he was going to the rock shelter back there under the mountain. We thought if we could learn his secrets, we might be able to make him leave us alone.

"We were wrong."

Chapter 14

Twenty-eight Years Earlier (1130)

Darkness enveloped the two boys as they crept along the path across the terraces. They had lost sight of Star-Watcher, but they were certain the rock shelter was his destination. Focused on the path beneath their feet, they paid little attention to the sky. They did not notice star-streaks* flashing across the dark dome above them.

Creeping to the edge of a terrace, they saw a small fire in front of the shelter.

"We were right." Nothai knelt and sat back on his heels.

"I'm glad he's got a fire. We can see what he does." Vachai lay on his belly and rested his chin on his forearms.

"Can he see us?"

"I don't think so." At that moment, a star-streak slashed the sky above Great-Grandfather. Vachai gasped, pointing. "Look!"

Nothai clapped his hand over his mouth when he saw how many stars were streaking across the sky.

The familiar moonless dome of night was covered with stars, both bright and dim. The corn meal path* Father Sky provided for spirits to follow into the Flower World glowed across the arc of the sky. Both boys had seen night skies many times. They had heard the people's stories. They had seen star-streaks from time to time, but they had never seen so many.

Staring wide-eyed at the sky, Nothai whispered, "What do you think it means?"

"Something bad's going to happen."

"To us?"

"Or to the people."

"Should we go back and warn them?"

Before Vachai could answer, Star-Watcher's reedy voice pierced the night.

> *Father sky, hear me*
> *Hear my voice*
> *Send me your power*
> *Give me your strength*
> *Help me do what I must do*

In the dancing light and shadows cast by the fire, he stood naked atop the rock shelter, his face lifted to the sky, his hands high in supplication. Great-Grandfather Mountain loomed dark behind him. Nothai started to rise. "We need to go back."

"No. I'm not leaving. If something bad's going to happen, it probably won't happen here, tonight."

Nothai sat again. "I hope you're right. Do you think he's making Father Sky throw the stars away?"

"No. We've seen star-streaks before." He studied the sky again. "Besides, he's not a fire-keeper yet— only a fire-keeper would have such power."

"But he will be someday."

"Maybe, but I still want to know what he's doing."

Mother earth
Hear my voice
Open your arms
To the one I send to you
Keep his spirit in your care
Seal his spirit deep in your arms

Vachai frowned. "He means to keep someone's spirit from crossing into the Flower World."

"Do you think so?"

"What else can it mean? We sing a different song when someone's spirit leaves them. We don't send them into Mother Earth's arms. We sing them into the Flower World on smoke and flames—" He swept his arm over his head along the dense trail of stars crossing the sky. "—so they can follow Father Sky's corn meal path."

"We have to go." Nothai began to tremble.

Vachai put his hand on his younger brother's shoulder. "I promise you. Nothing bad will happen—at least not now." He hoped it was not a hollow promise.

Chapter 15

Short Planting Moon 1158 (August)

And so we followed Star-Watcher, night after night. He danced around his little fire. One night, he threw something into the fire. We didn't know what it was, but he did it over and over again. Finally, whatever he threw into the flames immediately reduced it to smoke and ashes, and when he threw in something else, it flared up again. I didn't know what he was doing, but I didn't believe it was magic. He must have found something that allowed him to control the flames. It seemed like he was practicing, because the more often he succeeded, the happier he was—he would sing a song of thanks."

Tonrai nodded. To his brother, he said, "We must pay better attention the next time we gather in the plaza."

Vachai continued. "One night, I went by myself because Nothai had the flux. He opened moonflower pods and dropped the seeds and leaves into a pot. He settled it over the fire, and while it heated, he chanted words I didn't understand. When the steam rose from the pot, he used a forked stick to lift it and set it away from the fire. He knelt and leaned over the pot, arms stretched out, breathing in the steam. After a time, he lay down on the ground and appeared to sleep. I, too, must have fallen asleep because what happened could only have been a dream."

Chanu, Tonrai, and the boys waited in silence.

"I've never told anyone this—not even Nothai after it happened." He took a deep breath before continuing. "Star-Watcher's spirit rose from his sleeping form and danced in the air above him, shuffling his feet and chanting. The man was on the ground sleeping, but he was also dancing above himself." The older man shivered. "I don't like to remember it, to think about it."

Tonrai changed the subject. "Did you ever find out whose spirit he wanted to keep from crossing over?"

"We thought we did." Benai's back was turned with his father's leg resting on his shoulder. Tarukii had dozed off on Tonrai's lap. Vachai pointed at his youngest son, pressed a finger to his lips, and shook his head. "Other nights, he sat atop the rock shelter, watching the sky. We weren't sure what he was learning, but it gave me a chance to study the sky and the moon. I learned about the movement of the stars: how the old woman and the drinking gourd* circle the same dim star to the north and how predictable the moon's changes are."

Chanu grinned. "And you learned to follow the moon for planting."

"Yes. I told my father the corn we had planted under the new moon did better than corn planted at other times, and squash, beans, and cotton did better if they were planted during the half moon that followed a new moon. We discovered it was best not to plant anything when the moon was full. We scheduled the harvest when the moon was in its last phase. Following this pattern led to much better harvests, and we enjoyed a time of plenty."

"That's how you became a successful farmer."

"I think so. My brother and I were unable to uncover Star-Watcher's secrets, but we learned some valuable lessons that helped our people. I guess I owe that to him." He shifted his weight and lifted his leg from Benai's shoulder. "I need to stand. I've been sitting too long."

He reached for his walking stick and pushed himself up. "Bring me water, Benai, please." When the boy stepped away, Vachai spoke quietly to Chanu and Tonrai. "Within a very short time, Star-Watcher's father—our fire-keeper—died. He was a reasonably young man so it was a great shock to the village. And Star-Watcher became Fire-Keeper."

"Do you think he—?" Tonrai interrupted himself when Benai brought the water jar to his father, who simply shrugged in reply.

Vachai dipped the gourd into the jar, took a long drink, and poured the last few drops on the ground in thanks. "For one thing, he resents that I figured out how the phases of the moon affect farming. I'm not sure he had figured it out himself, but once he understood how my father used the moon, he knew why it worked. By the time his father died and he rose to the position of Fire-Keeper, my father was directing the planting, and I was helping. When my father died, everyone expected me to carry on. Other than Fire-Keeper, no one in council opposed it. He wanted to direct the planting and to raise himself above the rest of us—especially above me—in everything important to the people."

Chanu also took a drink. "Thank you, Benai." To his father, he said, "You said 'For one thing.' There is something else?"

Vachai sighed. "Star-Watcher had his eye on the prettiest girl in the village. She knew it and pleaded with her father to deny him if he asked. Her father agreed, and he was denied." He paused. "She married me."

Both Tonrai and Chanu stared open-mouthed at their father. Almost as one, they said, "Our mother?"

Vachai smiled. "She chose me, and I made an enemy for life." His smile faded. "For that reason, I do not doubt he is responsible for this." Leaning on his stick, he swung his free hand past his twisted leg. "And my brother's death."

Days later, Vachai limped across the plaza, leaning on his walking stick as he dragged his bad leg along. "I don't expect Fire-Keeper to be happy about Chief Elder's plan."

"Nor his suggestion for me to replace you on the council." Tonrai was not confident the meeting would go smoothly. "It will depend on how the other members receive the idea."

Dar and An-Nat joined them as they reached the base of the platform mound. The path to the top stretched its length, but it would be a challenge for Vachai.

"Greetings, Friend." Dar placed a hand on Vachai's shoulder, and he returned the gesture. "How are you doing?"

"I manage. Some days are better than others." Leaning on his stick, he grasped his thigh with the other hand and pulled his leg even with the other. "How are you?"

"I've been better." He held up one hand. "These knots keep growing on my knuckles, and they are painful. Sometimes, I can't bend my fingers to string beads, let alone make them."

It saddened Tonrai to think his mentor could not make the jewelry he had become famous for. "I'm sorry to hear that, Bead-Maker. Your skill has always been unmatched."

"No longer, I'm afraid." The older man turned to follow the path to the shaman's platform.

An-nat approached and also greeted Tonrai and his father, clasping shoulders in the traditional way.

Fire-Keeper stepped out of the Council House and frowned at those gathered below. "Come in. We're wasting time."

Tonrai waited for An-nat to mount the platform before he assisted his father to the top. When they were ready to go inside, Amureo, striding from behind the house, elbowed them out of the way and went in before them.

Of course, he has his own path to Fire-Keeper.

Chief Elder trotted across the plaza and up to the Council House. "Sorry I'm late, Friends."

Tonrai swept his arm toward the entry, indicating that Thandoi should go first. Then he took a firm hold on his father's upper body as the older man used his walking stick to bear some of his weight when he stepped down into the house.

Once inside, Vachai said, "Thank you, my friend," to Chief Elder who clasped his forearm and helped him negotiate the step.

A small fire brightened the otherwise dim room providing enough light for Tonrai to catch Fire-Keeper scowling at Chief Elder and then frowning when Tonrai followed his father inside. The shaman's staff, its feathers limp, leaned on the wall next to the entry. Hanging from a nub on one of the support posts were the two masks Fire-Keeper wore from time to time in ceremonies. Leather bags with unknown contents hung from another post, and, on the ledge in the back of the room, small jars stained with red, black, and white paints rested next to a stone palette. Several yucca brushes lay scattered on the ledge. Baskets of pinecones, dried flowers, and roots, unidentifiable in the dim light, sat on the floor in one corner.

Everyone but Vachai sat in a semi-circle around the hearth. Leaning on his walking stick, he said, "Forgive me for standing, but I find getting up and getting down quite painful."

"Of course." Fire-Keeper sneered. "You're not the man you once were."

It was all Tonrai could do not to react, but he would do his father no favors by alienating the shaman further. Besides, he was not officially on the council yet, and he needed An-nat's and Dar's goodwill.

Chief Elder began, "I have two matters to put before the council today. Our harvests have been scant in the past two turnings of the seasons, and it could get worse if we don't get the rain we need. Our seed supply is at risk. We cannot afford to allow the village to consume the entire harvest, even our small ones."

Fire-Keeper frowned and narrowed his eyes at Thandoi, but said nothing.

Chief Elder continued, "We need a steady hand to distribute the harvest equitably, to protect the seed supply for the next planting, and to guard the sacred seeds. For that reason, I propose we build a structure, a granary, and put Vachai in charge. His knowledge of planting and harvesting is unmatched in the village." He looked directly at the shaman as if daring him to suggest otherwise.

When Fire-Keeper shifted his gaze to him, Tonrai recognized barely checked rage in his pale eyes, along with a dark spirit writhing there. "Why is Artist here? He is not a member of the council."

Tonrai drew a cloak around his own spirit, met the shaman's gaze, and refused to be threatened. Fire-Keeper broke eye contact.

"That's the second matter we need to discuss. I invited him." Thandoi turned the conversation back to the issues at hand. "When I spoke to Vachai about building a granary and putting him in charge, he wisely pointed out that his role would be to serve the council by reporting to us and taking direction from us. He believed it was inappropriate, then, for him to be a voting member. He volunteered to resign, and I asked his son to consider replacing him."

Fire-Keeper scowled. "You made such a proposal without speaking to the council first?"

Thandoi remained calm in the face of the shaman's anger. "I did. But it is a proposal the council can accept or reject. We need to argue for or against both suggestions and make a decision."

Before Thandoi could invite those who had been silent through the growing conflict to speak, Fire-Keeper announced, "I suggest we put Amureo in charge of the granary."

Surprise registered on every face, but none more than on Amureo's.

The shaman continued. "Vachai is hardly capable of working on behalf of the village. Look at him. He cannot sit among us. He must stand and lean on his stick. The village will have no confidence in a cripple."

Tonrai nearly came to his feet, but his father's hard expression held him back. Vachai pressed his lips into a thin line as if suppressing the words he might like to say.

"Amureo is sturdy and wise. He will be a strong Granary Master under my guidance." The shaman glanced from man to man, intruding on their spirits by drawing their eyes to his.

Of those around the hearth, only Dar appeared drawn to the shaman's words. Tonrai remembered his father's comment that the old man was too easily swayed. It angered and saddened him that Fire-Keeper was taking advantage of a man he had so much affection for.

To Amureo, Thandoi said, "What say you, Amureo?"

"I—I would be honored to serve the village as—" He swallowed and looked at the shaman. "—Granary Master."

To Vachai, Thandoi posed the same question.

"I, too, deem it an honor to serve the village in such a role. Farming is critical to our survival, and the last few seasons have been too dry. We have to get more from the harvests, and I have some thoughts about modifying some of our practices, perhaps planting a very small tract to test some of my ideas."

When the shaman opened his mouth to speak, Thandoi raised his hand, palm out, silencing him. "An-nat, what say you?"

"I believe Vachai is best qualified to make such decisions for the village." He kept his eyes focused on the hearth.

"And you, Dar, what say you?"

The old man hesitated. With the shaman's eyes boring into his, he appeared to struggle with speaking. Everyone waited for his answer.

Vachai's walking stick clattered on the hard floor, breaking the strained silence and startling the seated men. Tonrai leaped to his feet and retrieved his father's walking stick, turned his back to the group, and grinned as he handed it to the older man.

"I beg your forgiveness, my friends." Vachai pushed the stick against the floor, lifting his shoulders and standing as straight as his back would allow.

Dar stared at the small fire in the hearth and spoke softly. "Vachai."

Fire-Keeper's shrill voice rose with him as he stood. "No. *I* will guide the keeper of the granary. *I* know when it's time to plant and harvest." Pointing at Vachai, he said, "He is a cripple and is useless."

"His physical form may be damaged, but his spirit remains strong. He has much to offer." Thandoi's voice reflected the anger he no doubt felt at the shaman's insult of his old friend.

"I will not allow him to defile the sacred seed supply. You will not overrule me. Amureo will be the Granary Master!"

Now, Thandoi stood, his bulk overpowering the shaman's slight form. "I would remind you, Fire-Keeper, each man in the council is entitled to an equal voice. You may think you can overrule us, but you are wrong. Your role is to provide the village with spiritual leadership and to keep the sacred coals burning, the coals passed to us from before remembering."

He met the shaman's eyes. "Vachai is my choice, An-nat's choice, and Dar's choice. We agree that Vachai has the knowledge to manage the granary. Only you and Amureo dissent, but you are overruled."

He turned to An-nat. "As Knowledge-Keeper, will you remind us of the traditional role of the council?"

An-nat stood. "Among our people, since before remembering, when Mother Earth and Father Sky created us, they commanded us to live together in cooperation, mutual respect, and harmony. The council is meant to protect the welfare of the people, and we speak on their behalf with equal voices. No decision shall favor one over the other." An-nat hesitated. "If I may be so bold, Chief Elder, I would like to point out that in recent years—since we moved inside these walls—our mutual respect for one another has diminished, with some villagers elevated above others. The effects of this change in our society are yet to be reckoned, but, in the meantime, the function of the council remains constant."

Fire-Keeper's pale eyes darkened, but he pulled his mouth into a poor imitation of a smile, curling his lip. "Of course, Chief Elder. I forget myself. Please forgive me."

Tonrai suspected his acquiescence would be short-lived.

"The matter is settled. Vachai is Onaati-Kaä's Granary Master." Chief Elder glanced back at the shaman. "And thank you for suggesting a title."

Fire-Keeper narrowed his eyes and glared.

Chief Elder went on. "We have now the matter of Tonrai's membership on the council." He glanced from one council member to the other. An-nat and Dar both nodded their approval, while Amureo and Fire-Keeper made no move. Thandoi glanced at Tonrai, saying, "Welcome to the council." To Vachai, he said. "Be prepared to report your plans for the granary at our next meeting." To the entire group, he said, "Good night, Friends," and he left the Council House.

An-nat and Dar, with Tonrai helping his father out the narrow entry, left Fire-Keeper and Amureo inside. Tonrai and his father said quiet good nights to the others and headed across the plaza to their house group. From inside the council house, they heard the shaman's shrill voice shouting at Amureo.

"He will not easily forget his defeat tonight," Vachai said as he limped along beside his son.

While Cheshonii and Anu built the granary behind Tonrai's house, Fire-Keeper made a point of observing them on several occasions. Vachai's recommendations called for the granary to follow the basic structure of a pit house, much like the houses they lived in, but smaller with the sides and roof covered with bean tree branches, sticks, slimwood, and dried grasses at a thickness nearly twice that used in the people's dwellings.

During construction, Fire-Keeper came daily to scowl in displeasure at what they were doing. "This is nothing more than a brush hut," he growled at Vachai. "How do you expect to keep the harvest and the seeds dry if it rains?"

"I'd be glad to plaster the entire structure, Fire-Keeper, but it would take a lot of water to prepare the mud. That's why we made the brush walls so thick. We'll plaster the roof now and the sides later when we can afford to use the water."

"Hmmmph. And how do you propose to house a full harvest in such a small structure? There's hardly room to lay out the corn to dry."

"We will build free-standing shelves woven from yucca fibers, one above the other We'll put the corn, squash, and gourds on the lower shelves and the corn stalks on the topmost shelves. We'll store the beans, squash, and gourd seeds in open jars and baskets on the floor."

"And how will you protect the sacred seeds?"

"Come with me." Vachai led him to the entry and invited him to look inside. The shaman stepped down into the dim interior. Vachai continued, "They will be kept in a seed jar and buried in the hole you can see near the east wall. We will cover the hole and place a large jar on top. They will be safe from rodents and other creatures that might intrude."

Fire-Keeper stepped outside and faced the farmer. "Why have you included a hearth? No one will live in this structure."

Vachai smiled. "Are you testing me, Fire-Keeper? Surely, you know that keeping a low fire burning will advance the drying process."

"Of course." The shaman spun on his heels and walked away.

Both Anu and Cheshonii stopped what they were doing and grinned at Vachai.

At the next council meeting, Vachai reported that the granary was finished and that the beans, corn, and squash they had planted in the spring would soon be ready for harvest. Even though they had lost some to the lack of rain, he was confident they would harvest enough to see them into the winter if they were careful with distribution.

"But will it be enough to keep our people from starving?" Fire-Keeper's voice carried his dislike for the farmer.

"It's hard to tell until we actually begin the harvest. In the meantime, I suggest we ask the women to continue collecting cholla buds, wild beans, and other foods from the desert and ask each family to contribute a portion of their collection for the good of the village. We can use one shelf in the granary to store their gifts for everyone to share when we need them."

While Fire-Keeper glared, the council approved.

Chapter 16

Short Planting Moon 1158 (August)

Ha-wani joined her mother-in-law under the ramada to prepare breakfast for the family. She glanced up at Fire-Keeper. He was in the plaza brushing away the shadow markings of yesterday's sun journey across the sky.

His back was turned, his bony legs bowed, and what little flesh hung from his upper arms flapped when he stretched them out. She couldn't hear the words he sang to the rising sun, but it was likely a song of gratitude.

"Vachai says the shaman's public display is for show. In spite of what he would have us believe, it is not his magic that keeps the sun in the sky."

"My husband knows as much about the sun and the moon as Fire-Keeper, and perhaps more, but it is not our place to raise doubts about the shaman's work." Li-naä stirred the fire under the pot. "Our place is to make sure our children understand how to observe the world around them and not be held captive by a shaman who manipulates and terrorizes the people."

"You are a wise woman, Li-naä." Ha-wani took both of her mother-in-law's hands in her own and, looking into her dark eyes, shared the gift of her spirit.

"Do I have to make the corncakes again?" Ra-naä stepped out of the dwelling, blinking against the morning sun.

Li-naä turned and handed her a basket of corn meal. "Yes. Thank you, Daughter." She glanced at Ha-wani and raised an eyebrow.

"At least you don't need to grind the corn this morning, Sister. The meal is ready, and I will help you." Ha-wani placed the flat rock above the fire.

"Where's Kokii? Why doesn't she prepare the corncakes?"

"She's still grieving for Nothai, and we must give her time to recover. She will rejoin us, and we'll be glad to have her corncakes again."

Ra-naä put her hands on her hips, frowned at Ha-wani, and demanded, "Are you saying mine aren't as good as hers?"

Ha-wani smiled at her sister's round belly protruding under her breasts and changed the subject. "Your baby is growing, Sister. Is the child active?"

"Active? This child is killing me. I couldn't sleep at all last night. I'll be glad when the thing is born, and I don't have to worry about it anymore."

Ha-wani gasped, instinctively cradling her own belly with her hands. "'Thing?' Ra-naä, don't speak of your child that way! When the baby is born, your responsibilities will be even greater."

Ra-naä pointed to Ha-wani's belly, still a bit smaller than her own. "Wait until your baby keeps you up at night. You'll know what I'm talking about."

"My baby is already active, but I love knowing he is growing inside me. I love it when he moves." She caressed the small swell of her belly. "It's as if he's talking to me, telling me he's there."

"Like I said, just wait. You won't like it either."

Alone in the dim light of their dwelling, Ha-wani held the necklace in her hands. Tonrai had made it with her sister's clay beads. Ra-naä had gone beyond the simple, round beads she had begun, and Ha-wani was impressed. She had crafted them into replicas of the pots the women under the ramada made that day, as well as other pots that had been a part of their lives. Later, she scored lines duplicating the decorations the women had painted on the pots. Her sister's work was original and beautiful. Ra-naä should be proud.

Now, holding the necklace, Ha-wani listened for her sister's song, wondering why it did not come easily from the clay. She closed her eyes and wrapped her fingers around the necklace, seeking her sister in the beads. When the song came, it was distant and sad.

I am alone
Mother Earth
I reach for you
To find myself
To find my place
To find my way
I reach for you

Mother Earth
I am alone.

Ha-wani's eyes flew open. Her sister had always
been so confident and sure of herself. *Could she really
be unhappy? Does she really think she's alone?* Somehow it didn't fit with the girl she had grown up with.
Could it be her pregnancy? Was she unhappy because
of the child? Or did Ha-wani not know her sister at
all?

She vowed to talk to her soon. To show her how
much she was loved.

Wearing the necklace of clay beads, Ra-naä asked,
"Are we ready?" She and Ha-wani were taking the
younger children to harvest the family's cotton,*
which grew in Great-Grandfather's Canyon* west
of the village. Unlike the sister crops* beside Elder
Brother Wash, which were shared by everyone in the
village, cotton was grown and tended by the families
who had a weaver among them.

The whole family participated in the planting; the
men tended it while it grew, and the women managed
the harvest. Li-naä was the weaver in Vachai's family
and was more than happy to turn the harvest responsibility over to her daughters-in-law. It had become
increasingly difficult for her to walk that far. The last
time she went to the cotton field, she could hardly
breathe when she got there and had to sit and watch
her children work.

"Do I have to go?" Benai frowned at his mother.

"Until you are ready to work equally with the men
in the fields, you will help with our work."

Pouting, he said, "But I do work in the fields. Besides, Chanu's teaching me to make arrow and spear points and knives. I don't want to be a farmer."

Li-naä laid her hands on the boy's shoulders, waiting for him to meet her gaze. "You chase the birds, rabbits, and rodents from the fields. You are getting skilled with your rabbit stick, and we appreciate the meat you provide us, but you are not doing men's work. You are smart, but it remains to be seen if you have the talent to do the work your uncle does. In the meantime, you will help with our family's cotton. And take an extra basket to collect barrel and prickly pear fruit on the way back."

"Yes, Mama." He picked up his baskets and said to Ha-wani, "I'm ready."

Again, the day was hot and still no promise of rain. The sky was a brilliant blue, and thin, impotent clouds hovered over the mountains. Beside the path, morning glories climbed over dry desert scrub offering a smattering of blues and purples where the green had faded. Butterflies floated around them, searching for what little nectar they might provide.

Kokii's boys, Chuwii and Tarukii, ran ahead of the others, playing tag and swatting each other with their baskets. Wokkai walked with her sisters-in-law, and Benai trailed behind.

Wokkai turned and walked backwards for a few steps in front of Ra-naä. "I love your necklace, Sister. When you make more beads, will you give them to my brother to make one for me?"

"If I did that, I wouldn't be the only one with a necklace such as this."

Ha-wani frowned, about to tell her sister how nice it would be to make a necklace for Wokkai, but before she could say it, she gagged and vomited beside the trail. Ra-naä laughed. "I told you being with child was no fun."

Ha-wani straightened up and dragged her forearm across her mouth. "I will admit this is unpleasant, but it reminds me I carry Tonrai's child and I am happy. Besides, it doesn't happen much anymore." She laid a hand on her belly. "He will have a son."

"What makes you think so?"

"His spirit came to me, laughing and reaching for my hand."

"I've had no such visitation from my child's spirit. I think you are making it up." Ra-naä, with chin held high, strode out ahead of her.

Ha-wani called after her. "And you will give Chanu a girl. You pretend not to care, but when you meet your child, you will understand."

Wokkai listened to the sisters' exchange, and now she spoke. "You got your baby from your nighttime joinings with Tonrai, didn't you?"

Surprised, Ha-wani stopped walking. "Why do you say that?

"You said your child will be Tonrai's son. If so, my brother did something to help make the baby. Your joinings are the only thing I can think of."

They resumed walking, and Ha-wani said, "You're clever, Little Sister. When you take a husband, you will make babies with him."

"I don't want a husband."

"Why? Soon you will be a woman, and your father will arrange your marriage."

"I don't want him to find me a husband." Her lower lip quivered, and tears spilled down her cheek. "I don't want to become a woman if he's going to find me a husband I don't want."

Ha-wani turned to Benai, still straggling behind them. "Run ahead, Little Brother, and catch up to the others. Tell Ra-naä we'll be along soon."

He trotted past, and, when he was out of earshot, she took Wokkai's hand. "Is this about Wood-Cutter?"

"I want him to be my husband, and I want to give him babies."

"You've talked to him about this?"

"Yes."

"Does he understand he cannot marry?"

"You said he could join with a woman. Why should he have to go hunting and make a trip to the sea to take a wife?"

Ha-wani sighed. "We cannot change what is. You need to talk to your mother." Still holding the girl's hand, she started walking again. "Let's catch up to the others."

Several mornings later, Wokkai awoke complaining of a stomachache, and a trail of blood ran down the inside of her leg. Her mother smiled happily. "Today, you are no longer a child. You are a woman."

"I don't want to!" The girl backed away from her mother and turned to Ha-wani. "Do I have to? Can we make it stop?"

Ha-wani looked past her to her mother-in-law, who stood gaping at her daughter.

Li-naä put her hands on her daughter's shoulders and gently turned her around. "What is it, Daughter?"

"I don't want to be a woman."

"We can't have this conversation now. I need to take you to the women's hut. If Fire-Keeper thinks I let you stay here to contaminate our dwelling, he will be angry—as will the men of the village. We would have to burn it."

"Do I have to go?"

"Yes. You have no choice. Come."

Ha-wani walked with them as far as the compound entrance. Ra-naä joined her as Li-naä and her daughter followed the path to the women's hut, Wokkai clinging to her mother and crying.

"I thought she was in a hurry to become a woman, although I don't know why. She'll end up like this once Vachai finds her a husband." She put her hands under her enlarged belly as if to pick it up.

Ha-wani hoped to steer the conversation in a different direction. "You did a wonderful job with those beads, Sister. Tonrai was impressed with your delicate designs. Next time we work with clay, you might make more beads. Such necklaces will make excellent trade goods."

"I might." She fingered the beads. "They are nice, aren't they?"

"They are. I think you've found your hidden talent."

"Hmmmph." Ra-naä looked toward Great-Grandfather to a distance Ha-wani didn't think had anything to do with the mountain.

"Sister, are you unhappy with Chanu?"

Ra-naä jerked her head around to look at Ha-wani. "Of course not. Why would you ask that?"

"I don't know. You seem so distant sometimes. And you're not really looking forward to the birth of Chanu's child, are you?"

"Being happy with my husband and being happy about having this baby are two different things."

"I don't understand. Getting married and having children is what Mother Earth and Father Sky put women here to do. Even though giving Tonrai children is my duty, it makes me happy."

Ra-naä stared at her sister. "You're serious. You think there is nothing else in this world for a woman but to birth babies for a man?"

"What else would there be?"

"I don't know, but I look out there across the basin at the mountains beyond Honey Bee, and I wonder what is there for me." She shaded her eyes from the sun with her hand, looking into the distance. With a hint of desperation in her voice, she whispered. "There must be something there for me."

"Someone other than Chanu?"

Ra-naä didn't answer right away, still looking out across the desert basin. "I don't think so. Chanu is pleasing to look at, and he knows how to pleasure me when we join."

Ha-wani flushed.

Her sister went on. "And he doesn't beat me. That counts for a lot."

Ha-wani put her hand on Ra-naä's arm. "More than anything, Sister, I want you to be happy. I am sure your husband loves you. And I'm glad we came here together. I can't imagine going anywhere without you."

Ra-naä looked at her sister, and, at the moment when their eyes met, Ra-naä cloaked her spirit and hid it from view.

When they broke eye contact, Ra-naä stepped back, beyond her reach. "I'm going to take a walk."

Ha-wani watched her sister walk away. She knew she hadn't said the right things, hadn't said anything that would give her sister peace.

While she was considering what she might have said, the hairs on her arm lifted and a chill ran down her spine. *Fire-Keeper.*

She turned and scanned the compound behind her but didn't see him. She looked in the direction her sister had gone. Nothing.

Shivering, she searched in the direction of the women's hut. He stood on the path, one hand raised, eyes closed, chanting. She couldn't hear what he was saying, but the words came to her: *Ha-wani. You are mine. Ha-wani. Mine.*

She shook her head and turned away from him.

"Let's walk. I'm not ready to go inside." The words and the voice startled her.

"What?" She spun around and found Li-naä standing before her, and she began to tremble.

"Daughter, is something wrong?"

"Fire-Keeper. Did you see him?"

"Where?" Li-naä searched the empty desert outside the walls.

Ha-wani pointed. "There on the path."

"No. There was no one on the path but me."

Taking a deep breath and rubbing her arms to warm them, Ha-wani said, "I'm sorry. I must have imagined it."

"Do you want to go inside?"

"No. You wanted to walk."

Together, they walked in silence toward the agave terraces. Desert grasses, now turning brown, lined the path, and orange butterflies fluttered through the snakeweed, their black-tipped wings dancing in the morning light. Above them, a hawk circled, calling *keee-eeee-keee-eeee* in the cloudless blue sky. Ha-wani's gaze slipped from the hawk to the grand and rugged sweep of Great-Grandfather Mountain. She followed the ridge to its descent into the desert basin to the west, the direction of her childhood village and wondering what, indeed, lay in those faraway mountains.

She remained silent, waiting for her mother-in-law to choose her words. She remembered her first visit to the women's hut when her own mother had told her what had happened to her and what to expect when she married. She suspected her mother-in-law had said as much to Wokkai.

Li-naä interrupted her thoughts. "My daughter said she wants Kutareo for her husband, but that can never be. I should have forbidden her to spend time with him. Now, I shouldn't put it off any longer. I must tell her father."

"Your daughter is warmhearted, and her spirit is generous. Wood-Cutter has changed since she befriended him. He no longer seems isolated and lonely. He smiled at No-wani yesterday when she thanked him for bringing firewood."

"She confides in you, and I appreciate your being there to listen, but I would prefer it if she came to me." The older woman's voice carried an edge of resentment.

"I'm pleased she trusts me, but when she talks of Wood-Cutter, I remind her that she should speak to you about such matters. You have been mother to me since Tonrai brought me here. I would do nothing to cause you pain."

"I'm sorry. I fear for my daughter. I can only see disappointment in her future if she insists on following her own path."

Chapter 17

Dry Grass Moon 1158 (September)

It's going to rain." Ha-wani inhaled the breeze sweeping across the desert from Great-Grandfather Mountain carrying the fragrance of rain.* Above the terraces and along the low hills under the mountain, creosote bushes released powerful aromatic oils triggered by the rain falling in the foothills.

"I can't remember when I last smelled rain." Li-naä lifted her face to the sky and breathed deeply.

In mere moments, strong winds followed the fragrant breezes, pelting the women with sand, ripping brush from the ramada coverings, flinging branches across the plaza, and slamming them into dwellings before lifting them into the sky. Dark clouds hurled sky fire into the mountains, and rain soon followed. The people sang for it to bless them and their fields while thunder reverberated across the ridge. Because the season for rain was nearly past, as violent as this storm might be, it could be their last chance to nourish the fields.

Ha-wani and Li-naä, with the other women, raced to get large, open-mouthed jars into the plaza, piling rocks around them against the wind, and singing for the rain to stay long enough for the pots to drink their fill.

The first drops, heavy and cold, smacked Ha-wani's back, sending a pleasant shiver down her spine. She scanned the gray sky, licking raindrops from her lips, savoring the cold relief washing over her. The mountains, always close, holding the village in their embrace, had disappeared, obscured by heavy curtains of rain. Now, from Great-Grandfather, a massive wall of rain bore down on them. When the bright glow of sky fire surrounded them at the same moment thunder vibrated in her ears, Ha-wani grabbed her mother-in-law's arm. "Inside! Quickly!"

They ducked into Li-naä's dwelling where Ra-naä, Benai, and her father-in-law waited.

"It comes?" No sooner had her father-in-law asked than the rain began to hammer the roof. "I should be out there helping my sons." Vachai sat on a bench like the one Chanu had built under the ramada. He leaned against a support post, his leg outstretched before him. Shadows from the hearth flickered across his sullen face. "They shouldn't have to do my work." Chanu and Tonrai, with Cheshonii's help, were lashing hide coverings on the platforms inside the granary in case the roof leaked.

Li-naä reached for her husband's hand as Chanu and Tonrai, dripping wet, ducked in through the entry.

"We wanted rain, and we've got it." Water dripped from Tonrai's hair and breechclout, settling in a puddle at his feet. "Cheshonii said to tell you the diversion dams down below and the check dams and channeling borders on the terraces are strong."

His father replied, "I hope the sister crops can withstand a flood. Cheshonii reports the corn and beans are well established, so they should be fine. If the rain beats the squash leaves into the ground and then a flood comes, they might not survive."

Tonrai moved the rolled-up sleeping mats from the ledge where rain dripped through the holes in the wall. "We must fix these breaks. The ones in my dwelling are even bigger. Maybe this rain will give us enough mud to close them—unless the rain just makes them worse."

Ha-wani knelt and added dry twigs to the hearth, which blazed up and filled the small house with warmth. Ra-naä waved a mat above the fire, fanning smoke out the entryway. "I can't stand this smoke. I think I'd rather not have a fire." Chanu moved closer to his wife and put one arm around her. He took the mat and fanned the smoke.

"Where's Wokkai?" Li-naä's expression reminded Ha-wani that the girl's relationship with Kutareo had become a matter of concern for her mother-in-law.

"She may be with Kokii and the boys. I'll go check."

Li-naä, also fanning the smoke from her face, smiled at her daughter-in-law. "Are you sure you want to go out in this?"

"I want to put your mind at ease. I'll be fine." Ha-wani stood and glanced at her husband. He, too, worried about his little sister, and she had promised him she would look after her.

Outside, she stood in the downpour and peered through the torrent. Somehow, she doubted Wokkai was there, but she stepped into the entry of the other dwelling. Only Kokii, Cheshonii, and the two younger boys were there, huddled around the hearth.

"Have you seen Wokkai?"

Cheshonii said, "She left the compound earlier—before the rain started. Do you think anything's wrong?"

"No. Her mother's worried about her being out in the storm, but she's a smart girl. She can take care of herself."

Ha-wani circled the plaza in spite of the downpour, calling out against the wind and the rain. Her hair clung to her shoulders, and her cotton skirt, which she had tied beneath her breasts, clung to her enlarging belly. She shivered, but the cleansing rain was welcome.

When she stopped to pull her long hair from her shoulders and twist it at the back of her neck, a cold hand gripped her arm. Startled, she turned to find Fire-Keeper, his eyes boring into hers. His double-knotted hair leaned precariously sideward under the weight of rain.

"What is it you seek, my child?" In the wind, his reedy voice triggered a shiver unrelated to the storm.

Unable to release her arm from his grip or to break eye contact, her spirit shuddered within. "My husband's little sister—"

Rain, pouring down his forehead, dripped onto the hooded lids over his pale eyes as he leaned closer, latching onto her spirit and drawing it toward his own. She no longer felt the rain, only the cold dread washing through her. She called on her spirit, searching for the protective wings.

She blinked.

Fat raindrops clung to his eyelashes, obscuring the darkness within. Wings enfolded her, and the dread was gone. She pulled her arm free and focused on a droplet reflecting the pale daylight, and, when it fell, she followed it through a wrinkle in his cavernous cheek, where it blended into the rain dripping from his jaw to his chest.

Ha-wani stood silent, watching the rain zig-zag through the sparse hairs on his chest, vowing to be better prepared for him in the future. Once again, she had almost fallen into his trap. She must not let it happen again. She needed to have her spirit ready at all times.

The corner of his mouth lifted. "You are shrewd, Ha-wani. In time, you will want to use your power, and I will help you."

Even though he had learned it during their first encounter when Raven brought her out of his spell, she cringed to hear him speak her spirit name. She tried to hide her discomfort. "I'm looking for my sister-in-law. I don't have time for you." It was dangerous to challenge him, but she allowed her voice to carry her dislike to his ears in the wind and rain.

He stepped back and scowled. "She's been seen with the wood cutter." He pointed to Amureo's house group. "She has only just become a woman, but he will never be a man. Your father-in-law has neglected his responsibilities to his family. And your husband, Ha-wani. He sent you into the storm to find his sister?"

"No one sent me. I—" She heard someone call her name and turned toward the shaman's platform mound. Wokkai stood at the entrance to his dwelling. Ha-wani glanced at the old man, this time challenging him directly, looking into his eyes with unguarded hatred. She turned away before he returned the challenge.

She ran to Wokkai and put her arms around the girl, standing limp in the diminishing rain. Something was terribly wrong. "What happened?"

"I don't know—he—I want my mother—"

Rain washed down Wokkai's face, still scabbed and raw from the new blue chin lines Healer-Woman had tattooed after her first visit to the women's hut.

Water dripped from her shoulders and across her young breasts, now full with nascent womanhood, revealing dark bruises on either side of an inflamed nipple.

With her arm around the girl, Ha-wani led her down from the mound. When they walked past Fire-Keeper, he said, "You had nothing to worry about. She was safe with me."

She put her hands on Wokkai's shoulders to turn her away from the shaman, and said, "No one is safe with you, Fire-Keeper." Her spirit rose with her anger and, again, she met his gaze. "Stay away from me and my family."

Chapter 18

Dry Grass Moon 1158 (September)

Ha-wani pulled her wrap around her shoulders shivering in the dawn wind, waiting for the first kiss of the sun. The sky above Great-Grandmother brightened, and the stars faded.

More than ever, this morning, she needed to clear her mind with the blessings of the wind and the sun. In the days since she had spoken rudely to Fire-Keeper, she struggled to understand why she had taken that chance. *Had he seen it as a threat? Of course he had; I intended to threaten him.*

She shivered again, but not from the cool air sweeping over her. She looked over her shoulder, thinking the shaman was behind her. More than once, she had experienced the same sensation, and each time, she saw no one. Somehow, even if the shaman himself were nowhere near, his specter seemed to follow her everywhere. She tried to dismiss her fear and concentrate on what to do for her sister-in-law.

Seeing Wokkai come from his dwelling, lost and confused, triggered rage she had never experienced before. While it had been her intent to resist him and to make sure he knew she would never allow him to control her spirit, she was afraid she had acted too soon. He would not suffer her disrespect for long. At what point would his intentions shift from capturing and controlling her spirit to destroying her and all she loved?

And what of Wokkai? She had been unable to sleep for several nights worrying about the girl.

What had he done to her? He had taken advantage of her; the bruises on her breasts said as much. But what else?

She shook her head, refusing to even think it.

Indeed, Ha-wani had begun to see Fire-Keeper as evil, but why had he singled her—and perhaps Wokkai—out?

Am I so different? Surely others ease into the spirit worlds as I do. Fire-Keeper tells me my spirit is strong. I have power within my grasp. But he wants to control the power he believes I have. Does he see such strength of spirit in Tonrai's little sister?

Closing her eyes, Ha-wani welcomed the wind, sharper and colder this morning than it had been for some time. It swirled around her, whispering, nudging her this way and that, as it did the trees and desert scrub surrounding her. She struggled to decipher its message. As her spirit Raven rose into the sky, Tonrai's sister appeared below.

Determined and purposeful, Wokkai glided along the desert trail deep into Great-Grandfather's canyon where the cotton grew. With no noticeable effort, she followed the twisting trail upward, danc-

ing lightly from rock to rock until she stood beneath Great-Grandfather's towers. She raised her face to the sky and sang.

A bighorn sheep, his horns curved into a full circle, leaped from rock to rock and paused, shifting his gaze to her. Sister doves circled above and landed with chattering wings on the ground around her.

From behind a boulder, a mountain lion lifted his head and peered at her; his golden eyes, rimmed in black. She turned to him as he climbed to the top of the boulder, lay down, and rested his chin on his forepaws, his eyes focused only on her.

A small stream gurgled from the base of the great pinnacle, tumbling over rocks, swirling around her feet, and rushing life-sustaining water into the canyon, its melody blending with Wokkai's song.

Within moments, a pale glow surrounded her, growing brighter until the image – and the song – faded into pure light.

The sun, now fully above Great-Grandmother's summit, filtered through her eyelids, brightening the darkness and warming her face. Ha-wani opened her eyes. *Wokkai?*

Inside their dwelling, Ha-wani found the girl kneeling beside her mother, learning how to spin thread from the cotton bundle* onto a spindle. Li-naä was going to weave her daughter's matrimonial ribbon.

"Is my father considering a husband for me?" Although the girl spoke to her mother, she directed her gaze to Ha-wani, who detected a note of dismay in her voice.

Li-naä did not look up from her work. "Not yet, Child, but he will send your brother to Honey Bee soon to discuss potential mates with Ha-wani's father. He will suggest a suitable young man."

Ha-wani wondered if she might go along and visit her parents, but she didn't ask.

Wokkai stopped rolling the spindle. "What if there are no young men? What if none of them have hunted successfully or gone to the sea?" Now there was a hopeful tone in her voice.

"Your father will have to wait." Li-naä sighed. "Is this about Kutareo again?"

Wokkai hung her head and whispered, "Yes."

"I told you before you cannot marry him. He is unlikely to ever marry, and you must obey your father's wishes."

"That's not fair!"

"You may not use that tone with me." Li-naä's voice was firm, but it did not reveal an angry spirit.

The girl leaped to her feet and ran through the entryway.

Li-naä looked helplessly at her daughter-in-law. "I haven't told her father about this. I'm a coward. He will not like it. And if Fire-Keeper even thinks we would permit such a thing, I hate to think what he'd do to the boy."

"Do you want me to talk to her?"

Li-naä sighed. "Yes."

Wokkai sat on the ground behind the dwelling, her knees drawn up, her hands covering her face, and sobbing. Ha-wani sat and wrapped an arm around her, saying nothing. Across the wall, sparrows and finches fluttered among the bushes and trees, singing and whistling. A pair of quail, topknots bouncing, popped up on the wall, followed by their half-grown youngsters, and surveyed the village inside. With wings fluttering, they jumped down, one at a time, in perfect succession, and inspected the granary, pecking around its base and searching for a way in.

When the girl's crying finally stopped, she drew a ragged breath and said, "Why do we have such a stupid rule? Why can't women decide for themselves who they want to marry?"

"We have followed these same practices since before remembering. Nothing changes."

"That's not true. We have changed some rules."

"What do you mean?"

"We used to send a party to the sea every year. I was still little, but I remember crying because my father was going and I didn't want him to leave, but he said he didn't have a choice. He had been named the leader, and it was an honor. We have sent our men to Great Water since before remembering, and the gifts they brought from the sea helped our village. But that changed. We stopped sending them a couple of years ago. Who decided that?"

"I suppose Fire-Keeper and the council made the decision. Your brother told me there had been several lean years with little rain and they needed to focus on feeding the village."

"Tonrai's on the council now. Maybe he could ask them to change the rules about marriage."

"I'm not sure they will listen to the idea."

Wokkai pulled herself from Ha-wani's embrace. "I thought you were on my side."

"I am, but I want what is best for you, although it may not be what you think you want."

Wokkai stood, lifting her chin and turning toward the compound entrance. "Great-Grandfather will tell me what to do."

Ha-wani followed. "May I join you?"

The girl turned, glaring at her. "What for? So you can tell me again I can't have what I want?"

"Could we wait to talk about this? I'd like to talk to you about something else."

"What?"

"You said Great-Grandfather would tell you what to do."

"Of course."

Ha-wani took her hand, and they walked along the path beside the agave terraces toward the rugged mountain. "Do you talk to him often?"

"Doesn't everyone?"

"I'm not sure. I visit the Sea Ania, the Flower World, and I talk to the dawn wind which comes from the Flower World. But I am not often drawn to the Huya Ania,* Great-Grandfather's Wilderness World."

"I am welcome there. It lies beneath Great-Grandfather's towers. When I sing to him, he listens, and, afterward, I know what I should do. He told me to befriend Wood-Cutter. But he didn't tell me what would happen after I did." She turned her gaze to Great-Grandfather's massive towers. "I need to ask him what to do now."

"I'm glad you have found your way with Great-Grandfather's help. But there's something else. You might think it has nothing to do with what we've been talking about, but it does."

"What is it?"

"Can you tell me what happened when you were with Fire-Keeper during the storm?"

"I remember what happened before I came back into the compound, but I don't remember anything else until you took me to my mother."

"May I help you remember?"

"You won't be angry about what happened before?"

"I promise I won't be angry." It was useless to try changing the girl's mind about Kutareo. It was more important to find out how to protect her from Fire-Keeper.

Ha-wani led the girl to the rock where she and Tonrai often sat to talk. She took Wokkai's hands and probed the dark pools of her eyes.

Join me
Trust me as I trust you
Let our spirits come together
Trust me
Join me

Wokkai stood with Kutareo in a grove of trees with straight trunks splitting into two or three thick branches above their heads. Dark clouds had gathered above them, but they paid no heed when the wind rose, and the trees sang of coming rain.

"My brother will use these trees to replace support posts in ramadas and dwellings." He cut a ring of bark off the tree a short distance from the ground. "The tree will die," he told her, "but not right away. I have to come back another time to cut it down." He had girdled two trees and was about to do a third when the storm hit.

He slid his knife into the sheath hanging from his neck and grabbed his ax. Wokkai caught his other hand, and they ran, ducking through branches until they were clear of the grove. Thunder roared in her ears, and sky fire hit a tree so close the concussion almost knocked them down. They stumbled through a gully that had been dry when they crossed it before, but was now running knee-deep in water. Wokkai lost a sandal, but they didn't go back for it.

Finally, the compound wall loomed dark before them. Exhilarated by the excitement of running through the storm, Wokkai pulled Kutareo to a stop. Rain washed down her upturned face, and she stood on her toes and kissed him. He stepped back so quickly, he nearly fell, but she gripped his hand and pulled him back to her. "It's all right, Kutareo."

"Are you sure? No one's ever kissed me before."

"I'm sure. And you can kiss me — if you want."

After a moment of indecision, he stepped close, lowered his head, and pressed his lips against hers. She wrapped her arms around his neck and leaned her wet body into his. At that moment, nothing else mattered; nothing else existed. Not even the rain.

When they stepped apart, Wokkai laughed and said, "I love you, Kutareo."

Before he could say anything, the glow of sky fire surrounded them, and thunder vibrated in the air.

"We need to get inside, but we can't be seen coming in together." At the entry between Amureo's house group and Fire-Keeper's platform mound, Wokkai peeked around the wall, but the rain was so heavy, she couldn't be sure no one was about. "You go first." She let go of his hand.

But Kutareo grabbed her hand again and blurted, "I love you, too," before dashing through the entrance and disappearing into the downpour.

Wokkai leaned against the compound wall and smiled, her face lifted to the rain. When she felt certain Kutareo had made it into his dwelling, she slipped through the entrance and worked her way along the wall. Once she cleared Fire-Keeper's mound, she would cross the plaza to her own house group. Paying attention to where she stepped, especially with a bare foot, she did not see the shaman until she bumped into him.

She stifled a scream and stepped back. "Forgive me, Fire-Keeper. I didn't see you." She tried to keep her eyes focused on the medallion hanging from his

neck, but she couldn't. Seemingly, of their own ac-
cord, her eyes gazed into his.

"But I saw you." His reedy voice carried
through the downpour to her ears, sounding like
nothing more than a whisper in the dark.

Her own image reflected in his eyes, with her
arms wrapped around Kutareo's neck, kissing him.
In spite of the cold rain, a warm flush of embarrassment swept her.

He lifted a bony finger and traced her lips with
his fingernail. As much as she wanted to get away
from him, she could not move. "You're a woman
now." He traced her new chin lines and drew a
circle around her nipple. "Your breasts are young
and firm; they will sag soon enough." He pinched
the nipple and twisted, but she felt nothing. "Your
woman's blood has flowed, and your power increases. You look just like she did at your age."

He took her hand. "Come."

In moments, she was enveloped by a warm, dry
darkness. The only sounds were the rain pounding on the roof and the shaman's heavy breathing.
A low fire burned in the hearth, and Fire-Keeper
turned her toward it. He stood at her back, pressing
his wet body against hers. Using both hands, he
fondled her breasts roughly. She concentrated on
the hearth, feeling only his body pushing against
her back.

"Bend over." When she did, something hard
slid between her legs. Fire-Keeper held her hips and
repeatedly thrust against her until, with an explo-
sion of breath and a grunt, he pushed her away. She
fell in a heap on the floor.

Silence surrounded her — even the rain had
quieted — and she raised her head. The dwelling
was empty and dark except for a dull glow from
the hearth. As she stared, the flame twisted up-

ward, transforming into the face of a thick, white worm, swaying back and forth and holding her in its gaze. From deep within its dark eyes, a black beetle emerged, its long, jointed antennae opening and closing, reaching toward her, coming closer . . .

She scrabbled away and huddled against the wall, burying her face in her arms, terrified.

Voices.

Outside.

Her mother?

No.

Ha-wani.

She stumbled to the entry. The air was damp, but the rain had stopped. Ha-wani was there. Ha-wani was talking to Fire-Keeper.

"Ha-wani . . . Ha-wani . . . "

Wokkai jerked her head up and whispered, "What did he do to me?"

Ha-wani didn't know how to answer.

"He joined with me? Does Fire-Keeper want to be my husband?" She wrapped her arms around herself and shuddered.

Choosing her words carefully, Ha-wani answered, "Some might call it a joining, but it cannot be because you did not consent. He does not want to be your husband, but he may want your spirit."

Wokkai gasped. "M–m–my spirit? Why?"

"He said, 'Your power increases.' He may believe your spirit has power that others do not. He has told me the same, and he threatens me. Perhaps he sees in us something he cannot find in himself."

"I don't understand."

"I'm not sure I understand it, but this I know: we must be prepared to fight his power or we will become like him."

"Fight him? How can we fight a shaman?"

"Not with knives or sticks, but with the strength of our spirits. With our knowledge of the Sea Ania and the Huya Ania."

"You mean Great-Grandfather will help me?"

"I think he will help you—help us—in this struggle with Fire-Keeper, but I would caution you not to use his help for selfish purposes."

"You mean, I shouldn't ask him to help me marry Kutareo." Wokkai lifted her eyes to Great-Grandfather's towers. "What should I ask him?"

"I'm not sure, but I think you will know when the time comes." She smoothed the girl's hair, tucking it behind her ear. "We do have one weapon we can use whenever he comes after us."

"We do? What is it?"

"His spirit name."

"You know his name?" Wokkai stared at her. "What is it?"

"I'll tell you in a moment, but, first, think about how important our spirit guardians are. Yours is Dove, and mine is Raven. Among our family and our closest friends, we share our names without fear. People who love us will not bring harm to our spirits. But when someone evil learns our spirit name, he might try to intrude on it and harm it. Because he didn't call you by name, it's likely he hasn't learned yours. That's good, so your spirit is still protected as long as you don't allow him to invade your eyes and discover it. He knows my spirit name."

Wokkai looked stricken. "Oh, no. I called you by name in front of him." Her tears began again. "I'm sorry."

Ha-wani put her arm around the girl. "No. You didn't reveal it. He already knew."

"How did he find out?"

"I'll tell you about it sometime, but, for now, let's talk about him. Once, I glimpsed something in his eyes, as you did in his hearth. I can't be sure, but my guess is the beetle whose larvae feed on the roots of the green stick tree* is his spirit guardian."

Wokkai frowned in concentration for a moment and brightened. "Yukui.* His name is Yukui."

Chapter 19

Big Cold Moon 1158 (December)

A melody rose into the night sky, calling the villagers to the plaza where a large fire blazed beneath the dome of stars. Usareo sat on the east side of the fire playing his flute, and Vaeleo, with his drum, sat west of the fire, inviting the people to winter storytelling. An-nat, who held the people's history, sat south with his calendar stick. Fire-Keeper, who would not appear until the people had gathered and were ready, would claim the north. Shadows, cast by the fire in rhythm with the flute and the drum, flickered across the faces of the people as they gathered, shaking gourd rattles and shuffling, circling around the fire. Many wore hide or woven wraps against the cold night air, and children snuggled against their mothers for warmth.

When the music stopped, Chanu helped his father to the ground and sat so the older man could lean against him. Ha-wani's heart hurt each time she witnessed her father-in-law struggle to stand or sit. This formerly graceful man had been reduced to a twisted shadow of himself.

Ra-naä, now heavy with child, knelt, sitting back on her heels and resting her belly on her thighs, glaring at her husband. "You could have helped me sit, you know." He did not answer.

Tonrai joined Ha-wani, and Wokkai sat on her other side. She had promised the girl she would squeeze her hand as a signal to lower her head and protect her eyes and her spirit from Fire-Keeper's touch.

He stepped from his dwelling and stood before them, naked except for his breech clout in spite of the cold. The brown skin of his neck, chest, and stomach sagged, and the lines carved in his cheeks were deepened by shifting light from the fire. He held his staff high, the colorful feathers floating above him.

"It is time." He swept his gaze across the gathered people, his pale eyes pausing to probe the eyes of one or more of the villagers. He descended the mound and paced before the crowd, the fire casting narrow shadows behind him.

"It is time," he said again, looking directly at Ha-wani.

Although she shivered at his invasion, Ha-wani squeezed the girl's hand, laid a hand on her enlarged belly, and held the old man's gaze. The protective wings of the raven opened. *Yukui, you will not have my spirit.*

Abruptly, the shaman's expression changed. He took a step backward and lost his grip on the staff. The crowd gasped as it clattered to the ground, the colored feathers slowly settling in the dust. The people whispered among themselves. The sudden fear on their fire-keeper's face was likely a shock to the people who were used to believing their shaman was fearless and steady.

He did not reach for his staff right away, perhaps collecting himself, perhaps considering how to use this lapse to his advantage. "Disharmony! We are beset by disharmony!" He pointed at it lying on the ground. "My staff—ripped from my hands and thrown to the ground. It is a warning. A warning we must heed."

Ha-wani believed she had hit the mark with his name, and she sensed the fear coursing through the gathered people. She placed a hand on Wokkai's knee. "Don't be afraid," she whispered.

Having regained his composure, but leaving his staff where it lay, the shaman announced, "It is winter, and the snakes are sleeping. They will not listen to our story and bring us harm. We are commanded to restore the harmony Mother Earth and Father Sky gave us. We must remember how the people came to be."

An-nat, the Knowledge-Keeper sang in preparation for telling the story of their creation.

Mother Earth and
Father Sky
You gave us life
You gave us the spirit worlds
We celebrate your gifts

After finishing the song, An-nat launched into the creation story*—a story everyone had heard from childhood, a story that usually gave them comfort. No matter what else might change in their lives, the story of their beginnings would never change.

Long ago, before remembering, before there was Here, the dwelling of Father Sky and Mother Earth stood alone in a vast emptiness. Mother said, "I long for children, but we cannot bring forth children without providing a home and the means for them to take care of themselves."

Father agreed, and together they set about their tasks.

Mother pondered on their needs for sustenance and survival while Father went out to create a world where their children would live.

A great thundering and roaring arose. Outside, she found a vast ocean of endless seas. Mother nodded. "Our children will be blessed by these waters."

An-nat's voice floated softly through the air, reaching every ear. He paused and sang the song of the waters. The people joined him.

> *Waters of life*
> *Waters of life*
> *Bless us with the waters of life*

An-nat began the song of the land, and the people joined in.

> *Mountains and forests*
> *And desert below*
> *Bless us with the mountains and forests*
> *And trees and plants to sustain us*
> *And rivers to carry the waters of life.*

When Mother next went outside, Father had brought waters to the desert through the sky. For winter, he gave them gentle, reassuring winter rains* to nourish their fields.

He created snow to blanket the highest parts of the mountains, providing a steady flow of meltwa-

*ter after the winter rains subsided and the spring
temperatures began to rise.*

He gave them summer rains — great drench-
ing downpours cutting gullies through the sides of
the mountains, carrying the water from the mountains to the children, irrigating their fields, filling
the washes and rivers in the desert, and transforming the barren desert into a lush, green, life-giving
oasis.*

*In the mountains, he carved deep pools to hold
water for the dry times.*

They sang again.

*Winter rains
Summer rains
Bless us with the waters of life*

*Next, in the great seas, they provided salt to sus-
tain us and shelled creatures to bless us with their
beauty. Together they created the sheep and the
deer to live in the mountains; the rabbits, rodents,
and squirrels to live in the desert; and birds of all
sorts to live high and low. They gave us the tools to
hunt these creatures.*

*But Mother Earth and Father Sky did not want
these creatures to compete with us for survival, so
they created animals to prey upon them. The great
birds, the mountain lion, the snakes, and the bear
balance our needs with those of the creatures.*

*When balance was achieved, they brought forth
our brother, Coyote, giving him the task of making
their children and placing them on the earth. After
he created the People, Brother Coyote admonished
us to protect our home and to take care of and protect each other. He taught us to respect the creatures and the gifts of the land and the seas. That is*

why we sing songs asking permission of plants and animals to take them for our needs, and we thank them for their gifts. They are our relatives, and we honor them as we honor each other.

Brother Coyote offered us the gift of se-daku,* that aspect of our spirits that protects us from evil, but cautioned us to live as Mother Earth and Father Sky demanded or we would lose that protection. He gave us the Sea Ania, the Flower World, where our spirits originated and where they go when we pass from this world. The flowers' essence cleanses and strengthens our spirit. He gave us the Wilderness World, where, during our lives, our spirits seek guidance and renewal.

When we see Brother Coyote rambling through the desert or listen to him singing at night, he reminds us of our duty to one another and to our Mother and Father.

They sang a final song.

Creatures of the mountains
Creatures of the desert
Gifts of the seas
Brother coyote
Bless us with harmony
Bless us with your gifts.

The people murmured their approval. Ha-wani was pleased that it reminded her of the story she had learned in her village where the Little Dove Mountains guarded them.

His staff back in hand, Fire-Keeper held it high and said, "That is how we came to be here, to live on this ridge below these mountains that have protected us and sent the waters they collect. From them, we have enjoyed the gifts of Mother Earth and Father

Sky, and our lives, though troubled at times, have been good."

His shrill voice rang out. "The towers rising from Great-Grandfather Mountain gave our village its name—Onaati-Kaä—Stone Towers Village. They reach upward, pointing to the sky and reminding us of Father Sky's power and of his gifts. The Wilderness World lies below his highest towers. We do not climb to the top of Great-Grandfather; the rugged peaks and cliffs are sacred and contain a dangerous magic."

Wokkai touched Ha-wani's arm. "Is it wrong for me to travel into Great-Grandfather's Wilderness World?" Her eyes reflected her fear. "Will he punish me?"

"I think not. You said you felt welcome, and he had offered his guidance. You have nothing to fear from Great-Grandfather." Although she smiled at her sister-in-law, she feared it was not the case with the shaman.

As if he had heard, Fire-Keeper spun and stepped in her direction, glaring at her. She squeezed Wokkai's hand but focused her gaze on the old man. He blinked, glanced in another direction and pointed eastward with his staff, allowing only the bells to speak in the momentary silence. "Great-Grandmother stretches out long and smooth. From her summit, she peeks over her knees as she collects precious waters from Father Sky in her lap and directs them through the canyons to the washes and gullies where we channel them to our fields. She has always invited us to climb to her heights to bring back the gifts she has to offer."

Ha-wani thought about Vachai, sitting on the other side of Tonrai, leaning against Chanu, his bad leg stretched out before him. He had struggled to sit on the ground with the others, and he would struggle more to stand when the evening was over. He had climbed Great-Grandmother to bring back her gift of water, but evil had been his companion. She wondered why Great-Grandmother had not punished Amureo for what she was certain he had done.

Fire-Keeper continued. "Now, Mother Earth and Father Sky are angry at us. They threaten to abandon us. We have failed them, and we are being punished. Little rains have fallen. It is a matter of time before none ever falls again." The people held their collective breath.

"The Great Light of Day burns our eyes, our skin, our seeds, and our spirits. There is little here to remind us of the gifts we once shared from Father and Mother. We must travel far to get little. The Hungry Time is coming. Each year the bean trees have fewer beans. We have seeds, but they wither and die. We must have rain to soften the rock-hard earth."

During the rain ceremony, the shaman had promised the rains would come, but they had been sparse throughout the summer with only a single heavy rain flooding the fields and promising a harvest that might not see them through the winter.

Now Fire-Keeper lifted his staff and shook it at the sky. Using the thunder voice he had first used at the rain ceremony, he demanded, "Why have you abandoned us? Why do you tease us with rain and then withhold it only to tease us again? Answer me! Why does each turning of the seasons bring fewer rains?"

A collective gasp went up among the people. Fire-Keeper had challenged Father Sky! Many hunched down as if destruction would rain upon them at that moment. Even Ha-wani shuddered.

To the people, he asked, "What will happen to us if Father Sky extinguishes the Great Light of Day and allows the Night's Eye to go to sleep forever?"

Vachai whispered, "I don't believe it. He intends to frighten us." But the people were alarmed.

Others likely remembered when Fire-Keeper persuaded them to build the compound and assigned roles to the villagers.

The shaman continued. "We will experience a darkness like none we have known. Because you have forgotten the teachings of Father and Mother, you are suffering here, as are those in the neighboring villages."

Ha-wani wondered about her parents and if they, too, were hearing these dire warnings. She leaned against Tonrai's shoulder, needing the comfort of his nearness.

Now, Fire-Keeper threatened them. "If you do not heed my warnings, I am afraid for you. We no longer live in harmony with the laws required by Father Sky and Mother Earth. Remember what you just heard in our creation story. Brother Coyote offered us the gift of se-daku, that aspect of our spirits that protects us from evil, but he cautioned us to live as Mother Earth and Father Sky demanded or we will lose that protection.

"Your se-daku is in danger. It is all you have to keep you safe—to protect you from evil." As he spoke, he raised his staff and shook it. "Look to Father Sky. Let him show you what will happen if you do not do as I say!"

While the crowd focused on the bells, tinklers, and feathers dancing atop the staff, Ha-wani kept her eyes on the shaman, who threw something into the fire, and, suddenly, the fire was reduced to embers.

Women screamed and covered the eyes of their children. Men shouted, "No!"

"This is what Father Sky will do to the Great Light of Day. We will be no more. We must protect our spirits and restore harmony." Once again, he shook his staff above him, and the people kept their eyes on the feathers. "Call on him, now. Everyone, call on Father

Sky." Again the people looked up, murmuring prayers. "Father Sky, can we be delivered from eternal darkness?" Again, he threw something into the fire. It blazed up violently.

The effect was stunning. The fire had been nearly extinguished, and now it was reborn. The people believed; Ha-wani read it in their faces. Fire-Keeper could deliver them from eternal darkness. He had won them over. They called out, "Fire-Keeper, save us!" They would follow him.

"Do not despair! We have hope. Father Sky and Mother Earth have shown me the way. We have not lived up to their intent for us. They are displeased and demand that you follow me. Only I can lead you out of the darkness."

Ha-wani observed the villagers around her. Crying women drew their small children into their arms, and the men moaned.

Fire-Keeper continued, the deep voice echoing like thunder. "We have disregarded their instructions. Look at the creatures they gave us. The hawk eats the snake who eats the rodents. The mountain lion eats the bighorn. Brother Coyote eats rabbits and squirrels. Mother Earth and Father Sky never intended the animals to be equal. Their harmony comes through how they sustain one another. Neither are we all equal. Those who live outside the compound serve those who live inside. It is a beginning, but there is more to do.

"Our efforts to live in balance and harmony have been a failure. Our laws—given by our creators—commanded us to live according to their will, but we have fallen short. We must renew our commitment and restore the balance and harmony they require.

"Our laws came to us from our Creators."

Honor your se-daku, your spirit body.
Use the power of your spirit to raise you up.

Share your spirit with those who share your goals.
Live in harmony with those who lead you forward.
Live and work in the roles decreed for you.
Know that what you do for the community, you do for
    yourself.

Tonrai frowned. He leaned close to Ha-wani and said, "He has changed our laws."

"They are not the laws your father shared with my father when they discussed our marriage. Your laws and ours were similar."

Others must have asked one another the same questions, perhaps speaking as Tonrai and Ha-wani spoke.

"SILENCE!! Listen to what the creators now demand of us. BALANCE!! They demand BALANCE!!" Fire-Keeper's thunderous voice rang across the ridge and echoed back from the mountains. "Consider this: they did not bring us forward until all was in balance for our survival.

"I have been on a vision quest and learned the new laws they require! Mother Earth and Father Sky appeared to me with instructions that I now pass along to you."

Balance your needs against the needs of your village.
Take only what will sustain you from the village.
Give more to the village than you take.
Live in harmony with the birds, the animals, the
    plants, and the waters.
Listen to he who will guide you to harmony and bal-
    ance as we have instructed him.

The shaman turned and disappeared into the Ceremonial House. The people sat silent for several moments around a dying fire. When he did not appear again, they rose and walked in silence to huddle inside their dwellings.

In Vachai's house, the family gathered. Kokii hugged Chuwi and Tarukii against her, both of them trembling with fear. Cheshonii, taller now than his father had been, stood behind his mother, his hand resting on her shoulder.

After helping his father lower himself to his bench, Chanu turned to his wife, wrapping her in his strong arms. Benai sat on the floor and lifted his father's bad leg to his shoulder.

Li-naä stood behind Wokkai with her arms wrapped around her, and Ha-wani leaned heavily against her husband.

"I have never experienced a night so dark." Vachai's soft voice was barely a whisper. "But it is not because the sun does not shine; it is because our shaman has instilled a dark fear in the hearts of our people."

"What can we do?" Li-naä gently smoothed her daughter's dark hair, tucking strands behind her ears. Wokkai was still getting used to wearing her hair loose. "What happens if the people believe what he says?"

"They already believe." Cheshonii, who spent most of his time with the farmers in the field, said, "Fire-Keeper has spread his dire warnings to those who live outside the walls. They far outnumber those of us who live inside, but they really believe that if our lives are better, then theirs will improve." He shook his head. "They don't seem to notice that it never happens. They no longer thank Mother Earth for her gifts. Instead, they pray to Fire-Keeper to protect them, forgetting it was he who condemned them to live apart and make our lives better with their hard work and to live only on the scraps we allow them."

"We must be strong and not fall prey to his madness."

At Tonrai's words, Kokii drew in her breath and covered each boy's ear with one hand, and pressed their other ear against her stomach. "Don't say such a thing aloud."

"What we must do," Vachai said, "is to remember the truth of what Mother Earth and Father Sky gave to us, the laws we have lived with since before remembering." He began to recite, "Honor your se-daku, your spirit body, and that of others."

The others joined him.

> *Never use the power of your spirit body to bring*
> *harm to another.*
> *Trust your spirit body only to those who trust you*
> *with theirs.*
> *Live in harmony with one another.*
> *Know that what you do to others, you do to yourself.*
> *As long as you live as we have taught you, all will*
> *be well.*

Chapter 20

Big Cold Moon 1158 (December)

I spoke with An-nat about Benai." Vachai stood inside the entrance to the dwelling leaning on his stick. Tonrai and Chanu, who had come in before him, stood to the side. "Come. Stand with me, son." Benai moved from his place by the hearth and stood by his father, looking puzzled.

Li-naä looked up from her weaving, her question unspoken.

He laid a hand on Benai's shoulder. "I asked him to take Benai in training as a Knowledge-Keeper." The boy said nothing.

Ha-wani, glanced at Tonrai and his brother. Neither appeared surprised, and she suspected the men had more news to share. Behind her, Ra-naä stirred but did not wake. She lay on her side with her knees drawn up against her belly. She had recently complained about the difficulty of carrying the extra weight of the child. This morning, she had moaned about a backache and asked Chanu to go with her to help her stand after squatting to relieve herself. She had returned to the sleeping mat without eating any breakfast.

After Fire-Keeper's pronouncements at the last gathering, and because the weather had turned unseasonably cold, the family spent most of their days together in Vachai's house, rather than outside under the ramada.

Li-naä asked, "Did the old man agree?"

"Yes."

"Our family is honored." She blinked back tears. To her youngest son, she said, "I will no longer be your mother when you move in with Knowledge-Keeper, but I expect you to honor us and your people by learning our true stories." Li-naä's expression was one of resignation.

Vachai turned his son to face him. "You are smart, and you are quick. You have a good memory." He chuckled. "I suspect you can recite our creation story as well as An-nat." The boy nodded. "You hear something once, and you remember every detail. I am certain you will have no trouble learning to make a calendar stick. You are being given a great responsibility. Do you think you can do this?"

Benai squared his shoulders and met his father's eyes. "Yes. I will do this."

Li-naä tucked her shuttle between the warp and weft on the loom* and put the thread Ha-wani had spun into her basket. She untied the loom from her waist, detached it from the support post, and carried everything to the corner of the dwelling, hanging the loom from a support timber. She turned to her husband. "You have more to say."

Vachai looked at his older sons, who grinned at their father. Chanu said, "She knows you well."

Tonrai declared to Ha-wani, "We've never been able to keep a secret from her."

Li-naä stirred the low fire in the hearth inside a circle of rocks. She placed a pot of water on the rocks above the flame and dropped in a handful of corn meal. "Sit. We will talk."

Vachai limped to his bench. Tonrai helped him down, and Benai sat, lifting his father's leg over his shoulder. Except for Ra-naä's, all eyes turned to Vachai.

"There is whispering among some of the people about what Fire-Keeper said at the gathering. Most believe him, and a few others, like us, do not. He claimed to have had a vision in which Mother Earth and Father Sky instructed him in these new laws, but I have known him since we were children. He is not to be trusted."

Tonrai picked up the conversation. "At the council meeting, Fire-Keeper repeated his new version of our laws, reminding us they had come to him directly from Mother Earth and Father Sky. He had the support of Amureo, of course, and Dar, who is increasingly frail and easily manipulated. Chief Elder was conflicted. He was reluctant to disagree with the shaman, but he was uncertain. I think he will not risk opposing him. He saw how the people reacted to Fire-Keeper's rantings, and he has to think about the welfare of the village. He won't want to put the whole village at risk. Those who might doubt the shaman will fall in line if Chief Elder endorses him. I fear only An-nat and I oppose him."

Chanu pointed out Fire-Keeper's magic at the gathering had been impressive to watch. "I suspect he not only terrified some of the people, but he made them believers with his fire tricks."

While the men talked, Ha-wani and Li-naä sat quietly, aware such matters were best left to the men. But finally Ha-wani could not remain silent. "Husband, may I speak?"

When Vachai and Chanu nodded, Tonrai said, "Of course."

"When Fire-Keeper held his staff high, he drew everyone's attention to the sacred feathers, but, with his other hand, he threw something into the fire, making it die. He threw something else to make it flame up. Surely, others know what he did."

Vachai nodded to his sons. "Yes. I have spoken of this. He practiced the trick when we were boys. Others may have seen what he did, but they will believe everything he says, even if it brings harm to them and their families."

"It was impressive," Chanu said.

Li-naä looked at her husband. "This is why you want Benai trained to keep our knowledge."

"Yes. Soon, An-nat will be obliged to weave the shaman's new laws into our stories, and I fear some of our past will be lost to those who come after us." He glanced at Ha-wani and Ra-naä, both of whom were carrying children who would someday—if the gods were willing—become leaders of the people.

Tonrai frowned. "Will he teach Benai new versions of our stories emerging from the shaman's new laws? Will he put aside the old stories?"

"If Benai starts now, he will learn the original stories. At least that is my hope."

In the silence following Vachai's comment, Ha-wani laid her hand on her round belly, wondering if Fire-Keeper would rob her son of his people's history. Tonrai put his arm around her shoulders and drew her close.

Li-naä handed her husband a drinking gourd filled with water. "You have not said all that is on your mind."

He drew in a long breath, and, with a look of resignation, said, "When the time comes, Tonrai and Chanu will take their families and leave."

Ha-wani turned to her husband. "Leave? But where will we go? When?"

"We have not discussed the details, but it will not be soon. My brother and I want our children to grow up knowing who we are. We are a people who have always respected and cared for one another. We are not this new vision of a people who raise themselves by putting others below them." Tonrai covered her hand with his. "My son will know the people are equal in the eyes of Father Sky and Mother Earth."

"Why do you speak of leaving? What is this all about?" Ra-naä roused from her sleep and struggled to sit up with Chanu's help.

He lifted her chin and rubbed his thumb across her cheek, smoothing the imprint of the woven mat she had rested on. "Do not worry, Wife. We are not leaving now, only discussing the possibility of having to go in the future if Fire-Keeper continues to change our laws and our beliefs."

"Good, because I don't want to travel with this—this—" She pulled her knees under her and lifted her belly, resting its weight on her thighs. "It's too heavy."

Chapter 21

Animals Get Lean Moon 1159 (January)

Make it stop!" Ra-naä's scream echoed off the mountains. With nightfall, most of the villagers had retired to their dwellings, but her voice carried beyond the women's hut.

Her pains had begun in the afternoon, and, while Wokkai went to fetch No-wani, Li-naä rushed to prepare the hut for the delivery of Ra-naä's baby. Wokkai was excited to be present at the birth of a child. Her mother had explained it was important for her to understand the process before marriage. Neither of them mentioned Kutareo, but Wokkai had no difficulty gathering the wood to build a fire.

Earlier, in their dwelling, No-wani, with her eyes closed, had laid hands on the young woman's belly, nodding with each contraction and ignoring her screams. She declared birth was imminent. She and

Ha-wani escorted the mother-to-be to the women's hut to await the birth.

Throughout the afternoon and evening, No-wani remained calm, assuring the young woman that everything was perfectly normal and the child would probably come during the night because the contractions were no longer coming in quick succession. Healer-Woman went about the business of preparing for Ra-naä's child slowly and deliberately. She sent Wokkai for a jar of water which she emptied into the pot over the fire.

Ha-wani knelt beside her sister, who squeezed her hand with each contraction. "Your child is coming, Sister. Isn't it wonderful?"

"Wonderful?" Ra-naä, who was lying on the mat, her knees drawn up and spread apart, shook her head. "Just you wait. Your turn is com—" Another contraction brought another scream.

"Breathe!" No-wani told her to focus on breathing through the contractions. "Don't push yet. Breathe evenly and try to relax."

When the contraction eased, Ra-naä shrieked, "Relax? The child is trying to kill me!"

"You will not die. Your child will be here soon." Although No-wani could say it with conviction, Ha-wani knew she could not promise the child would live. Three infants born in the last several moons had passed into the spirit world not long after birth. Even so, Ha-wani was comforted by No-wani's quiet attention to Ra-naä's subsequent contractions and the young mother's screams.

Finally, she nodded to Li-naä, who took her place behind her daughter-in-law, lifted her daughter-in-law's shoulders, wrapped her arms around the young woman's middle, and prepared to squeeze when directed. "On the next pain, you can push."

Ha-wani grimaced when her sister squeezed her hand so hard that the pain radiated up her arm. She held her breath and withstood it, knowing it could not compare with her sister's pain.

Wokkai, holding the deer skin blanket Chanu had made for his child, stood behind No-wani, her eyes filled with curiosity as Ra-naä screamed again. The girl leaned forward. "What's that?"

No-wani smiled. "The baby's head." To Ra-naä, she said, "Breathe now." She paused. "Now push—hard."

Ra-naä wailed while her mother-in-law squeezed, and the child slipped into No-wani's waiting hands.

Wokkai stared as No-wani ran her finger around inside the babe's mouth and then lifted the small bundle for her to see.

"Would you like to announce the child?"

"Me?" The girl's eyes grew wide, and she leaned closer to the child whose cries filled the small house. She took a deep breath and said, "My brother's child, born this night, is a girl."

Ra-naä collapsed against her mother-in-law in exhaustion. No-wani laid the infant on her stomach and delivered the afterbirth.

Li-naä placed Ra-naä's hands on the child. "Hold her."

Ha-wani was overcome with emotion. She laid an aching hand on the babe's head. "She's beautiful."

No-wani dipped her knife into the now steaming pot and used it to cut the cord. "Turn her." Ha-wani helped turn the baby on her side while No-wani drew a thin stick from the fire and blew out the flame, using it to seal the end of the cord.

Ra-naä turned her head and closed her eyes when Ha-wani dipped a cotton cloth into the warm water and washed the infant, who continued to cry.

"Make her shut up."

No-wani frowned at the new mother and swaddled the child in the deerskin. "Once she begins to nurse, she will quiet and go to sleep." She narrowed her eyes. "The child will cry when she is hungry or in need."

Li-naä helped her daughter-in-law lie down on her side, tucking the baby into the new mother's arms and helping the child find the nipple. The magic of the moment when the baby began to suckle was not lost on the women who attended the birth. For several moments, the only sound in the little hut was the child's soft grunting, sucking, and swallowing.

As the infant's tiny fingers, her perfect fingers, pressed her mother's breast in a rhythm matching the pace of her suckling, Ha-wani was overcome with love for this child. She sang a silent song for the child she carried. Ra-naä kept her eyes closed and turned her face away.

No-wani gathered her things, and Ha-wani walked out with her. The sky brightened behind Great-Grandmother, and a half-moon hung midway across the sky. Coyotes yipped and yodeled from somewhere close. They had no doubt smelled the odors of birthing and came to investigate. The old woman chuckled. "Brother Coyote and his friends might want this." She held up the wrapped afterbirth. "Be assured I will bury it where any wayward spirits arising from it cannot cause trouble."

"Thank you, Friend."

The older woman laid a broad hand on Ha-wani's arm. "You are worried your sister isn't interested in her child."

"I don't understand. She's paid no attention to her."

"It happens sometimes with new mothers. She will come around."

After two weeks in the women's hut, Ra-naä and her child were ready to join the family inside the compound walls. Ha-wani, who had gone to the hut daily to see her sister and the child, believed Ra-naä had adjusted. She held her child, rocked it in her arms, and hummed songs as the infant nursed. Sometimes, though, Ha-wani glimpsed a faraway look in her sister's eyes. *She misses her husband. She will be fine when she presents her daughter to Chanu.*

Chanu waited at the entrance to the compound, watching his mother, his little sister, and his sister-in-law bringing his wife and child to him. Tonrai and Vachai stood behind him.

When Ra-naä stood before him, unsmiling, she held the infant out to him. "Husband, I give you your daughter." A curve-billed thrasher whistled from his perch on the compound wall, bringing a note of optimism, a note that was somehow missing from Ra-naä's voice.

Chanu tentatively put one hand under the small bundle and then the other. Ra-naä withdrew, leaving the child in his hands. Holding the bundle close to his chest, he lifted the deerskin to meet his daughter. Ha-wani held Tonrai's hand on her belly, imagining the moment when he would meet their son.

Li-naä, Vachai—leaning on his stick—Wokkai, Tonrai, and Ha-wani walked in a circle around the new parents and sang.

We celebrate the family
We celebrate the child
We pledge our protection
We pledge our guidance
We celebrate the child
We celebrate the family

Together they went to their house group, where Kokii, Cheshonii, and the boys waited to meet the new family member. They joined the circle around the parents and the child and sang.

Father Sky, guard this child
Mother Earth, nourish this child
Give her long life
Mother Earth, nourish this child
Father Sky, guard this child

Chanu handed the child back to Ra-naä, and they waited while the men of the village filed past, each one kissing her tiny hand. The birth of a child promised the longevity of the village, and they pledged kinship. After a few men greeted her, she began to cry, whimpering at first, getting louder and louder, expressing her displeasure with each man's touch until she reached a crescendo that shocked the listeners.

When Fire-Keeper stood before them and took the tiny hand, she quieted and peered at the old man's face, her eyes locked on his. Quickly, Chanu placed his hand over her eyes, using his thumb to wipe her tears. Fire-Keeper cocked an eyebrow. "She is stronger than most." He kissed her hand.

Ha-wani cradled her enlarged belly, fearing the moment he might touch her child.

Chapter 22

Deer Mating Moon 1159 (February)

Ha-wani sat cross-legged on the floor holding her sister's baby atop her enlarged belly while Li-naä adjusted Ra-naä's sling.

She wrapped the length of cotton around the young mother's waist and crossed the ends over her shoulders. "Once you have it in place, reach behind and pull one end down through the band at your waist and tie the ends together." Again, she demonstrated. "With the baby nursing in the sling, you'll have both hands free."

Ha-wani wondered how many more times her mother-in-law would need to show Ra-naä how to bind the baby to her breast. Every time the new mother tried, she gave up in frustration and complained it was too much work. She'd pass the child off to Ha-wani or Wokkai or her mother-in-law and leave the dwelling, often not coming back until someone went looking for her because the baby was hungry. Now, in the child's curious eyes, Ha-wani recognized the strength of her spirit, even though she was still exploring the world in search of a guide. *Fire-Keeper knew. You will need that strong spirit, little one.*

With the sling in place, Ra-naä slid the infant in and helped her latch on to a nipple. She glanced at Ha-wani. "Your turn is coming—and, no doubt, soon."

Ha-wani resented Ra-naä's inference that having a child was a bad thing, but she chose not to reply in kind. "I think so. He is active. Last night, I was resting my belly on Tonrai's side, and he kicked so hard, Tonrai jumped."

"You're still convinced you'll have a son?"

"I am. Like your daughter, my son is strong."

Two weeks later, Wokkai ran to Healer-Woman's house group, very nearly crossing the boundary without an invitation.

No-wani was grinding dried leaves in a small mortar, but she interrupted the work and stood. "Is she ready?"

Breathless, Wokkai said, "Yes. Mother is taking her to the women's hut now."

Days earlier, Ha-wani had begun having contractions, but No-wani said to wait, telling her to walk, and, for days, Wokkai walked at her side.

Finally, on the fifth day, while they walked a circle around the ramada where Li-naä was weaving, Ha-wani bent over in pain, and water washed down her legs puddling on the ground.

By the time Wokkai and No-wani got there, Ha-wani's contractions were severe. The small fire in the hearth had not yet taken the chill out of the air, but perspiration beaded on Ha-wani's forehead and dripped into her eyes. The contractions were coming close together and with increasing ferocity. When the old woman knelt between Ha-wani's legs, she said. "I do not see the child's head yet."

Wokkai peered over the old woman's shoulder and gasped. "What—?"

"Shush, child."

To Li-naä, she said, "Let her lie flat." Li-naä lowered Ha-wani's shoulders to the mat while the older woman massaged her belly. "The baby is turned the wrong way." To Wokkai, she said, "Pour warm water over my hands. Wash your own hands and kneel here beside me."

Wide-eyed and nervous, the girl did as she was bid. This was nothing like Ra-naä's delivery when the baby slid easily into the world headfirst. This time, a tiny foot protruded from the birth canal.

No-wani instructed Ha-wani not to push. "Breathe slowly . . . in . . . out . . . good. Keep breathing and don't push."

As the old woman slid her hand into the birth canal, Wokkai whispered, "What's happening?"

"If I can get both feet together, the child can be born feet first, but . . . " Because Li-naä was talking to her daughter-in-law, reminding her to breathe evenly, only Wokkai heard her soft voice. "The baby's tangled around the cord, and my hand is too big. Either your sister-in-law or the child—or both—could be harmed." The old woman sat back on her heels. "Your hand is small. You must do it."

"Me?" She leaned away from the old woman. "What can I do?"

"Look at this hand." She held it up. "Your hands are small. When you slide your hand in, you will find the child's other leg wrapped around the cord; you'll know the difference between the child and the cord. Push the leg up and back so the cord is out of the way. Then you must wrap your hand around the two legs and hold them together."

No-wani shifted to the side, and Wokkai knelt between Ha-wani's legs. She glanced up at her mother, who nodded.

Tentatively, she touched the small foot protruding from the birth canal. When Ha-wani screamed with another contraction, the girl snatched her hand away.

To Ha-wani, the old woman said, "Don't push. Breathe." To Wokkai, she said. "As soon as the contraction passes, do it."

When No-wani nodded, Wokkai eased her hand into the soft, wet canal, sliding it along the child's leg until she felt the cord caught on the other leg. "I found it. Will it hurt him when I untangle his leg from the cord?"

The old woman replied, "I don't think so, but you have to save the baby—and Ha-wani."

"You mean—?" Wokkai had never been so terrified.

"Do it, Child."

At the same moment, Ha-wani was gripped with another contraction, which elicited another scream and squeezed the girl's hand against the unborn child. She held her breath.

"When the contraction eases, untangle the leg. Tell me when you have hold of both legs." She nodded to Li-naä, who lifted Ha-wani's shoulders and wrapped her hands around her middle.

Wokkai blew out a relieved breath. "I have them."

"Good. On the next contraction, tug gently while your sister-in-law pushes."

When it came, Li-naä squeezed her daughter-in-law's middle; No-wani massaged her belly. Wokkai didn't need to be told to put her other hand under the child's back as the rest of him arrived in the world. She couldn't move. The child was here. In her hands. She feared for his fragile spirit, struggling to come into the world with him.

"Good." The old woman took the baby and slid her finger around the inside of the child's mouth, and the baby began to howl. She shouldered the girl out of the way.

No-wani laid the child on Ha-wani's belly, cut the cord, burned the end, and bathed him.

Wokkai sat back on her heels, disbelieving and mute, as the walls closed in around her. Darkness swept over her, and an empty silence drowned out all sounds.

Whistling wings lifted her into the air, circling the women's hut and flying toward the walled compound.

Beneath her, the people went about their business. Women gathered under the ramadas making pots or weaving. The men stood in the plaza listening to Fire Keeper. Under the family ramada, her mother was preparing to weave, and Ha-wani, with a child strapped to her breast, was spinning the cotton thread.

But something was wrong. Now, under the ramada, Ha-wani held a girl child, a child older than the one just born. Ha-wani's boy child was nowhere to be seen.

She landed lightly on the ramada covering and sang, "cooo-AH-coo-cooo."

When Ha-wani looked up at her, sadness filled her eyes.

Now watching her sister-in-law caress her new-born son, Wokkai shed tears for her and the child Ha-wani would lose.

A little more than two weeks passed before Ha-wani was able to leave the hut and present her child to Tonrai. She had bled longer than usual, and she was still weak and sore as she walked with Wok-kai and her mother-in-law from the hut to where her husband and family waited to greet the child. It was a crisp, bright, sunlit morning, and Ha-wani reveled in the promise of her son's future.

She held her son to her breast and kept her eyes fastened on her husband as she approached. In his eyes, his spirit reached out in eager anticipation. Standing before him, she held the child out. "Husband, I give you your son."

Tonrai took the child. "My son."

Ha-wani stepped forward and laid a hand on the child's head. They stood close as the family walked the circle around them, singing in celebration of the baby's birth before going inside the compound. Once there, the rest of the family joined them, singing for Mother Earth and Father Sky to bless the child with a long life.

Tonrai gave the baby back to Ha-wani and the women of the village filed past to greet the child and kiss his hand. Fire-Keeper stood back, watching until all the women had passed. He stepped forward and addressed Tonrai. "You have blessed us with a boy child. May he grow to manhood and bless our people with the gifts of his labor." He did not look at Ha-wani or the child. By tradition, only women welcomed a boy-child, and the shaman would not have to touch her son.

Each morning, she sang her gratitude to the gods for her son's birth. Other women had not been as fortunate. The Hungry Time was upon them. Sochik's baby, so healthy at the saguaro harvest, had wasted and died. The wives of two farmers and their babies had died in childbirth within days of one another.

The last time the people had enjoyed full bellies was when they harvested and roasted the agave hearts. Now, though, with no winter rains, nothing grew in the fields. They would depend on scavenging for desert animals and collecting the greens growing in late winter's sun-kissed desert. Rats, rabbits, and desert squirrels remained plentiful, and children could hone their throwing stick skills hunting them.

When lizards came out of hibernation, they would be found resting in the sunlit trails and on nearby boulders. Instead of throwing sticks, which weren't always effective against the quick little reptiles, the children would set snares for them, although Tarukii's quick hands would catch a fair share. Between the creatures and wild greens, along with the first burst of cholla buds, the people could avoid consuming the corn, beans, and squash seeds they needed for planting.

Chapter 23

Yellow Moon, 1159 (April)

Under the ramada, Chanu knapped the point for the knife Tonrai was making for his son. Holding up the knife he was carving the giant cactus root with, Tonrai said, "Chief Elder made this knife for our father, who gave it to me before my first hunt." The blade gleamed black in the dappled sunlight streaming through the ramada covering. "I've only had to chip a new edge a few times."

"He is a master. I was fortunate to learn from him."

"And you learned well, my brother. Your points equal his."

"I can only hope so." Chanu held up the chunk of obsidian he was working with. At first glance, it appeared black, like most of the obsidian he had traded for, but when the light shimmered on it, the webwork of reddish-brown within it emerged. "This is the most valuable obsidian I have. It makes the strongest and sharpest points." He paused. "I intended to make a knife for my son, but Ra-naä gave me a daughter."

"You're more than generous using it for my son's knife, but will you have enough left to make another if your next child is a boy?"

"Yes, I have enough, but—" He stared into a distance Tonrai could not see.

"But what?" Tonrai stopped carving and frowned. "Something is bothering you, Brother. What is it?"

"What if I don't have another child? What if I never have a son to make knives and points for, to take hunting, to teach him what he needs to know to be a man?"

"Surely you will have a son."

Chanu focused on the sharp edge of the point he was making. "Ra-naä doesn't want another baby— ever."

It was impossible for Tonrai not to know his brother and his wife had not joined since their daughter was born. Sharing a small hut offered no privacy except darkness. He and Ha-wani had recently resumed their joinings after she assured him she was no longer sore and her torn flesh had healed. He suspected he knew the answer, but he asked, "How do you know?"

"She told me." He spoke quietly. "She said everything about carrying a child and giving birth to it was the worst thing that ever happened to her." His eyes clouded with unshed tears. "She said feeding the thing—" He choked on the word. "That's what she called her. She said the child was sucking the life out of her." He rubbed his eyes with his thumb and forefinger and drew a ragged breath.

Tonrai said nothing, sensing his brother needed time to find his way through the pain.

"We haven't found her name yet—she needs the protection of her spirit guide. Her spirit is strong, but it wanders. Ra-naä doesn't understand she has a duty as her mother to help the child find herself—or, if she does, she simply refuses."

"What can you do?"

"My daughter needs her spirit guide." He put his tools down and stood. "I will do it." He left the ramada and went inside the dwelling. When he came out, he had his daughter in his arms. Ha-wani followed with her baby at her breast in the sling. They joined Tonrai under the ramada.

Ra-naä came out and stood by the entry.

Chanu sat cross-legged on the ground and rested his daughter in the cradle of his legs. Sunlight danced through the ramada covering, and when he opened her deer hide wrap in the cool air, she opened her eyes in surprise but focused on her father. She had grown steadily stronger in the few months she had been here. Now, she waved her tiny fists and gurgled at him. "You are a fighter. You will need that strength."

Tonrai reached for his wife's hand, and she knelt beside him, as Chanu searched his daughter's eyes for her spirit.

"Ah, there you are." He smiled. "And what are you finding?" He was silent for a time, focused only on his child. Her spirit, thin and disconnected, moved aimlessly in the Sea Ania, without her guardian. "Go, Child. Go without fear. Your guardian is waiting." He said nothing more.

Her spirit gathered itself into a wispy cloud – bare-
ly more than a puff of smoke – and drifted about the
Flower World, pausing at times above a flower, a
tree, an animal, but moving on.

When she floated over a grove of giant cactus,
she hovered above it and descended, making passes
around and between them. She circled a tall, ma-
ny-armed cactus with a small hole near the top,
spiraling tighter and tighter until, finally, she flew
into the hole and disappeared.

Chanu sucked in his breath, but he did not move.
He did not let his eyes leave the darkness beyond the
opening.

Shortly, a pair of round, curious, golden eyes
framed by soft, white feathered brows stared at him
from inside the cactus.

Quickly, the bird flew out and landed on a bean
tree, disappearing among the branches. Chanu lost
sight of her, but, as the surrounding branches re-
ceded, a clear image emerged. Her speckled breast of
grey and white downy feathers and bright eyes ma-
terialized. No larger than the sparrows frequenting
the village, the owl's deceptive, compact body con-
cealed the strength and courage of this clever bird.

She sang a high-pitched, descending, "ME-ooo-
ME-ooo." She searched Chanu's eyes and lifted
tiny ear tufts. When he repeated her call, she kept
her eyes focused on him for several moments before
flying back to the cactus and disappearing into the
hole.

"Wichikai. Her name is Wichikai."
He wrapped her again in the deer hide, cradled
her in his arms, kissed her forehead, and whispered,
"Wichikai."

His wife, who had stood by the entry to the dwelling while he sought his daughters' spirit, turned and went back inside.

During his first month, Tonrai's son thrived, sucking greedily at Ha-wani's breast. They named him Muu-mai for his spirit, the little bee. She had seen him dart through the orange blooms of honeysuckle and mallow, drawing nourishment from the nectar.

It should have been a promising sign.

But in his second month, his spirit withered. "He won't take my milk." Ha-wani's eyes filled with tears as her husband knelt beside her. The child had cried himself to exhaustion and lay limp against her swollen, dripping breast. On the other side of the hearth, Ra-naä lay sleeping with her daughter. Wichikai suckled noisily, grunting, swallowing, and grunting again. It had been days since Ha-wani had heard those same sounds from her child.

"Do you want me to go to Healer-Woman again? She might have something else we can try."

"She gave me dogweed tea, but it didn't help." Ha-wani pointed to a small bowl beside the hearth. "Chinchweed tea,* much stronger than the dogweed. Li-naä warmed it for me." She dipped a finger and put it to the child's slack mouth. The drop fell past his lips, but he made no effort to swallow. "She said she had nothing else."

"There must be something we can do." Now, his tears threatened.

She brushed a gentle hand over her son's head. "I will appeal to Fire-Keeper. Maybe his magic—?"

"Fire-Keeper? He has failed to save others. He's a fraud. Why would you think he can save our son?"

She hesitated. "He has magic. Maybe not as much as he'd like us to believe, but he has used it on me. If I have the power he says I have and if he has the magic he claims, perhaps he will save my son in exchange for that power. I must submit to him."

Tonrai stared at her. "You would let him use your spirit?"

"It is the price I must pay."

"You cannot do this. I will not permit it."

In her eyes, his spirit reached angrily for hers, and, when she shifted her gaze, he demanded, "You would give him your spirit for his evil."

"Look at your son! Look at him!" She held the child out to him.

Tonrai turned away.

"Look at him, Tonrai. Your son is dying, and you can't look at him?"

"You look at him. He is going to die." He choked back a sob. "We have to face it. His spirit is already wandering." He blinked and pressed his thumb and forefinger to his eyes. "Fire-Keeper cannot save him, and I will lose both of you."

"I have no choice. If he saves your son, I will pay his price." She stood, untied her sling, and wrapped the child before handing him to his father.

He cradled the child in his arms. "My son? He is *our* son. Don't pretend you are doing this for me." When she turned to go, he put a hand on her shoulder. "Take my spirit with you. Let me stand with you."

She nodded, but when he sought her eyes, she closed him out again.

Ha-wani stood, her head down, at Fire-Keeper's boundary and waited for his invitation to speak. A ground squirrel slipped out of the hole it had burrowed at the base of the platform mound, stood still, watched her for a moment, and scurried back into its burrow when the shaman came to stand above her. "You come to me now, Ha-wani, but only because you want something for yourself."

She wanted to answer with his name, but the risk was too great. She had used it once and got the reaction she wanted, but she would not use it now, not with her son's life hanging in the balance. "Please, Fire-Keeper, my son has not wronged you. He is innocent." She kept her eyes downcast, careful not to meet his gaze. Now was not the time to engage his spirit in battle.

He came down from the mound. "He is a child. The village loses nothing with his death. Why do you bother me with a foolish request?"

She pressed her chin against her chest, wrapped her arms around herself, and squeezed her shoulders inward. Her breath caught in her throat. She had no answer. Among the people, even in her parents' village, a child's death—especially one so young—was unremarkable. A child had no value. They did not grieve the loss of one who had not contributed to the well-being of the village.

She concentrated on his sparse chest hairs, some now gray among the black, and found her voice. "His value cannot be measured at this time, but I have seen his spirit, and I know what his future holds— for us and for our people." She held the raven back lest he see the lie in her eyes and shifted her gaze to the ground at their feet. She sensed the change in his demeanor.

"What will you give me in exchange for your son's life?" He pinched her swollen breast, and, putting his hand to his mouth, he licked her milk from his fingers.

She struggled to give voice to the hateful promise. "I offer my spirit to your service."

"Bring him to the ceremonial hut in the morning, and, when your son lives, you will be mine."

With leaden steps, Tonrai walked with Ha-wani across the plaza. While they waited at the boundary for the shaman to acknowledge them, Tonrai turned to leave. She grabbed his arm. "Please, I can't do this without you."

With his head down, he pinched the bridge of his nose, wiped his hand across his forehead, and ran his fingers through his hair. The shell tinklers murmured, their song out of tune.

When they entered the hut, the hearth fire blazed with greasewood twigs. Baskets of dried leaves and seeds littered the floor, and masks and necklaces hung from the support posts. Pungent smoke filled the dwelling.

"Put the child here." Fire-Keeper indicated a mat next to the hearth. "Unwrap him."

Ha-wani knelt and unwrapped her son.

"Stand over there." She and Tonrai stepped away from the child.

The shaman lifted charred twigs from the fire and chanted while he fanned smoke over the child, his skinny arms sweeping through the shadowy interior of the hut.

*See-see-seemese-eee**
Koo-koo-koo waa-meh
See-see-seemese-eee
Koo-koo-koo waa-meh

Smoke swirled above her child, filling the room and stinging her eyes. She breathed in and out on behalf of her son, as if she could show him what he needed to do. Her throat burned and she suppressed a cough. In the stifling heat, then, the walls closed in on her. Her heart pounded in her ears, and she struggled to breathe. She clung to her husband's hand and resisted the urge to grab her son and flee into the open air.

Now, though, the child gasped and coughed, and he kicked and waved tiny fists in the air with more energy than Ha-wani had seen lately.

Hia-a-vih-tet-ooah oo-oo-si
Hia-a-vih-tet-ooah oo-oo-si
Hia-a-vih-tet-ooah aah
Hia-aap-see wah-meh

As the shaman swept the glowing greasewood twigs one last time over the child, ashes settled on his face and belly. The baby did not react. Fire-Keeper waved a spiny cactus joint over him and chanted again, drawing the bad spirits from the child's body and into the cactus.

Hia-aap-see kah-tuu-aah
Yeu see-meh
Hia-app-see kah-tuu-eee
See-see-seemese-eee

The shaman turned to her and held up the cactus joint. "I will take this far out in the desert and bury it. The poisonous spirits attacking him will not find their way back. The child will live. Take him home, and rub the ashes into his skin. I will come to your dwelling when the Great Light of Day first shines on the mountains in the west."

The shaman left the hut, and, when she bound the child to her breast and turned his face to her nipple, he did not suckle. She glanced up at Tonrai, his mouth closed in a thin, grim line. "Don't say it, please. I need to believe him."

For several days the family had kept busy and stayed away from Ha-wani and the baby. Perhaps they did not want to hear her heart break when the child took his last breath. Death was all too common among the youngest and the oldest, so they did not speak of it, nor did they hold on to hope. So many sad ceremonies—so many children and elderly taken into the spirit world. Under the family ramada, Vachai, weaving sandals, and Chanu, absently chipping the blade for Muumai's knife, sat with Li-naä, who said she was weaving a skirt; it had passed the point of being finished, but still she kept weaving. She did not look their way when she and Tonrai returned.

As the day wore on, nothing changed. When the sun neared the western horizon, she and Tonrai waited in the dim interior of their house, the child limp in his father's arms. She laid a hand on his head—it was hot, too hot.

Without waiting to be invited inside, Fire-Keeper stepped down into the house and handed her a small jar with dry, crushed leaves inside. He instructed her to fill it with warm water. When she did, a noxious odor enveloped her. She gasped for breath, and a wave of dizziness swept over her. While Tonrai held the child, Fire-Keeper poured a small amount of the liquid into the baby's mouth. Ha-wani's heart wrenched when he screamed and shook his head, and the nasty liquid dribbled down his chin. He had swallowed none of it. As the infant settled down to an exhausted moaning, the shaman lifted the jar above his mouth preparing to pour more liquid in. *No!* Without thinking beyond the child, Ha-wani grabbed the shaman's arm, and he spilled some liquid on the floor.

He jerked back and hissed, "Do you want your child to live?"

"Yes, I—forgive me, Fire-Keeper. I didn't think."

"Never touch me again." He turned and poured the liquid into the child's mouth, filling it to overflowing. This time, the baby choked and sprayed the medicine all over the shaman. Muumai struggled to breathe, but the possibility that he had swallowed some of the liquid both frightened and encouraged Ha-wani.

Tonrai had held his anger in check until the shaman left. "I don't think the medicine—or magic or whatever it was—will have any effect. What kind of medicine would he have that No-wani doesn't?"

"I don't know."

"You don't have to do this."

"I do."

Overnight, Muumai got no better. He refused to suckle even when Ha-wani strapped him to her breast with his mouth at a nipple. His touch caused her milk to run freely, soaking the sling and dripping down her skirt. She could only hope that, somehow, a bit of milk had gotten into his mouth and he had swallowed it.

During the night, she lay awake, her husband curled against her back, his arm across her wrapping the child she cradled in her arms. Within the dwelling, the only sounds were Chanu's snoring and her sister's child grunting and suckling from time to time.

Outside, an owl hooted.

Fire-Keeper had failed.

Chapter 24

Yellow Moon, 1159 (April)

In the morning, dazed, Ha-wani wrapped her son's tiny body in the soft hide of the young deer Tonrai had killed in anticipation of his son's birth. Later, it would have been his breechclout or a winter wrap. While Tonrai went to get Kutareo to bring fuel for the pyre, she knelt on the floor of the dwelling, rocking back and forth with her child in her arms, wailing. Until now, she didn't know the pain a child's death would bring. She sang for mothers who had lost children, mothers whose pain meant nothing to her people, mothers whose pain she now shared.

All through the winter, Kutareo had kept busy collecting wood for cremations, although Fire-Keeper had continued his new practice of burying the dead as he had done for Nothai.

When she was finally able to rise and face what needed to be done, she crossed the plaza and stood below the shaman's mound, clutching her dead child in her arms.

When he came to stand above her, he said, "I will direct the farmers to dig a hole."

"No. I will see my son's spirit rise into the sky on smoke and flames."

"It is no longer our way. He will be buried with the other children." He pointed to the corner of the wall where, on the other side, the village cemetery held the cremated remains of villagers who had died through the years, and where he now buried children without the benefit of fire.

His voice cut through her, but she persisted. "No. My husband is preparing his pyre now."

"I will not sing for him. The village loses nothing with his death."

"I will sing for him myself. I only need you to bring a sacred coal to light his way."

"And if I don't?"

"I will bring a coal from my own hearth. I will light his way without you." She turned and walked away.

Outside the compound, she watched her husband, Chanu, and Kutareo build the pyre. They dug a shallow pit and put together a small square of short logs with smaller branches and twigs filling the spaces. It would not take long for the fire to consume the meager pyre along with her son's tiny body. The cremation of an adult would take the better part of two days, but a child like Muumai would depart by nightfall.

Ha-wani carried her son to the pyre, tucking a shell frog necklace into the folds of the deer hide. Tonrai had made it to match the bracelet on her wrist. She turned it and rubbed her thumb across its incised face. Under a colorless, gray sky, the sun could not chase the chill that seeped to her bones. She would never be warm again.

Tonrai put in two small obsidian points so his son could hunt in the spirit world. Li-naä and Vachai, with Kokii and her sons, joined them. Wokkai stood to the side with Kutareo. Ra-naä stayed inside the compound with her daughter, but Chanu came and laid his broad hand on his brother's shoulder.

When Fire-Keeper came from the compound carrying a vessel, Ha-wani breathed a sigh of relief. A sacred coal would light his way, after all. The shaman set the pyre alight and returned to the compound without acknowledging Ha-wani or her family.

Ha-wani knelt, watching the flames dart in and out of the small twigs at the base of the pyre until the larger logs caught. She held her breath when flames reached the tiny bundle. The fragrance of burning wood gave way to a more acrid smell, and, when the smoke drifted over her, she breathed it in, searing her throat and relishing the pain in her chest. Great-Grandfather Mountain stood in the distance— strong, steady, and unchanged. She sang for her son.

> *Go now*
> *The flower world awaits*
> *vanseka weene*
> *Sea ania vovicha*
> *Go yonder to the*
> *Flower-covered wilderness world*
> *I will look for you there*
> *Go to the little flower world*
> *Sea ania vovicha*

Throughout the morning, clouds of gray smoke rose into a pale sky, taking with it Muumai's spirit. The others wandered back to the compound, but Ha-wani stayed, unmoving, watching her son depart.

Finally, when only fragments of bone and deer hide remained in the ashes, Fire-Keeper returned to collect them.

As the setting sun painted the slopes of the mountains red, Fire-Keeper scooped the child's remains into a small undecorated jar Ha-wani had given him. Nothing in his manner suggested a reverence for the dead or sympathy for her loss. When he placed the jar in her hands, she wanted to invade his eyes, confront his spirit, and to challenge him. Here. Now.

But it was not the time. Now that her son's spirit had safely crossed into the Flower World, they could bury Muumai with the other children.

Chapter 25

Yellow Moon 1159 (April)

Eyes closed, Ha-wani stood in the dim light of morning, certain neither the dawn wind nor the sun would make an appearance. But the wind arrived as it always did, washing cool air over her, and the first sliver of the sun peeked over Great-Grandmother, chasing the darkness from her eyelids but not from her heart. She opened her eyes and stared into the rising sun until the light was too fierce.

Nothing had changed. She was no different from other mothers who had lost their children and watched in disbelief as the sun rose and set each day. Like them, she, too, would go on, keeping her child in her heart if not in her arms. The thought triggered a painful swelling of her breasts and a flow of milk in anticipation of his suckling. Her heart broke anew knowing her milk would go to waste.

At the entrance to the compound, she met Kokii's boys on their way to hunt rabbits and ground squirrels with Benai who was enjoying a rare day off from learning the people's history. They carried throwing sticks, and snares hung at their waists, the young ones laughing and giggling and poking each other, while Benai, with an air of importance as the leader of the party, demanded they behave like men. When she approached, he stopped, and Chuwii and Tarukii stumbled into him. Wide-eyed and silent, they peeked around the older boy.

She studied each one, trying to imagine her son at those ages. After a ragged breath, she walked past them. Moments later, she heard them beyond the compound wall, again laughing and teasing.

Seeing Ra-naä under the ramada with Wichikai at her breast tore at her heart. Again, her breasts ached, and milk ran from her nipples. Ra-naä ignored her. Li-naä handed her a small bowl of broth. It warmed her hands.

Vachai, who had been talking with Tonrai and Chanu under the ramada, slid to the edge of his bench in anticipation of standing. "In the meantime, I could use your help in the granary. Whatever Fire-Keeper has in mind, the planting will go on—whether he likes it or not." Chanu helped his father to his feet, and they went around the dwelling to the granary.

Tonrai went with them without speaking. He had not forgiven her for turning to Fire-Keeper.

Li-naä took a bundle of cotton from her basket and handed Wokkai the spindle. The girl was getting quite good at spinning cotton.

After the men left, Ra-naä drew the sleeping child from her breast. "Will you hold Wichikai for a while? I want to take a walk." Without waiting for an answer, she stood and put her daughter into Ha-wani's arms.

"If she wakes up hungry, go ahead and feed her. You have plenty of milk."

Ha-wani did not watch her walk away. She stared at the child in her arms. Wichikai was soft and warm, breathing easily, squirming and grunting. She felt sturdy, even heavy, compared to—compared to—

She could not complete her thought.

With her thumb, Ha-wani rubbed dried milk from Wichikai's cheek and chin, and the child opened her eyes. Deep within, instead of the little bee she had seen darting in and out of red blossoms in Muumai's eyes, the curious, golden eyes of the little owl rested there.

Wichikai jammed her fist into her mouth, and, when it offered nothing, she began to cry. Ha-wani put the baby to her breast and helped her find the nipple, and the child settled into a contented rhythm of sucking, grunting, and sucking. Relief swept over Ha-wani as the ache in her swollen breast subsided, but it failed to diminish the pain in her heart.

"You will have other children." Her mother-in-law startled her when she spoke, but before she could respond, Li-naä went on. "Some will live, and some will go too soon to the Flower World. You will remember them and always carry them in your heart. You will never forget the pain." Her usually clear eyes clouded over. "It stabs you at times when you least expect it. You must hold it inside and go on."

"You have known this pain." It was not a question.

Li-naä nodded, staring into the smoldering embers of the cooking fire. "Tonrai might have had another sister and another brother had they lived."

Wokkai stopped wrapping the thread and stared at her mother.

"My first child—a girl—was born dead. To this day, I dream of her lost spirit searching but never finding her guardian." Li-naä's voice was barely above a whisper. She continued to smooth the raw cotton absently. "Then Tonrai was born. He was healthy and grew strong quickly. Chanu came soon after, and he's grown into a fine man. But after Chanu, I had another son. His spirit was the deer, like his father's. It should have meant he had promise. One day—" She glanced toward Great-Grandmother Mountain. "One day, I left him sleeping on the mat inside the house while I sat under the ramada with the other women watching our children play. He was wrapped well, and I knew I would hear him if he woke and cried, but he never made a sound. I sat there gossiping with the other women, and I didn't realize how much time had passed. When I went inside, his spirit had fled. He was gone. He had never been sick, had never refused the nipple. If I had only gone inside sooner—"

Ha-wani gazed at the contented child at her breast and realized that she, too, could still be lost. She held her a bit tighter as Li-naä continued.

"After Wokkai was born," she patted the girl's hand, "three times, I carried a child, and three times, I failed to bring them to birth. Finally, Benai came. From the beginning, he was bright and quick. He will be a fine Knowledge-Keeper, but I miss him living here with us. Unlike the others, though, I can visit him whenever I want. I miss them and think about them almost every day. But we are expected to pretend it is of no importance."

Ha-wani frowned. "Why? When babies died in my village, I never gave it much thought. Now, I understand how unfair it is to the mothers—and maybe the fathers. I think Tonrai feels the pain of loss as well, but he is still angry with me."

"He will come around if you give him time. He was always a perceptive child. I think he remembers his little brother and my anguish."

"Fire-Keeper said a child is of no value. He—and maybe some others—think I made a spectacle of myself with my grief and my insistence on a traditional cremation."

Li-naä smiled. "It doesn't matter what anyone thinks. Other mothers will follow your lead. You've given them a gift." She smiled at a wide-eyed Wokkai only now learning of lost brothers and sisters.

Chapter 26

Bean Tree Moon 1159 (May)

Do you use moonflowers* for medicine?" Ha-wani asked her question after No-wani acknowledged her.

"Why do you ask?" The old woman stopped grinding seeds in a stone bowl but remained seated under her ramada.

"I'm curious. When I was living at Honey Bee, our Healer-Woman collected the flowers, leaves, and roots, but my mother cautioned me not to go near them. I happened to see some blooming beside Elder Brother Wash yesterday, and they reminded me."

"Your mother was wise to tell you to stay away. They can be dangerous if you don't know how to handle them. You're likely to get sick."

"How do you use them?"

"I make ointments and liniments for sore muscles and minor injuries, but you dare not put it on broken skin."

"But you don't make a tea with them?"

"By the gods, Girl, no." No-wani frowned again. "What's this all about?"

"Nothing important. They are such pretty flowers. It's a shame they are dangerous." She glanced toward her house group. "I must go with the others to gather and grind beans* down at the grove. Thank you."

As she walked away, not only did she sense the old woman's eyes following her, but other eyes as well. Fire-Keeper. He had marked the sun shadow a few moments ago, but now he stood, his eyes exploring her, inviting her to turn and meet his gaze. She called on the raven and looked into his eyes. Dark wings enfolded her. *I know what you did, Yukui.* She broke eye contact before he could react, put her shoulders back and walked with confidence to join the others.

What Healer-Woman had just said and what Ha-wani had seen yesterday at sunrise persuaded her she was right.

When the rising sun had warmed her face, she closed her eyes and focused inward, inviting her raven spirit to come. She stretched her arms sideward and—

> *Lifting into the air, she circled the agave terraces where the farmers trimmed fleshy, blade-like leaves from several plants. In the winter, the agaves would provide a feast ahead of the hungry time — the time between the agave harvest and the first farming harvest of spring. Now, the outer leaves were trimmed and collected for their needle-like*

tips with long strands of fiber attached. The women used them to sew skirts, breechclouts, and leather seed bags for traveling. Men would strip the remaining fibers from the leaves for cordage, bow strings, basket weaving, and sandals.

She swung into a long arc and glided toward the walled compound, but a movement in the desert scrub to the east caught her eye. Fire-Keeper. Staying behind him, she wondered why he might be going to the wash below Great-Grandmother without using the path. He cut through the bean trees and hackberry scrub, frequently looking over his shoulder but failing to notice the raven who flew above him. When he climbed down the bank into Elder Brother Wash, she settled in a tree to watch.

Along the edges of the dry streambed, moonflowers grew in abundance, their showy white flowers brilliant against dark green leaves. He sang his thanks and knelt at first one and then another, cutting long stalks with both leaves and blossoms and putting them into a basket.

Moonflowers. Why did Fire-Keeper want poison flowers? When he stood, she took to the sky again, her wings whispering in the air. He turned in her direction, his hand shading his eyes against the morning sun.

Wokkai followed the women and girls off the ridge, along the trail towards Great-Grandmother. They were on their way to the grove beside Elder Brother Wash to gather and grind the early beans. Each woman carried a basket and her grinding stone.

While it was easy enough to gather beans from the trees close to the village and grind them under their own ramadas, this grove was large, and there were rock mortars nearby where they could grind them and bring home more flour than if they only collected them to take home.

As they walked, the women chatted amiably, keeping a close eye on the bushes bordering the path. The warm weather signaled the time for rattlesnakes, which would be coming out of their winter sleep and sunning on warm desert trails.

Saguaros growing along the slopes on either side of the trail stood guard, their arms reaching to Father Sky. As they passed, the women greeted their brothers. Nubs at the tops and on the tips of their arms promised an early bloom, followed by the harvest and singing down the rains—if such were still possible. The last two ceremonies had not brought the rains they needed. Perhaps the gods had indeed abandoned them.

Cactus wrens scolded as they passed, and small lizards crossed the trail before them, their tails curled up, mimicking the scorpion's venomous tail. Wokkai smiled, knowing they were not fooling anyone. The sun had climbed high, and the heat of the day was upon them.

The younger girls laughed and chattered, excited about this prelude to womanhood. For several weeks, they labored over the task of weaving their own baskets from willow twigs, creating their own designs of lizards, birds, and toads with the black fibers stripped from the wicked seedpod called ram's horn.

Wokkai walked with her mother and Ha-wani as a woman, carrying the basket she had made last year, tightly woven with a coyote track design circling the sides. She was particularly proud because Kokii said it was the finest first basket she had ever seen. Feeling like an adult, she smiled at the antics of the girls, who were increasingly involved in women's tasks, demonstrating their willingness to work hard and be good wives. She had done the same.

Had her mother told her father about her desire to marry Kutareo? She was reluctant to bring it up, but, as far as she knew, her father had not yet sought out a husband. But her mother had woven a new matrimonial ribbon and decorated it with small beads.

She caught up with Ha-wani. "You're quiet today, Sister."

"I'm thinking about Muumai."

"I'm sorry." Wokkai's own involvement in the child's birth made him special to her as well. She also grieved for him and for her sister-in-law. Knowing Muumai would die had been a terrible secret that still weighed heavily on her heart. They walked in silence for a short distance before Wokkai asked the question that was always on her mind. "Has my mother told my father to look for a husband yet? She hasn't said anything to me, but last night, I caught my father looking at me strangely. Like he thought I had done something wrong."

"Even if she didn't tell him about your relationship with Wood-Cutter, he might suspect it. He knows you spend time with him."

"I guess I'll have to wait." Wokkai sighed. "Will you tell me if he sends Tonrai to speak to your father? He wouldn't be able to walk there himself."

"I will ask your mother to tell you."

They followed the trail down the bank, past the rock mortars, and into the sandy bottom of Elder Brother Wash where it lay beneath Great-Grandmother's Knees. Breezes nudged the trees and cooled the women and girls after their long walk. They scattered among the trees along both banks, pulling beans and filling their baskets. The young girls squealed whenever a thorny branch snapped back and bloodied their arms. Wokkai laughed, remembering her own efforts to collect beans without getting scratched.

Several women climbed up on the rocks and set to work. It was cool in the shade, and Ha-wani focused on grinding the pods to a fine flour and separating the hard seeds from it. The women from Amureo's house group worked at mortars in the highest boulder. She was right below them with her back turned, and, although she was not interested in their gossip, she couldn't help but hear what they said.

Amureo's wife asked her sister-in-law, "Did you hear the argument between Chief Elder and his wife last night?" Ha-wani assumed they were taking advantage of the fact that Tatanikii's wife was with the girls collecting beans and couldn't hear them talking about what should be a private matter between her mother- and father-in-law.

"You couldn't miss it. His voice carried through the whole village. I suspect even those outside the walls heard."

"Could you tell what the fight was all about?"

"Apparently, she refused a joining."

"Refused? Can you do that?"

"Don't tell me you've never refused your husband."

"I refused once, and he beat me."

"I can get away with it from time to time, but I know better than to let him go too long without satisfying his desires."

"I wonder what it's like to join with Chief Elder. He's a huge man. I'll bet his man-part is twice the size of my husband's."

"I'd let him poke me any time he wanted."

Both women dissolved into giggles, but quieted when Tatanikii's wife climbed the boulder and traded places with Ha-wani. Because such work is hard, even for the most seasoned women, everyone pitched in taking turns on the boulders, relieving the others to go back to the trees to collect more beans. As the baskets filled, they set them aside and took an empty basket to fill. Under the trees, a refreshing breeze cooled them as they worked.

When it was Wokkai's turn to grind, she climbed to the mortars and set to work. The seeds inside the pods were rock hard and, once the pod was broken up, she sorted them into the basket and ground the pods into a fine flour. She fell into a rhythm, grinding, sorting, grinding again until she had filled several baskets. When all baskets were filled, each woman claimed her own, laid a woven cloth over it, anchored it with their grinding stone and headed back to the village.

The younger girls were quiet on the return trip, no doubt worn out from the work they had done this day. Tired, but proud to be doing women's work.

Ha-wani joined her sister-in-law, and they walked in silence under a cloudless pale sky.

When they neared the village, Wokkai stopped and turned to her. "I'm confused about something."

"What is it?"

"Kutareo."

"What about him?"

"His name."

"What do you mean?"

"Everyone calls him Kutareo because that's what he does. He cuts wood. Why doesn't he have a spirit name from the Flower or Wilderness World? He wasn't a wood cutter when he was a little boy. And he only calls his brothers Amureo and Panereo, which is what everyone else calls them because one is a hunter and the other a builder."

Wokkai went on, intent on her questions. "My father is Vachai, named 'corn' because he is a farmer, but his spirit name is Maasii, for the deer. I don't know why, but even we call him Vachai. I can't remember when my mother called him by his spirit name—well, maybe a few times at night."

Ha-wani smiled at the girl's apparent embarrassment at what she said. "I think it might be because the work he does for the village is so important to him. And he is proud of it. I'm sure his spirit understands."

"I hadn't thought of it that way. But it's different with Kutareo. Yes, he's proud of the work he does, but—I don't know. For some reason he said he is just Kutareo."

"Of course he has a spirit name, even if he doesn't know it."

"If he really doesn't know it, I'm going to help him find it."

Whistling wings lifted Wokkai into the sky, and she flew, arrow-straight, across the village and out over the desert, her tail fanned out behind her. She sailed higher and aimed for the grove. He was there, banding an old tree with an upright trunk. She settled in a nearby tree.

When he bent over to slice bark from the trunk, the muscles across his back, scarred from his brother's whippings, rippled with each movement. It pained her to remember how Amureo treated him. "Cooo-AH-coo-cooo."

He stood and squinted through the branches in her direction. Dappled sunlight danced on his dark face, and, when he smiled, his slanted eyebrows lifted, and he wore the quizzical expression she loved. His dark hair was pulled back and tied at his neck with a leather thong, with shorter strands hanging loosely around his ears.

She knew Kutareo cared for her, but why had he not shared his real name, his spirit? When she probed his dark eyes, searching, the darkness lifted and golden eyes, rimmed in black, gazed at her.

In the morning, Wokkai left the compound and crouched behind a hackberry bush near the opening behind Amureo's house group. When Kutareo came out, carrying his ax, he took the path down off the ridge. She followed, but kept her distance, watching.

He walked lightly, the ax over his muscled shoulder, his sandaled feet padding softly along the level trail. When the trail dropped steeply off the ridge, he stepped from rock to rock with uncommon grace. At the bottom of the ridge, he followed a turn in the trail, and she lost sight of him.

She had often wondered at his ability to move through the desert so quietly and so gracefully. Surely, those abilities related to his true spirit. As she rounded the same turn lost in thought, she almost bumped into him. He was standing in the middle of the trail, the quizzical look on his face.

"Why are you hiding? You don't want to walk with me anymore?"

She smiled. "I'm sorry. I'll walk with you now and explain." She took his hand. "Will you go with me to Spirit Canyon?"

"I need to girdle trees."

"I know. But this is important."

"But today is the day I'm supposed to girdle trees."

"It's all right, Kutareo. We can do that afterward."

At the entrance to Spirit Canyon, they stopped, each one lifting their arms to the sky. Each one asking permission to enter.

In silence, they followed the rocky trail upward to a rock outcrop where they could sit, looking back toward the canyon entrance and across the desert beneath Great-Grandmother. The canyon was remarkably green for as dry as it had been, and more birds than they could count fluttered among the trees, reminding her of the gifts of Mother Earth.

Wokkai held his hand in both of her own. "I didn't walk with you because I wanted to watch you. I wanted to see again the way you move through the desert. Have you never tripped over a root or a rock?"

He looked thoughtful, his slanted brows coming together in a straight line. "Not that I remember. Why?"

"Kutareo, tell me about your name."

"My name? What about it?"

"What is the name your family gave you when they helped you find your spirit guide?"

"My spirit guide?" His slanted brows leveled out again.

"You know my name. Wokkai. It means 'dove.'"

"Yes."

"Your name, Kutareo, means wood cutter."

"I know. I'm a wood cutter."

"Your brother is called Panereo because he is a builder. Your other brother is called Amureo because he is a hunter."

He nodded.

"What was your name before you started cutting wood for the village?"

"Before—?"

"Yes, what did your mother call you?"

His eyes welled, and he took his hand from hers, pinching the bridge of his nose. "I don't remember my mother." He slid off the rock and started down the trail. "I don't want to talk about this."

"Wait." Wokkai caught up with him. "Please talk to me. Don't you trust me?"

He turned back to her, his eyes clouded. "Don't make me talk about it."

She took his hands and clasped them to her breast. "I love you, Kutareo. Tell me. Please."

He took a ragged breath. "She died when I was born. I killed her."

"It's not your fault, Kutareo. Women die in child-birth. It happens, but the child should not be blamed."

"My brothers don't like me. They remember what I did."

"Amureo is a hateful man, and you don't deserve his whippings." She stepped closer, and, standing on her toes, she kissed him. "Your mother would have helped you find your spirit name, but since she died, didn't your father help you?"

"No. He didn't like me either. No one ever called me by name. When I became Wood-Cutter, I was proud to finally have a name, something people could call me, something that meant something. I don't have a spirit name. I don't have a spirit guide."

"You do. Everyone does. May I help you find him?"

She led him back to the rock and stood before him, holding his hands and looking into his eyes.

Join me
Trust me as I trust you
Let our spirits come together
Trust me
Join me

She flew into the wilderness world, sailing over the foothills beneath Great-Grandfather and into the canyon where the cotton grows. She followed the twisting trail upward.

When a bighorn sheep, his horns curved into a full circle, shifted his gaze to her, she probed.

No.

Sister doves circled above and led her with chattering wings to the trail beneath Great-Grandfather's towers. From behind a boulder, a mountain lion lifted his head and peered at her. She turned to him as he climbed to the top of the boulder, lay down, and rested his chin on his forepaws. She swept her gaze across his tawny coat and moved closer, probing. He lifted his head and made a low rumbling sound, purring in and out with each breath. The sound rolled through the canyon, echoing off its walls, and golden eyes, rimmed in black, looked back at her.

"Kawiusai," Wokkai whispered.

Kutareo blinked.

"Kawiusai. Your name is Kawiusai. Your spirit is the mountain lion."

Chapter 27

Big Rains Moon 1159 (July)

With the sun standing directly overhead, the heat of the day had become oppressive. The air hung heavy as the people gathered in the plaza. A rumble of voices filled the air as they sought out anyone who might know what Fire-Keeper called them here for.

When Anu and his family joined them, Ha-wani noticed shy glances pass between Cheshonii and Anu's younger daughter, Ma-taä, who had delicate features like Ra-naä. She suspected a budding romance, but, like Wood-Cutter, Tonrai's nephew had no hope of marrying unless he could make a trip to Great Water.

It had been a month since the saguaro harvest, and Fire-Keeper's predicted rain had not yet materialized—at least not in sufficient quantities to nourish the fields. Now, they had been summoned to the plaza.

"What do you suppose he wants?" Vachai stretched his bad leg out and massaged his thigh.

Chanu shrugged his shoulders. "I thought I might find out something from Amureo, but he was evasive. An-nat said he didn't know anything. Fire-Keeper has said nothing to him."

Finally, Fire-Keeper stepped out of the ceremonial hut and stood on the platform mound overlooking the plaza. When he pounded his staff on the ground, the bells sang, and the four feathers floated on air before settling to stillness. The crowd quieted as the people realized he was waiting.

"You!" He singled out some in the crowd, pointing at one and then another. "You are being punished. You have disappointed Father Sky for too long." His pointing finger lingered on Chief Elder, An-nat, and the others on the council. "They—our leaders—have refused to follow his traditions for too long. He has told me I may not summon the rains unless we send a party to Great Water."*

His reedy voice grated on Ha-wani's ears, and she focused on the bony toes protruding from his sandals at eye level. She whispered to Tonrai, "Again, he claims he can summon the rains."

"We haven't sent a party to Great Water because he directed us not to go."

"Silence!" He lifted his staff and shook it, sending the feathers in all directions. "You will not be blessed with rains if you have not honored the waters of Mother Earth and brought her gifts to our village." He chanted and paced back and forth along the length of the platform mound, revealing the carved mask he had fixed to the back of his head. It was an angry face, its brows painted into a frown, its mouth open. He stopped, and, holding his staff to the sky, he chanted again.

Te-oh-chee-ah ee-tom achaa-eh*
Te-oh-chee-ah ee-tom achaa-eh

The people joined in.

Bless us, Father Sky
Bless us, Father Sky

They shuffled around the plaza as they chanted, repeating the call to Father Sky. Dust swirled around them, clinging to their damp skin, as their sandals scraped against the hard ground, moving as one body, calling for a blessing.

When Fire-Keeper again pounded the ground with his staff, the feathers floated to a standstill.

"You must atone. You must honor Mother Earth. When the council declared you would no longer send a party to Great Water to collect her gifts, I warned them it was a mistake, that there would be consequences. They refused to listen. Only I can deliver you from Father Sky's anger."

Clearly, Fire-Keeper wanted the people to believe the council had betrayed them. Both An-nat and Chief Elder frowned at those who stared at them, and Vachai muttered to Tonrai.

In the crowd, someone—perhaps someone recruited by the shaman—shouted, "Tell us what we must do! We need your wisdom, Fire-Keeper! We depend on you and you alone!" Others joined in, creating a chorus of voices begging for Fire-Keeper's help. "Yes! Tell us," they called out. "Save us!" "What must we do?"

Fire-Keeper raised his bony arms, the staff in one hand, and the crowd quieted. "We will send a party to Great Water. We will bring back Mother Earth's

232 / Sharon K Miller   Big Rains Moon 1159

gifts and use them to honor Father Sky. Afterwards, he will allow me to summon the rains. I call upon the council to make amends for their mistake. On the seventh sunrise, our men will depart for Great Water." As the crowd cheered, he turned and went into the ceremonial house, the angry mask glaring at the people.

Several villagers muttered as Chief Elder made his way through the crowd to Tonrai. "Seven days? Is he mad?"

"Not so mad as he is cunning. His intent was to turn the people against the council. And if we are ill-prepared for this journey, he wins again." Tonrai turned to Ha-wani. "We'll join you later."

When Cheshonii started to leave with the women, Chief Elder surprised everyone by asking him to stay. They stood together at the edge of the plaza as the rest of the villagers scattered to their homes or to their work. Leaning on his walking stick, Vachai growled, "'The council declared.' He was the one who insisted we couldn't waste precious resources on a traveling party."

Chief Elder nodded. "Yes, but it's no use arguing with Fire-Keeper or trying to persuade the people otherwise. We need to make sure we put together a strong party, and you two," he pointed to Tonrai and Chanu, "must be part of the group. I'll not have the shaman make those decisions."

Both men agreed, but Chanu pointed out that Fire-Keeper would insist on Amureo going. "For that reason, it's important for An-nat to go. There'd be no question about who the leader is. Knowledge-Keeper knows the songs to guide us to the sea."*

Chief Elder agreed. "I will speak to him. In the meantime, we have much to do to get provisions and trade goods collected in time."

As one who had not yet attained manhood, Cheshonii listened, but he did not contribute to the conversation. Although Tonrai had no idea why Chief Elder asked the boy to stay, he could see how well Cheshonii fit into the group. He remembered the day his young cousin brought his father's body down from Great-Grandmother Mountain and how the boy had assumed his father's responsibilities. Nothai would be proud.

Interrupting Tonrai's musings, Chief Elder turned to the boy and said, "Several times, you have shown us you are ready for manhood. For that reason, you, too, will make this trip to Great Water."

Before his uncle and cousins could congratulate him, Cheshonii squared his broad shoulders, stood straight, and said, "I am honored by your offer, and, I would like to go, but I will be of more use here preparing the fields for planting. Vachai will need my help while his sons are away."

Thandoi smiled. "You surprise me once again. When we climbed Great-Grandmother to bring your father home, I thought you were reckless. You bordered on disrespect, but you proved your mettle that day. Since then, you picked up your father's work without hesitation." He laid a hand on the younger man's shoulder. "I know you are interested in a young woman, and I suspect you'd like to marry, but you decline the one chance you have to earn the right."

"Thank you, but there will be other trips. I will wait."

As the young man walked away, Chief Elder said, "Who knew a boy could become a man on his own terms?"

Both Vachai and Chanu nodded when Tonrai replied, "Perhaps we should examine our traditions someday."

"We'll see. For now, though, I think all the boys should stay here. If the one boy in the village most deserving of the trip declines to go, I can't see inviting any of the others."

Vachai pushed himself more upright with his stick and frowned. "That won't go over well with some."

"No, but we cannot delay the discussion." He turned to Tonrai.

The two men crossed the plaza and entered the Council House where Fire-Keeper, Amureo, An-Nat, and Dar sat around the hearth waiting.

Chief Elder wasted no time getting to the point. "We have little time to prepare." He glanced at Fire-Keeper. "Thank you for giving us leave to send a party to Great Water. I'm pleased to hear you acknowledge your mistake."

The shaman scowled and opened his mouth to speak, but Thandoi held up his hand, signaling silence. "We have been denied the blessings of the sea for too long." Again, Fire-Keeper frowned. "For that reason, this trip is critical. It must be made quickly and efficiently. Therefore, I propose we send only experienced travelers with no boys for initiation."

Amureo looked up sharply. "I object. I want my son to make his initiation trip. He has waited too long."

Again, Chief Elder signaled silence. "First, we must decide who of the men will go. An-nat will lead the party. His songs will guide them on the journey."

Knowledge-Keeper bowed his head. He held the one-hundred songs describing the route they would follow over long stretches of dry desert to the secret pools holding water and finally to the sandy dunes of the sea.

"Are we agreed?" Both Amureo and the shaman frowned but nodded agreement.

Dar said, "We need Tonrai to be in the party. He has the finest jewelry for trading, and he will bring the finest shells back to bless the village." When all the others nodded, Tonrai wondered why Amureo and the shaman voiced no opposition.

Tonrai spoke. "Thank you. I think my brother would be a valuable member of the party. His spear and arrow points are important trade goods, as well." Again, there was no opposition, but he was troubled by the satisfied expression on Fire-Keeper's face and his nearly imperceptible nod to Dar.

The shaman spoke up. "Amureo, of course, must be part of the group. He will see to it the party is well-fed along the way."

Thandoi stared at the shaman. "Fire-Keeper. You know the men do not hunt on these trips. They run from dawn to nightfall, stopping only at springs and rocky pools for water. They will not take the time to hunt, dress out, and cook an animal."

"Of course. In any case, Amureo will be an import-ant member of the party."

Tonrai spoke next. "We need a runner, Chief Elder. Your son is the fastest in the village, and we may need him to run ahead with messages from time to time."

Finally, the members of the party were agreed upon: An-nat, Tonrai, Chanu, Tatanikii, and Amureo, along with a few men from outside the walls to carry additional burdens.

Amureo stood. "My son must go on this trip. He is the strongest boy in the village. He will be a hunter and leader. There are none his age who can compete with him."

Tonrai suppressed a retort; Cheshonii could beat his boy in any contest and had done so on numerous occasions. Instead, he offered, "If we take boys on this trip, we will spend valuable time putting them through their initiation tests. It will slow us down. This is a trip we should make as quickly as possible, coming as it does before planting when we need everyone to be involved."

"The boys would be a distraction from our purpose." An-nat avoided eye contact with both Amureo and the shaman.

"What say you, Dar?"

Dar kept his eyes on the hearth and spoke quietly. "I agree."

"It is decided. No boys will go on this trip. They will wait until the next one."

Amureo's face contorted with anger. "You have no right to deny my son." He glared at Tonrai as if daring him to disagree. Boldly making eye contact with each member of the council, he said, "You are jealous because your sons and brothers are not worthy. My son will be Chief Elder one day, and you will learn your place in this village." His voice rang out so everyone in the village could hear. "You will regret interfering with his future. I will see to it he gets his due. You will pay!"

They sat in silence as Amureo bolted out the entry. An-nat was the first to speak. "I think we should take Amureo's threats seriously. We should not allow him to go with us to Great Water. He will cause trouble."

The shaman stood. "No. He is a trusted friend; he does not mean what he says. He will do the right thing as a member of the traveling party."

"I'm not sure I share your confidence," An-nat said, making only a brief eye contact in return.

Fire-Keeper narrowed his eyes, looking at each man. "You may deny his son, but you will not deny him."

Thandoi stood, signaling the council meeting was over. "As you wish, I will not deny Amureo this trip. He is a strong runner, and we need the strongest among us in this traveling party. I have spoken."

Excitement in the village was palpable, and the oppressive heat could not dampen the people's spirits. A trip to the sea would finally bring the rains they needed. Too much time had passed since they had sent a party to Great Water. The trade goods they took and the shells and precious salt they brought back would bless the village. But more important, the songs the men would sing to the vast expanse of water would surely mean Father Sky would allow Fire-Keeper to summon the rains. The Hungry Time had brought death and discouragement; this trip gave them hope for better times.

The travelers would equally share the burden of trade goods they would carry to Great Water to trade with the people who lived there. And they would equally share the newly acquired goods—dried fish, jewelry, beads, obsidian, turquoise, hides, and even clothing—on the return trip. The men gathered what they would need: extra sandals, drinking gourds, and newly repaired burden baskets, in which they would carry the trade goods going out and the gifts of the sea coming back.

With no time for the women to make new baskets or pots or weave new lengths of cloth, Kokii, Li-naä, and Ha-wani collected what they had made previously as contributions. Kokii offered six of her best baskets, and Ha-wani selected four pots and one jar she had made. After she brought them to the ramada, she picked up the small jar she had kept by the entry to the house. She had not yet found a good use for it, and it certainly could be contributed to the trading trip. She held it in both hands and closed her eyes, listening. Her song echoed quietly. *No. This pot is not meant to be traded. I don't know why, but it will stay here.*

Ha-wani drew in her breath when Li-naä brought out the long length of fabric she had woven past the point of being a skirt. Her mother-in-law had used her weaving as a distraction when Muumai was dying. "Someone may find it useful. Here, it holds a sad memory." When she gave Wokkai's beaded matrimonial ribbon, the girl looked surprised. "You don't seem to be in a hurry, Child, so I have time to make you another."

Wokkai hugged her mother.

Ra-naä sat cross-legged in the ramada with her daughter on her lap. With so much going on around her, Wichikai concentrated on everyone and everything. She gripped her mother's fingers and struggled to stand, only to plop down, and bounce up again as village women brought their best baskets, cotton fabrics, and pots to add to the collection. She jabbered and giggled each time someone stopped to greet her. Ha-wani could not suppress the pain that stabbed through her when she looked at her sister's healthy, active child. And she could not understand Ra-naä's bored expression.

Tonrai and Dar contributed beads, necklaces, and bracelets; Chanu contributed points and knives, including the knife he had made for Tonrai's son. He had resisted the idea, but Tonrai insisted. "You will make others for my sons."

Other than taking the knives they always carried in sheaths hanging around their necks, Amureo's bow and arrows, and Tatanikii's ax, they did not go as an armed group. In the past, they had never had trouble from other travelers, and they expected this trip to be like those the people had been making since before remembering.

The evening before their departure, Ha-wani and Tonrai walked along the path to the terraces, talking and watching the shifting colors the setting sun painted on the mountains. Ha-wani stopped and turned to her husband. "Once again, I feel I must warn you about Fire-Keeper and Amureo."

"No one has to warn me about Amureo. He is not a man to be trusted anywhere."

"I know, but we are certain he was responsible for Nothai's death and your father's injury. No one on this trip will be safe from him."

"I do not doubt it."

When he pulled her into his arms, she laid her head against his chest and listened to the beating of his heart, willing it to keep beating while he was away. "I love you."

"I love you." He brushed kisses on her forehead. "And I'm sorry."

"For what?"

"For forcing myself on you before you were ready. After Muumai's death . . . "

Tonrai's anger had simmered for weeks because she had gone to the shaman for help, and Ha-wani was cold to his advances. At night, she turned her back, leaving an empty space between them. Finally, one night he pushed her down on the mat and joined with her, not caring whether she was ready or not. When it was done, she rolled over and wept.

Afterwards, they fell into a regular routine of joining, but it seemed that neither brought their spirits with them to the encounters. They had become strangers.

"I promise I will keep my eye on Amureo. I know better than to turn my back to him. And when I come home, I will give myself to you without reservation. I will no longer hold my spirit apart from you."

"Thank you, husband." She took his hand and laid it on her belly. "You must return to me and our child."

"Our child? You are happy even though—?"

"Yes."

He picked her up and spun her around. "May the gods bless us with a strong, healthy child."

"I sing for it every day."

"Maybe your sister will give Chanu another child."

Chanu and Ra-naä had resumed their nighttime joinings, so it was possible she might be pregnant soon. If so, Ha-wani hoped Ra-naä would be happier with two children instead of one. But doubts lingered in the back of her mind, whispering in her ear, saying words she didn't want to hear. *My sister will never be happy.*

In the morning, the traveling party gathered outside the walls and was surrounded by the villagers. Together, they waited for the dawn wind to cleanse them and for the first kiss of the sun to send them off with the blessing of the day. Fire-Keeper held his staff high and chanted.

Bring the clouds
Bring the rains
From their home
In the sea
Bring the sea
To bless us

The people joined in, and they sang again.

The dawn wind swept over the travelers who, together, greeted it with upraised arms and the song. Behind them, the gathered people did the same, and when the sun had blessed them, the travelers turned to say farewell to their families.

Ra-naä, holding Wichikai at her breast in the sling, stood with Chanu. "I don't know why you have to go."

"It is my duty. I promise I will find the most beautiful shell in the sea and bring it back to you."

She smiled. "Prettier than the ones your brother will bring?"

He nodded and laid a gentle hand on his daughter's head. "Take care of my little one."

Ra-naä looked from her child to her husband and back to her child and whispered, "I do love you. . . . Both of you."

Tonrai wrapped his arms around his wife. "Do not worry, Wife. I will return."

"Travel safely, my love." She glanced past him at Amureo, who was bidding his wife goodbye, his son standing to the side scowling. Fire-Keeper approached him and handed him a small leather pouch which he slipped into his burden basket. Inside, she felt the spread of the raven's wings and remembered the shaman collecting moonflowers.

As Tonrai hoisted his burden basket to his back, she leaned close, helping to adjust his head strap. She put her hands on either side of his face, her thumbs tracing the lines on his cheeks. "Keep your distance from Amureo on this trip," she whispered. "Don't let him offer you anything to drink or eat."

"I wouldn't anyway, but what are you thinking?" He pretended to have difficulty balancing his load, giving them more time to speak.

"He and Fire-Keeper are conspiring again. The shaman collected moonflowers, which are poisonous. And he gave Amureo a bag of something."

When all burden baskets were in place, the men secured their drinking gourds to their waists and tied small leather sacks of seeds to their wrists. Ha-wani had filled her husband's with chia and squash seeds. They would have little else to eat while they were away.

Lifting her wrist, he rubbed his thumb along her bracelet and turned the frog so it could see them. "I will worry about you while I am gone. Fire-Keeper is to be trusted here no more than Amureo with us on the trail."

"May the gods watch over us both."

He nodded and kissed her again, his shell tinklers reminding her of the day they met. She had to stifle her fear that she might never hear them again.

As the men set out together at a run, Ha-wani and the others waved goodbye, and when they disappeared around a turn in the trail, she closed her eyes to sing again for their safety.

But this time the song eluded her.

Chapter 28

Short Planting Moon 1159 (August)

The morning star rose into a cloudless sky above Great-Grandmother Mountain. Throughout the compound, women ducked out of the dwellings, and muffled greetings among neighbors signaled the start of the day.

Ha-wani relieved herself outside the compound wall. When she stood, she considered the mountains, dark shadows standing against a brightening sky, and their importance to the people. From this angle, Great-Grandmother Mountain rose from the desert floor with her back to the rising sun, her knees drawn up into a long ridge sweeping to the north. Since before remembering, she had gathered the rains, pouring them into the canyon, and sending them into the washes to irrigate and bless the fields. South of the canyon, Great-Grandfather Mountain swung westward, his rugged towers and pinnacles rising abruptly into the pale morning sky. The embrace of these mountains comforted the people.

Now, sun spears flew through the canyon, and the towers and pinnacles glowed while the crevices and cracks below idled in darkness.

Walking into the dawn wind, she accepted its blessing and the revitalization of her spirit. Its song whispered in her ears as it wrapped her in the cold mountain air sliding down the slope before the sun rose above Great-Grandmother's highest ridge. Holding her arms out to the side and closing her eyes, she welcomed the first kiss of the sun and the day it would bring.

She lifted her eyes to the other mountain. The long ridges beneath Great-Grandfather, stretching like fingers across the land toward the village, were bathed in light as the sun rose above Great-Grandmother. These mountains, steadfast and solid, held the people in their embrace and gave them life. She didn't believe the shaman when he said they might abandon the people.

Will you bring them home today, Great-Grandfather? The full moon several evenings past had prompted prayers for her husband and the others to come before the moon rose full again. They should be back, but she had not felt the presence of Tonrai's spirit for many days. Such trips never took so long. She was not alone in her fear, but no one spoke of it, for speaking of imagined misfortunes made them real. She sang a song of hope and turned to the day, expecting only the fierce heat of summer.

Such heat in the right season usually brought rain, but now it delivered only perspiration to gather beneath her breasts and drip into the waist of her cotton skirt. A cicada buzzed in a hackberry bush and received answers from the scrub, their harsh sound combining to a high intensity. The people needed no such reminder of the heat.

At the family ramada, her mother-in-law raised the fire and put precious water in the pot to boil. Ha-wani bent down and stepped into the dim interior of her mud hut and brought out a basket of beans. Squatting near the fire, she split each pod, collecting the beans for what little flavor they would add to the water, and set the pods aside for grinding. Ra-naä and Kokii prepared the corncakes.

Later, Ha-wani left the walled compound and made her way west along the ridge. After passing Anu's house and greeting his wife and children, she passed several trash pits where houses used to stand. When families were selected to move into the walled compound, they dismantled their homes and brought the materials inside to build anew, leaving an empty pit. Now, they were of little value, useful only for holding that which no one wanted. Ha-wani paused at a burned-out pit where Fire-Keeper had buried someone like he had buried Nothai. She paused to sing a prayer for the spirit that may not have made its way to the Flower World.

All of these families were field workers and farmers. Fire-Keeper had reduced them to a lower class who worked for the benefit of those inside the walls. They accepted their fate without complaint. She passed by their huts, greeting them as she did each morning. Like those inside the compound, they knew where she was going and why. By the time she reached the overlook, dark shadows filled the contours of Great-Grandfather Mountain, showing ridges, deep cuts, and sheer cliff faces in stark relief, while the long ridges below were bathed in the glow of morning light. She turned her gaze to the west, searching for the small peak and notch at the end of Little Dove Mountains where her parents lived.

After she sang a blessing for her parents and the people of Honey Bee Village, she focused on the place where Great-Grandfather Mountain sloped downward, ending abruptly at the desert basin. Tonrai and the others would come around the mountain there. When they did, they would send Runner ahead to tell the village. Surely, today would be the day.

The path the men would follow was the same path she and her sister had followed with their new husbands. From where she stood, a traveler would only be seen in a few places where the scrub thinned. She focused on each, afraid to blink and miss a sign. But all was still. She searched again, but not even Brother Coyote passed. She sighed and turned back to the village.

Lizards darted into the shade of grasses along the path, while a collared lizard pushed himself up and down on a rock as she passed. "Hello, Friend. Your rock must be very hot." He paused only a moment to cock an eye in her direction. A jackrabbit huddled, unmoving, behind a bush, his long ears turned toward her. The birds were unexpectedly quiet this morning. *Even they cannot stand this heat.*

When she entered the compound, several villagers glanced in her direction and averted their eyes. Her posture and downcast eyes said the men would not come today.

Fire-Keeper was talking to Vachai, and her stomach clenched. He raised one thin arm in the air and gestured toward Great-Grandfather Mountain. She ducked behind her dwelling, held her breath, and listened.

His harsh voice, shrill in the morning air, grated on her ears. "Do you, Maasii, think you know more than me about the fields and the planting?"

Calling him by his spirit name was more than disrespectful. She winced, wishing Vachai would tell him he did, in fact, know more than the shaman about such things, but her father-in-law always managed to remain calm and never raised his voice.

Fire-Keeper continued, "Your being Granary Master means nothing to me. Father Sky tells me when to sow the seeds."

Vachai, his back bent and twisted, one leg almost useless, leaned on his stick. "We must get the squash and beans planted. I'm told the corn is up to my knees. If we don't plant the squash to shade the corn and beans,* we could lose them in the heat of summer, especially if the rains do not come." His voice carried a heavy burden of worry.

"You must be told how high the corn grows and how well the fields are doing. You cannot see for yourself. I will tell the men when to ready the fields for the shade crop. I will direct Amureo and the others to manage the planting. And I will summon the rain when we need it."

Once again, Ha-wani wondered why, if Fire-Keeper could summon the rain, he had not done so. Why had the village been denied nourishing rains for two full cycles of the seasons—almost two years?

And why did men have to risk their lives climbing to Great-Grandmother's pools to bring water for the village and the fields? Vachai's injury and his brother's death, which left Kokii with three fatherless children, happened because they took that risk.

"Amureo is not here, and he doesn't want anything to do with farming. He sees himself as only a hunter."

The shaman sneered. "He will be back soon, and I will take it up with him. In the meantime, you are of little use."

Her father-in-law, head lowered, turned toward the granary and his work there. Fire-Keeper turned in her direction and raised his voice. "Why do you hide, Ha-wani? Do you think I do not know you are there?"

She stepped around the dwelling, hating him anew for using her spirit name. Averting her eyes from his, she concentrated on his bony chest with its patch of sparse gray hair, his protruding rib cage, and his sunken belly. "I beg your forgiveness, Fire-Keeper. I did not wish to interrupt your conversation."

When he came toward her, she stepped back, seeing again the man who poured hateful liquid into her child's mouth. His rank odor enveloped her, and she struggled not to gag, breathing through her mouth. His ever-present shell pendant rested in the center of his chest. A rivulet of sweat dripped past it and zig-zagged through his chest hairs, coming to rest in his sunken belly button. Once again, he probed her downcast eyes, trying to penetrate, to glimpse the raven once again. Dark wings protected her.

He leaned toward her and whispered, "We will talk soon, Ha-wani. There is much I want to teach you." He drew his hand across the front of his breechclout and scratched his groin with a long, pointed fingernail. His man-part rose behind the covering. "Especially now that you have no child to occupy your time and your husband is away."

Shocked by his cruelty and the implication, she nearly raised her eyes to his, but Raven tightened her wings around her. *Not now. Not here.* Ha-wani clamped her jaw tight. Her heart pounded in her ears, and she shivered in spite of the heat. When she did not reply, he turned and walked across the plaza, his breechclout barely covering his sagging buttocks.

Chapter 29

Short Planting Moon 1159 (August)

S he had not taken the bracelet off since he gave it to her. Remembering that night stirred a longing deep within her. Now, as she waited for his return from Great Water, she turned the bracelet on her arm, placing the frog on top.

She scanned the horizon once again, sweeping her gaze along the path the men must follow to reach the ridge. Nothing stirred in the scrub.

She closed her eyes and lifted her arms sideward, seeking the touch of his spirit. For days, when the men first left, her spirit could touch his. Was the distance between them too far, or had something terrible happened?

A wordless song gurgled and clicked in her throat.

Black wings stretched out, swooshing through the warm air — down, up, down, up — effortlessly carrying her into the sky above the path. She sailed in enlarging circles, watching the path, catching glimpses of the villagers inside the walled compound and the farmers outside, going about their daily routines.

Great-Grandfather Mountain beckoned.

She soared in his direction and glided on air currents rising from the stony slopes as the sun warmed them. Another raven joined her, daring her to fly with him. They chased each other in and out of deep creases between the massive towers and pinnacles, turning cartwheels in the sky and narrowly dodging solid rock walls. When her companion turned upside down and glided along the ridge, she hesitated only a moment before flipping over as she sailed above the ridge, with a clear sky stretched out above her.

Turning upright, she bade her companion farewell and flew to the end of the mountain, sailing along the trail back to the overlook, landing softly on the path.

She opened her eyes and slowed her breathing. She had seen no one on the trail, but she had flown higher and farther than ever before. The sun shone down from a pale blue sky, a sky that moments ago she had sailed through, enjoying the cool rush of air around her. Here, no breeze stirred the scrub, and the day's heat was still rising. Exhilarated by the adventure but disappointed the men were not coming, she turned toward the village and nearly bumped into Fire-Keeper, who seemed to have materialized before her.

Before she could shift her gaze, he gripped her wrist, pulled her against him, and locked eyes with her. Ha-wani struggled, but once again he had taken her by surprise; Raven was not prepared to come to her aid at that moment.

A cold wave engulfed her, and the village and the mountains slipped away. She slid into darkness, into the pit again.

His rasping voice called. "I saw you. I saw the raven, but you cannot use your power against me. You cannot defeat me." She struggled against the darkness, against the voice.

At that moment, a pain shot through her arm, and she broke eye contact. She pulled free and ran back to the compound, stopping by the wall to catch her breath. Over her shoulder, the trail was empty. Disoriented, she ducked into the dim interior of the house. She leaned against the wall and tried to control her breathing, tried to make sense of what had just happened, trying to call her spirit. But Raven did not answer.

Moments later, Li-naä's voice penetrated. "Have you seen Ha-wani?"

Ra-naä answered, "She went to look for signs of the men's return."

Ha-wani pulled herself up and made her way to the entrance. When she stepped into the sunlight, her mother-in-law gasped. "Daughter, what happened?"

Blood pumped from her wrist and dripped from her hand. There was both dried and fresh blood on her skirt. She was confused and dizzy.

Her sister, with Wichikai strapped to her breast, grabbed a skin and wrapped Ha-wani's wrist tightly. Her mother-in-law led her to the ramada and helped her sit. "What happened?"

When Ra-naä unwrapped the skin, Ha-wani stared at the deep cut on the inside of her wrist.

"I'm not sure. . . . I was out on the ridge looking for the men." She shook her head. "I don't remember—"

Li-naä applied a poultice to the cut and re-wrapped her wrist. She gave her a cup of greasewood tea and took her inside to her sleeping mat.

She awoke the next morning and lay quietly trying to piece together what had happened. She had gone to the overlook. Raven had flown among Great-Grandfather's towers and pinnacles. Another raven joined her and taught her what ravens can do. She wrapped her hand around the bandage on her wrist and squeezed, remembering Fire-Keeper grabbing her and how the pain broke his spell.

It was very like that day in Honey Bee, when she had been disoriented and confused for several days after that first encounter. *He grabbed my wrist. . . . Did he have a knife? Did he cut me? He didn't know the pain would break his spell.*

That evening, her mother-in-law examined the injury. "It's not terribly deep, but keep it wrapped for a few days, I think."

"Thank you, Mother."

"And you don't know what happened?"

She didn't answer right away. She needed to put it all together for herself first. "I'm sure, with time, I will remember."

A few days later, when she removed the wrap, Li-naä asked, "Where is your bracelet?"

The cut had closed and was healing, but, until the wrap was gone, she hadn't missed the bracelet— the beautiful shell bracelet Tonrai had made for her. *Have I lost him, too?* Her heart ached for its loss and for her husband's absence.

Fire-Keeper. Raven had been caught off guard in the exhilaration of her flight. But Fire-Keeper didn't have a knife. He didn't cut me. It was the broken bracelet* that cut my wrist. Tonrai's bracelet saved me.

Ha-wani left the walled compound, walking toward the overlook, searching the path and the scrub on each side. *Maybe I will find it. Maybe Tonrai can fix it.*

Summer flowers had finally made a quiet appearance. In years of plentiful rain, brilliant colors flooded the desert. Now, meager blue lupines stood watch over a sparse blanket of yellow poppies and pale pink owl clover. She scanned the ground around the overlook. *If I find it, I might feel the presence of his spirit and know he is coming home.*

But it was not there. She studied the open places on the trail below searching for any sign of the men. Again, she saw no one. She gazed at Great-Grandfather's massive stone towers and the deep ravines cut between them and imagined herself flying along the rugged ridge, peering into those creases and circling those towers.

A gurgling croak issued from her throat and echoed against the mountain. *Raven. I called upon my spirit, and she carried me to Great-Grandfather's heights. And Fire-Keeper saw it. Once again, he caught me unaware. He knows what I can do. If my spirit is vulnerable, I must work harder to resist him.*

Chapter 30

Short Planting Moon 1159 (August)

T hey come! They come!"
   Ha-wani's shout rang through the midmorning air. She had seen Tatanikii running along the path, but she did not wait for him. Surely, the men were not far behind. Villagers, inside and outside the compound, ran from their dwellings and surged down the path.

   Finally, they were coming home. She ran with the others, her sister behind her. Kokii's boys and Wokkai had outdistanced them. At the overlook, she stopped with several other women and waited for the men to come into sight. She glanced once at Runner, who was speaking quietly to Chief Elder. She returned her focus to the path, standing on her toes, stretching to her fullest height, hoping for the first glimpse of her husband when the group emerged from the scrub.

   Youngsters scampered down the hill and ran to meet their fathers and brothers who had been to the sea. The men shouted happy greetings to the children, dropping their baskets and waving to the women on the hill. Ha-wani scanned the enlarging group for Tonrai, afraid he was not among them. *Where is he?* Her heart stopped beating momentarily before pounding against her chest wall when he appeared on the trail. His unmistakable broad shoulders, his brown skin glistening in the sunlight. Her breath exploded from her lungs, and she shouted for joy. As the men started up the hill with the youngsters happily running in circles and shouting, she ran to meet her husband.

Tonrai swung his burden basket to the ground and swept her into his strong arms. He covered her face with kisses, and she clung to him, her heart singing words of thanks for his safe return. He pushed her away and looked into her eyes. Something fearful, something dreadful lay heavy on his spirit.

A shiver ran down her spine. "Please," she prayed, "please let all be well," fearing her life, along with the lives of everyone on the ridge, was about to change.

Knowing he would share the story of the journey as soon as he could, she asked no questions. They joined the noisy and joyful procession moving in a body toward the compound wall. Youngsters and the men who had stayed in the village relieved their fathers and brothers of their baskets. As they walked along the ridge toward the compound, Ha-wani sensed a tension among the men. She pushed it behind her and thought only of Tonrai's return. Other than the day her mother had given her to Tonrai, this was the happiest day she had known, and she desperately hoped nothing would ruin it.

When they reached the compound, she paused in her excited chatter to catch her breath. Her heart bursting with happiness, she turned, expecting to see Ra-naä and Chanu celebrating his homecoming. Instead, An-nat, like Tonrai, dusty and tired, stood talking to her sister and Li-naä, who held Wichikai. When he walked away, Ra-naä collapsed, sobbing, against her mother-in-law, who wrapped her in a strong, brown arm and wept with her.

Ha-wani looked wide-eyed at her husband, her mouth open but empty of words, hoping that, if she couldn't ask, maybe she would not have to hear it.

He could barely glance at her before looking at the ground.

Taking his hand, she said, "Tell me."

"It was on the way out . . . " When he reached for the shell bracelet with his thumb, he stopped and turned her hand over. "Where's your bracelet?"

"It broke, and I lost it. Tell me what happened."

He rubbed his thumb lightly on the raw scar. "It was on the way out. The day of the third sunrise when we arrived in the Desert of Burned Rock."* Ha-wani tried to still the fierce beating of her heart as she imagined this awesome place. For generations, her people had told stories about the frightful things that had happened to travelers and traders in this scorching land. Anyone who wanted to travel to Great Water had no choice. They had to cross it. She said nothing as Tonrai continued.

"We had not yet reached the dark mountain where travelers climb to the top* to see Great Water for the first time. We encountered a band of refugees from several days west of here. Apparently, their drought was much worse than ours. They had given up their village and, bringing almost nothing with them, were going south in search of a new homeland. They were hungry and tired, and their children and old people were dying." Tonrai's voice shook. "We tried to help them, but we had to think of our obligation to the people, to our families. We had to complete our journey."

"Yet what of your brother? Was it because of these people he has not returned to us?"

"Yes, but they were only a part of it." He took her arm and pulled her into the shadow between the house and the compound wall. It was here they had first pledged their devotion to one another.

She searched his eyes. In them, his troubled spirit reached for hers, and, although she was afraid, she forced herself to offer her own spirit, in solidarity, with him. She was wrong to have shut him out when Muumai was dying. She promised herself she would never do that again. In times of trouble, they must be one.

Chapter 31

Short Planting Moon 1159 (August)

He surveyed the village that had always been his home, took a deep breath, and allowed the story to unfold.

The small group of eight, led by An-nat, Knowledge-Keeper, carried with them only a little food— seeds in a small leather pouch attached to their wrists. Each man carried his own drinking gourd, but they carried no water. They could run for a full day without water, stopping at the traditional springs and pools each night. With luck, they would find sufficient water to quench their thirst and send them on the next day.

The first night, they found only damp sand lining the bottom of the spring. An-nat sang to the spring, digging to find a small bit of muddy water. Each man stepped forward, sang his thanks, and dipped his gourd into the ground, taking only enough to dampen his parched throat and giving a small amount back to Mother Earth in thanks. In the morning, they continued toward the dark and formidable mountains where they would surely find pools filled with water.

On the second night, the spring was dry, and, at sunrise, when they set out, each man put a pebble in his mouth to ward off thirst. On the third day, they arrived at the Desert of Burned Rock, running along a path worn smooth by travelers who had crossed this hardpan desert since before remembering. Lining both sides of the path were dark, burned, and crusted rocks, rocks that would tear their sandals to shreds if they ventured far from the trail. Each man had brought with him an extra pair, knowing they would be needed for the return trip.

At a place where another trail intersected with the one they were on, they encountered refugees traveling southward. As the group approached them, much to Amureo's displeasure, An-nat asked Tonrai to speak for their group. He stepped forward to meet the short, squatty man who appeared to be their leader.

The man sought Tonrai's eyes and squeezed the handle of the ax he carried in his sash. With the threat made clear, he spoke, "I am Ladenki, Leader of Twisted Snake Village. My people have traveled far, and they are hungry. You will give us your food."

Unlike his suffering people, Ladenki was strong. Tonrai suspected he had helped himself first to whatever food or water had been available. He stood nearly a head shorter than Tonrai, but he kept his fists clenched, flexing the hard muscles of his chest and arms, displaying enormous strength. He would be formidable in a fight. Hanging from his neck was an elaborate necklace of small blue shell beads, holding a large, blue, iridescent shell—bigger than any Tonrai had seen. On either side of the shell were two bear's teeth and bright red and yellow feathers clustered together. Tonrai had never seen a blue shell of this sort. He had only ever seen one bear's tooth, and it belonged to An-nat. Each item on the necklace was precious and rare, and Tonrai knew they represented personal wealth. Even if trading this wealth to feed his people had been possible, Tonrai suspected Ladenki was not of such generous spirit.

"We come from Onaati-Kaä, the village of the Stone Towers. We will share what we can, and our Knowledge-Keeper will sing for you, but afterwards, we must go. Our journey is long." Though Tonrai met his gaze, he kept his spirit neutral, expressing neither fear nor threat.

Each member of Tonrai's party lowered his burden basket to the ground, standing in front of it, ready to defend it, if necessary. It was not only their food that was at risk. These people would take the trade goods if they had a chance. Tonrai untied the small bag of chia and squash seeds from his wrist and offered it to Ladenki. He gave all he had brought for himself.

At this, three other men in the group—one of them Chanu—stepped forward and handed their wrist bags to Ladenki. It was a generous offer. Tonrai and the others had given up fully one-half of their remaining food supply. The rest would see them to Great Water, where, in part, they would trade for food for the return trip.

Ladenki accepted each man's gift, looking them directly in the eyes and offering no thanks. He sought to intimidate the remaining four men—those who had not offered their supplies. He brought his free hand to the pendant hanging from his neck. Almost imperceptibly, he lifted the shell from his chest as he met each man's eyes. Only Amureo reacted, narrowing his eyes and licking his lips. When he raised his eyes and met

Ladenki's gaze evenly, Tonrai knew they had made a bargain.

An-nat sang them blessings, requesting an abundance for these people and their needs. When it was done, Tonrai retrieved his burden basket, swinging it up and around his back. As he adjusted his head strap and shifted the weight of the basket into position for travel, he bade Ladenki and his people farewell and resumed his journey toward the sea. Each of his men followed suit. Tonrai sensed Ladenki's penetrating gaze following his every step.

To make up for lost time, they ran without talking. It was after dark by the time they arrived at the base of the dark mountain and found the pools. The lowest tank was dry, so again An-nat sang, and they climbed to the second tank. A shallow pool of precious water gleamed in the light of the nearly full moon. As before, each man came in turn, sang his thanks, and dipped his gourd into the dark surface, only taking enough to dampen his throat and giving a small amount back to the earth. Tradition demanded no one take more than he needed, as the lives of other travelers depended upon the water in these pools.

Amureo drank his fill.

They planned to spend the night on the eastern side of the mountain and run to the top in the morning where they would catch their first glimpse of Great Water in the distance. It had always been a critical initiation for the boys who came on trips in the past. To pass the test, they were to run to the top without stopping. Success here meant they were much closer to a declaration of manhood. Tonrai remembered his first visit and his first glorious glimpse of the sea beyond the mountain.

An-nat shared his seeds with Chanu. Amureo likewise offered seeds to Tonrai, but he refused. Because even the slightest generosity on Amureo's part would be suspect, he would have declined anyway, but he remembered what Ha-wani had said about Fire-Keeper collecting moonflowers. In his peripheral vision, Tonrai saw Hunter slip the offered bag of seeds into his basket and take out another that he ate from.

The moon was high as they set up for the night. Each man cleared the ground of rocks and stones and used them to mark his sleeping area. They settled down in the half-light of night, each inside his own circle of rocks. Tonrai kept an eye on Hunter, who seemed to focus on the darkness from which they had come. Tonrai was certain Ladenki was not far from their camp. Before Amureo lay back in his circle, he tapped his chest and smiled. Tonrai was sure that now there would be trouble.

Although he would have preferred to sleep with his head toward the sea, as most men did, Tonrai positioned himself to watch Amureo through slitted eyes. He began to breathe deeply and evenly, hoping Hunter would think him asleep. Shortly, Amureo rose, picked up his bow and arrows, and slipped into the darkness.

Before Tonrai could get to his feet, Chanu was standing and ready. He, too, had seen all. Without words, they awakened the others and warned them to be prepared for an attack. Each man readied what weapons he had and waited.

Chapter 32

Short Planting Moon 1159 (August)

Before dawn, Ledenki, along with three of his men
and Amureo, attacked." He hesitated, drawing
a ragged breath. "Amureo's first arrow found Chanu,
but before he could load another, I managed to knock
him down and throw his bow out of reach. As much as
I wanted to, I could not stop and tend to my brother. I
had to help An-nat, Tatanikii, and the others.

By the time it was over, my brother lay dead,
and Amureo was gone. Two of Ladenki's men were
dead as well. Tatanikii killed one—gutted him with
his knife—and An-nat the other. Don't ever let anyone tell you that Knowledge-Keeper is getting old;
he fought as well as any of us. One of Ladenki's men
had me down choking me when An-nat grabbed him
by the hair, pulled his head back, and slit his throat.
He saved my life." He glanced at Great-Grandfather's

rugged ridge, but Ha-wani didn't think he saw it. "It was hard on him. Nearly every night afterwards, he sat awake chanting quietly. I'm sure he'd never killed a man before, but, then, neither had Tatanikii. None of us had.

"I knelt beside my brother's body all night, talking to—" Tonrai's voice cracked, and he swallowed, but his eyes were dry. "Talking to his spirit."

While her tears flowed, Ha-wani took her husband's hand and held it to her heart. She suspected he had cried all the tears he had.

"At sunrise, An-nat sent Runner and one of the other men to find dry wood and brush to cremate my brother and the others. It was unlikely Ladenki and his people would come back to claim them, and, even though they attacked us, we couldn't leave their spirits to wander." Tonrai took a deep breath. "We had to stay there for several days. And, because we couldn't depend on our short supplies, I took one of the men, and we went hunting. We brought back a couple of good-sized lizards.

They built two pyres. One for Chanu and another larger one some distance away for the attackers. "Since we carried no coals with us, we made a fire using hand drills, lit the pyre for the men from Twisted Snake, and sang briefly for their spirits." He frowned. "It was hard. Like the other men, I didn't want their spirits to rest, to find their way out of this life. They didn't deserve it. But An-nat reminded us that they, too, were Ladenki's victims."

She touched his cheek, drawing her finger the length of one tattooed line, hating to imagine her husband preparing his brother's body for the cremation and knowing he would have to tell his parents about it when he got home.

As if reading her mind, he said, "I didn't want to believe it was real. How could I come home without him? I didn't want to see my parents' pain when they learned of his death." He went on to say that two days later, when Chanu's body was consumed, they covered his remains with rocks and prepared to continue to Great Water. The other pyre, with two men on it, would likely burn for at least two more days. "We did not stay for them."

He lifted his eyes again to the massive towers of Great-Grandfather and went on. "In the morning, before setting out for the sea, we ran to the top of the mountain and stood, our backs to the rising sun, catching our first glimpse of the grand expanse of blue water stretched out before us."

When he turned back to her, she was glad to hear enthusiasm in his voice. "Along the shore, the water is turquoise but fades into a deeper blue further out. The air hangs heavy with moisture—not thick, like here after a monsoon rain, but refreshing. You can taste the salt in the air." He ran his tongue over his lips as if remembering. "Between the mountain and Great Water, sand dunes,* pale in the morning light, stretch to the sea. Almost nothing grows in those sands. We had already passed through a desert that looked like it was made of solid rock, a desert so hard in places you couldn't dig a hole. In spite of that, trees, desert scrub, and cactus grow out of cracks in the surface. It's an unforgiving place where a man alone can count himself lucky to survive."

Ha-wani stood, rapt, trying to visualize it.

"And the mountain itself is different from these." He swept his arm from Great-Grandmother to Great-Grandfather. "It, too, is rocky, with scrub growing in cracks, but there are deep depressions,* like bowls with steep sides and rounded bottoms. This village and ten more its size could fit inside some of the largest ones."

"I cannot imagine it." If her husband were a man prone to exaggeration, she might think he was being less than truthful.

"When we reached the top . . . " He paused as if trying to find the words. "I had seen it before, but every time is like the first time. In the distance, a flock of birds took to the air from the rocks near the shore line, wheeling about over the water and diving for fish. They are strange-looking birds; they have blue feet."*

Ha-wani laughed. "You're making that up, Ton-rai. Whoever heard of such a bird?" She was glad he could make a joke after what he had been through.

"It's the truth, Ha-wani. The first time I got close to them, I couldn't believe it, and I was looking right at them." He was silent for a moment, gazing again toward Great-Grandfather. "That morning, I pointed and said, 'Chanu, look,' but he wasn't there." His dark eyes clouded, and he swallowed hard. "I don't remember ever not having my brother—"

His voice broke; he dragged his forearm across his eyes and took a ragged breath. "Finally, we moved on, without him. . . .

"We circled the mountain and set out along the dunes toward the sea. No one spoke. No one took his eyes from the sea. In silence, we ran to the water's edge, watching it roll toward us and roll away and then roll toward us again." He demonstrated the water's movement with his hands. "When Knowledge-Keeper began singing, we walked forward until the water was swirling around our feet. It was cold, but it felt good after such a long journey." He sang the song quietly, never taking his eyes from Great-Grandfather's rugged ridge.

By the sandy water I breathe in the odor of the sea,
From there the wind comes and blows over the world,

By the sandy water I breathe in the odor of the sea,
From there the clouds come and rain falls over the
world.

"We were greeted by the villagers and welcomed by their chief when we arrived at Oönaho-ara.* They are friendly and willing to trade, but we have to bargain. They don't easily give their trade goods away. They have men who actually go into the sea and dive into its depths to collect the creatures whose shells we trade for. We watched some of them work. They dive to see who can stay down the longest, holding their breath the whole time they are under water." He shook his head. "I walked into the sea up to my knees. I could feel the pull of the water as it flowed in toward the beach and then back out again. I can't imagine going in over my head."

It pleased Ha-wani to hear enthusiasm in his voice once again. It had been such a painful journey, she was glad to hear pleasant memories.

Tonrai told her they traded their goods for salt and shells, but they also collected some themselves. "Before we left, we sang songs of thanks to Father Sky and Mother Earth for giving us the gifts we would bring back to our village. I waded once again into the shallow water at the edge of the sea, hoping my feet would remember its pleasant cool as we crossed the desert going home."

On their way back, the men kept watch for Amureo and Ladenki, although they didn't expect them to stay in one place. "We found Hunter's body not far from where we were attacked. The back of his head had been smashed in." He drew in a ragged breath. "In spite of his treachery, An-nat built a pyre and sang for his spirit to find peace. After two days of watching the pyre, we covered his remains with rocks and set out for home."

While she was enchanted by her husband's descriptions of the strange land by the sea, she shared his grief. Knowing what she did, Ha-wani was not surprised by Amureo's betrayal, but she knew others in the village would be shocked. Surely, Fire-Keeper would be angry at the loss of his ally. She suspected he had enlisted Amureo to make sure neither Tonrai nor Chanu came home.

"I must go to my sister. She will need me." She took one step toward the family house group then turned back to her husband. "I'm so glad you came home to me!" She threw her arms around him, and they held each other.

Tonrai pushed her gently away. "Do you know for sure . . . I mean . . . "

She laughed. "I have missed my second visit to the women's hut, so, yes, I'm sure."

"I'm glad." He kissed her again. "I'm sorry . . . "

She put her finger on his lips. "Don't say it. We are fortunate to still have one another." She laid her hand on her still-flat belly. "This child will be a blessing."

"Go. I must meet with Chief Elder and Fire-Keeper. They will need to tell the people what happened."

They walked together a short distance, she going directly to their hut and he going on to the Council House. Ducking her head at the opening and stepping down into the dim interior, she found Ra-naä sitting on her heels before the hearth, rocking back and forth, sobbing. Li-naä sat nearby, holding Wichikai and weeping. Vachai sat on his bench holding his walking stick upright between his knees and leaning forward, resting his head on his hands. Ra-naä waited only a moment before grabbing a small pot. Rising up, she hurled it at her sister and screamed, "Get away from me!"

Ha-wani blocked the pot, which fell aside, shattering on the floor. Shocked and confused, she backed toward the entry. "Sister—" She looked at her mother-in-law.

"Go," Li-naä said softly. "I'll talk to you later."

Ashamed, Ha-wani stepped back into the sunlight. *Ra-naä knew what was in my heart. She knows I'm relieved it was Chanu and not Tonrai.*

She focused her attention on the massive tower standing in the middle of the complex assortment of stone and rock structures on Great-Grandfather Mountain. She sang a song of thanks for the safe return of her husband and a song of grief for her sister and for her brother-in-law.

She had no song for her fear of tomorrow.

Chapter 33

Short Planting Moon 1159 (August)

Tonrai joined the council in the Council House to discuss how the trip might affect the ceremonial acceptance of the gifts from the sea. Amureo's treachery was another matter.

The men's return might have meant the gods were smiling on them, but never had a trip to the sea brought evil upon them. Would the blessings be lost?

In the ramada, Ha-wani knelt at the grinding stone working mindlessly until Li-naä tapped her gently on the shoulder and handed her a basket. Neither of them spoke. Ha-wani picked out the seeds to save and small bits of stone from the flour and filled the basket.

Li-naä dragged the back of her hand across her eyes before taking the basket of flour and dropping a handful into the cooking pot, enriching the thin gruel that had become a daily staple. The ground squirrels Tarukii and Chuwii were skinning and gutting would add substance and flavor to the stew. She worked the remaining flour into a dough for bread. Ra-naä, her eyes swollen from crying, came out and sat under the ramada with Wichikai strapped to her breast. She stared silently into the flames under Li-naä's pot.

Throughout the village, everyone was busy, but the atmosphere was tense. Small children hung close to their mothers. In other years, the time between the men's return from the sea and the ceremonial presentation of the gifts was filled with excitement and joy. Now that the news of Amureo's treachery had been whispered around the village, the atmosphere was strained.

Amureo's wife stayed out of sight in her dwelling, while his son stood at their boundary, his arms crossed over his muscled chest, glaring at everyone as if daring them to say a word about his father.

The celebration would go on as planned, but Fire-Keeper and Chief Elder would likely set a subdued tone. The shaman's insistence that Amureo go on the trip would be remembered as a terrible mistake. Ha-wani wondered who would take the brunt of his anger. Because he would not be gracious in this defeat, she did not doubt that she and her family might be his target. She would pay attention to his whereabouts as much as she could.

As the sun climbed above Great-Grandmother, the village awakened and murmured "good mornings" with hesitant smiles of anticipation. However, even as they gathered in the plaza, an uneasiness spread through the community, and their anxiety increased. The ceremonial fire had been dutifully prepared, needing only the shaman to bring it to life with sacred fire and Knowledge-Keeper to sing the songs.

Finally, the men emerged from the council house, unsmiling and sober. That is, except for Fire-Keeper. While Tonrai and the council members kept their eyes downcast, Fire-Keeper held his head high and swept his gaze around the assembled villagers. There was defiance in his action, and, for one moment, Ha-wani found herself looking into his eyes. There, in the depths, his twisted spirit, deformed by hatred, writhed. His eyes came to rest on her own, and she braced herself to repel his assault, dark wings lifting. But, then, it was over.

Tonrai had walked into the space between them. She appreciated her husband's efforts to protect her, but she knew a confrontation with the shaman was inevitable. *I must never let him take me off guard again. I must be ready.*

Fire-Keeper remained on the platform mound while the council members joined their families in the plaza. He surveyed the crowd, pausing to stare at some, waiting silently for their attention. "My people," he began, his reedy voice quavering almost imperceptibly, "we are gathered to celebrate the gifts of Great Water. The seasons have turned two times since we had such a celebration." Now his voice achieved the power he had reserved for times when the people needed persuasion. Sounding like a low rumble of thunder, he said, "Great-Grandmother and Great-Grandfather will forgive you for your previous failures, and their blessings will follow."

There was a murmur among the people as some wondered if this could be true given the evil they had suffered. Tonrai bent close to Ha-wani's ear. "He takes no responsibility. I don't know what he and Hunter had planned, but I suspect Amureo's actions betrayed him, too."

Fire-Keeper's sweeping gaze silenced them. He came down from the platform mound and stood at the edge of the plaza. An-nat handed him a vessel, which he lifted toward the south. "Great-Grandfather, we honor you." Turning to the east, he sang, "Great-Grandmother, we honor you." He touched a twig to the sacred coal in the vessel. He lifted it, now flaming with the sacred fire of the people, the same fire that had ignited their fires since before remembering. He sang to the flames, thanking Mother Earth and Father Sky for this precious gift, and calling forth the spirits of Great-Grandmother and Great-Grandfather.

As the fire sprang into life, the crowd murmured its approval. It was a good sign.

But when Usareo took a seat on one side of the fire and began the ancient song that had welcomed travelers back from the sea since before remembering, he played it differently. Instead of playing the notes on his flute in quick succession, he played with a solemnity they had never heard before. Vaeleo joined him, pounding his drum slowly in time with the flute. The celebratory song had become a dirge.

Each of the men who had gone to Great Water came forward, carrying the gifts he'd brought back, and they all formed a circle around the fire. Now Chief Elder spoke, but his voice carried the same sorrow presented through the song.

"Our brothers have traveled far to bring the gifts of Great Water to the people."

At this, An-nat stepped forward and gave him a basket. Turning towards the crowd, he said, "This I offer on your behalf; you are my kinsmen." Thandoi held up the basket for all to see. He reached inside and scooped a handful of precious salt, lifting it high and allowing it to pass through his fingers back into the basket. The crowd, momentarily forgetting the dark cloud that had accompanied the travelers, murmured approval. Now that they had salt, the meat they dried would last longer.

Tonrai rose and stepped forward. He placed his basket before Thandoi, and, to the villagers, he recited the traditional pledge: "This I offer on your behalf; you are my kinsmen." Thandoi raised Tonrai's basket and lifted from it a large shell. Its iridescence glowed in the firelight. The people gasped at its beauty. Thandoi lifted handfuls of smaller shells that sang a staccato song as he poured them back into the basket.

Tonrai left the circle and joined his family, which had remained near their own family ramada, standing apart from the crowd. Vachai sat on his bench with Li-naä kneeling at his side, his hands clasped in hers. Neither could bring themselves to watch the celebration of the gifts of Great Water without Chanu.

The gifting ceremony repeated itself five times as each of the other travelers presented his gifts of more salt and shells, along with tobacco and dried fish, a delicacy they rarely enjoyed.

When all the gifts had been presented and placed in the center of the circle, Vaeleo's drum beat a steady cadence, and the music of Usareo's flute floated gently on the air. An-nat began to sing, and Fire-Keeper lifted a length of wood from the fire and swept its flaming end around and over the baskets, purifying them with the smoke of a sacred fire.

When he concluded the blessing of the gifts, Fire-Keeper picked up one basket and made his way through the crowd to An-nat's house group. An-nat followed with another basket. No-wani waited under their ramada with a pot of steaming water resting on her fire-stones. From his basket, the shaman scooped a handful of salt. Facing Great-Grandmother, he held it above the pot, and said, "We bring the sea to Onaa-ti-Kaä," and sprinkled the salt in the water.

The crowd whispered their approval. Taking the other basket from An-nat, he reached inside and lifted out a handful of dried fish. He held it up and faced Great-Grandfather. "We bring gifts of the sea to Onaati-Kaä." When he dropped the fish into the water, No-wani stirred the pot. Within moments, the aroma of cooking fish carried to the crowd, familiar to some, and brand new to others.

Tonrai took a deep breath and closed his eyes for a moment. "I had probably smelled cooking fish before when I was younger, but the first time it meant something to me was the year before my first trip. We hadn't moved into the compound yet, and, during the ceremony, my father told me I would be going to Great Water the next year. I looked at the gifts of salt and shells and fish differently because I would go and bring them back." He paused, gazing toward Great-Grandfather, but Ha-wani sensed he was look-ing at something far beyond the rugged ridge. "There is—was—less than a year between me and Chanu, and we always did everything together—our first hunt, everything. He thought he should go to Great Water too, but our father said no." Ha-wani took his hand.

He went on. "We had a fight. Not an argument. A real fight. He bloodied my face." He rubbed the thin scar on his lip. "I deserved it. I kept bragging about going and leaving him at home." He lowered his head and pinched the bridge of his nose.

Ra-naä, who had not spoken to Ha-wani since the men returned, must have heard Tonrai's story. She stepped past him, unwrapped her sleeping child from her breast, and handed her to Ha-wani. "You hold her for a while. I'm tired." She turned and went back to their dwelling.

Ha-wani stared after her sister, but when the baby stirred and searched for a nipple, Ha-wani's milk began to flow. Tonrai helped her wrap the sling while the child suckled and grunted contentedly. She laid a gentle hand on the child's head and said, "She's beautiful." A pain stabbed through her, and she thought again of her son. Tonrai wrapped a strong arm around her shoulder and pressed her to his side. Although Ha-wani wished her sister would pay more attention to Wichikai, she cherished the feeling of a child at her breast. Because Ra-naä so often passed her daughter to her to nurse, Ha-wani's milk had not dried up after Muumai's death, and her pregnancy had not had an effect on it.*

The crowd around them began to stir. It was time to taste the sea. With the drum and flute infused now with a hint of energy and celebration, An-nat invited the people, beginning with the eldest, to come forward with their drinking gourds or bowls, to dip them into the pot, and to swallow a bit of the sea, saving some to give back to Mother Earth. As each received his or her portion, each one joined the others in the singing, walking rhythmically in a circle, shuffling their feet, and preparing the ground to receive the rain Father Sky would surely send now. As the number of voices increased, the sound echoed from the mountain slopes beyond the village.

Ordinarily, after tasting the sea, the young men who had accompanied the others on the trading trip would experience the manhood ceremony. Fire-Keeper would pack tobacco into his pipe and blow smoke over each young man, welcome him as a kinsman, and wish him prowess in hunting, running, crafting, or whatever role he would assume within the village. And after the young man had climbed Great-Grandmother, spending one moon in her Wilderness World, the Huya Ania, in fasting and prayer, the parents of eligible girls could begin "courting" him. This time, though, no boys would become men.

Amureo's son, still standing where he stood when the ceremony began, barely concealed his rage. He was handsome, strong, and thick shouldered like his father. Under other circumstances, he would have had his manhood ceremony by now had there not been the drought years keeping them from Great Water or if this trip had been planned in the traditional way.

She wondered what fate the council would choose for the boy and his mother. Amureo's wife and son would bear the responsibility for Amureo's treachery.

Chapter 34

Short Planting Moon 1159 (August)

The following evening brought another ceremony, one not nearly as uplifting as the blessing of the gifts. The punishment Amureo would have received would be visited upon his wife and son.

Once again, the villagers gathered in the plaza, but this time, no celebratory fire burned; only a small one. No songs would be sung at tonight's ceremony. Amureo's wife and son sat on the ground beside Chief Elder. Hunter's wife kept her head down, her silent tears flowing. The boy, however, kept his head high. Most of the villagers were forced to avert their eyes from his. Ha-wani reached for Wokkai's hand and whispered. "Before this is over, you must take Kutareo from the compound. He will be vulnerable to that boy's anger."

"You're right." She scanned the crowd over Ha-wani's shoulder. "There he is." He was standing alone beside the compound wall behind Amureo's house group.

Wokkai wove through the crowd to take the young man's hand. Because everyone's attention was on Chief Elder and Amureo's family, no one else was likely to see them go. Ha-wani breathed a sigh of relief.

Thandoi announced the decision of the council. The boy and his mother were to be expelled from the village, but because they had not participated in Amureo's treachery, they could remain connected to the community.

"You will move from your dwelling to the rock shelter* at the far end of the agave terraces. You," he said, pointing to Hunter's son, "will maintain the check dams and keep the irrigation channels free of debris. You will not make tools or weapons, and you will not hunt."

To Amureo's wife, he said, "Your cotton field will be turned over to another family. You may make baskets, but not pottery. You may collect beans from the trees, but you will not share in the harvest of corn, beans, or squash. You will live only with the things you can carry from your dwelling in one trip and whatever you can collect from the desert. Beyond the supervision of your son's work, no one from the village will communicate with you, and you may not re-enter the compound for any reason."

Ha-wani couldn't believe they would do that to Amureo's family. It was too harsh. They had nothing to do with his betrayal. She frowned at Tonrai, her eyes asking why? Others who may have thought the punishment was too much talked among themselves.

Tonrai bent to whisper to her. "I was the only dissenting voice on the council. Fire-Keeper insisted. In that way, I guess he thought people might forget his role in sending Amureo along with us. I didn't think Chief Elder would go that far, but he ultimately gave in."

The punishment was a humiliation, but, while Amureo's wife quietly accepted the banishment with humility, the boy was furious. His father was a skilled hunter, and he would have likely achieved the same status.

He had grown tall and strong and handsome. Many thought he had a bright future—that is, if he didn't inherit his father's bullying ways. He had been eager for his first trip to Great Water and the manhood rituals. Now, there would never be a trip. There would be no wife. He would remain unmated; he would not be a hunter; he would be lower than the farmers, someone who worked for them. When Thandoi finished proclaiming their punishment, the boy stood and surveyed the elders, forcing them to avert their eyes.

"I will not be denied. You will regret this." He turned and walked, head held high, beyond the glow of firelight and into the darkness.

Among the villagers, some gasped at the boy's threat, and others muttered.

"Silence!" Fire-Keeper pounded his staff, and the crowd quieted. "This evil that has come upon us could have the power to undo what we achieved with bringing the blessings of the sea. For that reason, I will call a council of shamans from neighboring villages to determine if other villages have suffered similar issues. We must protect ourselves from the wrath of

Father Sky and restore his benevolence if we are to survive." He paused, sweeping his pale eyes across the gathered people, stopping from time to time to linger on a particular person. "And we must find the one who walks among us with an evil heart."

When he finally appeared to single out someone in the crowd, others turned to see. It was not Amureo's son he had targeted. Tonrai took Ha-wani's hand and led her through the whispering, staring crowd to their house group.

Chapter 35

Small Rains Moon 1159 (October)

After the Treachery, as it came to be known, life in the village changed, but for no one more than Ha-wani. Other than An-nat and No-wani, most villagers refused to speak to her, viewing her with suspicion, and no women other than Li-naä and Kokii ever sat with her under the ramada, weaving or making pots. No rains fell after the gifts from Great Water were celebrated. They would wait until the saguaro harvest to call down the rains unless the gathering of the shamans could offer relief.

Their arrival brought hope to the people. They came from the villages closest to Onaati-Kaä: Honey Bee and Sleeping Snake from one end of the Little Dove Mountains and Rattlesnake and Seepwillow from the other.*

Fire-Keeper had instructed the people to make the visitors welcome. Each one would bring one or two men along with him, but those individuals would not be welcome inside the Ceremonial House where the shamans would meet. Instead, they would wait in the plaza around a fire with the men of Onaati-Kaä, who were expected to make them welcome.

With so many visitors to the village, the shaman directed the women to cook a mid-day meal for them. They sent the boys out to snare rabbits, ground squirrels, and gophers, but they were remarkably unsuccessful. Even without meat for the stew, it still seemed like a festive occasion. They collected winter greens, wild tepary beans, and barrel and prickly pear cactus fruits from the desert.

While some of the women made a stew with wild greens and beans, Li-naä cooked and strained dried cactus fruits to make a sweet beverage, and Kokii used stored mesquite flour to make flat breads. While they worked, the shamans from the other villages and their escorts started arriving and gathering in the plaza.

As much as she wanted to help her mother-in-law with the food preparation, Ha-wani feared the village would reject their offerings if she did. Instead, she sat under the ramada spinning thread and watching a sleeping Wichikai.

She didn't know where Ra-naä had gone. Her sister's quiet moodiness since Chanu's death had worsened. She rarely spoke to the family and spent less and less time with her daughter, walking out in the desert nearly every day.

At that moment, a stranger approached, interrupting her thoughts.

When he stopped at the boundary and waited, Li-naä said, "You are welcome,"

"I am told I would find two women from Honey Bee here. I bring word from their parents." The man was tall and thin, but he was no one Ha-wani remembered.

Ha-wani's heart soared. "I am from Honey Bee. Are my parents well?"

"They are. Your father sent this." He handed her a small, leather pouch.

Trembling, she opened it, and, when she turned it over, two worked stone effigies dropped into her palm, one brown and one black, both birds. The black one, her spirit raven, was worked smooth and shiny with its wings tucked to its sides, a sharp beak, and indented eyes. Ra-naä's brown bird was smaller but no less detailed. "Thank you," she whispered. Taking a ragged breath, she went on. "Tell my parents we are well. My younger sister has given them a granddaughter. Her husband, though, has gone to the Flower World. I will soon give them a grandson."

"I will carry your greetings." He turned and walked back to the gathering of men.

By sundown, the visiting shamans and their escorts had gone, and the village was quiet.

In the morning Fire-Keeper called everyone into the plaza and told them the plans he and the shamans had made the day before. Ha-wani stood with Tonrai on the outside of the crowd. In fact, Vachai's whole family stood apart from the rest.

Fire-Keeper stood on his platform mound above the people and raised his staff. "Along with our neighbors in the other villages, we will make an offering to Mother Earth. Each of you, and each of the people in the other villages will offer your most precious beads, the smallest ones you have. We must impress Mother Earth by giving much back to her. By collecting the smallest treasures in the greatest numbers, we can return to her much of what we have taken from her spirit. She has been generous with us; we must be generous in return. She will be pleased and will ask Father Sky to bless us once again.

"I pledge to you that I will sacrifice even as I ask you to do so." He brought his staff down and reached up to touch the two bells hanging there. "I will offer these bells to Mother Earth."

A collective gasp went up among the people. Years ago they had learned the bells had come into his family before remembering. They had been passed from generation to generation. The mystery of where they came from and who made them went unsolved, but the bells were the most precious things the shaman owned, and the people believed they carried much of his magic.

"I have no son to pass these bells to. It is fitting that I give them to Mother Earth. Go now, and begin collecting your gifts. The Council of Shamans will gather here in five moons, bringing their gifts. Together we will honor Mother Earth. Our gifts will restore the harmony we so desperately need." He turned and disappeared into the ceremonial hut.

Beyond the agave terraces, Amureo's wife and his son had settled in the rock shelter. The boy grudgingly maintained the check dams, seeing little or no water, but he didn't care. Most nights, he slipped quietly into the granary to help himself to a bit from each of the stores. He didn't know where the sacred seeds were; otherwise, he would have taken them all. He carried away small amounts, hoping not to arouse suspicion, and, to be safe, he scattered rat droppings around the entry and occasionally tipped a basket over, hoping rodents would take the blame.

His mother never questioned his theft of grain, and, as a result, they ate reasonably well when the rest of the village often went hungry. He discovered an advantage to living in the rock shelter—no one from the village came to visit, so he didn't have to hide anything. He followed the younger boys when they went to set snares for rabbits and other small game, going back later to remove their catch, reset the snares, and erase any signs that someone had been there.

He practiced moving quietly in the dark and found he could slip in and out of dwellings while people slept, taking whatever might be of use to him. Dar's family used the vacant dwelling in their house group as storage—extra pots, gourds for Vaeleo's drums, shells, and stones for Dar's jewelry making. As a rule, Akamai kept his nighttime ventures spread out over time, taking only one thing, hoping the villagers would either not miss the item or believe they had misplaced it or, finally, believe the gods were punishing them for their failure to bring harmony back to the village. He got a fine chunk of obsidian from Knowledge-Keeper's dwelling and used it to make a knife, one of the skills he taught himself. He discovered he was far more capable than even his father had imagined.

He hunted the ridges of Great-Grandfather, ignoring Fire-Keeper's warning that the high canyons were forbidden. The bighorn sheep were plentiful, and he learned to anticipate their movements at those heights. He was careful not to be seen by the hunters from the village—although they rarely entered the high canyons he frequented. When he brought a bighorn home to his mother, she laughed. He was glad to make her happy again. They stripped and dried the meat and cured the hide, gleeful that while the village might be starving, they ate well.

And he followed the woman who often walked alone in the desert.

He studied her path, learning when she walked, where she walked, and how long it took her to get to specific places along the trail. His father had killed the husband of this woman. Now, he would make her his.

One day, when she left the compound and started down her usual path with the sun glinting off her dark hair, he was struck again by her beauty, and his need rose. He smiled, knowing it would not be long before he could put aside his self-pleasures and share pleasures with a woman. That he had never had a woman before did not deter him. He had often watched his parents. There was no mystery.

He ran through the scrub to wait for her.

Except for frequently passing Wichikai off to her sister, Ra-naä had little to do with Ha-wani. She blamed Tonrai for Chanu's death. "It should have been Tonrai who died." She said this more than once to her mother-in-law. "Why am I the one who lost my husband? Ha-wani has everything, and I have nothing."

At moments like this, Li-naä would put her hands on her hips and frown. "You have your daughter—a precious gift from my son."

More often than not, Ra-naä would pass the baby off to her mother-in-law, saying. "If she's so precious, you take care of her."

She had quit helping with the cooking, and she never joined the women to make pottery or to weave baskets. Among their people, she was free to marry again, but her behavior drove men away; apparently she didn't care. And because her sister nursed the child more than she, her own milk had dried up, something that pleased her. She took to walking along the ridge outside the compound wall and keeping to herself nearly every day.

On one of those daily walks, she rounded a turn in the path and stopped short. A man sat on a boulder beside the trail. She took a step backwards and nearly turned around.

When he did not turn to speak, she assumed he didn't know she was there. She examined this stranger, taking note of his muscular arms and strong profile. He was wearing nothing but his breechclout, his knees up and forearms resting on them as he looked out across the basin. The sun had set his brown skin glistening.

When he finally turned and met her gaze, she recognized him. "You! What are you doing here?" Her dark eyes flashed with hatred. "You're supposed to be back there in the rock shelter." She pointed.

"The sky is beautiful, don't you think?" His voice was deeper than she remembered, and he spoke softly.

She had no intention of talking to this boy whose father had killed her husband. The sky was clear and a deep blue, and she retorted, "Without rain clouds, no." She put her hands on her hips and glared at him.

"Of course, you're right. It would be nice to get a gentle winter rain."

As his eyes swept from her face to her feet and back again, she enjoyed the moment, knowing he was admiring her long brown legs, her narrow waist, and her breasts still round but not heavy with milk. He licked his lips, and her nipples hardened under his gaze.

When he probed her eyes, she opened them to him.

He slid from the boulder and stepped close, his eyes locked on hers; she could not deny the warmth spreading through her. He was narrower at the waist and taller than Chanu.

It was dangerous to be interested in this young man, but it was also exciting. Saying nothing, she started walking again.

He fell in beside her, and they walked quietly for some distance. He did not touch her, nor did he speak.

They came to a place where the path diverged, and he stopped. "I have to go down to the terraces and fix one of the dams. May I walk with you again?" He smiled, and Ra-naä was dazzled.

"Yes, I think so," she said, glancing briefly into his eyes and taking pleasure in the scandal she would create if anyone knew.

He inclined his head, saying, "I am Akamai." He smiled again and strode down the slope.

Ra-naä noted the rippling muscles in his strong legs and the careless swinging of his arms. When she started back towards the compound, she thought, "Well, it wasn't *him* who killed my husband."

Chapter 36

Small Rains Moon 1159 (October)

When the boy dropped two jackrabbits at his mother's feet, he was surprised to see her face twisted in fear. He turned. Fire-Keeper stood on the trail watching them.

"What will he do to us?" His mother was terrified.

"You mean to make our lives more miserable?" He shook his head. "I will handle him, but not here." Akamai strode down the path, calling on his spirit, Rattlesnake. He stood before the shaman, his head high and his shoulders back, meeting his gaze. "Why do you come to our place of exile? No one in the village is to come near us."

"Such rules do not apply to me." Fire-Keeper narrowed his eyes but kept them fixed on the younger man's. "I am your shaman."

Akamai scoffed. "My shaman? You are nothing to me."

"You may not speak to me like that, boy."

"You think you can tell me what I may not do? You call me 'boy' to remind me of my place? To remind me I am nothing?" He nodded in the direction of the village. "To remind me that you and those other fools are somehow in charge of my destiny?"

"Do not stir my anger, boy."

Akamai clenched his fists and stepped closer, his face inches from the older man who did not back down. "Your anger? Your anger is nothing compared to mine. You think I am not a man? It is not a trip to Great Water that makes a man. I went on my own vision quest without your blessing. I will choose my destiny. I do not need you, and I will not grovel at your feet." He stepped back and spat on the ground in front of the shaman.

Although he flinched at the insult, Fire-Keeper laughed.

Akamai had not expected that. He had challenged the shaman and should have had to defend himself. He didn't believe in the old man's magic because he had seen how often his father had helped create the shaman's illusions in the past. He stood his ground and waited.

"Your father was my man, but he chose badly. He had a job to do on that trip, and he failed to complete it."

"What are you talking about? What was he to do for you?"

The shaman waved the question aside. "He only succeeded in part before getting himself killed. He was a selfish man, thinking only of himself, caring nothing for your mother and you."

"Don't speak ill of my father." This time, Akamai stepped closer, leaned in, and circled the old man, forcing him to follow his every movement, turning with him.

"I will speak of him as I wish. If he cared for you, why did he choose to ally with those strangers? Why did he help them attack our men? If he had survived, he could not come back here unless he had killed them all. What a stupid man."

Akamai, trying to sort out what Fire-Keeper was saying, waited for him to go on.

"If he had done as I instructed, he would have come back, having seen to it that two men sickened and died."

"You mean—?" His father was to kill both Flint-Knapper and Artist. "But why would he do this for you?"

"He thought he would be Fire-Keeper someday."

That explained his father's relationship with the old man, but the "job," as the shaman put it, didn't make sense. How could his father kill two of the group without the others knowing? Akamai didn't think his father was clever enough. Amureo was, in fact, a stupid man, although he would never say it aloud. He suspected, too, the old man had no other ally in the village who would do his bidding as Amureo had done. "If you have come to me with the same promise, forget it. I have no desire to be Fire-Keeper."

"No, of course not. But we can use your exile here to our advantage."

Akamai said nothing. He was only interested in himself.

"I know you have been in and out of the compound, stealing from the granary and from the people."

"And?"

"Some are convinced the gods have turned against us. They are afraid."

Akamai smiled. "So what do you want me to do?"

"I want you to keep doing what you are doing, but if you are caught, I will not come to your defense."

He scoffed. "Don't worry about me, old man. You intend to use their fear to your advantage. But what do I gain?

"I suspect you hope to leave here and strike out on your own. I can see to it you leave with priceless trade goods."

"And where would I get 'priceless trade goods?'"

"You leave it up to me. Keep on doing what you are doing. I will tell you when you can leave and I promise you will leave a rich man."

Akamai nodded, and the old man walked away. *He will give me nothing. I do things on my own terms*

.

Ra-naä met him on the path almost daily but always where they would not be seen from the compound or by anyone who lived outside the walls. In fact, he led her far out into the desert so they would have complete privacy. He took his time, watching for Ra-naä to make the first move.

Indeed, she began to close the space between them, occasionally brushing his arm with hers; she would touch his arm and point to a hawk or another bird. He suspected she wanted to touch him as much as he wanted to touch her.

Finally, one day, before going to meet Ra-naä, he told his mother not to be surprised if he brought someone back to the shelter with him. She smiled and went back to her weaving, sitting outside with her back to the shelter opening.

At the end of their walk, Akamai took Ra-naä's hand and without saying a word, led her to the rock shelter. His mother ignored them when they approached. Inside the shelter, they lay together on Akamai's mat. She was his first, and he was pleased she used the advantage of her years and experience to teach him how to pleasure a woman.

Chapter 37

Big Cold Moon 1159 (December)

I t's true," Ra-naä said. "Just ask Healer-Woman."
    In the dim light of the women's hut, her sister sat with four other women, chattering and giggling when Ha-wani bent down, a little clumsily, to put a basket of corncakes on the floor next to the hearth.

"Are you saying she can give me something to keep me from having any more babies?" The woman sitting next to Ra-naä was the wife of one of the farmers.

"Yes. If you like your night time joinings but don't want more babies, Healer-Woman can help."

"Like them? I have been pregnant twelve times and only have five children to show for it. I almost never get to come to the women's hut. My husband is after me all the time even when I'm still sore from

giving birth. For him, rutting season is year-round."
The other women laughed.

Before Ha-wani could raise a question, one of the other women remarked to Ra-naä, "You don't have a husband—may his spirit rest easy—so why should you worry about it?"

When Ra-naä lowered her head and reached for a corncake, Ha-wani wondered, *Was that a smile? Surely not.*

"Of course I don't have to—now." Ra-naä broke off a piece of the cake and studied it before continuing. "But Healer-Woman's remedy kept me from getting pregnant after my daughter was born. I hated being pregnant, my back aching all the time, needing help getting up and down, my breasts starting to sag— look at them now." She lifted her shoulders, showing off her firm, round breasts. She pointed to the farmer's wife. "And yours. You've been pregnant twelve times, and now your breasts hang to your waist."

When the others laughed, the woman folded her arms across her body without laughing.

Ra-naä went on. "And yours, Sister. Your breasts almost reach your enlarging belly. They'll be at your waist soon. How can you look forward to giving birth again?"

Ha-wani laid her hand on her own round belly, remembering how easy Wichikai's birth had been for her sister compared to the difficulty of Muumai's birth.

"Was it really so bad?" The whispered question came from the youngest of the women, one who had only recently been married.

The farmer's wife placed a hand on the young woman's knee. "Giving birth is not as bad as she would have you think. Don't be afraid." The girl didn't look confident.

After a moment of uncomfortable silence, Ra-naä said, "Look at you, Sister, you've grown fat and round."

Ha-wani replied, "My son will be here soon."

Ra-naä scoffed. "A son? Again, you pretend to know."

"Yes, Sister, I know."

Ra-naä waved her sister's comment away. "You think you're smarter than anyone else."

Without responding, Ha-wani put the second basket of corncakes on the floor. "I will bring more food in the morning."

Outside the women's hut, she sang a song for the child she carried and for the one she had lost. On the path back to the compound, she couldn't help but think of what Ra-naä had said. She had resumed joinings with Chanu after Wichikai's birth. Maybe whatever Healer-Woman had given her worked. She had not gotten pregnant before Chanu . . . Ha-wani couldn't finish the thought.

Lost in thought, she didn't see Fire-Keeper standing in the path until she nearly bumped into him. "Oh—Fire-Keeper, forgive me." She lowered her chin, focused on his feet, and called upon her spirit. She would not let him take control again.

He stepped aside.

Without speaking, she started along the path, taking only shallow breaths in an effort to repel his fetid odor. He fell into step beside her. She focused on the grasses beside the path and on the prickly pear and barrel cactus devoid of fruit. This was a well-traveled path between the compound and the women's hut. They were stripped of fruit as soon as they ripened.

"Your child will be here soon."

She drew in a sharp breath. Only women or husbands were to speak to a woman about her pregnancy. For another man to comment on a matter so personal was rude. She stopped walking and turned toward him. "Please, Fire-Keeper, do not speak to me of matters that are no concern of yours." Inside, she felt the lift of dark wings as she met his pale eyes.

"I will make it my concern when you come to me to save yet another child."

As he returned her gaze, she shielded herself with a broad wing. "To save another child? You saved no child of mine, Fire-Keeper. Your impotent effort did nothing for my son."

"Take care, Ha-wani. I do not take rejection lightly." He leaned toward her. "Do not underestimate me."

"Believe me, I don't, but neither should you underestimate me." In his eyes, the slug writhed and transformed into the beetle with long, jointed antennae.

Raven stretched her wings, tilted her head, and peered curiously at the creature, her heavy black beak coming closer and closer, reaching toward him. In one swift movement, Raven pecked, as all birds do when an insect or worm presents itself.

At the sudden movement, Fire-Keeper jerked backward and blinked, breaking eye contact.

At the same moment, a stone bounced off the shaman's shoulder,* landing harmlessly beside the trail. Startled, he spun around, presumably looking for the person who had thrown it. When a hoarse croak sounded from above, he looked into the sky. A raven wheeled in a circle, flapped heavy wings, and dove directly at him. Fire-Keeper held his forearm across his face and ducked as the bird sailed over his head, lifted high into the sky, and flew toward Great-Grandfather Mountain.

When he stood straight, Ha-wani remained focused on his eyes.

He clearly struggled to compose himself, to restore his sense of superiority. She had won this round. He was right. She did have power.

The shaman stepped again to the side of the path and swept his arm forward, inviting her to walk on, saying, as he always did, "We will talk again, Ha-wani."

"I'm sure we will, Yukui." She heard his sharp intake of breath as she passed.

Chapter 38

Big Cold Moon 1158 (December)

Holding Wichikai in her arms, Ha-wani studied the family cluster of three huts and the ramada with its cooking area and workspace, its roof of slim-wood, and sticks. Nothing had changed. Everything had changed.

Ra-naä was gone. She was in the dwelling last night when they went to sleep, but she was nowhere to be found today. When they awakened this morning, Wichikai lay bundled on her sleeping mat alone. Ra-naä's drinking gourd, her hide wrap, her spirit effigy, and Ha-wani's extra pair of sandals were gone as well. The absence of the effigy should have persuaded Ha-wani she was gone, but Ha-wani kept hoping to find her, hoping she was just walking in the desert.

Frantically, she searched the desert on all sides of the compound. Of those who would talk to her, no one—inside or outside the compound—had seen Ra-naä.

That night, Tonrai held Ha-wani in his arms, a sleeping Wichikai nestled between them. "She's gone, my love."

Through tears, Ha-wani asked, "But why? Where would she go alone?"

"I don't know, but she hasn't been happy since Chanu died."

"She seemed more cheerful lately. I thought she was looking ahead instead of behind."

"Maybe leaving was what she was looking forward to." He stroked Wichikai's soft hair.

"But leaving her daughter? Surely she couldn't walk away from her child."

He took a deep breath. "Ha-wani. Who's been caring for her?"

Reluctantly, she admitted the truth. "Your mother. Me. But still—"

"You would still be nursing her if she hadn't quit taking your nipple."

Recently, the child had abruptly refused her breast but cried hungrily. No-wani told her pregnancy sometimes changed the taste of the milk. She advised them to wean her even though she was younger than most. Li-naä had taken over the job, and the little girl thrived.

"Do you think she went to Honeybee to see our parents? Can we go tomorrow to find out?"

"If she intended to visit them, don't you think she would have told you? Would she have sneaked out before sunrise?"

"But—"

"She's gone, my love. We are Wichikai's parents now."

Someone shouted. People ran across the plaza.

Tonrai struggled out of the dream. As he forced the cobwebs from his mind, an acrid smell registered. Smoke poured through the breaks in the back wall of the dwelling. He nudged Ha-wani, "Get up. Quick. We have to get out." He helped her up and pushed her, with the child, outside.

The granary was on fire. Behind their dwelling, heavy smoke poured through its brush walls, which quickly ignited. Within seconds flames engulfed the entire structure. Whirlwinds of orange flames spiraled into the sky, and flaming tendrils reached toward the back wall of their dwelling.

Tonrai grabbed Cheshonii and pointed. "My house is next if I can't protect it." Breaks and cracks in the exterior plaster exposed the wood and brush interior. Only an ember or two would kindle a fire that would destroy the dwelling. "Get as much as you can out."

Benai, who ran from the Knowledge-Keeper's dwelling, helped Cheshonii carry pots, jars, and baskets to the ramada, along with their sleeping mats, hides, winter wraps, and Tonrai's baskets of beads, stones, shells, and jewelry-making tools.

Cursing himself for not repairing the holes, Tonrai ran into the space between the structures where the fire-wind carried red-hot sparks toward his house. One arm up, his forearm protecting his eyes, he swatted them away and slapped those landing on the thatch, ignoring those burning his shoulders and chest. Inhaling air thick with heat and smoke, his chest hurt. Coughing and choking, he almost didn't

hear Cheshonii shouting. When the words penetrated the heat, smoke, and his desperation, he knew
he had lost the battle. Flames danced a circle around
one of the larger openings in the mud plaster. His
vision blurred and his eyes burning, he stumbled to
Ha-wani, holding a whimpering Wichikai, and held
her as their home burned.

Vachai leaned on his stick, his cheeks wet with
tears, whether from the smoke or from grief, Tonrai
couldn't tell.

Most villagers protected their own ramadas and
dwellings in case embers drifted to them. When the
brush covering on Dar's ramada ignited, Usareo and
Vaeleo knocked the burning part down and stomped
out the flames. Vaeleo suffered a severe burn on his
leg.

When the sun rose above the mountain, the granary was no more than smoldering ashes and embers
with only one support structure remaining upright.
Their dwelling had collapsed on itself, smothering
most of the flames, but still burning around the
edges and beneath the shattered roof.*

Overnight, Li-naä had struggled to breathe. She
wrapped the cloth around her face and sent Wokkai
to No-wani for the tea she needed to quiet her angry
chest.

Anu and one of the farmers brought their hoes
in the morning and dug into the ashes and embers
of the granary, spreading them out, giving them air
to burn themselves out and cool. Another day would
pass before anyone could sift through the debris to
see if any of the seeds had survived. Vachai held no
hope

Tonrai and Cheshonii combed through the debris bringing what they could to their father under the ramada. Tonrai sat with his father sorting through what they had pulled from the ashes. The smaller pots and jars broke when the platforms gave way, scattering the seeds and grain to burn on the floor. Tonrai retrieved the sacred seed jar. It was not broken.

Vachai poured some of the seeds into his hand and pushed them about with his finger, searching for any viable ones. "They do not look good."

Fire-Keeper and Chief Elder stood outside the ramada, watching.

To Vachai, Fire-Keeper said, "You are responsible for this loss." The shaman turned to Thandoi and said, "I warned you against giving him this responsibility. Now we have lost everything."

"We need to find out how the fire started before we accuse the Granary Master."

At the same moment, Anu approached the ramada. "The check dams for the agave terraces are all destroyed, and the rock shelter is abandoned. I sent someone to inspect the diversion dams down below."

"What do you mean 'the rock shelter is abandoned?'" Fire-Keeper scowled at the farmer.

Tonrai couldn't help but wonder why Fire-Keeper was more concerned about the rock shelter than the dams.

"Amureo's wife and son are gone. The shelter has been cleared out and whatever they left has been thrown on the trash heap. He took an ax to the dams."

"An ax? He was not supposed to have an ax." Thandoi frowned.

"He was not supposed to have a lot of things, and he was not supposed to hunt, but from the number of

bones on the trash heap, he's been hunting plenty."
Anu turned to Vachai. "Have we lost everything?"

"I'm afraid so. The sacred seeds are lost, too."

Fire-Keeper scowled. "This is your fault. You will
pay for this." He turned and stalked away from the
group.

Thandoi turned to the others. "I think we know
who started the fire. We were wrong to punish him
and his mother as we did."

Tonrai shook his head. "Perhaps, but the boy was
too much like his father. We would have had trouble
with him in any case."

The smell of smoke and ash lingered over the village, and no wind rose to blow it away.

At the council meeting, Chief Elder invited Vachai to
report on the losses.

"All the seeds for the next planting are lost. We
recovered the sacred seeds, but they are parched.
They will not serve the shaman's needs."

For the first time, seeing Vachai leaning on his
stick before the council, Tonrai realized his father
had become an old man.

"The corn from the last harvest was laid out on
the drying platforms." Vachai's voice shook. "We have
squash to harvest yet, but we will depend on the desert to feed us for a while."

Thandoi's mouth tightened into a thin line. "Thank
you, Granary Master."

Tonrai stood and helped his father out of the
Council House and off the platform mound. He limped
across the plaza, his head down.

Back inside, Tonrai returned to his seat on the floor. The conversation had continued without him.

"And you think the boy started the fire?" Dar scratched his chin with a knotted finger. Tonrai had not noticed how bad his hands had become. No wonder he didn't make jewelry any more.

"We think so," Thandoi said. "There's no other explanation."

Up to this point, Fire-Keeper had been uncharacteristically silent. Now, he stood. "I have warned you the gods would abandon us, and once more we have failed to restore harmony." He pointed his staff at Tonrai. "There are those among us who have brought these misfortunes upon us."

Tonrai frowned. "Are you saying I brought trouble to our village, Fire-Keeper?"

"You brought her here. You and your father brought both of them here—those women from Honey Bee. They are the reason the gods have turned against us."

Tonrai narrowed his eyes but kept his voice low. "I would remind you our troubles started long before my wife and her sister arrived here." He stood, his fists clenched at his sides.

Fire-Keeper glared into Tonrai's eyes, but Tonrai held his gaze and took a step toward the older man. Chief Elder held up his hand and shouted, "Enough. I will not tolerate this behavior in the Council House. Looking pointedly at Tonrai, he said, "You will sit and make no additional threatening moves toward Fire-Keeper."

"Forgive me, Chief Elder." Tonrai returned to the floor, but he did not turn his eyes away from the shaman.

To Fire-Keeper, who remained standing, Thandoi said, "You will explain your accusation."

"We have concluded Amureo's son torched the granary. I believe Tonrai's sister-in-law helped him."

An-nat spoke up. "Surely you are wrong. Amureo was responsible for her husband's death."

"She took up with the boy some time ago. They have been sneaking around together, and she has been seen going into the rock shelter with him. With his mother sitting outside."

Tonrai closed his eyes. Ha-wani's heartbreak would be intensified by this revelation.

Dar spoke up. "Bring her to us. Demand an explanation. If what you are saying is true, she must be punished."

Dar appeared angrier than Tonrai had ever seen, but when a look passed between him and Fire-Keeper, he understood. The shaman had a new ally. Dar had always been a man of honor, a man Tonrai admired, from whom he had learned so much. Now, with his hands knotted and twisted, he had lost the skill that was his source of pride. Perhaps the shaman had taken advantage of his vulnerability now that he had little else to offer the village.

Tonrai stared at the hearth and said, "She's gone."

"Gone?" Thandoi's head jerked up. "What do you mean?"

"We haven't seen her since the day before the fire. If what Fire-Keeper says is true, it's likely she left with Amureo's son and mother."

After a moment of silence, An-nat laid his hand on Tonrai's shoulder. "And her daughter?" It was no secret among the villagers that she cared little for her child.

"Her daughter is here. With my wife."

Thandoi spoke. "Which brings us back to Fire-Keeper's original charge. Do you also accuse Tonrai's wife?"

Fire-Keeper smiled. "She has magic. She could destroy us all if we are not careful. She attacked me more than once. Fortunately, my magic is stronger. I—"

Tonrai interrupted. "My wife has no magic."

Thandoi raised his hand, palm out. "Let Fire-Keeper speak." He nodded to the shaman to continue.

"I don't have to remind you we have been denied sufficient rain after these women came here. When did we last have a good, drenching rain fall on the village?"

Knowledge-Keeper ran a finger down the calendar stick. "Over a year ago. The wind blew our ramada roofs away. We thought our long wait was over, but the rain stopped abruptly. We haven't had such a rain since."

"Exactly. I conjured that rain." The shaman began to pace around the dim room, the fire casting his shadow against the walls above the hunched shadows of the council. "It could have saved us. It signaled the end of our suffering. I had eaten nothing for three days while I sang to Father Sky, urging him to bring us rain. I pushed myself to the limits of my power, knowing I might have died."

At moments, his shadow appeared disconnected from him, its movements somehow divorced from his own. When he swept his arm upward, the shadow's arm did not follow right away. Tonrai glanced at Dar, who was watching the shadow, fear written all over his face.

Tonrai stared into the fire, doubting the old shaman had brought rain any time. *Could anyone remember what the fire-keeper had done in the days before that day? Unlikely.*

"When the rain was at its heaviest, I stepped out of my dwelling, intending to go to the center of the plaza to celebrate, to thank Father Sky for sending the rain and to sing for more. Your wife stood in the middle of the plaza." He pointed again at Tonrai.

"If I recall, she went out to look for my sister."

"You recall nothing. She was looking for no one. She stood in the center of the plaza, her arms upraised, singing a song. The words of her song disturbed me.

> *I am not the enchanted light blue cloud**
> *I am just the black cloud blowing under.*
> *I am moving over there.*
> *I, on the flower-covered distant earth,*
> *I am here and going there*
> *I am just the black cloud blowing under.*
> *I am moving.*

"I had never heard that song before. While she sang, she pointed to the north, commanding the rain to leave us. When she stopped singing, the rain stopped falling on the village and raced across the desert to quench the thirst of other villages. Then she pointed her finger at me. I felt like I had been slammed by sky fire. Her voice pierced me like an arrow when she said, 'Stay away from me. If you challenge me, I will destroy you."

Chapter 39

Animals Get Lean Moon 1160 (January)

You never told me about your encounter with Fire-Keeper during the storm last year." Li-naä's words startled Ha-wani. Some time had passed since Tonrai had told the family about Fire-Keeper's accusations against her.

When Tonrai came back from the council meeting, he sent Wokkai to An-nat's house group to ask permission for Benai to come home for the night. Cheshonii, Kokii, and her younger boys joined them in Vachai's dwelling. They were crowded around the hearth, but

Tonrai didn't think they should talk in the ramada where others may hear.

"I'm sorry I have brought trouble to the family." Ha-wani struggled to hold back tears.

"Nonsense." Vachai held up his hand. "You have brought no trouble on us."

With Wichikai sitting in the cradle of her crossed legs, leaning against her enlarged belly, Ha-wani said, "I cannot deny the trouble my sister has caused."

When she stroked Wichikai's head, the child turned around and wrapped her little arms around Ha-wani's round middle. "Mama?"

Now, her tears fell freely. Ha-wani smiled at the child. "I'm right here, Daughter."

Tonrai put his arm around her shoulders and pulled her against him.

Li-naä wiped a tear and asked, "Why has Fire-Keeper singled you out like this?"

"Before my sister and I married Chanu and Tonrai, I had a disturbing encounter with him at Honey Bee." Tonrai registered surprise. He loosened his embrace and let her sit up straight. "It frightened me, but, when my father arranged our marriage, I put it aside." She continued to stroke Wichikai's head, and, although the child struggled to keep her eyes open, she fell asleep against Ha-wani's belly. "I had seen him with our Fire-Keeper. I assumed he was a shaman from a neighboring village, but I didn't know which one. When we arrived here and he greeted me, I was terrified."

"I remember. You nearly fainted when you met him. You never told me about meeting him at Honey Bee." Tonrai took her hand.

"I had gone to greet the dawn wind. As always, I sang and closed my eyes to await the sun's first kiss, and, when I opened them, he was standing before me." She shook her head, trying to dismiss his image.

"When I asked him what he wanted, he said he was looking for a wife with a powerful spirit. He wanted me for his wife."

Wokkai slid closer to her mother, who absently put her arm around her daughter, saying, "I never imagined how powerful he must think your spirit is."

She exchanged a glance with Wokkai. "He locked his eyes on mine, and I could not break eye contact. I found myself in a pit. There was no way out. His spirit surrounded me, attacked me, and, when I thought I was lost, Raven lifted me out of the pit and freed me from his grip."

"He was testing you?"

She nodded. "I think so. I had not yet been marked, so I lied and said I was not yet a woman." She touched the lines on her chin. "When I told him my father would choose a husband, he used my name, and I was shocked, but my spirit had defended me, so I shouldn't have been surprised. Before he walked away, he said 'You will be my wife.'" I was terrified for days, but then my parents told me that Ra-naä and I would marry two young men from Onaati-Kaä. I put the shaman's threat out of my mind."

Tonrai nodded. "That's why you thought he had at least some magic? You were right. During our council meeting, I saw a bit of that magic myself."

"If he could close me in a pit like that, I wasn't sure what else he could do."

"And since you've been here, he has continued to intrude on your spirit?" It was the first time Kokii spoke.

"Yes. Sometimes, Tonrai has protected me by stepping in the line of his gaze, but I have found, more often than not, I am capable of repelling his intrusion when we meet."

"Which only persuades him he is right, and, now, he must either capture your spirit or destroy you."

Cheshonii, who was a man of few words, summed it up for the group.

Li-naä glanced from one to the other, "What should we do? How can we help?"

"For now," Vachai said. "We must protect one another. Don't forget Fire-Keeper was responsible for the deaths of my brother, my son, and this." He swept his hand along his thigh. "I do not doubt that Amureo was acting on his orders."

Now, under the ramada, Ha-wani needed to tell her mother-in-law what Wokkai had asked her not to. "I didn't tell you about the encounter. And I didn't tell you where I found Wokkai that day."

"What do you mean?" Li-naä lifted a jar of stew from the firebox and put on the flat griddle-stone for Kokii's breads.

"Do you remember what happened when I brought her home?"

"She ran into my arms and cried. I thought she was afraid of the storm. But that wasn't it?"

"No. I encountered Fire-Keeper in the plaza, but I did not sing to the rain nor did I send it away. But I did tell him to stay away from me." She hesitated. "I also told him to stay away from my family."

Kokii looked up from flattening the dough for the griddle, one eye looking toward Ha-wani and the other aimed over her shoulder. "You spoke to Fire-Keeper like that?"

"Wokkai was in his dwelling."

Kokii's mouth dropped open, and Li-naä pressed her hand to her chest. "In his—"

"When she came out, she was confused and upset. She told me later what he did to her."

"What he did—" A dark cloud passed within Li-naä's eyes. "Why didn't she tell me?"

"She didn't remember it until later. And she asked me not to tell you."

"Once again, my daughter turns to you instead of me."

Ha-wani again recognized the hint of resentment in her mother-in-law's tone. "I'm sorry, Li-naä, but he may think Wokkai, too, has a powerful spirit. If she does, she has not yet learned to control it."

"Actually, there may be something else behind his interest in my daughter."

"In any case, I fear he will turn his attention to her if he is convinced I will never yield to him."

Chapter 40

Deer Mating Moon February 1160

The fragrance of roasting agave* floated in the air, stirring a confident hunger in Ha-wani. She had not had much of an appetite as her pregnancy advanced, but today the agave smelled good. The villagers would eat well for as long as the agave lasted. And they were hopeful their misfortunes would be reversed when the shamans came to prepare their offering to Mother Earth, who would bring the blessings of Father Sky.

The day was cool and the sky was clear. Anu and Cheshonii had prepared the ceremonial pit oven in the plaza days before, layering rocks at the bottom and building a fire on top of them. When the wood was burned to coals, they layered agave leaves over the coals and laid three agave hearts in the pit. More agave leaves covered the hearts, and the pit was filled with sand. Out on the terraces, four additional pit ovens were being prepared, and roasting would be phased in over a number of days to extend the agave distribution to the people. When the agaves had been consumed, Hungry Time would be upon them.

In the evening, when Anu opened the pit oven, the people gathered with their bowls for the feast. Families joined other families under their ramadas, and small children curled up on the ground near their parents and slept—their hunger, along with everyone else's, satisfied.

With the exception of Anu's family, most villagers avoided contact with Ha-wani and rarely spoke to her. Anu brought his family inside to eat under Vachai's ramada. Sochik's second child, a boy, was close to Wichikai's age; they played together, chattering in a language known only to toddlers and testing the ability of the adults to catch them before they wandered off. Wokkai took charge of them for their mothers, especially because Ha-wani was heavy with child and back pains plagued her.

Anu's daughter, Ma-taä, and Cheshonii were clearly in love, but they had no hope of marrying until he could go to Great Water. Ha-wani could see how the tradition was unfair to young men like him and Kutareo.

Tonrai brought her a bowl of roasted agave, but she had lost her appetite. Her back pains had increased, and she was miserable. She asked him to help her inside to lie down. Before they reached the entry, she stopped and bent over. A powerful contraction slammed through her, and she felt the baby pushing.

She caught her breath and said, "He's coming!"

The women under the ramada sprang into action, while the men simply stared. Sochik grabbed her son, and Wokkai passed Wichikai along to Ma-taä before she dashed out of the ramada to get No-wani.

Li-naä and Mochik escorted Ha-wani to the women's hut, stopping several times along the way to wait for a contraction to pass. Inside, two wide-eyed young women were waiting out their first time there. They scrambled back against the wall in silence.

While the women lowered Ha-wani to the mat, Wokkai rushed in carrying a water jar. "Healer-Woman is right behind me." To Anu's wife, she said, "Would you mind building up the fire and warming the water?"

Li-naä knelt behind Ha-wani, massaging her shoulders, saying, "Relax. Breathe. Don't push yet."

Wokkai knelt between Ha-wani's legs and panicked. "The baby's coming. Where is No-wani? She was behind me."

Mochik dashed out the door while Wokkai splashed the cold water over her hands.

A massive contraction gripped Ha-wani, who clamped her jaw tight, groaned, and pushed. Wokkai had no choice but to catch the child as it came into the world, wet, slippery, and howling. She grinned but waited through another contraction as Ha-wani expelled the afterbirth.

When the new mother began to breathe easily, she leaned back against her mother-in-law and closed her eyes.

Wokkai waited until she opened them and announced, "My brother's child, born this day, is a boy." She laid the baby on Ha-wani's belly and stared at the placenta and afterbirth, trying to remember what to do. *Where is No-wani?*

With both hands, Ha-wani caressed the child, who continued to cry and flail his arms and legs.

Finally, Mochik brought No-wani through the entry. Her knees were bloody, and she was holding her arm against her body, grimacing in pain. "She fell. She thinks her arm is broken."

Mochik helped lower Healer-Woman to the floor where she could lean against an upright post with her legs stretched out. When she caught her breath, she surveyed the scene before her and said, "Did you clear the baby's mouth?

Wokkai shook her head.

"Do it, Girl. Don't you remember anything?"

Wokkai retrieved the infant and ran her finger around the inside of his mouth before handing him back to his mother, who caressed his small head and back, smiling through her tears.

Wokkai looked over her shoulder at the old woman. "What do I do now?"

"You'll find a knife in my bag. Dip it into the water, and cut the cord about this far from the baby's belly." Using her thumb and forefinger, she showed the girl the length.

Wokkai turned the child toward her and struggled to cut into the tissue. The boy had quit crying. He seemed to be watching her every move. "I'll try not to hurt you," she whispered to him. When she finished, blood trickled from the short length of cord still attached to the infant. "It's bleeding."

No-wani pointed to the hearth. "Pull a stick out of the fire, blow the flame out, and press it against the end of the cord."

Wokkai pressed Ha-wani's legs farther apart so she wouldn't burn her, and, with a shaking hand, she took the cord between her thumb and forefinger, cupping her palm beneath it. She didn't want to burn the child or Ha-wani with a wayward ember. She jumped when No-wani spoke.

"Don't wait. Do it."

She squeezed the cord and pressed the hot stick against the end, hearing the sizzle and breathing in the odor of burning flesh.

"Now get a clean cloth from my bag, and wash the child. And you'll have to take care of burying the afterbirth."

Wokkai washed the baby, but she wished she had done a better job bringing it into the world. *It's not my fault she fell.* She tried to hold back her tears.

When the child was clean and wrapped tightly in deer hide, Li-naä lowered Ha-wani's shoulders to the floor and nestled the child in her arms, helping him find the nipple. They laughed tearfully when he latched on and began sucking greedily.

Wokkai sat back on her heels and, with her head down, spoke quietly to the old woman. "I'm sorry."

No-wani frowned. "For what?"

"I did everything so badly." Her lower lip quivered, and she wiped her tears with the back of her hand.

"By the gods, girl. What makes you think you did badly?"

"You said—you—" She didn't want to suggest No-wani had been rude. She couldn't find the words.

"Because I scolded you? I talk mean when I'm in pain. And this is truly painful." She pointed to a bump in her forearm.

"I'm sorry. Is there something I can do?"

"The birthing is out of the way, so you and she," she nodded toward Mochik, "can fix this for me."

Wokkai's eyes widened. "How?"

The old woman explained how Mochik should hold her from behind, keeping her upper arm tight against her side while Wokkai gripped her hand and pulled. For the girl, this sounded worse than helping Ha-wani's baby into the world, although Ha-wani's baby did it all by himself. When they were ready, the old woman told them, "Once you start pulling, don't quit, even if I scream, don't quit. When you hear it pop, we've set it aright. And you can put a splint on it."

Anu's daughters, Sochik and Ma-taä, with the children sleeping in their arms, waited under the ramada with Tonrai and Cheshonii when Mochik brought No-wani back to her dwelling.

Tonrai met her between An-nat's house group and theirs, and Mochik smiled. "Your wife and your son are both fine."

He breathed out, realizing he had been holding his breath. One milestone reached. Now, he prayed to the gods: *Let him grow to be a man.*

At the ramada, Mochik smiled at her daughters. To Tonrai, she said, "Your mother and your sister will stay with your wife tonight."

When Sochik stood, her son automatically wrapped his legs around her middle and put his head on her shoulder. "What happened to No-wani?"

"She fell and broke her arm, but she will be all right. She's a tough one."

"On her way back from the birthing?" Sochik stroked her son's back.

"No. She did not get to the women's hut until after Tonrai's sister delivered the child."

"Wokkai delivered my son?" His momentary disbelief turned quickly to pride, and his smile was wider than they had seen in some time.

Mochik turned to her older daughter and said, "I'm exhausted. Let's go home and put the boy to bed." To Ma-taä, who was still holding a sleeping Wichikai, she said, "You stay here tonight. That child needs loving arms around her." She nodded to Cheshonii, who was standing behind her younger daughter. "Your mother will understand."

Chapter 41

Green Moon 1160 (March)

When the sun stick cast no shadow, the shamans began to arrive with their escorts. After the first gathering, each of the shamans recruited others from other villages throughout the desert basin.* This time, there were no less than thirteen shamans, each one bringing from four to seven escorts.

The people of Onaati-Kaä, like those in the other villages, had collected the beads from matrimonial ribbons, from sashes and belts, from hair pins, and from anything they had ever decorated with tiny red, black, and blue beads. Each shaman would contribute on behalf of his village, promising the villagers that the gods would reward them for their gifts.

Kutareo had prepared a structure in the center of the plaza for the ceremonial fire, one larger than the village had seen for a while. Usareo and Vaeleo sat on either side welcoming the visitors with flute and drum. Today, because of the lack of sufficient water, Vaeleo had no water in the bigger gourd basin to moderate the sound of the half-gourd he used as a drum. He depended on striking it at different spots and using the rim and sides of the basin to vary the sound. An-nat, with Benai at his side, sat ready with his calendar stick, recording the arrival of the guests. Benai scraped a rasp in time with the flute and drum.

Each arriving group took places around the fire, looking cautiously at the others. All the visiting shamans carried staffs with feathers and tinklers, but not all of them had bells like Fire-Keeper's. Their faces, chests, and arms were painted in bright colors. From under the ramada, Ha-wani observed each had one or more men standing close, not watching them, but watching everyone else.

"I wonder if some of our visitors have reservations about cooperating with shamans they might never have met." Li-naä stood with Kokii and Wokkai, as the crowd of men continued to grow larger.

"I suspect some are rightfully concerned, especially about our own shaman." Li-naä grunted as she hefted the jar of stew to take to An-nat's house group, where the food would be made available for the guests.

Kokii joined Li-naä, carrying a basket of flat breads for the feast.

Wokkai turned to her sister-in-law. "You told my mother about what Fire-Keeper did." It was not a question.

"I did. I could not lie to her when she asked."

"I wanted to protect her from the truth." She wrapped her arms around her middle as if shielding herself from the memory.

Ha-wani smiled. "That is so like you, Sister. But we need to be prepared. I'm not sure of these other Fire-Keepers, but ours will do anything to enrich himself. He will not leave these treasures in the ground for Mother Earth. He has persuaded the others, but he has not persuaded me."

"What can we do?"

"I have a plan."

An impressive crowd of men had gathered on the plaza by the time Fire-Keeper came out to welcome them. No women had accompanied the visitors, and the women of Onaati-Kaä stood apart, watching from their ramadas.

Fire-Keeper held his staff high, signaling for silence. He passed his staff to Dar, who handed him a bowl. Each of the visiting shamans stepped forward. Kutareo had stacked short lengths of wood for the ceremonial fire in alternating layers in the center and had leaned long branches and logs against the stack, building a pyramid taller than the tallest man there. He had filled the spaces between the outer lengths of wood with dry leaves and thin strips of kindling.

When all of the shamans were in place, Fire-Keeper lifted the bowl above his head and shouted, "We light this fire to honor Mother Earth. We ask her to carry this blessing to Father Sky in her smoke. May he bless us in return."

The shamans repeated his words in unison, handed their staffs to their attendants, and knelt to place sacred coals from their own villages in the wood structure. They reclaimed their staffs, which they held high as the fire spread through the pyramid. Soon the wood was blazing, and Usareo, Vaeleo, and Benai played their instruments in rhythm with the crackling, rushing, song of the flames.

Watching from the ramada, Wokkai smiled. "No one builds a fire better than Kutareo."

Li-naä put an arm around her and sighed. "Once again, your matrimonial ribbon is delayed. I started a new one, but I've given your beads to the collection. Your sister-in-law gave the beads from hers and from her sister's ribbon."

"I don't mind, Mother. Like you said, I am in no hurry."

Ha-wani had wept when she took the beads from Ra-naä's ribbon, remembering the day her father had bound her and Ra-naä to Tonrai and Chanu. She would redecorate her sister's ribbon one day for Wichikai.

"I'm not sure we can put it off much longer. Your father mentioned it was past time to send Tonrai to Honey Bee to see about finding you a husband."

"Then you haven't told him about my desire to marry Kutareo?"

Li-naä sighed. "Not in so many words, but he is not blind. He sees you with him and has begun to worry. The boy is not permitted to marry."

The girl hesitated. "What would he say if—if—" She seemed to have trouble saying it. "—if Fire-Keeper asked for me?"

"Fire-Keeper? Child, don't even think that."

"He wanted Ha-wani, but, now that he knows she will never agree, he has turned against her. What if he comes after me again? If he thinks I have a strong spirit, will he come after me?" She began to cry.

Li-naä put her arms around her daughter and held her. Then she stepped back, holding her daughter's shoulders and bending to meet her eyes. "Never, Wokkai. He didn't get the wife he wanted many years ago, and he will never have you."

In the plaza, the shamans stopped shuffling around the fire and squatted or sat cross-legged.

Fire-Keeper welcomed the visitors and announced that the collection of treasures would commence with the contributions of Onaati-Kaä. Dar handed him a pot. He held it aloft, his rasping voice carrying through the village, grating on Ha-wani's ears. "We agreed to offer Mother Earth the smallest gifts of our hands, gifts she gave us, gifts adorning our persons, gifts honoring our Mother each time we wore them. By choosing the smallest, we can offer the greatest number of gifts." As he poured the beads from the pot into a bowl, the crowd murmured with approval.

He put the bowl and the pot on the ground at his feet and reached for his staff. He cut the bells loose and held them up. "These bells are from before remembering. They have been passed through countless generations in my family. They are my most precious possession."

He held them to his lips for a moment and dropped them into the bowl. Some of the watching shamans gasped.

"Come. Bring your gifts." He held the bowl before him as shaman after shaman came forward.

Each poured his gifts into the bowl, saying, "We honor you, Mother Earth, and ask your blessing." Several shamans who had bells on their staffs, perhaps moved by Fire-Keeper's generosity or feeling pressured to match his gift, removed the bells and dropped them into the bowl.*

When the collection was complete, Fire-Keeper poured the treasures into the pot and laid the bowl over the top. While the shamans took the offering to the desert, their companions and escorts remained around the fire, enjoying a meager feast of bread and stew.

Watching the shamans file out of the compound behind Fire-Keeper, Ha-wani turned to Wokkai. "Are you ready?"

The colorful and impressive procession left the compound and followed the path off the ridge with Fire-Keeper in the lead. They crossed Elder Brother Wash, walking in single file, each holding his staff aloft with feathers flying and tinklers dancing. There were, however, no bells singing.

Cheshonii, Anu, and the other farmers, weeding the fields in preparation for a lean planting of the sister crops, stopped their work as the shamans passed by. The people had contributed all of the seeds they had in their personal stores after the granary burned. A good harvest would restore the seed supply rather than feeding the people. They would continue to depend on the generosity of the desert to keep from starving.

As the shamans passed the brush house where Nothai and Vachai's families had waited after the accident coming down from Great-Grandmother's pools, a flock of doves fluttered up from the path, scattering noisily in the brush. Overhead, a pair of red-shouldered hawks circled, waiting for rabbits or other small creatures to run into the open when the procession passed by. A curved-bill thrasher whistled at the intruders, and mockingbirds dodged from tree to tree with flashes of white. Bean and green stick trees had begun to blossom, but for now the desert had not turned golden.

When the trail diverged, going down to the bean tree grove and the rock mortars, the group went the other direction, following the trail upward, climbing a long hill. At the top, surrounded by desert scrub and brown, dry grasses, with Great-Grandmother at his back, Fire-Keeper pointed to the west with his staff. In the distance, the expanse of Little Dove Mountains marked the locations of the closest villages. Honey Bee sat at the southern end, with Sleeping Snake beyond. Rattlesnake sat near a small canyon a little north of mid-range, with Seepwillow at the far northern end. The rest of the shamans, no doubt, could see features identifying their homes. Onaati-Kaä, of course, lay between them and Great-Grandfather. Here, at the top of this hill, in sight of their villages, they would offer gifts to Mother Earth, imploring her to act on their behalf to secure blessings from Father Sky.

Around them, doves foraged in the dry grasses, searching for seeds and insects, while ravens cartwheeled and called above them in the pale sky.

Fire-Keeper held the pot up, standing beside a hole he had prepared earlier, and sang.

Mother Earth
Hear us
We bring you gifts
Returning that which you gave us
Shaped now by our own hands
Mother Earth

Hear us
Bless us with the waters of life
Bless us with the waters of life

The other shamans joined in, their voices lifting into the sky, carrying across the desert to their people, and bonding their gifts to the earth.

Fire-Keeper knelt and placed the pot in the hole. He lifted the bowl that covered it, and each shaman, one after the other, turned and lifted his staff to his own village, pledging their gifts would bring the blessings they sought.

After they covered the hole, wrapping the gifts in Mother Earth's bosom, the shamans silently filed off the hill and back to Onaati-Kaä, the visitors then collecting their escorts and leaving the compound. The sun, sliding behind thin clouds forming in the west, turned the sky gold before shifting into red and painting Great-Grandfather and Great-Grandmother with a crimson glow. A single raven circled above as they followed the trail away from Onaati-Kaä

.

Chapter 42

Green Moon 1160 (March)

Ha-wani came out of the dwelling with the infant strapped to her breast and Wichikai on her hip.

"Let me help you." Ma-taä reached for Wichikai, who giggled and wrapped her arms around the girl's neck.

"Thanks. She's getting bigger every day."

"And your little one? How's he doing?"

"He's fat and happy. The gods have blessed me." She suppressed her inclination to add, "this time." She suffered the same pain each time she thought of Muumai. It had eased somewhat with the coming of Mocho-okoli, who was thriving—at least for now.

They joined Kokii and Li-naä under the ramada for breakfast. Ma-taä sat with Wichikai in her lap, and Kokii handed her a flat bread and a small bowl of gruel. The child took the bread, dipped it into the bowl, and bit off the soft edge.

Kokii went back to the fire to put more flat bread on the griddle rock. "Did my son stop at your dwelling this morning?"

"Yes. He and my father went to the terraces together."

As Ha-wani switched her baby from one breast to the other, she glanced up. Fire-Keeper stood at the boundary. Li-naä stepped between him and her daughter-in-law. "Is there something I can help you with, Fire-Keeper?" Her voice carried her dislike of the shaman.

"No." Frowning, he spun and walked away.

He went to the sun stick and swept away yesterday's shadow markings.

The day was clear and cool. Thin clouds floated over the mountains to the west and over Great-Grandmother, but it was doubtful that many saw hope in them.

"He wants to talk to me," Ha-wani said, unwrapping Mocho-okoli and handing him to her mother-in-law.

"Are you sure you want to talk to him?"

"I'll be fine. I will talk to him in the plaza, in full view of everyone."

Instead of crossing the plaza in a straight line, as the shaman had done, she swung around in a wide circle past Chief Elder's house group, greeting him and his wife with a simple nod. At An-nat's group, where Dar's family also lived, no one—with the exception of No-wani—offered a glance in her direction. She stopped at the boundary with her eyes down.

"Good morning." No-wani was under the ramada cooking breakfast. Her broken arm was still in a splint and strapped to her side.

"Does your arm still give you pain?"

"Not so much, but it remains weak. I fear it will never be quite the same again. How is your son?"

"He seems to be thriving." In her peripheral vision, Ha-wani knew Fire-Keeper was watching. She enjoyed thinking he was annoyed.

"I'm glad. If you need anything for him or his sister, don't hesitate to ask."

"How is my husband's brother?" Benai was still training with Knowledge-Keeper.

"He is a bright boy. My husband took him across the terraces to the base of Great-Grandfather for stories about the mountains."

"I'm on my way to speak to Fire-Keeper," she said, knowing the old woman would watch every move. "I wish you a good day."

When she stood before Fire-Keeper, her eyes cast downward, focusing on his bony toes, she said, "Good morning, Fire-Keeper. The gods have blessed us with a sunny day. May we hope those thin clouds bring us rain?"

"What did you do with it?" He sounded as if he were speaking through a clenched jaw.

"With what?" She noticed his second toe was longer than the big one.

"Don't play games, Ha-wani. Where is it?"

After the shamans presented their offering to Mother Earth and started back to their villages in the glow of a red sunset, Wokkai entered the compound and joined her mother under their ramada. Moments later, Ha-wani entered from the other side, pausing to glance at the wreckage of the granary and what had been her home since she married Tonrai. She gave her mother-in-law a basket of desert greens in exchange for her son, strapping him to her breast. When Mocho-okoli latched on to a nipple, Ha-wani breathed a sigh of relief. "I needed this." She caressed the boy's head, smoothing the thick, dark hair. "The plaza is back to normal after Fire-Keeper's big ceremony."

Li-naä dropped a handful of greens into a steaming pot. "Yes. The shamans and their noisy escorts are gone, and the children are back outside running and playing. I much prefer the noise of the children."

Ha-wani laughed. "So do I." In the plaza, Chuwii and Chief Elder's youngest boy were chasing Builder's girls, who were squealing with delight.

Stirring the stew in the pot, Li-naä asked, "Do you think this offering to the gods will bring us rain?"

"I would like to believe it will. Mother Earth may look favorably on the gifts of our people." She turned to Wokkai. "I promised Mochik I would bring her some of these greens. Would you like to join me?"

When they were outside the compound wall, Wokkai said, "What now?"

"We must make certain the treasure is not there when Fire-Keeper goes back for it. It will soon be dark, and there is no moon, so I don't think he'll go tonight. That means we must act tomorrow morning."

"How will we explain leaving the compound with digging tools? If he goes back for it, he will remember we weren't here."

"We will not be gone from the compound, and Fire-Keeper will know we never left."

Wokkai frowned. "How?"

"Kutareo. You told me once he can move through the desert so quietly sometimes the animals are not aware he has passed."

"So we will send Kutareo to move the treasure?"

Ha-wani nodded. "And we will not ask him where he took it."

"You trust him to do this?"

"I do. And Fire-Keeper will never suspect him."

"And I will send Dove to guide him while we sit under the ramada?"

"Yes."

Wokkai glanced up at the rugged ridge watching over the village. "I will ask Great-Grandfather to help me be here while Dove is with Kutareo. But what will we do if Fire-Keeper gets there before we do?"

"Your father has arranged for him to be busy."

Wokkai's eyes widened. "Did you tell my father what we are doing?"

"No, but he suspects something. He trusts me enough to ask Chief Elder to bring Fire-Keeper to his ramada early in the morning to talk about the spring planting and restoring the sacred seeds. You and I will be here in full view, here in our ramada, spinning thread for your mother."

"Where is it?" Fire-Keeper bored through her lashes, peering into the line of her lower eyelid, reaching, pulling. "You stole the offering to Mother Earth."

Dark wings wrapped her. "The ceremony was yesterday, and you and the other shamans took it somewhere. I haven't left the compound. Perhaps one of the other shamans—"

"Don't play innocent, Ha-wani. You were foolish to reject me, but, now, you have gone too far."

Raven lifted her shoulders, stood straight, and gathered dark wings into flight. She wheeled away from him, wings whoosh-whooshing through the air. When she turned back, she sailed over his head, her primary feathers spread apart, like fingers, brushing across his double knot and pushing his hairpin askew.

Below her, he transformed into the gigantic beetle that had terrorized her in Honey Bee. The double knots in his lank hair unwound and stretched out and upward into long, jointed antennae. His mouth twisted into a pair of sharp, talon-like mandibles, and, on either side of his neck, a row of pointed horns rose from the skin. As his arms lengthened and each leg split into two, he dropped to the ground. The skin on his long, narrow back hardened into a shell that reflected the sunlight.

His eyes flattened, and a shield slid over them. He had shut her out. She rode the wind in a circle above him.

She should have the advantage — an earthbound beetle against a raven with strong wings and powerful beak.

But then his shell parted, and wide, translucent wings emerged from beneath it. He rose clumsily into the air, flying one way and then another, without grace, but with deadly intention. His eyes still probed her own, but she found no way to penetrate the shields. She wheeled into a turn considering her next move. But his antennae reached across the distance and slithered around her neck, under her wings, and across her back like snakes. She could fly, but only in his direction.

Folding her wings against her sides, she dove at him — now on the ground, his cloaked eyes still boring into hers.

She wheeled past, pulling herself free, wings outstretched, primaries spread. She circled and

*landed before him. A deep "crrr-uukk, crr-uukk"
issued from her throat, followed by "tok-tok-tok-
tok."*

*Above them, four ravens circled — calling,
croaking — and when he glanced up, her black eyes
sought the edges of his, and the shields fell away.*

*She poured her strength into those eyes, chal-
lenging him. The image of Yukui, the shaman
holding his staff, rose from behind the shields.*

*"You think you have the upper hand, Ha-
wani. You think you are stronger than me." His
thunder voice rumbled. "You succeeded in identifying my spirit and determining my name, but I
never allowed you to see what lies behind the beetle. You failed to learn my true power." He thrust
his staff into the air and shouted in his thunder
voice. "I — AM — THE — RAIN!"* Thunder reverberated along the mountain and echoed across the
land.*

Rain began to fall.

*The Raven spoke. "If you are the rain, why are
our people struggling? Why have you not nourished the fields?"*

*"I have reasons. Do not doubt me. Do not
doubt my power! I have offered only enough to
keep them alive. When they are needy, they depend
on me." He thrust his staff into the air again, and a
powerful wind swept her, tumbling wildly into the
sky. Drenching rain pounded her, and she struggled to push her wings through it, turning a cart-
wheel into the wind, flying sideways, and upside
down.*

*Suddenly, she found her strength, the power
of her wings, and each time the wind slammed her,*

she shifted her angle of flight taking advantage of it, allowing it to lift and propel her forward.

A dark shadow loomed, and she turned away, unable to see clearly through the drenching rain. It stayed before her: Great-Grandmother's Knees, the long ridge rising before Great-Grandmother Mountain. She flew into the trees above Elder Brother Wash, settling under a canopy of leaves, shaking water from her feathers, breathing deeply. The tree swayed with the wind, but she clung to the branch and focused on the landscape below.

Rain fell heavily on the desert, a rain uncommon for this time of year. Winter rains, which so far had been scant, normally linger over the fields and seep into the ground quenching the thirst of the crops, and winter was nearly past. This was a heavy summer rain, promising little more than flooding of the too-dry desert. The first planting of corn was only recently in the fields. A flood would wash the first sprouts away, and the crop would be lost.

She peered through the heavy curtain of rain. "Yukui, where do you hide?"

"I am here. In front of you. Behind you. I am all around. Do you not believe I am the Rain? Do you not understand I can destroy every living thing with my rain? I can flood the land until even Great-Grandmother drowns." His voice rang with thunder and sky fire streaked across the sky.

Ha-wani's spirit flinched, then stiffened. "Perhaps you can summon the rain, Yukui, but Mother Earth and Father Sky will not permit you to destroy their children. They will take your power and leave you with nothing."

"Pfaahh!" Thunder vibrated in the air. "Mother Earth and Father Sky. They are nothing! They exist only here before you. What you see. What *you can touch. Mother Earth is nothing but the dirt we stand on. Father Sky is nothing. If they do exist, their power can't compare to mine!"*

Wind churned the rain, swirling it around her. For a moment she felt as if it were pulling her into a whirlpool like she had seen when water churned through a flooded wash, sweeping trees and debris against the banks. She pressed her wings to her sides and clung to the branch.

She shouted, "If that is true, why do we have rain two days after you offered a gift to Mother Earth?"

"I brought it." Yukui's thunder rumbled and the whirlpool subsided.

"But you say the offering disappeared, and you accuse me of taking it. I never left the compound."

"You used this – your raven spirit." Thunder rolled in the distance and the rain eased.

"Quooo-rrrkkk!" She laughed aloud. "Look at me, Fire-Keeper. This is my spirit – a raven. I am strong, but my spirit is built to fly, not to dig something out of the ground and fly away with it. My spirit's form cannot do what a raven cannot."

"It was you." Thunder crashed, and the trees swayed violently.

She tightened her grip on the branch, swaying with the tree. "I remained in the compound. My spirit would have needed me, Ha-wani, to retrieve the treasure. But I'm not here to talk about your treasure, Yukui. I want to talk about what you did to my son."

"I did nothing to your son."

"The liquid you poured into him was made with moonflowers. You killed him."

"He was dying anyway. He was nothing." Sky fire struck a tree further up the slope, and thunder crashed around her. The tree she clung to swayed

violently, and the damp air filled with the odor of a quenched fire.

"I promised you my spirit in exchange for my son's life. That was what you wanted."

"You lied." Thunder vibrated in his voice. "You would never have given me your spirit. You only offered because you needed something."

When her branch settled, Raven said, "Of course, I lied. You think I would give you my spirit for your evil?"

"You should not have rejected me." Thunder rumbled in the distance.

"You rail at the People demanding they live by the laws given by Mother Earth and Father Sky. But you lie to them, telling them the laws have changed. You use your power to harm others. You forget that what you do to others you do to yourself. Mother Earth will punish you."

"Mother Earth will do — nothing." Instead of the thunder voice, Fire-Keeper's shrill voice intruded on the last words.

"She already has, Yukui. I'm surprised you haven't figured it out."

"You talk in riddles. Tell me what you did with the offering." No thunder echoed off the mountains, and no sky fire threatened.

"I did not take it, but I know who did."

"Who?"

"You and the other shamans made an offering to Mother Earth and asked her to seek Father Sky's favor."

His response was almost a child-like squeak in the silence. "Yes?"

"Look around us. Your drenching rain has settled into a rain that will nourish the fields, not destroy them." She lifted a wing and swept it toward Elder Brother Wash, flowing full but not flooding

over the banks. "Our farmers are manning the diversion dams. Every village in the desert basin is
celebrating the success of their offering."

"You distracted me!" He thrust his staff in the
air, but the skies remained quiet. Again, he thrust
it high, his rasping voice demanding a flood.

"There is only one explanation, Yukui. Mother Earth accepted your gift and did what you
asked." Raven spread her wings and, in the gentle
rain that was falling, flew along the flowing wash
where the farmers were diverting its waters to the
fields.

Ha-wani and Fire-Keeper had remained in the plaza
throughout the wind and rain. The roof of his ramada
had blown off, and Panereo's was damaged. Villagers
had scrambled to collect blowing baskets and family
belongings, running into their dwellings to wait out
the storm.

Vachai stood at the entry looking out at the rain.
"I've never seen rain like this in Green Moon. We
don't get thunder and sky fire this time of year, but
if the men get the diversion dams into place and they
hold, it will work to our favor. The corn has only just
sprouted."

"The offering—do you think—?" Li-naä was afraid
to say it.

He shrugged. "We can hope. It's settling now into
a winter rain, the kind we need." With his stick, he
pushed himself up the step and out into the fresh, cool
air.

Wokkai followed him outside. She pointed at the two figures standing in the plaza, both of them drenched from the earlier downpour. "Look."

Fire-Keeper, his twisted hair disheveled and hanging to the side, thrust his staff into the air, the wet feathers clinging impotently to the stick. He thrust it a second time.

When nothing happened, Ha-wani walked away.

Again and again, the old shaman shook his staff at the rain and the sky and howled. His chilling screams carried throughout the village and beyond, into the rain-soaked desert, and then slowly faded into silence.

Chapter 43

Yellow Moon 1160 (April)

From under the ramada, Ha-wani glanced around the village. The rain had brought enough water to make the mud plaster they needed to repair holes in the dwellings, making some of the houses look almost new. Even so, a pall hung over the people.

She had been here, just a short distance from her parents' village for two full turnings of the seasons, but she had not been home to visit since her marriage. She passed through the opening in the compound wall and out along the path. A light breeze blew dried blossoms from the bean and green stick trees, just as it did the day she became Tonrai's wife. Blue, yellow, and pink flowers covered the hillsides—more than she had seen in years. The desert was alive again.

Across the broad basin, the blue and purple mountains shadowed the horizon beyond her home village, and she remembered childish dreams of traveling into that unknown distance. Those mountains, whose colors changed with the sun's crossing each day, were beautiful and strange, inviting and frightening. She had been curious, but her sister apparently could not resist. What was it Ra-naä had said? "There must be something there for me." Ha-wani hoped she had found it.

She turned her gaze towards the massive cliffs of Great-Grandfather. They had become her strength. She could not imagine life without these mountains here watching over her. The village had so much promise. It was cradled by the curve of the mountains and blessed by a network of canyons which had, in other years, brought water to the village and to their fields. The long ridge on which the village stood was surrounded by potential sources of water.

In years past, Elder Brother Wash, to the north, flowed year-round, and the two smaller drainages to the east and to the west carried water whenever it rained on the mountains or when the snow melted in the spring. There had been sufficient water to irrigate the crops and live a contented life here. The recent rains might hold a promise of more to come, but would that promise be broken? Even Honey Bee had struggled when the washes dried up and rains fell infrequently. Since before remembering, these villages had survived on those scant rains, and they would go on.

They would go on without Ha-wani and those who were leaving with her.

For now, Onaati-Kaä had the promise of a good harvest. The diversion dams had held with little damage and had directed the water to the fields. Most of the young corn had survived, and the soil held the moisture. Now the farmers prepared to plant beans. The wells in the sand of the wash held much-needed water. Everyone believed that Mother Earth and Father Sky had finally smiled on them, that harmony had been restored, and that their gifts had been received and blessed.

In the days following the rain, Fire-Keeper went about his usual routines but limped as he marked the sun shadows on the plaza. He had little to say to anyone. One morning he failed to emerge from his dwelling. That in itself was unremarkable because, in the past, he had been known to go into the desert before sunrise to sing thanks to Mother Earth for her blessings. Surely the recent rain was such a blessing.

By sunset, he had not returned, and no one had seen him. The sun had completed its journey across the sky, casting new shadows over yesterday's markings. Chief Elder and Dar investigated and found Fire-Keeper on the floor of his dwelling, unable to get up, struggling to talk, and paralyzed on one side of his body. He lay with terror in his eyes, moaning and drooling as they built up the fire to give No-wani more light when she knelt to examine him.

"I have seen this once before. It happened to my grandmother. He will not live through many more sunrises." No-wani pushed herself into a standing position and pressed her bad arm around her middle with the other. She left Chief Elder and Dar standing with mouths agape.

Before long everyone knew what had happened. The villagers, on both sides of the compound wall, were alarmed. They had never been without a Fire-Keeper. Who would tend the sacred coals? Who would lead them in honoring Mother Earth and Father Sky? Most forgot their shaman had often ill served them; the lack of a spiritual leader was terrifying.

Fire-Keeper died a day later. Kutareo prepared the pyre, and An-nat, as Knowledge-Keeper, sang the shaman into the Flower World. Ha-wani wondered if Fire-Keeper would have preferred being placed in the ground with his staff, feathers, and mask, along with gifts brought by the people. When his body had been consumed, the people drifted back to their dwellings silently.

Vachai's family kept to themselves, aware of the distrust stirring the emotions of the villagers. Onaa-ti-Kaä was without a Fire-Keeper, and most blamed Tonrai's wife.

Later that day, when the remaining members of the council met to discuss the future of the village, Tonrai expected to be questioned about the confrontation between his wife and the Fire-Keeper.

In the Council House, Dar, An-nat, and Tonrai greeted each other quietly. Chief Elder began, "We will need to expand the council soon, but, in the meantime, we must make some decisions. I have asked An-nat to preserve the sacred coals on behalf of the village. For now, the responsibility will lie with Knowledge-Keeper. Should they die out, I fear we will all be lost. Does anyone object?"

When no one responded, Thandoi glanced at Tonrai, who sat silent. "Can you tell us what happened between your wife and Fire-Keeper the day of the rain?"

"No." Tonrai kept his focus on the low fire in the hearth. "I don't know. I only know Fire-Keeper had threatened my wife on numerous occasions. He was obsessed with her. On the day it rained, they simply stood face to face in the plaza. What passed between them I cannot say."

Dar and An-nat lowered their heads as Chief Elder continued. "I have spoken with others on the council and with people in the village. We are agreed that your wife must leave Onaati-Kaä."

Tonrai took a deep breath. "I have lived in Onaa-ti-Kaä all my life. As I said when I presented the gifts of the sea, the people here are my kinsmen. But I will not stay if my wife is not welcome here. We will go."

When he stood, the others did as well.

An-nat placed a hand on Tonrai's shoulder, and Tonrai returned the gesture. "Go in health, my son. And may the gods stand with you."

Tonrai nodded. When he and Chief Elder grasped shoulders, the older man said, "You have served our village well, Artist. Thank you."

When Tonrai turned, Dar stepped to the side, hesitant, his downcast eyes filled with tears threatening to flow down his wrinkled cheeks. When Tonrai laid his hand on the old man's shoulder, he lifted his head and met the younger man's eyes. After a moment, he raised his hand and gripped Tonrai's shoulder in return. "Thank you, Dar. You were my friend, my teacher, and my guide. I will carry your gifts with me wherever I go."

The old man struggled to speak. "I have disappointed you, my son. I will carry my sorrow into the Flower World."

"You made choices you thought were right." He caressed the knotted hand on his shoulder. "The spirit of your gifted hands, if it can be so, will be with me always."

The night before their departure, Vachai's family gathered in their dwelling, making plans for those who were leaving.

With tears flowing, Wokkai begged her mother, "Why can't I stay? You and my father will need someone to help you. We can't leave you alone. I can't leave—" She couldn't say what was in her heart. She couldn't leave Kutareo—Kawiusai. Who would be there for him? His brother had paid little attention to him after the Treachery. Now he would have no one.

"I promise you, Daughter, you will be fine. You must go with your brother." Her voice cracked. "There is nothing here for you." Li-naä's tears fell openly, and Wokkai clung to her.

At that moment, Anu, Mochik, and Ma-taä came in, followed by Cheshonii and Kokii along with her younger sons.

Vachai, who had been sitting on his bench, struggled to his feet and leaned on his stick. Before speaking, he looked into the eyes of each of those assembled around him. They returned his gaze. "Some of you will be leaving this village tomorrow." Li-naä and Wokkai sobbed openly. "We will never see one another again, but you will take with you our love and the strength of our spirits. And, as we prepare to say farewell to you, there is unfinished business we must attend to. Tradition has long dictated the way we live, but I have learned not every tradition serves our people well." He nodded at Cheshonii, who took his place beside Ma-taä, standing next to her father.

Anu spoke, "Cheshonii, I give my daughter to you for your wife. You may bind Ma-taä's spirit to yours." He gave him her matrimonial ribbon. Cheshonii turned Ma-taä's right hand over and laid the ribbon across her palm. Holding it between their hands, he used his free hand to wrap it over and around their clasped hands several times. "Ma-taä, I bind your spirit to my own. You are my wife."

Kokii, standing to the side, clinging to her younger sons, wept. Tarukii and Chuwii would be leaving with their older brother.

Wokkai was surprised at how easily they had defied tradition. Before she could ask her question, her mother took her confused daughter to stand beside her father. Li-naä signaled Tonrai, who stepped outside and came back with Kutareo at his side.

When Vachai invited Wood-Cutter to stand beside Wokkai, she whispered to her father, "You are sure?"

"I am sure, Daughter." To Wood-Cutter, he said, "Kutareo, I give my daughter to you for your wife."

"No." Wood-Cutter spoke softly, but everyone heard.

In the shocked silence that followed, the young man said, "My name is Kawiusai. Kawiusai." He looked at Wokkai with his ever-present quizzical expression.

Her smile was radiant.

"Kawiusai, I give my daughter to you for your wife. You may bind Wokkai's spirit to yours." He handed him the matrimonial ribbon her mother never got around to decorating again.

Because he had likely never seen a marriage ceremony, Wokkai turned her palm up and told him to lay the ribbon across her hand. He did. "Now, put your hand on top of mine, and wrap the ribbon around our hands." He wrapped it over and around their clasped hands several times.

After Vachai leaned forward and whispered to him, he said, "Wokkai, I bind your spirit to my own. You are my wife."

In the dim pre-dawn light, Ha-wani rested her hand on Tonrai's strong shoulder, watching him peck two circles, one inside the other, into the rock. He squatted, using a hand stone and a hammerstone to engrave the image.

When he drew rays extending from the outside circle, she knew it was the sun. A sun that would greet itself each morning when it rose over the ridge behind her. *Here, on this rock, we leave our mark, his mark. Others will come here and find it. They will wonder who brought the sun from the sky and placed it here.**

When he stood and turned, his shell tinklers singing, the morning rose behind her. He took her hand and drew her aside as the dawn wind swept them and the first kiss of the sun found its own image, warming it with hope for the journey ahead of them.

They followed the path back to the village to gather their belongings and go where the sun might lead them. Bean and green stick trees hung heavy with blossoms, and yellow poppies covered the desert beneath the mountains. Lupine and owl clover splashed the golden carpet with blue and pink. Birds chattered in the scrub, and red-shouldered hawks circled above them. The desert had come alive with promise.

Ha-wani gazed along the mountains cradling the village and across the basin to the distant mountains. The mystery of what lay beyond would finally be solved. She wanted to be optimistic, especially for her son and the generations to come.

The day was clear, and a steady breeze blew through the trees and scrub, singing a desert song she would carry with her wherever they went.

In the compound, An-nat and No-wani walked Benai back to his parents' dwelling. The old man laid a hand on Benai's shoulder, saying. "Take our stories with you, and keep them sacred. Take our knowledge wherever you go."

Benai, not quite tall enough to reach the older man's shoulder, returned the gesture and, looking solemn, said, "Thank you. I will do as you bid." He turned and showed his calendar stick to his parents, running a finger across newly incised lines. "This tells of the day we left Onaati-Kaä."

Others in the village stood silent beneath their ramadas, aware of their impending departure, but none came to bid the young people goodbye. In spite of the gentle rains that had fallen on the village and the fields in the past two days, many blamed Ha-wani for Fire-Keeper's death. Chief Elder's devotion to his old friend, Vachai, was the only thing that had kept them from driving her from their midst without delay.

The new family packed their burden baskets, and Ha-wani strapped Mocho-okoli to her breast. Tonrai, Wichikai with Ma-taä holding her hand, Cheshonii, Benai, Tarukii, Chuwii, Kawiusai, and Wokkai gathered at the opening in the compound wall, waiting for Ha-wani.

She took one last look at the baskets and pots under the family ramada. They were the gifts of countless women's hands. They held the songs and stories of the years before and after she had come here. She would make new ones for their new life when they settled somewhere else.

The first pot she had made under this ramada leaned against a corner post where it had been since their house burned. She had never found a particular use for it, but now she would give it back to Mother Earth. Here, in this place, where she had lived with her husband and the family who had welcomed her, where these mountains had embraced her, she would leave her song.

Kneeling on the west side of the compound, near the wall, she traced the pot's red lines with a finger, and, for the briefest moment, she saw a pair of delicate women's hands, pale, not dark like her own, uncovering the broken pieces.*

She filled the pot with dirt, packing it tightly, hoping Mother Earth would protect it and keep it whole, all the while knowing that even the fragments would carry her song and a bit of her spirit. She dug a hole and tucked it into the ground.

*Someday, when these walls have collapsed, and only the mountains remain, a stranger may pass this way and hear my song.**

She caressed the child strapped to her breast, saying, "It pains me to leave your brother behind, but his spirit will linger here where he was born, and, someday, someone will know him, as well."*

As she sang, the song floated on the wind, around the rocks, into the canyons, and across the land to be picked up by other winds, in other times—a small, far-away sound that those who really listen will hear.*

The earth is our mother
Who sustains us
She honors us with gifts
We respectfully use her gifts
And honor her by giving back
The gifts of the earth
The gifts from the earth
The earth is our mother
Who sustains us . . .

If you enjoyed this story, please consider posting a review on Goodreads, Amazon, and other online book retailers.

Author Notes

Visit my Pinterest board for *The Clay Sustains* to see pictures representing many of the things described or explained here. Entries marked with a caret (^) symbol indicate images that may be found at www.pinterest.com/buckskinbooks/the-clay-sustains.

Chapter 1

Dawn wind: As the sun rises behind a mountain to the east, warming the air on the opposite slope, the warm air pushes the heavier cold air down the western slope. Often, the coldest temperatures are recorded just before sunrise. The ritual of welcoming the dawn wind is designed to cleanse the body and prepare the spirit to face the day and whatever might come. It comes from the spiritual beliefs of the Yoeme.

Neither move nor break eye contact: Just as contemporary people say *the eyes are the window to the soul*, some ancient cultures took it literally. For Ha-wani's people, their names are drawn from their spirit guides, and those names are not shared beyond family and intimates. To look into someone's eyes is a threat to them and their spirit.

"Harsh croak gurgled in her throat. . . . Raven's wings lifted . . . ": Ha-wani's spirit guide is the raven. Because her spirit guide helps her, the man now knows her spirit name. Ravens are reputed to be one of the most intelligent birds, capable of solving complex problems. Acrobatic flight is common. They have been known to fly sideways and even upside down.

Fire-Keeper: the village shaman, keeper of the fire (coals that have been kept burning for generations).

Chapter 2

Pit house: A simple brush- and dirt-covered house built over a pit, one to two feet deep. The pit kept the house cool in summer and warm in winter. The house consisted of one rectangular, square, or oval room, with an entryway extending from one of the house's long walls. Posts supported the roof and a framework for the outer walls. Beams were laid across the major support posts and covered with a network of saguaro and ocotillo ribs. The whole roof was covered with brush. The walls were also covered with brush or bundles of arrow weed and reeds.

Finally, the whole structure was covered with mud plaster and dirt. A smooth, mud-plastered floor was laid inside, and a hearth was just inside the entryway. People slept on woven mats, laid directly on the floor, or on low sleeping platforms. Cooking and eating pots, large storage baskets, awls, arrows, and grinding tools were kept on the floor or on the ledge at the base of the walls, and light objects, such as baskets, were hung from walls and posts. Storage pots and various tools stood along the house walls.^

Onaati-Kaä or Stone Towers Village: Fictional name for the prehistoric Hohokam village situated on what is now Romero Ruin in Catalina State Park, near Tucson, Arizona. This site is thought to have been occupied by the Hohokam from approximately 550 – 1450 (although it might possibly date to 450), with the most intensive occupation from around 850 – 1000. Archaeologists believe that after 1150, the primary occupation was within the compound wall with limited occupation outside the wall. Some archaeologists speculate the decline and final abandonment of this village, as well as many others in the Southwest, came about from the stratification of the social structure and the rise of an upper, perhaps priest, class.

Honey Bee Village: A prehistoric Hohokam village in what is now Oro Valley, Arizona, near the Tortolita Mountains. Throughout the Tucson Basin, there are numerous prehistoric sites from the time of the Hohokam, an agrarian people who, archaeologists believe, occupied the area from approximately 200 BCE (Before the Common Era) to 1450 CE (Common Era). It is unknown why they left and what became of them. The Tohono O'odham, a Native American tribe who lives in Southern Arizona and Northern Mexico, claim the Hohokam as their ancestors.

"Blue lines . . . from mouth to chin": Tattoos made in vertical lines from the mouth to the chin that mark the achievement of womanhood. Such tattoos have been used during the modern era by some members of the Tohono O'odham nation, possibly for different purposes.

Bean and green stick trees: Mesquite and palo verde trees.

Leather thong from which tiny shell tinklers hung: the spire end (the tapered point of a spiral shell) from the interior of *Olivella dama*. When strung on different lengths of fibers, they rattle against one another. Comparable to the metal tinklers used on the costumes of Native American dancers.

Chapter 3

Umbo: highest part of the shell of a bivalve or univalve mollusk, situated above the hinge.

Great Water: The Hohokam traveled to the Sea of Cortez (Gulf of California) to get salt and shells and to trade with the people who lived there.^

Shell: *Glycymeris gigantea*, a clam from the Sea of Cortez.^

Hunting stick: a blunt stick or wooden club used to kill small game. It is curved slightly, somewhat like a boomerang, and rotates rapidly when thrown. Also known as a Rabbit Stick.^

Hammerstone: a rock used as a hammer.

Pine sap and fermented liquor from the giant cactus: Pine sap protects the shell surface while the cactus liquor etches the design into the shell.

Slimwood: The ocotillo is a desert plant with several woody, spiny, whip-like branches that may grow as high as twenty feet. The branches were used for roofing ramadas and building the internal structures of pit houses.^ Today, they are often used to make a living fence.

Ball game: Many Hohokam villages in the Tucson Basin and elsewhere in Arizona left behind large, oval depressions thought to be ball courts where they may have held celebrations, ceremonies, and/or played a ball game similar to one known in Mexico.^

Chapter 4

Agave terraces: The Hohokam cultivated agave for a variety of uses, including food. Archaeological evidence indicates they grew and harvested agave on the terraced slopes south of the Hohokam site in Catalina State Park.

"They are coming": Archaeologists speculate that, during the later years of Hohokam history, there was movement between the Hohokam and the northern Pueblo cultures.

Bells ringing: The archaeological record indicates that Hohokam must have traded with people in what is now Mexico, acquiring copper bells which have been traced to Jalisco, Mexico.^

Feathers: The archaeological record indicates that the Hohokam also acquired parrot or macaw feathers of many colors from Mexico. Red, blue, yellow, and white represent the four sacred directions (North, South, East, and West).^

Sleeping Snake: Another Hohokam village near Honey Bee Village excavated by archaeologists. "Rattlesnake" is a fictitious village.

Chapter 5

Rabbit stick: a blunt stick or wooden club used to kill small game. It is curved slightly, somewhat like a boomerang, and rotates rapidly when thrown. Also known as a hunting stick.^

"The half-light of night": In the desert, when the moon is full, it is like twilight, and the moon casts shadows.

Chapter 6

Saguaro: The large, many-armed cactus which
grows only in the Sonoran Desert. It has come to
represent Arizona.^

"Calling down the rains": A practice continued
today by the Tohono O'odham Indians. After harvesting the saguaro fruit, they allow it to ferment
into liquid form. They then call down the rains
by drinking and throwing up, thereby returning
the liquor to the land. The ceremony today is con-
ducted on June 24, San Juan/Saint John's day,
after which the monsoon rains usually begin.

"We call upon our brother": This song, associated with the saguaro harvest, along with some
others, but not all, is a variation of a Tohono
O'odham song.

"Cicadas signaled a hotter one to come": In the
desert, cicadas disturb an otherwise quiet desert
with loud buzzing when the temperature reaches
100 degrees or more.

Harvesting poles: Long lengths of saguaro ribs
lashed together to make a pole long enough to
reach the top of the tallest saguaros. A short
length of greasewood is lashed near the top,
allowing the person to pull or push a ripened
fruit from the cactus. These poles continue in use
today.^

**"Snapping off the dried blossoms and slicing
the fruit open":** The saguaro flower dries as
the fruit develops. The end of the dried blossom
where it connects to the fruit is a hard, flat,
sharp-edged disk. It can be used to slice into the
fruit.

Sotol spoon: The narrow leaves of *Dasylirion
wheeleri*, or Desert Spoon, when removed from
the plant resemble a stalk of celery. When dried,
they can be used as a spoon.

The Rain House: The pit house in the camp reserved for fermenting the juice of the giant
cactus. Saguaro fruit juice ferments very quickly,
usually within two days.

Chapter 7

Gourd water-drum: a drum made of two half-
gourds—the larger one with water in it, the
smaller one turned upside down in the water.^

"The little red spiders": This song is a variation
of a Tohono O'odham song recorded by Ruth
Murray Underhill, in *Singing for Power: The
Song Magic of the Papago Indians of Southern
Arizona*. All of the songs from this point in the
chapter are taken from Tohono O'odham songs.

Seedpod of ram's horn: the seedpod of Devil's
Claw.^

Chapter 8

Great-Grandmother's pools: Currently Romero
Pools, depressions in the rock formations at the
top of Romero Canyon in the Santa Catalina
Mountains. The pools fill with rainwater and
snowmelt and usually contain water.^

Chapter 9

The trail to the pools: Currently Romero Canyon
trail, approximately five miles long and gaining
about 1,000 feet in elevation.^

Chapter 10

***Sea Ania* or Flower World:** In Yoeme spiritual
tradition, the *Sea Ania* is thought to be a place
of complete beauty and harmony. It is located
beneath the dawn in a place filled with flowers,
water, and natural abundance of all kinds. The
author has used this to identify where one's

spirit goes after death, but it is also a place which someone who is in close touch with their spiritual side can actually visit during life. *Ania* means "world" in the Yoeme language.

There are five such worlds in Yoeme culture: *Sea Ania* or Flower World; *Yo Ania* or Enchanted World; *Tuka Ania* or Night World; *Tenku Ania* or Dream World, and *Huya Ania* or Wilderness World. Each of these may be thought of as physical places, as well as states of being.

Chapter 11

"Vanseka weene": In the Yoeme language, "go now."

"Go now, Maisokai": Nothai's spirit name is Maisokai for his spirit, the tarantula.

"Sea ania vovicha": The Flower World awaits.

Cremation and burial: Sometime during the Classic period, the Hohokam began practicing inhumation (burial) instead of cremation. No inhumations were excavated at Romero Ruin.

"Iansu weene Itom Ae Aniawi": Go now to Mother Earth.

Chapter 12

Big River: The Santa Cruz river passes through the Tucson Basin. The Hohokam collected clay from multiple sources, but the clay used by the Hohokam during the Tanque Verde Phase (Hawani's time) came from the west branch of the Santa Cruz. The Tanque Verde Phase dates from approximately 1100 to 1250 CE.^

Puki: a shallow clay saucer which is used to begin shaping a pot.^

Chapter 13

Sotol spike: *Dasylirion wheeleri,* or Desert Spoon, a desert plant that produces a flower stalk every few years. The dried sotol stalk is a popular source of hiking sticks in the Southwest.

Granary: This event probably predates the use of granaries for central storage of grains by a few centuries according to the archaeological record. When they came into use, they were not likely to be brush shelters like this one. This brush shelter is more like those from the Early Agricultural Period (approximately 2000 BCE – 50 CE). It is modeled on the structure built by Allen Denoyer, Preservation Archaeologist for Archeology Southwest, at Steam Pump Village and later burned intentionally for research purposes.

Sun shadow marks: Fire-Keeper keeps track of the sun's journey across the sky by making a series of marks on the ground showing the length of the shadow from a stick standing in the plaza.

Taruk: Tarukii's spirit guide is the roadrunner, a fast-running bird in the cuckoo family. In the Yoeme language, *taruk* means roadrunner.

Chapter 14

Star streaks: Meteor shower.
Corn meal path: The Milky Way.

Chapter 15

Old woman and the drinking gourd: The constellations Cassiopeia and Ursa Major (the big dipper) circle the North Star.

Chapter 16

Cotton: The Hohokam cultivated cotton and used it to make clothing.^

Great-Grandfather's Canyon: Currently called Alamo Canyon, it cuts into Pusch Ridge on the north side of the Santa Catalina Mountains.

Sister Crops: Corn, beans, and squash are planted together with each one benefiting the other. Corn grows tall; beans planted next to it climb the stalk; squash planted around the corn and beans provides shade for the roots of all three, assisting in holding moisture in the soil.

Chapter 17

"Fragrance of rain": When we say, "The desert smells like rain," we are referring to the fragrance of the oils the creosote bushes release when it rains.^

Chapter 18

Spinning thread from a cotton bundle: After the harvested cotton has been seeded and flattened to align the fibers, the spinner pulls fibers from the bundle, twisting, and turning the spindle as the thread wraps it. The spindle is a straight stick with a weight at the end.^

Huya Ania: The Wilderness World in Yoeme culture, which may be either a physical place or a state of being. Mountains are considered sacred, spiritual places where, traditionally, the people went to pray and to acquire spiritual help and renewal.

"The beetle whose larvae feed on the roots of the green stick tree": the palo verde beetle, *Derobrachus geminatus,* a longhorn beetle native to the American Southwest. They can reach up to three and a half inches in length, possibly longer. They have long antennae, and spines on the thorax which form a collar around the "neck" of the beetle. They have wings and can fly, although awkwardly. In the larval stage, they are a large, white grub.^

Yukui: In the Yoeme language, *yuku* is the name of the palo verde beetle.

Chapter 19

Creation story: This story combines the elements of a number of different creation stories from different cultures. It does not represent the creation story of any past or present culture.

Winter rains: Native Americans in the Southwest refer to winter rains as *female* rains. They are gentle rains that take the time to soak into the soil and nourish the fields.

Summer rains: These rains are considered *male* rains. They are great drenching downpours with lots of noise. Summer floods often wash away healthy soil and provide little nourishment.

Se-daku: Variation of *seataaka*, which is a Yoeme (Yaqui) concept meaning "flower body" or the human living spirit. It is that part of a person's being that protects him/her from evil people and spirits during the person's lifetime. In order to maintain and keep the *seatakaa* in life, the person must follow the right path as taught by the traditions of the people. Whatever happens to your body cannot harm your *seataaka*, and no one can damage or destroy it.

Life is part of a cycle: you were already living in the universe; your living spirit comes in the physical body for a brief journey on this earth; and your spirit resides within you and connects you to everything—a perfect being within your body. What you do to others, you do to yourself. *Seataaka* allows you to survive this life. When you leave this earth, your *seataaka* still exists and can return.

Chapter 20

Li-naä's loom: She is using what is called a back-strap loom, which is held to the weaver by a strap around her waist and secured to a tree or post on the other end so the threads can be held taut.^

Chapter 23

Dogweed and chinchweed tea: for colic and gastrointestinal distress.

Fire-Keeper's songs over the baby: These songs use a number of Yoeme words—*simese'e* (go away), *kokowame* (death), *hiavihtetua* (revive), *hiapsiwame* (life), *ka-tu'i* (bad), and *yeu siime* (come out)—but do not represent an actual Yoeme song.

Chapter 26

Moonflowers: the sacred datura (*Datura wrightii*), also known as jimsonweed, devil's trumpet, deadly nightshade, and belladonna. All parts of all Datura plants are poisonous and can be fatal if ingested. Native American shamans have been known to use Datura to initiate visions.^

Grinding beans: Scattered around the Tucson Basin, archaeologists have found numerous bedrock mortars, depressions in large boulders and rock formations, where women likely ground mesquite beans. As they ground the pods, they also ground depressions into the rocks. Such mortars are often located near large stands of mesquite trees. This is seen as evidence that prehistoric people ground the beans on-site rather than carrying them back to their villages to grind.^

Chapter 27

Trip to the sea: Archaeologists have discovered prehistoric trails worn into the hard desert surface leading to the Sea of Cortez (Gulf of California). Researchers believe that the prehistoric peoples of the Southwest traveled there to trade and to get salt.

In modern times, the Tohono O'odham made salt trips to the sea. A map of the ancient trails can be found on the Pinterest board for this book. These trips were made in a surprisingly short time for the distance they covered. According to stories told by the Tohono O'odham, their people ran to the sea and back, so it is likely the Hohokam did as well. From the Tohono O'odham Village to the salt flats of the Sea of Cortez, the distance is 300 miles round trip.^

Te-oh-chee-ah ee-tom achaa-eh: *Te'ochia itom achai* translates from the Yoeme language as "Bless us, God."

"Knowledge-Keeper knows the songs . . . ": For the Tohono O'odham, songs were important to guide the travelers on their trips to the Gulf. The trips were made primarily for salt and to acquire "medicine power." They believed the sea held everything, including the clouds and the wind. The rain came from the sea. The songs provided the runners with directions and landmarks to look for in order to get to their destination.

Chapter 28

" . . . plant the squash to shade the corn and beans: Squash is one of the "sister crops": corn, beans, and squash. Once the corn begins to grow, the beans are planted next to it so the beans can climb the stalk. Squash, which has broad leaves, is then planted around the corn and the beans to shade the soil so it holds moisture.^

Chapter 29

Broken bracelet: In *The Clay Remembers*, when Anna, the archaeologist, holds a broken shell bracelet Margy found during a pit house excavation, it brings her into touch with Ha-wani's spirit and her experience with Fire-Keeper when it broke. Ha-wani would have lost it when she huddled inside the pit house.^

Chapter 30

Desert of Burned Rock: Now called the Pinacate Biosphere Preserve, the Pinacate is located in Mexico on the route to the Sea of Cortez (Gulf of California). It is a volcanic desert made up of volcanic cones, calderas, and a volcanic mountain.^

"Dark mountain where travelers climb to the top . . . ": Travelers might have done this because, from the highest peak, the Sea of Cortez is visible. It would have provided the first opportunity for them to glimpse the sea.

Chapter 32

Sand dunes: located between the Pinacate Peaks and the Sea of Cortez (Gulf of California).^

Deep depressions like bowls: volcanic craters in the Pinacate Peaks.^

Bird with blue feet: The blue-footed booby is a large seabird common to the Sea of Cortez.

"By the sandy water . . . ": The song Knowledge-Keeper sang at the water's edge is a traditional song of the Tohono O'odham connected with expeditions to obtain salt.

Oönaho-ara: a fictitious village by the Sea of Cortez. In the Yoeme language, *oona* means "salt," and *ho'ara* means village.

Chapter 33

"**Her pregnancy had not had an effect on it.**": Nursing during pregnancy is more common than some may think. However, sometimes, when a nursing mother gets pregnant, the nature of her milk changes, and the nursing child may refuse it.

Chapter 34

Rock shelter: Near the base of Pusch Ridge (Great-Grandfather Mountain) is a large rock shelter which has been designated as an archaeological site and was possibly used by Hohokam farmers tending the agave terraces.

Chapter 35

Sleeping Snake, Rattlesnake, Honey Bee, and Seepwillow: Hohokam villages along the Tortolita Mountains. Sleeping Snake and Honey Bee are documented in the archaeological record, and the town of Oro Valley, Arizona, has preserved part of Honey Bee as a public park. Rattlesnake and Seepwillow are fictitious villages.

Chapter 37

"**A stone bounced off the shaman's shoulder . . .**": Ravens have been known to play games like this.

Chapter 38

The granary and pit house fire: The granary, without a protective mud plaster exterior, would have been more vulnerable to fire. Such structures were common during what is known as the Early Agricultural Period (see Chapter 13, Granary note), although Edward S. Curtis's *North American Indian* provides a photograph of a "Papago [Tohono O'odham] brush house" of similar construction in 1908.

Tonrai's pit house, even with its mud plaster exterior, was vulnerable because the mud easily deteriorated, exposing the interior wood and brush walls.

"I am not the enchanted light blue cloud": The song Fire-Keeper claims Ha-wani sang, stopping the rain, is a variation of a Yoeme deer song, not associated with rain.

Chapter 40

Roasting agave: The archaeological record describes pit ovens (roasting pits), found in areas where agaves were cultivated and thought to be used for roasting agave hearts.^

Chapter 41

"Shamans recruited others from other villages . . . ": There were numerous Hohokam villages during the same period in the Tucson Basin and beyond the Tortolitas.

The collected beads and bells: The Romo cache was found in 1949 by a man named Ray Romo on a hill in what is now Catalina State Park, near Tucson, Arizona. It was an ancient Hohokam pot cupped over a larger Hohokam pot containing 25 copper bells and 100,000 tiny beads.

Archaeologists have dated it to the Hohokam era, possibly between 950 CE, when the Hohokam population began fragmenting, and 1150 CE, after which the Hohokam began to vanish from the Tucson Basin. They speculate it might have been some kind of offering through which those who had collected these treasures sought a blessing from their gods or sought to secure the welfare of the village.^

Chapter 42

"I – AM – THE – RAIN!": His name, Yukui, means not only "palo verde beetle, but also "rain" in the Yoeme language, perhaps because rain brings these beetles into the open.

Chapter 43

Tonrai's sun sign: a pictograph of two concentric circles with rays drawn out from the outside circle. It is featured in *The Clay Remembers.*^

"Delicate women's hands, pale, not dark like her own, uncovering the broken pieces": In *The Clay Remembers,* Anna finds the broken pieces of the same pot. It broke when Esperanza was leaving the ridge in *The Clay Endures.*

" . . . know I was here": In *The Clay Endures,* Esperanza found the pot. It had remained intact for more than seven centuries.

" . . . someone will know him, as well": In *The Clay Endures,* a dark child appears in Esperanza's dream to take her son to the spirit world.

" . . . the song floated on the wind, around the rocks, into the canyons, and across the land to be picked up by other winds, in other times—a small, far-away sound that those who really listen will hear.": from Byrd Baylor's, *When Clay Sings.*

Book Club Questions

1. There is an old adage that the eyes are the window to the soul. Many Native American and other indigenous cultures believe that the eyes provide access to a person's spirit; therefore, to look into someone's eyes is to trespass on that spirit and to, possibly, bring it harm. How does the opening scene illustrate that belief?

2. Some native cultures believe that our spirits are guided by an aspect of nature, most commonly an animal or bird. What do you learn about the shaman's spirit guide and Ha-wani's spirit guide from the opening scene?

3. Do the characters seem real and believable? Can you relate to their predicaments?

4. Who is your favorite character? Why?

5. Do the actions of the characters seem plausible? Why? Why not?

6. When one (or more) of the characters makes a choice that has moral implications, would you have made the same decision? Why? Why not?

7. What is Wokkai's role in the story? What is Fire-Keeper's interest in her? Discuss her relationship with Kutareo.

8. Is there a minor character that outshines a more central character? Explain.

9. Discuss the dynamics between: (1) Ha-wani and Tonrai; (2) Ha-wani and Fire-Keeper; and (3) Ha-wani and Ra-naä. In what ways does Ha-wani's relationship with each of them change over time?

10. Why does Ha-wani insist on turning to Fire-Keeper when her son is dying. Discuss the conflict between her and Tonrai regarding seeking the shaman's help.

11. What is unique about the setting of the book and how does it enhance or take away from the story? How does the setting figure as a character in the story?

12. What specific themes does the author emphasize throughout the novel? What do you think she is trying to get across to the reader?

13. How has the society of Onaati-Kaä changed since the wall was built? Why do the villagers so easily fall into line with Fire-Keeper?

14. What is the impact of Fire-Keeper's changes to practices related to sending a spirit into the Flower World? On Ha-wani? On others?

15. How do boys become men?

16. How do girls become women?

17. Are there parallels to gender differences in today's society?

18. Throughout the story, what main ideas—themes—does the author explore? (Consider the title, often a clue to a theme.) Does the author

use symbols to reinforce the main ideas? If so, what are they?

19. What passages strike you as insightful, even profound? (Perhaps a bit of dialog that's funny or poignant or that encapsulates a character.)

20. If you could ask the author a question, what would you ask?

21. What, if anything, sets this book apart from others you've read in a similar genre?

22. Is there a particularly striking scene for you in the novel? Share it with the group, and then discuss why and how it impacts you.

23. Are there parallels between this story and current events?

24. Are there parallels between the spiritual traditions of Ha-wani's family and her people and modern day religious traditions?

25. Which characters change or evolve throughout the course of the story? What events trigger such changes?

26. What do you think of the story's ending?

27. What three words would you use to summarize this book?

28. The author's inspiration for this series grew, in part, from Byrd Baylor's small book, *When Clay Sings,* wherein she said, "...everything has its own spirit--even a broken pot. They say the clay remembers the hands that made it...." (See the full quotation in the epigraph before Chapter 1. How does this apply to *The Clay Sustains* and to the other books in The Clay Series if you have read them?

29. Have you read the other books in The Clay Series? If so how does this book compare? If not, does this book inspire you to read the others?

30. If you have read *The Clay Remembers* and/or *The Clay Endures*, what connections did you find between the events of this story and the events in the first two books?

31. Did you enjoy *The Clay Sustains*? Why or why not?

About the Author

Sharon K. Miller fell in love with words at a young age, and writing became a big part of her life from that moment on. Her fascination with the archaeology and history of the Sonoran Desert and the indigenous cultures who left their stories etched on and buried in the land inspired the books in The Clay Series—the interconnected tales of the three women separated by centuries.

Additionally, she collaborated with Cristy Kessler on *Surviving Healthcare: 5 Steps to Cutting Through the BS, Getting the Treatment You Need, and Saving Your life* (2015) and co-authored a successful university textbook, *Doing Academic Writing in Education: Connecting the Personal and the Profession* (2005), with Janet C. Richards.

Miller lives beneath the back range of the Santa Catalina mountains near Tucson, Arizona, with her husband Jim, their son Jeff, and a rambunctious dog named Hannah who give her the space and time to write.

—

"If you have never been called a defiant, incorrigible, impossible woman, . . . have faith, . . . there is yet time." ~from *Women Who Run With the Wolves*, by Clarissa Pinkola Estés.

Connect with Me

Visit www.sharonkmiller.com
to join my mailing list. Look for announcements about
upcoming book talks/walking tours of the Romero
Ruin site at Catalina State Park.

Other Sites
www.buckskinbooks.com
about.me/sharon.miller

Social Media
@authorskmiller

Blogs
authorsharonkmiller.com
boxeldersandblackberries.wordpress.com

Pinterest
www.pinterest.com/buckskinbooks/the-clay-
remembers/
www.pinterest.com/buckskinbooks/the-clay-
endures/
www.pinterest.com/buckskinbooks/the-clay-sustains

Contact Me
sharon@buckskinbooks.com

References

All Books in The Clay Series

Alcock, John. *When the Rains Come: A Naturalist's Year in the Sonoran Desert*. Tucson: University of Arizona Press, 2009.

"Ancient Salt Trails and Oases Project, The: Connecting the Past to the Present." https://www.desertmuseum.org/center/salttrails.php.

Arellano, Anselmo F. *Las Curanderas: Traditional Healers in New Mexico, Mother Earth Living*. www.motherearthliving.com/health-and-wellness/.new-mexico-shealing-tradition.aspx?PageId=3. 1997.

Ashmore, Wendy, and Robert Sharer. *Discovering Our Past: A Brief Introduction to Archaeology*. Mountain View: Mayfield Pub., 1996.

Bahr, Donald M., Juan Smith, William Smith Allison, and Julian Hayden. *The Short, Swift*

Time of Gods on Earth: The Hohokam Chronicles.
Berkeley: University of California, 1994.

Baldwin, Gordon C. *The Warrior Apaches: A Story
of the Chiricahua and Western Apache.* Tucson:
D.S. King, 1965.

Ball, Eve, with Nora Henn and Lynda A. Sánchez.
Indeh, an Apache Odyssey. Provo: Brigham
Young University Press, 1980.

Barnett, Franklin. *Dictionary of Prehistoric Indian
Artifacts of the American Southwest.* Flagstaff:
Northland Press, 1973.

Barter, G. W., ed. *Directory of the City of Tucson for
the Year 1881.* San Francisco: H.S. Crocker &
Co., Printers, 1881.

Baylor, Byrd. *And It Is Still That Way: Legends
Told by Arizona Indian Children.* El Paso: Cinco
Puntos Press, 1998.

Baylor, Byrd. *When Clay Sings.* New York: Aladdin,
1987.

Beals, Ralph H. *The Contemporary Culture of the
Cahita Indians.* Smithsonian Institution.

Bureau of American Ethnology, Bulletin 142, Wash-
ington, D.C.: United States Government Printing
Office, 1945.

Bennett, Robin Rose. "Wild Carrot (*Daucus carota*):
A Plant for Conscious, Natural Contraception,
USDA Plant Profile." Sister Zeus www.sisterze-
us.com/qaluse.htm. 2009.

Bernard-Shaw, Mary, Henry D. Wallace, Linda
Mayro, and William H. Doelle. *Archaeological
Testing at Los Morteros North and a Mitiga-
tion Plan for the Site of Los Morteros*, Technical
Report No. 87-10. Tucson: Institute for American
Research, 1987.

Bezy, John V. *A Guide to the Geology of Catalina
State Park and the Western Santa Catalina*

Mountains. Tucson: Arizona Geological Survey, 2002.

"Blue-Footed Booby." Wildscreen Arkive. http://www. arkive.org/blue-footed-booby/sula-nebouxii/.

Bowden, Charles. *Frog Mountain Blues.* Tucson: University of Arizona Press, 1994.

Boyer, Jeffrey L. "Is There a Point to This? Contexts for Metal Projectile Points in Northern New Mexico," *Papers of the Archaeological Society of New Mexico*, No. 38. Albuquerque: Archaeological Society of New Mexico. www.academia. edu/4160733/Is_There_A_Point_To_This_Contexts_ for_Metal_Projectile_Points_in_Northern_ New_Mexico.

Braddock, B.H. "How to Make and Use a Throwing Stick," Wilderness Arena: Wilderness and Urban Survival Guide. http://wildernessarena.com/ supplies/weapons/throwing-sticks.

"Breastfeeding." American Pregnancy Association: Promoting Pregnancy Wellness. http:// americanpregnancy.org/breastfeeding/ breastfeeding-while-pregnant/.

Caid, Bill. "Los Pinacates Volcano Field: Unimogs Dominate the Altar," Trip Report. http:// billcaid.com/2005/PinacatesNov2005/PinicateTripReport2005.html. November 8-13, 2005.

Colwell-Chanthaphonh. *Massacre at Camp Grant: Forgetting and Remembering Apache History.* Tucson: University of Arizona Press, 2007.

Cornett, James W. *Indian Uses of Desert Plants.* Palm Springs: Nature Trails Press, 2011.

Cornett, James. "Mistletoe Depends Upon Bird," *The Desert Sun.* www.desertsun.com/story/life /home-garden/james-cornett/2014/12/06/mistletoe-depends-upon-bird/20039567/. 2014.

Cremony, John C. *Life Among the Apaches.* San Francisco: A. Roman and Company, Publishers,

1868. (Digital reproduction by Digital Scanning, Inc., 2001.)

Crider, Destiny L., Cathryn M. Meegan, and Steve Swanson. *The Hohokam Preclassic to Classic Transition Part II: Modeling Socioeconomic Changes.* Tempe: Arizona State University, Department of Anthropology. n.d.

Curtis, Edward S. *The North American Indian, v.02.* Cambridge: The University Press, 1908. http://curtis.library.northwestern.edu/site_curtis/

Dancey, William S. *Archaeological Field Methods.* Edina: Burgess, 1981.

Dart, Allen. "Prehistory-Hohokam: Hallmarks of the Hohokam Culture, Origins, Subsistence, Settlement Systems, Social and Organizational Systems, Interaction-Action," Series of PowerPoint presentations. Tucson: Old Pueblo Archaeology.

"Datura and Brugmansia Species as Sacred Plants and Medicines," http://www.lycaeum.org/leda/docs/16271.shtml.

Denoyer, Allen. "Burning Down the (Pit) House, Part 1." Preservation Archaeology Blog, Archaeology Southwest, May 19, 2017.

"Depression During and After Pregnancy." U.S. Department of Health and Human Services, Office of Women's Health. www.womenshealth.gov.

"Desert Foods for a Healthy Living." Native Seeds/SEARCH. www.nativeseeds.org.

Doelle, William H., and Deborah L. Swartz. "Hidden Times: The Archaeology of the Tortolita Phase," *Archaeology in Tucson: Newsletter of the Center for Desert Archaeology*, Vol. 11, No. 2. Tucson: Center for Desert Archaeology. Spring, 1997.

Fagan, Damian. "Medicinal Plants Found in the Deserts." http://www.desertusa.com/flowers/wild-medicinal-plants.html.

Ferg, Alan, ed. *Western Apache Material Culture: The Goodwin and Guenther Collections*. Tucson: University of Arizona Press, 1987.

Fish, Suzanne K., and Paul R. Fish, eds. *The Hohokam Millennium*. Santa Fe: School for Advanced Research Press, 2007.

Fish, Suzanne K., Paul R. Fish, and John H. Madsen. "Evolution and Structure of the Classic Period Marana Community," *Anthropological Papers of the University of Arizona*, Number 56. Tucson: University of Arizona Press, 2001.

Fontana, Bernard L. *Entrada: The Legacy of Spain and Mexico in the United States*. Tucson: Southwest Parks and Monuments Association, 1994.

Gargulinski, Ryn. "Why Lizards Do Push-Ups? And Other Tucson Wildlife Tidbits You Need to Know Before You Die," *Tucson Weekly*. www.tucsonweekly.com/TheRange/archives/2011/05/20/why-lizards-do-push-ups-and -other-tucson-wildlife-tidbits-you-need-to-know-before-you-die. May 20, 2011.

Giddings, Ruth Warner. *Yaqui Myths and Legends*. Tucson: University of Arizona Press, 1959.

Gold, Alan. "Indian Uses of Desert Plants: Indian Harvest Methods and Preparation of Pinyon Pine, Chia, Agave." http://www.desertusa.com/desert-activity/indian-desert-plants.html

Gregonis, Linda M., and Karl J. Reinhard. *Hohokam Indians of the Tucson Basin*. Tucson: University of Arizona Press, 1979.

Griffith, Jim. "El Dia de San Juan," Special to the *Arizona Daily Star*. June 14, 2013. http://tucson.com/news/blogs/big-jim/big-jim-el-dia-de-san-juan/article_1963ed22-cb14-11e2-8346-0019bb2963f4.html.

Gronemann, Barbara. *Hohokam Arts and Crafts*. Scottsdale: Southwest Learning Sources, 1994.

Hanson, Roseann Beggy, and Jonathan Hanson. *Southern Arizona Nature Almanac: A Seasonal Guide to Pima County and Beyond*. Tucson: University of Arizona Press, 1996.

Hassler, Lynn. *The Raven: Soaring Through History, Legend, and Lore*. Tucson, Arizona: Rio Nuevo Publishers, 2008.

Hatch, Stephanie. "Traditional, Processual, and Post-Processual Archaeology," *Archaeology, Art History, Religion, Ancient Cultures, Anthropology, and Nature*. http://stephaniehatch.blogspot. com/2010/02/traditional-processual-and-post. html. 2010.

Hayden Papers. *Francisco Romero Documents*. Tucson: Arizona Historical Society.

Heilen, Michael. *Uncovering Identity in Mortuary Analysis: Community Sensitive Methods for Identifying Group Affiliation in Historical Cemeteries*. Walnut Creek: Left Coast Press, 2012.

Hernandez, John. *Blood Along the Cañon del Oro— Tully & Ochoa Wagon Attack*. April 4, 2013. www.copperarea.com/pages/blood-along-the-can-on-del-oro-tully-ochoa-wagon-attack-2/.

Hester, Thomas R., Harry J. Shafer, and Kenneth L. Feder. *Field Methods in Archaeology*, Seventh Edition. Mountain View: Mayfield Pub., 1997.

History.com Staff. "Struggle for Mexican Independence." http://www.history.com/topics /mexico / struggle-for-mexican-independence. 2010.

History.com Staff. "Veracruz." http://www.history. com/topics/mexico/veracruz.

"Homes in the Gold Coast Historic District of Chicago." http://www.74elm.com/photo-gallery/.

"Honey." http://www.dermnetnz.org/treatments/ honey.html.

"How to Grow a Three Sisters Garden." Native Seeds/SEARCH. www.nativeseeds.org.

Huckell, Lisa W. *Archaeological Assessment of the Proposed Catalina State Park*. Arizona State Museum Archaeological Series. Tucson: University of Arizona Press, 1980.

"Illinois Grounds for Dissolution of Marriage." www.divorcesource.com/ds/illinois/illinois-divorce-laws-674.shtml, http://www.illinoisdivorce.com/family_law_articles/grounds_for_divorce.php.

Kallevang, Britta. "Beliefs of the Pápago Tribe." http://classroom.synonym.com/beliefs-papago-tribe-6515.html.

Kane, Charles W. *Medicinal Plants of the American Southwest*. Boston: Lincoln Town Press, 2011.

Kessel, John L. *Friars, Soldiers, and Reformers: Hispanic Arizona and the Sonora Mission Frontier, 1767-1856*. Tucson: University of Arizona Press, 1976.

King, Dan. *General Hohokam Pottery Descriptions*. www.rarepottery.info/protect /articles.htm. July, 2004.

Lavin, Patrick. *Arizona: An Illustrated History*. New York: Hippocrene Books, 2001.

Malville, J. McKim, and Claudia Putnam. *Prehistoric Astronomy in the Southwest*. Boulder: Johnson Books, 1993.

Marks, Tracy. *Becoming Woman: Apache Female Puberty Sunrise Ceremony*. www.webwinds. com/yupanqui/apachesunrise.htm. 1999.

Martin, Patricia Preciado. *Beloved Land: An Oral History of Mexican Americans in Southern Arizona*. Tucson: University of Arizona Press, 2004.

Martin, Patricia Preciado. *Images and Conversations: Mexican Americans Recall a Southwestern Past*. Tucson: University of Arizona Press, 1996.

McNamee, Gregory, ed. *Named in Stone and Sky: An Arizona Anthology*. Tucson: University of Arizona Press, 1993.

Miranda, G. "Racial and Cultural Dimensions of 'Gente de Razón' Status in Spanish and Mexican California," *Southern California Quarterly, 70*(3), 265-278. www.jstor.org. ezproxy2.library.arizona. edu/stable/41171310 doi:1. 1988.

Molina, Felipe S., Herminia Valenzuela, and David Leedom Shaul. *Yoeme-English / English Standard Dictionary: A Language of the Yaqui Tribe in the American Southwest and Northern Mexico*. New York: Hippocrene Books, 1999.

Molina, Felipe. Yoeme History and Culture, personal communication, 2014.

Molina, Felipe. "Yoeme Spirituality," *Yoeme History and Culture Project, Volume 5*. Unpublished.

Muehrcke, Phillip C. and Juliana O. Muehrcke. *Map Use: Reading, Analysis, Interpretation*, 4th Edition. Madison: JP Publications, 1998.

Nahban, Gary Paul. *The Desert Smells Like Rain: A Naturalist in Papago Indian Country*. San Francisco: North Point Press, 1982.

Nabhan, Gary Paul. *Gathering the Desert*. Tucson: University of Arizona Press, 1985.

National Register of Historic Places. *Registration Form: Ghost Ranch Lodge*. U.S. Department of the Interior, 2012.

National Park Service, "Tumacocori—the Ultimate Primary Source." https://www.nps.gov/tuma/ learn/education/upload/2nd%20Unit%201%20 The%20O%27odham%20PRINT%20826%20KB. pdf.

New Perspectives on the West, "William Clarke Quantrill," *The West Film Project*. Public Broadcasting System, 2001. www.pbs.org/weta/ thewest/people/i_r/quantrill.htm.

Niethammer, Carolyn. "A Summer's Gathering," *Edible Baja Arizona*, Issue 1. Summer 2013.

Officer, James E. *Hispanic Arizona: 1536-1856*. Tucson: University of Arizona Press, 1987.

Olin, George. *House in the Sun: A Natural History of the Sonoran Desert*. Tucson: Southwest Parks and Monuments Association, 1994.

Overstreet, Daphne. *Arizona Territory Cook Book: Recipes from 1864 to 1912*. Phoenix: Golden West, 2004.

Pablo. "Duerme Ya" (Sleep Now), *Lullaby written to the theme from "Pan's Labyrinth,"* 2008. https://answers.yahoo.com/question/index?qid=20080918 102717AAFdsjU.

"Palo Verde Beetles." The Dragonfly Woman: Aquatic entomologist with a Blogging Habit. https://thedragonflywoman.com/2011/04/04/an-appreciation/.

Phillips, Steven J., and Patricia Wentworth Comus, eds. *A Natural History of the Sonoran Desert*. Tucson: Arizona Sonoran Desert Museum Press, 2000.

Pirate Medicine: "Gunshot wounds." *Pestilence and Pain During the Golden Age of Piracy*. http://pirates. hegewisch.net/Pestilence_Pain.html #gunshots. n.d.

Pluralism Project, Harvard University. "Apache Initiation Dress." http://pluralism.org/religions/native-american-traditions/native-peoples- experience/apache-initiation-dress/.

Potter, Lee Ann, and Wynell Schamel. "The Homestead Act of 1862." *Social Education*, Vol. 61, No. 6, 359-364. October, 1997.

Record, Ian W. *Big Sycamore Stands Alone: The Western Apaches, Aravaipa, and the Struggle for*

Place. Norman: University of Oklahoma Press, 2008.

Redish, Laura. "Native American Vocabulary: Apache Words." www.native-languages.org/ apache_ words.htm.

Reid, J. Jefferson, and David E. Doyel. *Emil W. Haury's Prehistory of the American Southwest*. Tucson: University of Arizona Press, 1986.

Reid, Jefferson, and Stephanie Whittlesey. *The Archaeology of Ancient Arizona*. Tucson: University of Arizona Press, 1987.

Saguaro Sings Down the Rain. Tucson: Tohono Chul Park, n.d.

Saxton, Dean, Lucille Saxton, and Susie Enos. *Dictionary: Papago-English, O'otham-Mil-gahn, English-Papago, Mil-gahn-O'otham*, Second Edition. Tucson: University of Arizona Press, 1983.

Scholes, Walter V. "Benito Juarez." Encyclopedia Britannica Online. www.britannica.com/biography/ Benito-Juarez. 2016

Shelton, Richard. *Going Back to Bisbee*. Tucson: University of Arizona Press, 1992.

Shelton, Richard. *Hohokam*. Tucson: Sun/Gemini Press, 1993.

"Spanish Djarr, Pieces of Eight." https://en.wikipedia.org/wiki/Spanish_djarr. 2016.

"Songs Connected with Expeditions to Obtain Salt." Recorded and Edited by Frances Densmore, Library of Congress Collections of the Archive of American Folk Song, Papago Music, Bulletin 90. Bureau of American Ethnology, 1929.

Spicer, Edmund H. *Cycles of Conquest: The Impact of Spain, Mexico, and the United States on the Indians of the Southwest, 1533-1960*. Tucson: University of Arizona Press, 1962.

Stein, Pat H. *Homesteading in Arizona, 1862-1940: A Component of the Arizona Historic Preservation*

Plan. Phoenix: Arizona State Historic Preservation Office, 1990.

Stockel, H. Henrietta. *Women of the Apache Nation: Voices of Truth*. Reno: University of Nevada Press, 1991.

Sutton, Mark Q., and Brooke S. Arkush. *Archaeological Laboratory Methods: An Introduction*. Dubuque: Kendall/Hunt, 1998.

Swartz, Deborah L. *Archaeological Testing at the Romero Ruin, Technical Report 93-8*. Tucson: Center for Desert Archaeology, 1993.

Swartz, Deborah L. *Archaeological Testing at the Romero Ruin, Technical Report 91-2*. Tucson, Center for Desert Archaeology, 1991.

Swartz, Deborah L. and William H. Doelle. "The Romo Cache and Hohokam Life," *In the Mountain Shadows*, 27:1. Archaeology Southwest, 1996 and 2013.

Thiel, J. Homer. "People of the Presidio: Family Records from the Tucson Presidio," *Supplemental Media Content for Archaeology Southwest*, Vol. 24, Nos. 1-2. Tucson: Center for Desert Archaeology, 2010.

"UA Engineers Help Save and Reconstruct the Past," *Arizona Engineer* 20.1 University of Arizona, College of Engineering and Mines, 2006.

Underhill, Ruth Murray. *Papago Woman*. Prospect Heights: Waveland Press, 1979.

Underhill, Ruth Murray. *People of the Crimson Evening*. Palmer Lake: The Filter Press, 1982.

Underhill, Ruth Murray. *Singing for Power: The Song Magic of the Papago Indians of Southern Arizona*. Tucson, Arizona: University of Arizona Press. 1938, 1993.

Van Ness Seymour, Tryntje. *The Gift of Changing Woman*. New York: Henry Holt and Company, 1993.

VanPool, Christine S. "The Signs of the Sacred: Iden-
    tifying Shamans Using Archaeological Evidence,"
    Journal of Anthropological Archaeology 28
    177–190. (2009)

Wagoner, J.J. "History of the Cattle Industry in
    Southern Arizona, 1540-1940," *University of
    Arizona Bulletin, Social Science Bulletin No. 20.*
    Tucson: University of Arizona Press, 1952.

Walker, Charlie. "Sotol (Desert Spoon), www.
    swordofsurvival.com/2010/11/sotol-desert-spoon.
    html.

Ward, Andy. *Palatkwapi: True Southwest.* www.
    palatkwapi.com. 2014.

"Weatherby 9 Lug/Magnum." http://en.wikipedia.org/
    wiki/Weatherby_Mark_V. n.d.

Weaver, Donald E, Susan S. Burton, and Minnabell
    Laughlin, eds. *Proceedings of the 1973 Hohokam
    Conference.* Ramona: Acoma Books, 1978.

Wechel, Edith te. *Yaqui: A Short History of the
    Yaqui Indians.* www.manataka.org/page129.
    html. n.d.

Weiser, Kathy. "Arizona Legends: Fort Breckinridge,
    Built Again and Again." www.legendsof america.
    com/az-fortbreckinridge.html. 2016.

Yetman, David. *Sonora: An Intimate Geography.*
    Albuquerque: University of New Mexico Press,
    1996.

Zentner, Joe. "Hunting For Food in the Desert:
    Gathering Wild Plants." http://www.desertusa.
    com/desert-activity/desert-food-hunting.html

Zucker, Robert. "Treasures of the Santa Catalina
    Mountains: Naming the Santa Catalina Moun-
    tains," *Entertainment Magazine.* n.d. www.emol.
    org/treasurescatalinas/santacatalinas.html.

Zucker, Robert. "Lost Mission of Ciru." *Entertain-
    ment Magazine.* http://www.emol.org/treasures-
    catalinas/missionofciru.html. n.d.